A Jared Buck M...

TO DIE IN KANAB

The Everett Ruess Affair

Council Press
Springville, Utah

TO DIE IN KANAB

The Everett Ruess Affair

a novel by

JACK NELSON

ISBN 13: 978-1-55517-953-3
ISBN 10: 1-55517-953-3

Published by Council Press, an imprint of
Cedar Fort, Inc., 925 N. Main, Springville, UT, 84663
Distributed by Cedar Fort, Inc. www.cedarfort.com

LIBRARY OF CONGRESS CATALOGING-IN-PUBLICATION DATA

Nelson, Jack A. (Jack Adolph), 1930-
   To die in Kanab : the Everett Ruess affair : a novel / by Jack A. Nelson.
   p. cm.
   ISBN 1-55517-953-3 (acid-free paper)
   1. Ruess, Everett, b. 1914--Fiction. I. Title.

PS3614.E4457T65 2006
813'.6--dc22

                                                2006029165

Cover design by Nicole Williams
Cover design © 2006 by Lyle Mortimer

Printed in the United States of America

10 9 8 7 6 5 4 3 2 1

Printed on acid-free paper

DEDICATION

This novel is dedicated to those hardy souls who have found solace in the solitude of the lonely canyons of southern Utah—and especially to those wanderers who never emerged from that unforgiving land and still lie mostly forgotten among the red cliffs and the sagebrush.

ACKNOWLEDGMENTS

Many of the events in this novel are based on actual happenings, such as the ranchers' rebellion against the federal government for confiscating their cattle on the Escalante-Grand Staircase National Monument. I take off my hat to the record-keepers and conscience of our society—the American press. In addition, I want to express appreciation to Johnny Rustywire, to whom I owe thanks for my version of his story "The Goat Woman—Asdzaa Tlizí." Johnny has a web site with his Navajo stories that are worth reading: www.rustywire.com/starship/grymtn.html.

CHAPTER 1

Some mysteries never die, Sheriff Jared Buck mused as he watched the limousine pull into the Kane County parking lot. *It was strange,* he thought. Over the years people had disappeared in these red-rock canyons of southern Utah on a more or less regular basis. But none of them had caught the nation's attention like Everett Ruess, the seemingly enchanted artist and writer who after all these years had not faded from the public's interest. The mystery of the young vanished wanderer seemed never to go away.

And now this movie company was resurrecting the whole puzzling affair. He watched them disembark from the limousine into the September heat of late afternoon. At this moment, the sheriff was tired, hot, and angry that the County Commission had not given him permission to have the air conditioning repaired. October would be here soon, they had reasoned, and it could wait until spring. Jared Buck was lean and sinewy with a craggy face set off by a slightly crooked nose. On his office walls, along with the official state and county certificates, hung photographs of nearby mountain scenes and of the deep canyons and colorful cliffs of the area where he liked to roam in his free time.

Across the room, his deputy rose and stared out of the window with a grin. Angus Terry was a short, bearded, balding man who had shown up from Kansas a dozen years earlier and was slowly melding into the southern Utah landscape.

"Looks like your movie people finally got here," Angus said, a grin splitting his wide face.

With a resigned nod, Jared rose, stretched, and gave a weary shake of his head. "Better make 'em feel welcome, I guess," he muttered

"A buck says they're gonna be a big pain in the butt." Angus chuckled.

On the street the usual string of tourist cars rolled by, flanked by the occasional rancher's pick-up truck. The officers watched the three men pause to remove their suit coats as the heat hit them. Behind them, a tanned brunette with flowing hair in the barest halter top and shorts got out, opened a can of soda, and motioned the men to go ahead without her.

The deputy shook his head. "That young heifer's goin' to sunburn her heinie if she ain't careful."

But Jared's eyes were on the approaching men. In front, the tall man with a trim moustache had a manicured look about him that put him out of place in this country where Levi jeans and wide-brimmed hats were the norm.

Three days earlier, Jared had received a call from Hollywood informing him that the Majestic West film company would be coming to Kanab to do preliminary planning for a feature film about the Everett Ruess disappearance. An imperious voice had informed him that the executives would expect red-carpet treatment. The man striding in the lead wore a blue silk shirt with a dark gray tie, set off by two-tone wingtip shoes. Jared wondered if he was the one who had come across as so arrogant on the phone.

Jared was just under six feet tall, but this man towered above him. As the men pushed open the glass front door that read "Kane County Sheriff," Jared rose and motioned them in. His secretary, Myra, had gone for the day.

"Gentlemen." Jared nodded as they entered.

The tall man paused to wipe his brow, but didn't offer to shake hands. He was middle-aged, with a chiseled face that was set off by thick brown hair pulled into a ponytail. Jared guessed that at one time he had aspired to be an actor.

"Whew, hot out there," the producer said. "Officer, I'm Alex Carlton, president of Majestic West Films. My business associates," he said, gesturing to a mid-thirties, athletic-looking man who nodded and reached to shake hands, "Ronald M. Murdock, and Maury Peralto, both from the East Bay Bank of Oakland."

Jared noticed the deference given to Murdock. The third man, Peralto, was older, squatty, with a rumpled look about him. "Jared Buck, and my chief deputy Angus," he replied. "So you're here to make a movie?"

Carlton drew himself up with a deep breath. "Not just any movie—an award-winning movie."

Jared smiled. "So how can we help you folks?"

"Sheriff, we're not here just to make a movie," Carlton said, cocking his head and arching an eyebrow is if sharing a secret, "but to solve an old murder for you!"

In spite of himself, Jared blinked. "What do you . . . oh, you mean Everett Ruess's disappearance." He tried to keep the annoyance out of his voice; he didn't like cuteness.

Carlton turned to Murdock and nodded. "That's our plan. Of course, it won't be easy, we know, but we're determined."

With that, Jared nodded and waved the men to the hardwood chairs that sat against the wall. Angus, leaning against the windowsill, had a bemused expression. Since 1934 the disappearance of Everett Ruess had aroused endless speculation among the locals.

The son of middle-class, artistic, and intellectual parents from Los Angeles, Ruess was already a gifted writer and artist who hiked throughout the Arizona desert and the Navajo Reservation at age seventeen in search of solitude and beauty. He was an engaging, affable youth who knocked on people's doors and expected to be taken in. In that way, he had become friends with such well-known artists and photographers as Ansel Adams, Maynard Dixon, and Dorothea Lange. His mother had seen to the publication of some of his writings.

Riding a burro named Pegasus, he had tramped throughout the desert regions of Arizona and Utah, exploring, making friends, and gaining a reputation as a likeable eccentric. He sold some of his paintings and sent back articulate letters, obviously intended for publication, detailing his love affair with the spectacular desert country. In 1934, when he had visited nearby Escalante at age twenty with his burros, it was the last time he was seen. The haunting mystery had garnered national attention, and the fascination had never really died. Books had been written about him, and his letters and journal had been published.

Jared Buck leaned back in his chair and scrutinized the movie producer. "Of course, he's been dead about 65 years, you know."

Carlton nodded. "Yes, but the legend's never faded." He paused, gazed at a picture on the office wall of a great stone arch with snow-clad peaks in the background, and in a stentorian tone he quoted, "*'He was a hunter, brother, companion of our days'*— that's what Edward Abbey wrote about him."

Jared frowned. "Abbey also wrote that Ruess might still be alive in some canyon somewhere, living on prickly pear and lizards," he said, enjoying the look of surprise on Carlton's face. Undoubtedly the man considered him a country hick who wouldn't know Edward Abbey from Westminster Abbey. "Look. . . ." He paused, trying not to let his frustration show. "This is wild, inhospitable country. Do you have any idea how many people have disappeared in these canyons, never to be found? Or how many die or who nearly die that we have to go out and rescue?"

The younger man named Murdock shrugged. "That makes it all the more exciting. This movie will focus on how Everett Ruess met the challenge of this wonderful land."

Stifling a chuckle, Jared leaned forward. They seemed a determined lot. Now his job was to keep them from getting lost or killed. "Well, maybe a movie about Everett Ruess is not a bad idea," he agreed, "considering the state of Hollywood these days. So I guess this is the right place. Been lots of movies made here, so the mayor will be happy for the business."

Through the years actors like Frank Sinatra, Charlton Heston, and Ronald Reagan had strolled the streets of Kanab while starring in films ranging from westerns and Biblical epics to space dramas. Sinatra had even donated money to build the municipal swimming pool. The picturesque cliffs of the red-rock country, the deep canyons, the lonely mesas that looked southward toward the Grand Canyon—all these combined to make the town well-known around Hollywood. When western movies had been in vogue, the movie crews had meant dollars for the local merchants. Often, it also meant headaches for the sheriff's office, keeping them out of trouble.

The producer gave an emphatic nod of agreement. "We're checking out locations, and at the same time seeing if we can solve the mystery of his murder—perhaps find his grave." Carlton drew himself up to his full height and stared out the window that looked beyond the town to the mesas that dropped off southward. "We're going to be doing some exploring." He nodded to the younger man. "Mr. Murdock here will no doubt be financing this venture, and he wants to see some of the grandeur of the area."

"That's right," Murdock confirmed. "I'm excited by this story. It looks like it has tremendous potential." He paused and gazed intently into Jared Buck's eyes. "I see it sort of as payback for the space I take up in this world," he said.

"I see." Jared nodded, noting the cliché.

Murdock hunched forward, intensity shining in his eyes. "When I learned about Ruess, I felt he was a kindred spirit," he said earnestly. "I wanted his ideals—and his story—to be more widely known."

"Okay," Jared said, nodding. He liked Murdock. He seemed sincere—maybe even naïve—unlike the smooth-talking Carlton. In his ten years as sheriff he had dealt with enough con-men to recognize them instinctively. He noted that the other man, Peralto, was sweating profusely with a frightened look on his face. "But you mentioned murder," Jared said. "What makes you think Ruess was murdered?"

"We've talked to some sources," Carlton said with a wink. "Names have even been mentioned, though the guilty ones are dead now."

"What kind of sources?"

"Well. . . . You know, some people in recent years have talked," Carlton said in a secretive tone. "Some people who are getting old now who were around then."

Only a year earlier the magazine *National Geographic Adventure* had featured an article about a search for the fate that befell Everett Ruess. The article repeated the speculation that he had been killed by two cattle rustlers that he had stumbled upon—relatives of some of the families still ranching in the area. Or, that he had been done in by renegade Navajos. Most of the locals, however, felt that the most likely scenario was that the youth had simply fallen into one of the deep slot canyons that gutted the red-rock wilderness. For a lone traveler, even a broken leg would usually mean death in the desert. It happened on a more or less regular basis, but it happened mostly to tourists who didn't respect the untamed land.

"We've been to Escalante," Carlton said, pronouncing it like an outsider; local people dropped the final "e" sound. "And we simply wanted you to know we're out there exploring Ruess's trail."

"I see. So what can we do to help?" Jared asked.

Carlton took a quick step forward. "Some people were kind of close-mouthed. But maybe you know something that might help solve this . . . riddle."

"Afraid not," Jared said with pursed lips and a little shake of his head.

"Well, we'll make out all right," Carlton replied with a toothy smile. "We have a guide and transportation arranged."

"A guide's a good idea," Jared agreed.

"Who is it?" the deputy wondered.

"Henry Winslow," Carlton answered. "He's a guide on the Colorado River, and he's supposed to know this country like the back of his hand."

Jared Buck gave a quick nod. "I know him. The main thing is, be sure you have plenty of water. And I don't mean a quart of Evian. And stay out of the canyons if the weather is cloudy. At this time of year, even on a clear day a flash flood can sweep down those slot canyons like a racehorse, and there's no place to escape to." He thought of mentioning the dozen European tourists who had died a few miles away only three years earlier when they had been caught in such a flood, but decided not to.

Against the window, the deputy leaned forward with a knowing smile. "Maybe your guide can also find Burt Loper," he said. "Famous. One of the first to take people down the Colorado in the Grand Canyon. He disappeared on the river back in the 1930s when he was eighty years old. Never been found."

Carlton shot the deputy a withering glance. "I don't think sarcasm is necessary here," he rebuked.

"Never mind," Jared said, frowning at his deputy. Sometimes Angus was a smart alec, and more than once it had got him into trouble. Jared attributed that quirk to the fact that he was short, and that most of his black hair had fallen out when he was barely twenty-three. He had been through two marriages since he had arrived. Still, he was likeable, and efficient in his job.

Jared handed Carlton his card. "Just be careful," he warned. "This is scenic country, but it's tough and unforgiving."

"We're headquartering at the Cinnamon Cliffs Motel," Carlton said. "I just wanted you to know."

"We appreciate that." Jared wondered why they weren't staying at the Parry Lodge in the center of town where the stars traditionally stayed, but he decided that Carlton probably hadn't known about that.

When the producers went out, Jared gave his deputy a questioning look. "Everett Ruess again. The old 'killed by cattle rustlers theory.' What do you think?"

"I think every time somebody finds some old bones the first thing they think of is Everett Ruess," he answered.

After the article had appeared in *National Geographic Adventure*, several parties had come to search for signs of the fate of

7

the vanished wanderer. Twice in the past year Jared Buck and the county rescue squads had had to search for missing hikers from these groups. They had found one San Diego man who was nearly dead from dehydration, and had brought him up a series of cliffs by stretcher.

Jared shrugged. "Some of these things never get solved. They're still speculating about the Lincoln assassination—not to mention Kennedy." Indeed, after the magazine published the article a year ago about the disappearance of Everett Ruess, Jared had found himself intrigued by the character of the young poet and wanderer, and he had read everything he could find on the case. He had gathered articles and studied two books—one containing Ruess's letters and the other his journal. He often carried one of the books when he hiked into the red-rock canyons.

"And 'Mooch' Winslow for a guide," the deputy continued, amused. "He's liable to rob 'em blind before it's over."

Jared nodded glumly. He had known Mooch Winslow to be a troublemaker. Several years earlier, Jared had tried to help the local game warden pin a case on him for guiding out-of-state trophy hunters into prime deer areas after the season had ended, during the winter months when deer were vulnerable from hunger and the cold. Trophy heads of mounted mule deer could bring thousands of dollars as a designer item, and afterward there was no way of knowing if the head had been taken illegally. It had become big business. They had made a case against Mooch, but he had beaten it on a technicality. Nevertheless, the man did know the country well.

"I just hope we don't have to climb some cliff to rescue them or pull their bodies out of a slot canyon. But," Jared shrugged, "all the world loves a mystery."

"Maybe he'll just try to steal that brunette," Angus said, watching through the window as the men got back into their vehicle, his focus on the young woman climbing into the motor home. "I take it back, about her sunburnin' her heinie," he said wryly. "I think that young lady's tanned all the way up."

CHAPTER 2

As his Land Rover inched along over the rocks in Hackberry Wash next morning, Mooch Winslow tried to hide his smirk each time his Land Rover lurched. In his rear-view mirror he watched his passengers cringe in distaste as they were tossed back and forth. But at his side, Ron Murdock seemed to be enjoying the little canyon, while Peralto and Carlton behind him obviously had no taste for traveling over rough roads.

As for the girl, she seemed to weather the road without problems, hanging on to Carlton's shoulder for stability. Mooch caught her eye from time to time and was rewarded with a smile. He would have to be careful, he reminded himself, for he could ill afford to lose this job.

"Does this road get any better?" Carlton asked with a groan.

"More of the same," Mooch replied with a laugh. "But these petroglyphs up ahead are worth it."

"This is great," Murdock said with enthusiasm, obviously enjoying the experience. "I bet not many people get up here."

Several times Mooch slowed to point out rock drawings left by the ancient Anasazi on cliffs they passed, but he promised a more dramatic panel ahead.

In a few minutes he pulled to a stop in the shade of a high, gray cliff. Muttering, Carlton slid from the Rover and stood with

9

his hands on his hips. "Absolutely atrocious," he said with a shake of his head at the creek bed they had traveled.

Ron Murdock emerged and walked toward the rock face, where prehistoric drawings of dozens of animals, elongated hunters, and strange figures were etched into the patina of the stone. "Wow, well worth it," he said with a low whistle. He approached and stood in awe before the drawings of what he recognized as bighorn sheep. Above the animals a strange, coiled line represented nothing he could recognize.

"What do these mean?" he asked the guide.

Mooch came and stared at the figures. "The animals—obvious, I guess that's what they hunted. But the geometric shapes and circles . . ." he shrugged. "I don't think anybody knows."

It was hot in the wash, and Peralto had emerged from the Rover to stand fanning himself. "You said we had some cold beer?" he called to the guide.

Ten minutes later they were lolling in the shade, having sandwiches and drinks that Mooch had pulled from the cooler. Suddenly, a shot sounded from above and a bullet ricocheted with a zing from a rock next to the truck. Mooch Winslow made a flying leap for the protection of the Rover, but the others stood looking puzzled.

"Better get down," Mooch called. "Some idiot hunter is up there."

Quickly the others scrambled toward the truck. "Stupid fool!" Carlton yelled out as he ducked.

Mooch raised his head. "Watch where you're shooting!" he shouted toward the top of the cliff.

As if in answer, another shot rang out, followed by the explosion of the front tire.

Until now, Mooch had assumed a stray shot had come their way. Crouching behind the rear fender, he now sucked in his breath. "Everybody stay low!" he called. "Some bastard's really shooting at us."

Peralto had crawled onto the floor in the rear seat, and the girl lay sobbing across the front seat. Carlton hunkered on the ground near Mooch, half under the truck.

"Do something!" Carlton screamed at the guide.

"I am." Mooch turned and frowned at him. "I'm keeping my head down."

Another shot shattered the silence of the canyon, again followed by a small explosion as the other front tire burst. Mooch made a face, calculating how much these tires cost.

At this, the brunette gave a little scream of terror. Mooch could see Peralto lying with his eyes squeezed shut in fear. The guide reached to nudge Carlton.

"If you still got that cell phone, call the sheriff—right now." He gave him the number.

* * *

The call came as Jared Buck was sliding some eggs and bacon onto his plate from the frying pan. His Alaskan malamute Sitka sat nearby, watching intently and savoring the smells.

"Don't even think it," he warned the dog as the phone rang and he reached to picked it up.

"Jared Buck," he said.

The voice was nearly hysterical. "Sheriff, get here quick— somebody's trying to kill us!"

Jared frowned in surprise. "Who is this?"

"Alex Carlton," the reply came in an almost hysterical shout. "They're shooting at us!"

"Okay, okay. Calm down. Where are you? And who's shooting at you?"

There was a frustrated silence. "S-somebody. . . . I don't know! We're a long ways . . . toward Page."

"Listen, is your guide there? Let me talk to him." It was obvious that Carlton was in no shape to talk.

"All right, but hurry!" Carlton's voice had turned high and whiny.

Jared could hear shuffling, then another voice.

"Jared?"

"Hey, Mooch, what's goin' on?" Jared asked.

The guide's voice was calm, almost philosophic. "Well, looks like somebody doesn't like somebody."

"You sure it wasn't a stray shot?"

"Not likely. The first one zinged over our heads. Then the next one blew first one tire on the Rover, then another. The shootin's stopped, but you better get out here."

Jared nodded. It was Saturday, and he had donned his Levis and an old flannel shirt in anticipation of a day in the mountains. "Okay. I'll be right there. Where are you?"

"Up Cottonwood Canyon along the Cads Crotch, and about three miles up Hackberry Canyon. You know it?"

"Yeah, I know it. I'll find it. Can you get away from there on that flat?"

"Well, with two flat tires in front, we're bogged down good in the sand. You better call them over at Red Rock Rentals and tell 'em to get a couple of mounted tires out here for our Land Rover."

"Is anything else going on now—how long ago was this?"

"Maybe five minutes. I thought that tall guy was goin' to crap his pants. We're still hunkered down here by the Rover."

"Okay. Hang on, Mooch. I'll be there quick as I can. Stay low and keep in touch by phone."

He hung up, and then scraped the eggs and bacon into the dog's dish next to the door. He had hoped to take Sitka to go exploring up on Boulder Mountain to scout out the elk situation for the upcoming hunt.

"Okay, so we don't go hiking today," he said as he quickly slipped on his khaki shirt and adjusted the badge on his chest. Jared Buck lived alone and was used to talking to Sitka. Even before cancer had taken his wife Sunny seven years earlier, he had always talked to his dogs. Since that time, Sitka had made the loneliness easier.

"Sitka, keep an eye on the place, hear?" he said as he sprinted down the steps. Buck paused a brief moment to be sure there was water in the dog's pail in the shade of a cedar tree in his yard.

The malamute was a large animal, rangier than most of its breed, wolf-gray with the typical black mask. Sitka sat and watched with begging eyes as his master spun away down the dirt lane toward the main road.

*   *   *

The highway eastward toward Page runs south of the towering red and gray cliffs that mark the end of the Paunsaugunt Plateau where Bryce Canyon National Park lures thousands of visitors every year. As he sped along, the sheriff kept his lights flashing. He didn't bother with the siren because there was little traffic this morning. As he drove, he called Mooch Winslow several times on his cell phone, instructing him and the others to stay out of sight until he arrived. The shooting had apparently ended, Mooch informed him, but they were taking no chances. After thirty minutes, Jared turned off onto the dirt road of Cottonwood Canyon. As he bounced along he kept an eye open for anyone who might be leaving the area. If he had not already gone, the shooter had only two ways to leave the area on the dirt road—south, to the Page highway, or north some forty miles to emerge near Bryce Canyon on the Escalante highway.

After another fifteen minutes of bone-jarring jostling over the rocky trail used only by hunters and adventurers up Hackberry Wash, Jared spotted the red Range Rover mired in the sand in the shade of a hillside. It was covered with red dust and the people huddled inside were barely visible.

"Everybody okay?" Jared called as he jumped from his Jeep, scanning the hillside and the cliff beyond them. All appeared calm. Mooch Winslow was sitting in the shade of his Rover, smoking. With a disgusted expression, he motioned to his front wheels. Sure enough, the two front tires were flattened, with exit holes the size of a quarter in each.

"Looks like it's over now," Mooch said, rising with a glance over the top of the truck. "They're pretty shook up inside, though."

Slowly, heads appeared and the door opened a crack. Alex Carlton rose from where he had been half-lying on the ground next to the guide, but stayed in a low crouch. "You're sheriff here," Carlton said in a low voice, as if the assailant might hear him. "You better do something."

Jared studied the cliffs above and shrugged. Ron Murdock peered from the door of the vehicle, and then got out and came around to stand staring up at the rock face. Clearly shaken, Murdock nevertheless managed a grin. "Boy, Sheriff, you didn't tell us this part of the West was still wild. I hadn't expected this."

Jared gave a little shake of his head. "Nobody did. Where'd the shots come from?

Mooch pointed to the top of the sandstone cliff above. The rock was pockmarked with holes caused by eons of weather, some large enough to hide in. At the top of the cliff a few juniper trees jutted skyward where they had gained a foothold in the rock.

"Sounded like up there," Mooch said, grinning. "Damn, I haven't been shot at since Vietnam. Kind of takes me back." The guide was dressed the part, wearing a safari shirt and an Aussie hat tied up on one side—all set off by a handlebar mustache. Although he was slender and wiry, in that outfit he reminded Jared of Teddy Roosevelt.

Jared gave a grim shake of his head. He had been too young for the Vietnam war. "Anybody see anything?"

"Not a thing," the guide said, adding a low whistle. "We had just got out to look at some of the rock writing and were just lolling around when 'Bang!'" He peered into the back of the Rover and called, "Hey, Mr. Peralto, looks like it's over. You can come out now."

The rotund figure of Peralto emerged, white-faced, but stayed bent over in the shelter of the car. "You sure they're gone?" he asked nervously.

"Looks like it." Jared nodded. "But I'll check around just to be sure."

Again Jared examined the tires, figuring the bullet path.

He studied the cliff. It was at least two hundred feet tall, nearly straight up. With a scowl he considered the possibilities. It could have been a chance encounter with some smart-aleck vandal. But maybe someone knew where the party was going and had waited—which meant that Mooch had set up the whole thing. It would have been a stupid trick for the guide to do, and his only likely motive would have been to make his service seem more important. Not likely. Or they had been followed and when they stopped they were stalked from above.

"You see any other vehicles in the last few miles?" he asked the guide.

"Nothing. But I wasn't watching."

Now Alex Carlton got out of the Rover and stood staring at the cliffs. He turned and, his hand still shaking, wagged a finger at Jared Buck. "Sheriff, this is serious stuff. I want something done about it."

"Who knew you'd be here?" he asked. "Did anything happen in Escalante that might've got somebody riled up?"

Murdock stepped forward. "I don't think so. A few people looked disgusted when we told them about the film project and didn't want to say much, but that's about all."

"Anybody special?"

Both Murdock and Carlton shook their heads.

Jared studied their faces. "I'd like a list of those you talked to," he said. "But I'm going to look around first." He waved a thumb toward a plume of dust a quarter mile down the road. "That's probably Hank from the rental place. He'll replace the tires and get you out of here."

"I don't like it," Carlton said, looking grim. "Somebody is out to get me."

Jared scratched his ear and searched the man's eyes. "Any particular reason you think it's you that somebody's after?"

"Well no, but . . ." Carlton flushed.

"Could have been pranksters," Jared said, tucking his thumbs in his belt. "Of course, maybe somebody's mad at Mooch there. It's his truck."

With a laugh, Mooch rocked back on his heels. "Jared, you know everybody loves me."

"Seriously," Jared said, letting his eyes sweep past each of them. "Anybody here have any enemies that would want to do this?" No one answered, but each gave a little shake of his head.

"Hey, can I come out now?" a feminine voice called. The brunette who had earlier worn the bikini slowly stepped from the truck. Her tears brought on by the fright had left little tracks on her cheeks.

Her appearance seemed to reassure Carlton and he motioned toward her, but still his eyes kept searching the cliffs above. "This vision of sunburned loveliness is Chandra—my friend." He slipped an arm around her waist to show possession.

Jared nodded.

She smiled broadly, her teeth sparkling. She eyed Jared appreciatively. "A pleasure, I'm sure," she said in a voice oozing with honey. "I'm a script consultant. I'm sorry I didn't come in yesterday." She was in her twenties, poured into a pair of skin-tight jeans and a well-filled, embroidered tee shirt. Jared wondered how long it would take Mooch to get into trouble with this bunch.

She started to say more, but was interrupted by rattling and banging that signaled the arrival of Hank with two spare tires.

*   *   *

By the time that Mooch Winslow's Rover was bouncing over the rocks toward Cottonwood Creek and the highway, Jared had already climbed to the top of the cliff. On top the ground was mostly slickrock, with an occasional sagebrush or clump of cheatgrass that had found enough soil to subsist in. Carefully, he scanned along the cliff top, looking for tracks or ejected cartridges. The rock was cut by deep gullies that not even a Jeep could get across. For two hours he slowly hunched along for a half mile in each direction. All that he spotted in the sand were a few weathered twenty-two empties and some shotgun shells where someone had practiced at tin cans tossed into the air. The cans, riddled with holes, lay rusting, brown against the lighter cinnamon sand. Apparently it wasn't too difficult for the shooter to approach on top, for others had done it before.

Feeling stymied, he next traced and retraced the little road in the bottom of the canyon, but the sand and rock showed no tracks other than those made by the trucks of Mooch Winslow and Hank. Aside from the inevitable beer cans and a little old trash, there was no sign of anyone stopping or leaving the road.

He was puzzled about the motive. It was true that Mooch had offended people all over southern Utah and northern Arizona with his shady dealings. With his swagger and underhanded methods, it was possible someone had finally decided to put a scare into him. He was known as a womanizer, and Jared Buck was well aware how often that resulted in a shooting. Rumor was that it was Mooch's aggressive coming-on to female clients in the Grand Canyon that had finally cost him his river-guide position there.

By late afternoon, Jared had given up the search, and he turned back to find Angus in the office, handling the report of an over-eager vacationer who had rolled his dune buggy, resulting in crushed ribs and a broken leg. Angus had accompanied the man to the hospital in Kanab, followed by a tearful wife in her Miata.

CHAPTER 3

By the time Jared had finished his report regarding the shooting that Saturday, it was after eight. With a glance at the clock, he picked up the phone.

"Sheriff Calder?" he asked. Jake Calder was sheriff in Panguitch, Garfield County, to the north. "Jared Buck here. Yeah, fine. Say, I'm wondering if you've run across a California bunch up there in a big limousine. They say they're making a movie about Everett Ruess."

He heard a long-suffering sigh. "Yeah, they been here. Big, tall, slick fella, and a couple others. One was a fat, little guy?"

"That's them."

"Hell, they liked to talk my leg off, pumping me about Ruess," Calder complained. "Ever since that article in *National Geographic Adventure*, people been pourin' in here out to find that kid's bones. Damn fools."

"I know what you mean. But I got a problem. Somebody took a couple shots at them today."

"They did? At that California bunch?" Jared heard Jake stifle a chuckle. For many local people the influx of Californians fleeing the urban blight, buying up choice property, and building huge homes—not to mention the liberal ideas they brought with them—had made the newcomers about as popular as the hantavirus. "Probably just some rabbit hunters. Stray bullets, most likely."

"Don't think so. They blew out both front tires of Mooch Winslow's Land Rover."

"That so? Hmmm." The Garfield County sheriff paused to ponder the situation. "Well, Mooch Winslow ain't the most popular guy around here. Probably some mad husband."

"Maybe, but in that case they would've probably shot Mooch dead—or at least blown his engine apart."

"That's so," Calder agreed.

"Tell me, has this bunch been talking to a lot of people about Everett Ruess? Maybe somebody doesn't want this movie made."

"Well . . . yeah. I know they hung around the Hell's Backbone Cafe all day," Jake replied. "Wednesday, I think it was. And I hear they were out to Cal Oxborrow's place on Hole-in-the-Rock Road. And I think they was gonna talk to Ira Crahorn." Sheriff Calder's voice went hard. "You know, that damn magazine said that Matt Oxborrow and Mose Crahorn killed the Ruess kid back in 1934 because he caught them brandin' somebody else's cows. Old Joe Heaton said so, anyway."

Jared nodded. "I read that." Through the years, Jared had heard all sorts of rumors about Everett Ruess's death, ranging from suicide to his being murdered by rustlers to his having fallen into the Colorado River and drowned. "What do you think?"

"Oh, both dead long time ago, of course," Jake replied. "And Mose Crahorn was probly stealin' cows, all right. He was a mean cuss. But there ain't a year goes by that somebody don't disappear in this country and never gets heard from again. Don't know why all the fuss now—except that that New York magazine writer stirred it up after all these years."

Jared contemplated for a long moment. "Well, Jake," he said finally, "if he was murdered I suppose we ought to look into it. And I need to find out who's using these guys for target practice before somebody gets hurt. Maybe I'll drop around and talk to Heaton and the others."

"I can tell you one thing." Sheriff Calder's voice dropped in tone, "The Oxborrows and the Crahorns may not make you too welcome. They don't like being told their grandpas was murderers."

* * *

In the morning Jared Buck rose early, invited Sitka to sit next to him, and headed north on the highway toward Escalante. Usually he was getting ready for church at this hour, but something about the shooting yesterday bothered him, and he didn't want it to get out of hand. Seven miles north of Kanab, he turned onto a dirt road that led up a canyon where a small stream intermittently appeared through the sandy bottom. After a mile, he pulled into the yard of a small, rundown frame home.

An old man in overalls, sitting in a straight-backed chair on the porch, rose as Jared got out of his Jeep. He was shorter than Jared, with shaggy hair turned salt-and-pepper, but with the same hollow cheeks and square jaw as Jared.

"Hello, Pop," Jared said as he reached to shake his father's hand.

"Jared, good to see ya." That was about as effusive as Levi Buck ever got. He was a stern man who liked living alone. He had not been blessed with a sense of humor. "I was just gonna fix me some steak and eggs. Come on in."

"I can't, Pa. I gotta get over to Escalante and see some people."

"Sure you can." The old man's steely gaze fixed on Jared. "Hell, you gotta come have a meal now and then, or what's the use of havin' a son."

With a shrug, Jared acquiesced. Things had not always been good between him and his father. As a teenager, Jared had stepped in when his father had loudly berated his mother. When the man struck her, knocking her down into a collapsed heap, Jared had torn into him, screaming and calling him names. But he was only fifteen, and his father had thrown him bodily from the porch, where he had lain sobbing with a bruised shoulder.

Three days later Levi Buck had disappeared, and it was not until the following Christmas that he sent a card with a short note saying that he was now living in Montana and that he liked it there. He did not return until Jared's twenty-fifth year, when he had come for Jared' mother's funeral. He had then settled into their old home, but it had taken two years before the wall between father and son began to melt.

The sizzle of frying meat brought Sitka inside from the mountainside where he had been chasing ground squirrels. The dog nuzzled the leg of the man who stood at the wood stove holding the spatula.

The old man arched an eyebrow at his son. "That's the begginest dog I ever seen."

"Yeah." Jared gestured with his thumb toward the door. "Go on, Sitka. Out. Go find your own meat." Reluctantly, the dog went, and Jared closed the door.

As they sat down to eat, Jared looked at the meal, and then at his father. "Pop, I got a favor to ask of you."

"You do?" He seemed incredulous. "What kind of favor?"

Jared took a bite of egg, considering. "You used to know old Joe Heaton, didn't you?"

Levi Buck nodded, chewing heartily. "Sure. Cocky son-of-a-bitch when he was young."

"Well, he's attracted some attention lately. He says he knows what happened to Everett Ruess. Remember the young guy who disappeared about sixty years ago?"

Levi Buck looked up sharply. "Hellfire, anybody who knows this country knows how easy it is to get caught in some canyon by a flash flood or fall off some rock. What does Joe say?"

"He says Mose Crahorn got drunk one night years later and told him that he and Matt Oxborrow shot Ruess. But he never said anything 'til now."

The old man rubbed his stubble of grey whiskers in contemplation. "Maybe. They were mean cusses. Or maybe old Joe Heaton just wants to get his name in the papers."

"Can you go with me to talk to Heaton?" Jared asked. "He might open up to you." Jared had seen pictures of both men together when they were in their twenties, hunting deer and working in cattle roundups.

"When?"

"I'm headed there now."

The old man nodded, and continued eating. When they finished, he gathered their plates and dropped them into a pan in the sink. He got his wide-brimmed hat and they went out onto the porch. From behind a weathered barn, Sitka came tugging a heavy reddish-brown hide, black at the neck. The dog had chewed the still-fresh remnants of meat from the hide.

Jared stifled a groan and shook his head. "Pa, I knew that wasn't beef we were eating, but I wasn't going to mention it." The elk hunt didn't begin for another two weeks.

"That so?" Levi asked with a twinkle in his eye. "Hank Morton gave me that quarter of beef."

"Then what about that hide?" Jared asked motioning at the elk hide that Sitka had reluctantly left to join them.

"Road kill," the old man replied.

With a disgusted shake of his head, Jared led the way to his truck. His father paid little attention to the game laws, figuring that since his grandfather had settled this country a hundred years earlier, he had some vested rights in the wild game. More than once that attitude had got him in trouble with state authorities.

* * *

The highway to Escalante ran through red-rock country into the pines, and then turned east on Highway 12, past the edge of the colorful pinnacles of Bryce Canyon National Park. Beyond the park, the road dropped to what seemed the fringe of the world, hugging a narrow hogback of yellow and pink sandstone for three miles where the edges dropped away on either side toward what looked like an infinity of space—and a moon-like landscape of tortured rock. There was barely room for two cars to pass. Each time he traveled it, Jared chuckled to himself. Some tourists from the East and from the plains states refused to cross the hogback, and had instead turned around and traveled the extra hundred miles to reach Capitol Reef National Park by a less nerve-racking route.

In the distance—beyond the strange rock formations, sitting more than fifty miles away—Jared could clearly see the hump of the sacred Navajo Mountain that rose on the reservation south of Lake Powell. Sitka rode in back with his head stuck out the window over Jared's shoulder, savoring the cold wind of the morning.

The men rode mostly in silence, but for a time, Levi Buck talked about his times with Joseph Hyrum Heaton, from the time they were boys together until they worked rounding up wild cattle from the gullies and brushy coulees of the Arizona strip. Then he fell silent, lost in reverie, and Jared did not interrupt his reflection.

Escalante sits at the foot of the majestic thirty-mile-long Aquarius Plateau that rises to more than 10,000 feet. The plateau, covered with spruce and grass and dotted with lakes, made the town a quiet ranching center. Set among scenic cliffs, the town that Jared now entered had changed since the establishment of the Grand Staircase-Escalante National Monument. Several motels now lined the streets, and a new Bureau of Land Management Monument center had a parking lot that was usually filled with tourist's cars. As witness of the conflict engendered by the monument, two blocks farther along, a large wooden sign on a vacant lot read: "Public Lands are for all the public—wilderness is for only a few people."

Most telling of all of the changes that had occurred, however, was a new log building with a large sign declaring "Escalante Outfitters," with an equally large sign beneath that said "Expresso." That sign always evoked a bittersweet chuckle from Jared, for he was uneasy with the swelling tide of newcomers into the area that was quickly changing the pioneer character of these towns. Luckily, he told himself, this country was big and dramatic enough that it would take a century for them to ruin it.

On that day in 1934 when Ruess had come riding into Escalante on his burro, townspeople had speculated on what the young man was up to. Ruess was a slender, tanned youth with soft features and an engaging manner that made him immediate friends. He was different from the other drifters who occasionally wandered through town. He was polite, well-mannered, and interested in everything around him—always pausing on the dirt streets of the little town to chat. Above all, he was interesting himself, and when he set up camp under a gnarled cottonwood across the river from town, he had soon won over the younger population. Around his campfire he told stories, sharing his dinner of deer meat and potatoes with the local boys. He explained that he had come to "look the country over" and make some drawings. Together they rode on horseback through the canyons, searching for arrowheads and pottery shards. He even paid the dime admission to the local movie house for a few of the boys, where they saw "Death Takes a Holiday."

In turn, they showed him the Indian petroglyphs etched into the sandstone walls of remote canyons by the ancient ones seven centuries earlier.

At that time, in all of the United States, no town was more remote than Escalante. The picturesque area had been settled little more than half a century earlier by cattlemen and ranchers who were part of Brigham Young's colonizing plans of settling the West.

After a few days in Escalante, Ruess had mounted one of his two burros, waved merrily to his youthful admirers, and set off southward on the Hole-in-the-Rock trail toward the Colorado River—to disappear into the annals of unsolved quandaries of a mysterious land.

*   *   *

When they reached an old brick home on the edge of town, Jared pulled up under a huge cottonwood that shaded the yard.

The lawn was well-kept, with flowers in their last fall bloom lining the house. A slender, fragile-lookng man was just emerging from the backyard, dressed in a suit and tie and hobbling along with the aid of a cane.

Levi Buck got out and gave a pitiful shake of his head. "That you, Joe Heaton?"

The man straightened himself up and studied them without recognition. "Course it is," he replied crossly. "Who'd you expect lived here?"

"Levi Buck, Joe. Guess you don't remember the hardscrabble times we had poppin' brush together rounding up cows for the Heaton ranch." Levi extended his hand as recognition slowly lit Joe Heaton's face.

"Well, I'll be cussed," he exclaimed. "I thought you was dead, Levi!" Heaton gave Levi's hand a fragile shake.

"Too ornery to die, I guess," he joked. "But you, Joe, you don't look worth a damn."

At this, the frail man gave a hearty laugh. "Nope, I guess the Lord's just gettin' me ready to go. Fact is, I'm tired of hangin' on. I want to see my Clara again."

Jared stepped forward. "Mr. Heaton, I'm Jared Buck, the county sheriff down in Kanab. Can we talk a minute?"

Heaton looked from one man to the other, made the connection between the two. "Well, I was just headed for sacrament meetin', but . . . what about?"

"Everett Ruess. I know that . . ." Jared paused when he saw the craggy features of the old man contort into a pained look.

"These people are dang near driving me crazy—ever since that magazine fella came and wheezled me into tellin' him what I kept still about all these years."

"What people?" Jared asked

"Lots," Joe snorted with a look of disgust. "You name it."

Jared chewed on his lip for a moment. He wondered if that magazine writer knew what a Pandora's box he was opening when he wrote his story. "Did some movie people come and see you, Mr. Heaton?"

Heaton grimaced, and Jared thought he was going to have a coughing spell. "They dang nigh wore me out," he said, choking slightly. "Kept comin' back, hasslin' me. The big one almost accused me of doing in the Ruess boy, and I was only ten at the time. Can we sit down?" He motioned to a log bench in the shade under a tree, and they sat there.

Jared didn't speak while the man caught his breath.

Finally Heaton stared up into the leaves of the cottonwood above that were rustling in the slight breeze. "What I told 'em was what I told the magazine fella—and it's just the way I remember it," he began. "I was ten when this young traveler came into town. Had two burros with him. Oh, he was a delightful sort—young, handsome, sandy-haired fella who smiled a lot. Ever'body took to him right off. He camped on the edge o' town, down there in the trees." Joe paused to point with his cane to a flat spot next to the creek where a house now stood. "Course, there wasn't no house there then. But stories. . . . I tell ya, never heard nobody tell a story like he could. Some of us boys took him deer meat and we roasted it over a fire ever' night. And he told stories that . . . ," Joe paused to look into their eyes and be sure they understood, "that makes television seem like the dullest thing ever invented." He shook his head. "We liked the young man, all right. Then he took his burros and headed south. Never saw him again."

Jared cleared his throat. "What about Mose Crahorn?"

Joe Heaton gave a reluctant nod. "Mose was lots older than me. But one night, about fifteen years after the Ruess boy disappeared, I ran across him tryin' to get home. He was so drunk he couldn't hardly move, so I took him. Along the way he was babbling. When I stopped in front of his place, he started braggin' that he and Matt Oxborrow had done in the Ruess kid. Way down near the Colorado River. Maybe he was just a braggin' drunk. I don't know."

For a moment nobody spoke. "I see," Jared said. "Did these movie people mention they were talking to others around here."

Heaton tried to shrug, but his shoulders didn't work well. "Maybe," he offered. "I heard they were talking to anybody who knew about Ruess." He chuckled. "Course, there's hardly any-body left who even saw the kid. They've all gone down there—with my Clara." He motioned toward a patch of green among the sagebrush that was the town cemetery. "Be goin' myself soon. Now, brethren, I missed the opening music already. Don't want to miss the sacrament and talks. Who knows how many more meetings I got left in me." He struggled to his feet, balanced for a moment to get a grip on the cane, and then straightened himself. "Levi, good to see you. You got your life in order yet?"

Levi grinned. "I'm doin' okay, Joe."

"Remember," Heaton said, cocking his head, a twinkle in his eye. "Old time is swiftly flying." With that, he began to hobble toward the road.

"You want a ride to church?" Levi called. The red-brick Mormon chapel in the center of town was four blocks away.

"No, thanks. Still able to get there on my own power." With that, he paused and turned back. "You know, we've had lots worse things happen here—shootings, rustlers, lots of people who went into the desert and never came back. I don't know why this Everett Ruess thing keeps comin' back. Seems odd."

Without waiting for their response, he turned and, with his halting gait, walked toward the center of town, humming an old Mormon pioneer tune as he went.

CHAPTER 4

When Jared arrived at his office, he was already aware that Angus Terry had been up most of the night. Angus had been on Sunday call when a fight between two groups of motorcyclists and dune-buggy fanatics had broken out at the Coral Pink Sand Dunes State Park a few miles west of town. The deputy was called to help the state park rangers quiet things down and get one knife victim to the hospital. With the summer waning, people came from as far as Salt Lake City and Las Vegas to get in one last outing at the popular playground.

"Well, at least nobody got killed." Angus jerked his thumb toward the dunes as Jared plopped down at his desk.

"Let's hope it stays that way."

"You find out anything about our movie friends up in Escalante?"

Jared clasped his hands behind his head and stared at the ceiling before answering. "Not much. I took Pop along and Joe Heaton told us Mose Crahorn bragged to him that he and Matt Oxborrow did the kid in—like the magazine said. But I've heard that over the years half a dozen guys have admitted to killing Ruess."

"Fifteen minutes of fame." Angus chuckled. "That's what Andy Warhol says everybody gets. I guess that's why a guy would admit to that."

"I guess so. You see anything of our California friends today?" Jared inquired.

"I bumped into Mooch this mornin'," Angus replied. "Said he was taking them down to the rez."

"The rez?" Jared looked puzzled. The huge Navajo Reservation was just across the forty-mile stretch of Lake Powell that bordered the county. "I guess they're followin' Ruess's trail, all right. Well, if they get in trouble down there, the tribal police can handle it. We can quit worryin' about them."

Angus stirred his coffee and looked contemplative. "Too bad. I'd like to've seen more of that brunette."

"You don't have good luck with brunettes, remember?" Jared said with a grin. Both of Angus's wives had had the same deep brown hair as Chandra Maroney, the friend of the movie producer.

"Aw, you didn't have to bring that up," Angus said, chortling. "So now what you got planned for today while I sit here and catch up on my sleep?"

"Oh, you got a few chores to do. And I still got some checkin' to do on the Ruess thing."

Angus tucked his thumbs in his belt and cocked his head. "Hell, Jared, I think you got fascinated by this disappeared kid too. The mystery of it get to you?"

With a flick of his hand, Jared dismissed the notion. "Oh, if there really was a murder, even back then, I suppose we ought to look into it."

"So now what?"

"Talk to some of the people who might know something about it—people who may have had their strings pulled by this movie bunch. It could be one of them who did the shooting up in Cottonwood Canyon."

He pulled out the file on Everett Ruess that he had kept ever since the magazine article had appeared, and began to refresh his memory. Along with the magazine article, there were several newspaper pieces, and two books dealing with the vanished wanderer. He thumbed through the book of the young adventurer's letters.

The youth had the habit of simply knocking on anyone's door and expecting them to make him welcome and take care of him. Many Navajos thought he was a witch because he would simply walk into their hogans and make himself at home. But his audacity and innocence earned him friends, and he had learned enough of the language to be able to converse with them. In his journal he told of sitting most of the night around a campfire with Navajos he met, drinking coffee, eating mutton, and singing the Navajo chants. He found the Navajo songs fulfilling, and he told of riding his burros through the canyons singing them to offset the loneliness.

After Ruess had disappeared from Escalante, decades of searches had failed to uncover the fate of the young adventurer. Because he had touched lives, and because he wrote with such fervor and romanticism of his adventurers, his disappearance had attracted national attention. Jared read from a letter that Ruess wrote to a friend in 1934.

> *Once more I am roaring drunk with the lust of life and adventure and unbearable beauty. I prefer the saddle to the streetcar and the star-sprinkled sky to a roof, the obscure and difficult trail, leading into the unknown, to any paved highway, and the deep peace of the wild to the discontent bred by cities. . . . I have the devil's own conception of a perfect time: adventure seems to beset me on all quarters without my even searching for it. . . . Alone I shoulder the sky and hurl my defiance and shout the song of the conqueror to the four winds, earth, sea, sun, moon and stars. I live!*

On that day in 1934, when Ruess had left Joe Heaton and the other boys, he had ridden his burro southward along the Escalante River down toward Hole-In-the-Rock, long before the Colorado River had been dammed to create Lake Powell. It was rugged going across land that was cut by deep gorges and canyons, all of them leading downward toward the giant river that had created the Grand Canyon and drained the Rocky

Mountains to run to the Sea of Cortez and the Pacific.

In later accounts it was generally agreed that Ruess had run across Mose Crahorn and Matt Oxborrow somewhere south in Kane County where they were hunting cattle. They had camped together for a night, shared a meal, and—according to the two cowpunchers—the next morning Ruess had gone with his burros on down the canyon.

Two months later, a search party found his burros in lonely Davis Canyon, just above the Colorado near Hole-In-the-Rock. None of his camp gear or clothes were ever found.

The place called Hole-in-the-Rock was a near shrine for local Mormons because in 1879, Brigham Young had sent two hundred hardy souls to colonize south of the Colorado River near what was now Moab. After intensive searching for a suitable crossing for their wagons upriver from the Grand Canyon, the colonizers decided to cut a way down through the sheer cliffs that towered above the river. For weeks they toiled at the herculean task in the sandstone, using hand tools and dynamite to create a path of sorts down to the river. The wagons had to be taken apart and lowered by ropes, rafted across, and then reassembled on the other side. Eventually the colonizers settled the town now called Blanding on a high plain next to the Abajo Mountains, where wresting a living from the hostile land on the edge of Indian country proved to be heart-wrenchingly difficult—but it was done.

It was near the crossing where the last sign of Everett Ruess was found.

*   *   *

That afternoon as Jared Buck drove the dirt road that was a shortcut up Johnson Canyon toward the Oxbow Ranch of Cal Oxborrow, he pondered his job in this lonely country. His county stretched from the dunes on the west 120 miles to Bullfrog on Lake Powell on the east, and from the Arizona border on the south nearly to Escalante on the north. It was mostly federal land, with a few ranches and mines scattered among the more-habitable parts that old homesteads sat on.

When President Clinton signed a bill establishing the Grand Staircase-Escalante National Monument north of Kanab, it prevented the development of a major coal mine on Kaiparowits Plateau that environmentalists said would devastate one of the great natural areas of the nation. On the other hand, it was a wildly unpopular move with most southern Utahns. In that beautiful, hardscrabble land, jobs were few, and there were cries that the land was being locked up by "bureaucrats in Washington." Protest meetings were held, the president was hanged in effigy, and Utah congressmen protested that the president had acted underhandedly—even illegally.

During the turmoil, Jared had kept his peace. In a place where "environmentalist" was a dirty word, he found himself happy that some steps were being taken to preserve the pristine land. During his college days as a wildlife student at Utah State University up north in Logan, he had come to appreciate that the mentality of "get in, cut it out, get out" held by many westerners was short-sighted, a hold-over from the nineteenth century when timber and water and land were seen as inexhaustible.

So, he kept quiet when his friends railed against those who talked preservation. There was a place he drew the line though. When the Sierra Club campaigned to drain Lake Powell to try to restore Glen Canyon to its original state, he only shook his head at the stupidity of it and wondered why they would ruin their credibility when they had backed so many good causes.

The most interesting place in his county, he felt, was the polygamist commune at Big Water, where Alex Joseph held sway. Joseph was a charismatic, tall, romantic-looking figure who openly practiced what was forbidden in his state, with twelve comely wives.

Of course, the Mormon Church had forbidden polygamy more than a century earlier. These days, the quickest way to get excommunicated from that body is to espouse polygamy. However, periodically, some apostate groups would crop up, calling themselves such names as "Church of the First Born," or "Church of the True Order."

One such was the settlement that straddled the Arizona-Utah line just east of Kane County. It was originally called Short Creek, but its name had been changed to Colorado City after a disastrous federal campaign to stop the practice had backfired in the 1950s. Sweeping down on the town, federal marshals had arrested most of the men and snatched the numerous children up and put them in foster homes. The resulting publicity in such publications as the *Saturday Evening Post* had shown that the children suffered horribly from the broken families thrown on welfare, and that the press coverage just strengthened the cause, as more alienated souls from around the nation found a reason to adhere to. It was decided that they were best ignored and left to molder in the seedy little community.

Jared had little sympathy for such men, who took advantage of the leniency and led their families into poverty and what he considered degradation. When he was occasionally dragged into the situation, he found an excessive amount of spousal abuse and incest. These he helped prosecute to the fullest extent of the law.

But Alex Joseph was something else. He made no pretense at religious motives. A tall, strapping man with a sense of humor, he went on national talk shows to tell of his adventures of living with twelve wives. Articulate and charming, he had chosen his mates exceptionally well. Not only were they attractive, but two were attorneys, one was a physician, and his flock also included a school teacher. The others had similar skills that they contributed to the well-being of their family and their community. They had settled onto a flat near Lake Powell that they called Big Water on the far eastern edge of Jared's jurisdiction. They seemed to cause no trouble. Jared liked Alex Joseph, and from time to time, he stopped off to chat and was warmly welcomed.

All in all, he liked his job, with its far-flung vistas and the long drives between destinations. The travel gave him time to contemplate his place in the universe. Over all, it resulted in a sense of peace.

* * *

It was late afternoon when his Cherokee rattled down the dusty lane towards the headquarters of the Oxbow Ranch belonging to Cal Oxborrow. The man had expanded the holdings his grandfather had built early in the century. Cal had gone off to college and learned not only modern agricultural methods but, more importantly, how to work the system. He had become politically prominent, and was able to increase his livestock grazing allotments on the lush national forest lands northward, enabling him to extend his holdings considerably. He was now a powerful man in the community.

When Jared pulled up in front of Oxborrow's ranch house, Cal was just coming out of his barn. The rancher grinned and touched his broad hat in greeting when he recognized the sheriff. Oxborrow was one of those western men who wore their belts slung beneath an overhanging belly, but Jared knew that at one time Cal had been a bulldogger on the rodeo circuit, and his arms still bulged beneath his denim shirt as evidence that his prosperity had not caused him to abandon hard work.

The rancher's face clouded when Jared asked about Carlton and the movie group. "Yeah, you'd think after all this time. . . ." He let the sentence hang and shook his head. "Well, I was civil to them, sheriff, but I sure wanted to throw them off my place. Why dredge all that up now? My family. . . ." He shrugged.

"Yep, I can understand that. But Cal," Jared said, "somebody took a couple of shots at them. Shot up Mooch Winslow's truck."

"They did?" Cal seemed genuinely surprised. "Who do you think would do somethin' like that?

"I don't know," Jared admitted. "You got any ideas?"

Oxborrow held up his hands in protest. "Hey, none of us. We didn't have words or anything."

"I expected so, but I have to check everything," Jared replied. "And Mooch has riled the feathers of lots of folks around here. Maybe they were sendin' him a message."

"More'n likely." Oxborrow paused to knock some mud from his boots against the wooden fence.

Jared waved to Oxborrow's two teenage sons, who were shooting baskets by the barn—bare-chested in the afternoon heat. They stopped, and basketball on his hip, the oldest waved back. Kelly Oxborrow was a tailback on the Kanab football team—the position Jared had played on the same team twenty years earlier. The younger was a sophomore and played receiver. Jared liked the boys.

"Hey, Kelly," Jared called. "You guys better kick butt when you play Pine Valley this week."

They both grinned widely. "You got it, Sheriff!" Kelly called back.

Cal Oxborrow was still standing by his fence pondering what Jared had told him as Jared drove away.

* * *

The sun had nearly set when Jared's Jeep pulled up to the broken gate of the Crahorn ranch. Ira Crahorn stood watching with his thumbs tucked into his overalls and a scowl on his face as the dust settled.

Jared took a deep breath before he opened the door. He wasn't eager to face old man Crahorn. Twenty years earlier, the previous sheriff had sent the rancher for a three-year vacation at Point-of-the-Mountain prison after he was caught stealing cattle over by Hanksville. And twice since he had been sheriff, Jared Buck had jailed him for barroom brawls. He was a surly and cantankerous man, and it probably didn't help his mood any, Jared guessed, that the magazine had named Crahorn's father as having confessed to killing Everett Ruess after he had stumbled into their camp those many years ago.

Ira Crahorn narrowed his eyes and spat tobacco juice onto the dirt as Jared approached.

"You lost or sunthin'?" Crahorn asked without a smile. He was a small, wizened man with deep crevices in his face. His shirt was stained with the remnants of several breakfasts.

"Howdy, Mr. Crahorn," Jared said, pushing his hat back and wiping his brow. It was still hot, and he remembered he hadn't eaten yet today. "Just checkin' on something. Somebody took a few shots this morning at some people from Hollywood down in Cottonwood Canyon."

"That so?" The old man squinted with suspicion. "Hit anybody?"

"Nope. Shot out the tires of Mooch Winslow's truck though."

Crahorn chewed on his lip as he considered this. "Damn shame. Too bad they got missed. Them sonsabitches was here couple of days ago. Somebody oughta remind them to mind their own damn business."

"That so?" Jared inquired. "They come askin' you about the Ruess kid, did they?"

The old man made a gruff noise in his throat and spat again. "California dudes. Acting high and mighty, like they owned the place and me along with it."

Jared puckered his lips and nodded. He didn't think that the old man had gone gunning for the film people, but he had to follow the trail. "Were you around on Friday morning, Mr. Crahorn?"

"Hell!" snorted the rancher. "You think I took a potshot at those bastards? I bet you'd like to pin that on me," he said accusingly, his eyes narrowing in hostility.

"Nope, I hadn't figured you did it," admitted Jared "Had to ask though."

Crahorn gave a little shake of his head. "Not a bad idea though, them dragging up all that crap that happened so long ago. They better let the dead stay dead."

Jared squatted down against the fence, thinking. He pulled a brown piece of cheatgrass and began to chew it, letting the silence settle over them. "Seems like that magazine stirred things up proper when they wrote about Everett Ruess disappearing like he did," he remarked. "Anybody else come around asking you about him?"

"Too damn many." Crahorn stared sullenly into the sky. "Now why don't you just ride along, Sheriff. I got work to do."

Jared rose and dusted his knees with his hat. "All right, Ira." He touched his hat in farewell, started to go, and then turned back to face the old man. "Tell me, did your father ever talk to you about Ruess?" he asked. "I guess he and Matt Oxborrow were the last ones to see the kid."

With a look of disgust, Crahorn gave a violent shake of his head. "You think he killed the kid, don't you?" he accused. "Hells bells, if anybody killed him, it was probably some outlaw Navajo or that crazy lion hunter."

"John Lilly?"

"Hell yes. My old man told me once he thought it was probably Lilly did away with the kid."

Jared frowned as he considered this. Ever since he was little, Jared had heard stories of John Lilly's exploits—living alone off in some remote shack in the canyons, surrounded by his dogs and obsessed with the need to pursue and kill mountain lions. In earlier years he had made a living of sorts off the bounties paid for dead lions by the state and the stockmen's associations for the protection of their sheep and cattle.

Once Jared had run across the lion hunter on the Dirty Devil River near the Arizona border. While on a search for a missing plane, Jared had gone through a morass of canyons and mesas north of the Grand Canyon and had discovered a tumble-down shack with smoke coming from the chimney.

Lilly had given him a cool welcome, but had offered him some beans and coffee. With his startlingly blue eyes peering from beneath a leather hat and a white beard hanging down over a shirt and jacket that had not seen soap and water in years, the lion hunter was a local legend. Jared had often thought that if he had lived anyplace else, the old man would probably have been institutionalized. Still, he assumed he didn't hurt anybody, and he moved from place to place at a whim so he was hard to keep track of.

"Old Lilly, huh?" Jared mused. "Well, maybe that's possible."

"Damn right," Crahorn answered. "An' we don't need no movin' picture people rilin' the water no more."

Jared took a deep breath as Ira Crahorn turned without a goodbye and trudged toward his house. Jared glanced up at the frame building that looked like it was left over from pioneer times and caught a glimpse of a curtain being moved. Mrs. Crahorn was a mousy little woman with a chronic cough and not much else in life. Jared had often felt sorry for her.

"Maybe not, Mr. Crahorn," he called. "But it looks like they're determined."

With that, Jared turned, got into his truck, and sat a moment, pondering. *John Lilly.* He wondered if the old man was still alive, or if he had died alone and unnoticed in one of his primitive shelters. In any event, not a very likely suspect. But some day, when he had time, he would look him up.

CHAPTER 5

At the Cinnamon Cliffs Motel the next morning, Jared Buck greeted the pot-bellied clerk in the western shirt behind the counter. "Cletus," he asked, "is that movie bunch up yet?"

"Sorry, Jared. They left about eight with Mooch Winslow." The clerk thumbed toward the rooms. "That girl, the looker, she's still here though." With a leer, he added, "You might want to talk to her—she's still in. I been watchin'."

Jared frowned. "I might, Cletus. But strictly business."

"Sure," Cletus said with a smirk.

* * *

On the third knock, the door opened a crack and then swung wide. Chandra Maroney stood there in a robe, half open at the neck.

"The sheriff, I do believe," she said musically. "Come on in." She stepped back and gave a grand welcoming gesture.

Jared cleared his throat, not moving. "Better not," he declined. "I just wanted to report what I found up in Escalante."

"You found the shooter?" she asked.

"No, Ma'am. I just talked to some of the ranchers there. Some of them are not too happy about this movie. Some of their families were involved with Ruess, you know." He fidgeted in the doorway.

She laughed. "Ma'am? Isn't that right out of 'Gunsmoke' or something? I don't think anybody's ever called me that."

"Sorry."

"No matter. Well, let's hope they don't start shooting again. That could put a crimp in this project."

"I see." Jared had removed his hat, and now he turned it over and over. "Tell me, how far along is this movie they're talking about anyway?"

She fluffed her hair before answering. "Well, they're checking out locations now—getting a few establishing shots."

For a moment, Jared studied her face. She was in the process of putting on makeup, and Jared marveled at how thick she was laying it on. She would have been pretty without it, albeit slightly jaded. His own Sunny had worn little makeup. She hadn't needed it. "So it's a done deal?" he asked.

"Not quite. Ron Murdock has committed only to exploring the project. The other ten million is on hold until he's convinced it's going to work."

Jared considered this. "I see. Young, isn't he, to be worth that much?"

"His father left it. We should all be so lucky." She looked skyward as if in supplication. "He's got some idealistic bones in him. Wants to commemorate the ideals of this young guy—Ruess."

Jared pursed his lips as he contemplated this. "And your job?"

The woman gave him a coy look, and leaned back against the doorway. "Script supervisor," she answered. "And maybe . . ." she arched her eyebrows and worked her tongue over her lips, "maybe a small part for little Chandra."

"I see," he said with a grin. He tried to avert his eyes from the split in her robe. "So, where've the boys gone? Part of my job is to keep them out of trouble."

She shrugged. "Over into Arizona, out to the Indian reservation. Me, I'm not cut out for roughing it. So I stayed here to explore your little town."

"It's an okay place. Miss . . . Maroney, was it?"

"Chandra, to you. Tell me, what's there to do here? It looks pretty dead."

"Some folks think so," he said with a smile. "But St. George is only ninety minutes away. Not much there, either, unless you're into golf or scenery. Then Las Vegas is another hour and a half if you're desperate."

She let her eyes wander over his face. It was decidedly rugged, if not handsome. "I uh . . . I don't suppose you could find time to show a girl around?"

Jared gave a nervous shake of his head. "I'm pretty tied up right now," he said. "This shooting and all. But my deputy Angus might have time. But thank you, Ma . . . Miss Maroney."

She laughed, began to close the door, and wriggled her fingers at him. "Well, I tried," she said cheerfully.

*   *   *

When Mooch Winslow's Land Rover pulled into the parking lot at the visitors' center at Navajo bridge, a half-dozen Japanese tourists were milling around the telescope that looked over the Colorado River below, where it tumbled, still blue, before it swept into the Grand Canyon.

The newcomers stretched their legs, swigged a cold beer from the cooler that Mooch Winslow offered them, and then headed inside to escape the morning heat. As they entered the flagstone building, a gray-haired, burly park ranger nodded a greeting. A young Navajo woman was at the cash register, just finishing a sale of Grand Canyon memorabilia to two German tourists.

"Mornin', folks," the ranger said, giving a nod of recognition to Mooch Winslow. "Welcome. Is Mr. Winslow here treating you right?"

"So far," Ron Murdock said pleasantly.

But Alex Carlton shook his head. "That's if you don't count getting shot at yesterday."

"That right?" The ranger arched an eyebrow at Mooch Winslow. "Well, Mr. Winslow's usually good for a little excitement. It comes with his tours."

"Nah, just a mistake," Mooch protested. "Some trigger-happy deer hunter, most likely."

"Good. We need to take good care of our guests. Can I help you folks find anything?" The badge he wore on his uniform read "Al Coots."

Carlton cleared his throat. "Everett Ruess," he said. "That's who we're looking for."

"The lost Ruess fella, eh? Well, here's a couple of books about him," said the ranger. He led them to a bookcase against the wall, searched a moment, and then held out two paperbacks.

Murdock took them, and almost lovingly ran his fingers over the volumes. "I've devoured these back home. But we can use a couple more copies."

The park ranger gave a contemplative nod, and sidled closer to them. "Of course," he said in a confidential tone, "you won't find out much about what really happened to Everett Ruess in those books."

"What do you mean?" Carlton demanded.

"I mean, they don't tell what really happened to that young, adventurous free spirit."

"And you know?" Ron Murdock was incredulous.

"Sure, but I don't usually mention it to people. It ruins their illusions."

Peralto, the quiet member of the group, stepped forward. "So what do *you* think happened? We're puttin' lots of money in this thing. A film like this costs bucks."

The park ranger paused to rub his graying sideburns. "Making a movie about it, eh? Interesting." He contemplated them for a long minute, and then gave a little nod. "In that case, I guess I can tell you fellas what really happened to Everett Ruess."

"You actually think you know?" Murdock asked, his eyebrows arching in surprise.

The ranger gave a little laugh. "Heck, of course I know where

Everett Ruess is. In Lebanon, Missouri. Came there in 1935, riding a mule. Liked the country so much he stayed."

"Come on!" Carlton almost spat the words.

"What makes you think that?" Murdock asked, has jaw hanging half open.

"I saw him—often," Coots said, hunching closer and speaking in conspiratorial tones. "Why, my father told me when he was a kid that young Ruess came ridin' in like he owned the town. Full of stories about the West and the Indians he'd lived with. Then he met young Jessica Boone—everbody said she was the perttiest girl in Missoura. He got smitten but good. Her father offered him a half section of land along the Missoura River. Settled down there. I saw him lots when I was growin' up."

Murdock looked confused, not sure if he was the butt of a joke. But the ranger appeared perfectly serious. Alex, however, turned away in disgust, while Mooch Winslow stood leaning against the flagstone wall, wearing an amused grin.

"What's all this about then?" Murdock held up the two books by way of challenge.

Al Coots chuckled. "Well, old Ruess kind of enjoys the mystery about him. Doesn't want to give up a good thing. So he sits there up on that hill in the big house in Lebanon looking out over the river and laughin'. He's quite a character. Good story teller. You should hear him tell about the time down around the Lukachukai trading post when he walked into a hogan and the Indians thought he was a witch. Fed him proper with lamb stew an' then took him to a squaw dance. One of the young Navajo girls grabbed him and pulled him into the dance. If he would've danced until morning with her they would've been married."

Murdock blinked, his brow wrinkled, and then he tentatively said, "You are joking, aren't you?"

"Joking? Now why would I joke about a thing like that? My family's been friends of Jacob Ruess—that's what he goes by there—for the past fifty years. Joking? No, sirree."

Alex Carlton huffed and pulled himself up to his full height, glaring at the park ranger. "Look, we know when we're getting our legs pulled."

With a chuckle, Coots waved his hand toward the expanse of red rock vistas out the window. "Well, sir, I wouldn't want to be the one to disillusion you about Everett Ruess. Fine man. But you can look all you want to over this whole grand region, down the canyons and the gullies and up on Navajo Mountain, if you want. But if you really want to find the famous Everett Ruess, you better hit I-70 for Lebanon, Missoura."

Ron Murdock laughed, only half convinced that he was being kidded. "Okay, but I guess we'll need the books anyway. Thanks, uh—" he read the man's badge, "Mr. Coots." Murdock paid the woman at the cash register and glanced over at the park ranger, who sat watching them without a smile as they went out the door into the morning sun.

CHAPTER 6

In their favorite corner of Houston's Café, Angus cocked his head and regarded his boss with an amused smile. "So, you're buying into this Everett Ruess thing too, eh?" he said over the noise of the brunch crowd.

Caught in the middle of a bite of steak and eggs, Jared nodded glumly. "Maybe. Like I told Sheriff Calder over in Panguitch, if there was a murder—even if it was sixty years ago—we should probably check into it."

"And he bit on that?" Angus asked.

"Sort of."

Angus's wide face broke into a grin. "Like nobody's tried before!"

"Well, some new things been happening," Jared said. "With that magazine article, and now this movie, I just thought I'd check out a few things." Jared was used to Angus' contrariness, so it didn't ruffle him.

Angus laughed. "But you'd probably have to arrest Cal Oxborrow's grandfather, or maybe Mose Crahorn, even though they're dead," he joked. "And you'd likely not be too popular hereabouts."

"Well, in some circles I'm not too popular now, I guess," Jared responded. "Over the years more than one miscreant had threatened him after being jailed, but so far nothing serious had happened aside from a few midnight phone threats. Several times, Sitka had awakened him with furious barking at what Jared suspected were prowlers, but little damage was ever done to his place.

The door swung open, and Mooch Winslow entered, laughing. When he spied the two lawmen eating, he approached and pulled up a chair without waiting to be invited. The guide was not one of Jared's favorite characters, but at times he had a flamboyance about him that gave him a certain charm.

"Jared, Angus," he greeted them, "now this is some fun, ain't it? These Hollywood characters."

Angus sized him up with a grin. "Anybody shootin' at you guys any more, Mooch?"

"Aw, that was just somebody playin' around, I guess. But I would like to get paid for my two tires that got blowed away. You find any likely suspects yet, Jared?"

"Not yet," Jared said with a shake of his head. "But, Mooch, you know there's an awful lot of boyfriends and husbands out there who don't think too kindly of you."

"Naw, those are all rumors, Sheriff." He laughed, not displeased.

"Any more problems with that bunch?"

Mooch screwed up his face. "It's about like herdin' cats. They don't like rough roads much, which is about all we got out in this country. We went out to Kaibito lookin' for some old Navajo they'd heard about. Hell, nobody remembers anything about what went on sixty years ago."

"But, Mooch, " Angus put in, "I thought you guys were going to solve this Everett Ruess mystery."

"Not my idea," Mooch replied with a dismissive flick of his hand. "But as long as they pay me three hundred a day, I'll take 'em to hell-an-gone lookin' for his bones. Why, I took them in some canyons where I never even been. Couldn't see the sky in some places. They already shot some film."

"They're pretty green," Jared said. He looked up as Chandra Maroney swept into the restaurant, followed by a pale, thin man with hollow cheeks. When seated, she saw Jared and smiled in recognition.

"Look." Mooch indicated the man with a nod. "I guess you haven't met that gent—if you can call him that. He's their cameraman. Got in late two nights ago. Then we left early for Pariah Canyon and over to the reservation."

"How'd that go?" Jared asked.

"Fair," Mooch answered with a shrug. "Now they want me to take them out to Standing Rock."

"That so?" Jared took a sip of his Coke, leaned back, and studied the man across the room. Chandra looked up, saw him, and wiggled her fingers to beckon him.

Mooch Winslow was not about to let this pass. "Hey, Sheriff, you got somethin' goin' there?"

"Nothing like you do, Mooch," Jared said with a frown. "But I suppose we better go meet the new guy. You ready, Angus? See you, Mooch."

Jared rose, put on his hat, and the two officers wended their way through the tables to where Chandra Maroney sat, watching them with a pleased expression.

"Good morning, Sheriff Buck," she cooed. "I guess you haven't met our cameraman. Willie Silvis, Sheriff Buck."

Silvis, looking bored, simply nodded.

"Oh, don't mind him." She frowned at Silvis. "He spent yesterday tromping around your desert for ten hours. But to be honest, he's usually surly anyway. Right, Willie?"

He didn't even look at her. "If you say so, Chandra," he muttered.

Jared wanted to get acquainted. "I understand you guys got some good film."

Silvis looked up at him, shrugged, and almost brightened. "You might say that. Matter of fact, I never seen anything like those long shots and the narrow canyons—the different colors."

Angus laughed. "Yeah, but there's no place to hide if you're caught in there after a flash flood. And that can be without a cloud in the sky."

Silvis studied the deputy, half in doubt.

Jared nodded. "He's right. Just be careful and watch the weather. Your guide knows how it works."

With a glance in the direction of Mooch Winslow, Silvis shook his head. "That guide is an ass."

Jared considered this, and finally laughed. "Maybe so, but he knows how to stay alive in this country. You want to listen to him."

Jared frowned when his cell phone rang. It was the newest deputy, Porter Cannon, obviously alarmed. "Sheriff, come quick," he said excitedly. "We got a big problem brewing here!"

"At the visitors' center?" Jared asked, his frown deepening.

"Yes, hurry! I think there's going to be fighting." His voice bore a hint of panic. Cannon had been on the force only a few months. He was identifiable by the fact that he always wore every accessory possible on his belt—handcuffs, mace, nightstick, pager, and anything else that buckled on.

"Okay, be there in five minutes," Jared said with a deep sigh. He hung up and motioned to Angus. "Trouble at the monument again. Let's go."

"Same thing, huh?" the deputy said, hiding a smile. "The cowmen and the eco-freaks just can't be friends."

A few days earlier Jared had interceded when a half dozen protestors had set up a table with their literature next to the visitors' center of the Grand Staircase-Escalante National Monument on the edge of town. They were vociferous in their demands that all cattle grazing be stopped on the hundreds of square miles of scenic land encompassed by the new monument.

The agreement was that they would remain three hundred feet from the visitors' center with their literature, but they had violated that and the feisty monument ranger, a middle-aged strong-willed woman from Grand Junction, insisted that an arrest be made. Jared had reluctantly issued a ticket to the young leader and that had quieted things down. Now it seemed to be starting all over again.

*   *   *

As he pulled to a stop in front of the center, a crowd was milling near the entrance. It was a mixture of tourists, townspeople, local ranchers, and a few environmental activists that the locals liked to label "outsiders"—some from the Salt Lake area. Porter Cannon was at the rear of the group, pacing nervously. When he saw Jared, he looked relieved. The sound of angry voices rose above the occasional laughter from those who were merely spectators.

"What's happening, Porter?" Jared asked as he strode up.

The deputy shrugged and looked nervously around. "It looks like there's going to be some fights," he said.

Angus walked up and stood, watching with folded arms. "Nobody's pulled a gun yet, have they?" he said, joking. He seemed amused by the whole thing, a fact that irritated Jared Buck.

Already there had been major damage done. A couple of years earlier, an environmentalist extremist had poured sugar into the gas tank of one of the Garfield County bulldozers working surreptitiously to pave the scenic Burr Trail that led down off the plateau to Bullfrog on Lake Powell. The County Commission wanted the trail paved, while the National Park Service wanted it left in its pristine state and had obtained a court order to that effect. On the other hand, since then, visiting environmentalists' tires had been slashed, and some said that anyone with a Sierra Club sticker on his car that stayed at a local motel would have a smashed window by morning. In Jared's view, both sides harbored idiots, and he just tried to keep the peace.

The crowd parted as a huffing Elizabeth Hansen, in a creased Monument Ranger's uniform, strode up and confronted the officers. She was known as a no-nonsense director, and the anger on her red face told Jared that this would not be an easy dilemma to solve.

"It's about time you got here, Sheriff," she blurted. "What are you going to do about it?" She waved her arm at the group, where a thin young man with a ponytail, wearing a Mexican chaleco vest and worn Levis, was being confronted by two men in cowboy hats and boots. They were all shouting.

Jared nodded, and began to work his way through the crowd. Jared was well acquainted with Mark Herrington. Indeed, he had warned him that he would be arrested this time if his group didn't keep their distance as agreed. Now they had moved their table right next to the visitors' center sidewalk.

Herrington had raised his voice to a shout. "This is not your land!" he screamed. "It belongs to the public, and the cattle are destroying what belongs to all of us."

He was answered by a snort from a heavy-set cattleman whom Jared recognized as Caleb Smoot, whose ranch was just over the line in Arizona.

"Listen, you snot-nosed little puke, you don't know nothin' about this country," Smoot shouted. "For a hunnert and thirty years my family been usin' the same grazing ground up there— buildin' fence, stock ponds, watchin' it grow, takin' care of it." As he spoke, his cheeks puffed out in his anger. "We know you and your Eastern pansies want this as your private playground, but this is our livin'."

Herrington leveled a finger at the rancher's face as he interrupted, shouting, "And a fine mess you've made of it too!"

Another rancher stepped forward, smartly-dressed in a leather vest and polished boots. It was Cal Oxborrow, a member of the Kanab City Council and a well respected member of the community. He nodded to Jared, and then turned his attention to Herrington.

"That's not true, son," he said in a calm voice. "It's only the drought that has hurt the range, not the grazing. In fact, some studies show that grazing actually helps the range by stimulating growth of grass."

Herrington placed his hands on his hips and glared. "Then where's all that grass that was belly deep to a horse that the pioneers wrote about?"

"Son, you're thinking of somewhere farther north," Oxborrow said with a laugh.

Herrington turned to the crowd. "Don't you see what's happening here? It's your land they're ruining for the benefit of a few families! We can't let that happen! We won't let that happen!" A chorus of shouts erupted from different segments of the group, agreeing and disagreeing.

Above it all, a shrill voice rose above the din—a voice that Jared recognized. It was the dominating tones of Kathryn Thompson—better known as "Cattle Kate," a wizened, ebullient, and charming antique of a woman who had no fear of man or beast in defending her ranching rights. As owner of the T-Bar Ranch west of town, she had gained fame all over the Rocky Mountains for carrying on a running feud with the Bureau of Land Management over her grazing allotments.

"You dimwits!" she shouted at the three workers behind the table offering flyers about cattle grazing on the monument. "You can't come in here and take our cattle and our way of life. Shame on you for even trying! These are generations-old rights!" There was some pushing and shoving in the crowd as two separate arguments broke out among the onlookers. Jared felt a strong poke in the ribs that caused him to take a step forward.

It was Ranger Hansen. "Sheriff!!" she demanded.

In response, Jared pushed forward and faced Herrington across his table of literature. "Mr. Herrington, we've got the same deal as last time," Jared said, keeping his tone friendly. "You know you have to have your table three hundred feet from the center."

Herrington regarded him coolly. "We need to get the message across, Sheriff," he said. "it's the future of the land that's at stake here."

"Yep, I know that," Jared replied. "But I also know the agreement was for you to leave room for people to come to the center without being bothered. You can still pass out your literature."

Herrington flipped his ponytail. "Sorry, Sheriff. We're not moving."

Jared shrugged in resignation. "Afraid I'll have to arrest you then," he said. He knew that this was Herrington's plan. To get arrested meant attention from the press and spreading their views in every newspaper in Utah, maybe throughout the West. Jared hated to be used like this.

"Have at it then," Herrington said, extending his wrists for the handcuffs.

Jared glanced at Angus, who had come to his side in support. "If that's your choice," he said, giving Angus the signal to put the cuffs on him. "Read him his rights."

As Angus adjusted the cuffs, a young woman in shorts and a khaki shirt burst from the crowd and leaped upon the table. "Wait!" she screamed. "It's your land that's being raped!" she pleaded with the crowd. There were a few catcalls.

In response, she broke out in a Woodie Guthrie song in a lilting, loud voice that quieted the crowd: "This land is your land, this land is my land, From California to the New York Island."

As she sang, her presence was so powerful, and her voice so compelling that soon others joined. Jared watched as Angus and Porter led Mark Herrington to the sheriff's car. Some members of the crowd gathered around to offer encouragement to the young arrestee.

"Have a good time, Mark," Jared called.

"I'll do that, Sheriff," Herrington said cheerily.

As Jared turned back, the song was finishing and the protestors were hauling their table back to the appointed area. He turned when he felt a tug on his sleeve, and saw Cattle Kate standing before him with her hands on her hips.

"Sheriff Buck, are you going to do something about my cows?" she demanded.

"Hello, Kate," he said. "Sure sorry. But I don't know what I can do." He knew that the Bureau of Land Management had impounded nearly fifty head of her cattle for not removing them from the monument when ordered. He was torn. He had known the woman all his life. His mother had worked in the Relief Society at church with her.

"This could nearly break me, Jared," she announced. "I won't give up without a fight."

"Surely there's something your lawyer can do, Kate." Jared

said. "But I know the feds are hard to work with."

Her face went stony. "Hard? They're impossible!"

"I know."

"And Jared, they're goin' to try to sell my cattle." Her voice was thin. He had never seen her emotional before. Then her voice grew hard. "I won't let that happen."

"Kate, I'll do anything I can."

In the end, he drove back to his office frustrated and sad. There was little to be done for her.

CHAPTER 7

When the phone rang in the office the next afternoon, Jared was greeted by Mooch Winslow's voice.

"Jared? Mooch."

Jared grinned, leaned back, and put his boots up on his desk. "So, back in town?" he asked. "How's it going with your Hollywood friends?"

"That's why I called. We just got back from the rez. You know, these SOBs are driving me nuts."

"Aw, but they're paying good money, Mooch. You should like that."

There was a long-suffering sigh on the other end. "Jared, these guys think they own the world—especially that Carlton guy," Mooch complained. "Treats everybody like peons. Anyway, you better go on over to the Standing Rock post. Carlton got us thrown out of there! You never saw such an insulting bastard as he was. You know old George, the owner?"

"I know him." Jared had often stopped in at the trading post to chat.

"Well, Carlton called him a liar," Mooch informed him. "Someone's told him that one of the old Navvies knew Ruess way back. George told him to go away. Carlton got mad as hell. George's young clerk—I think his name is Sam—got into it with Carlton. I tried to step into it, but Carlton hit the kid and bloodied his nose before I could stop him. Then he kicked him when he was down."

Jared groaned in disgust. "Then what?"

Mooch Winslow made a frustrated noise. "Got 'em out of there. I read Carlton the riot act. Told him the Navajo Police would toss him in the slammer for a few weeks if we didn't hightail it."

"Carlton's a little big for his britches, sounds like," Jared said.

"That's not all," Mooch said after a pause. "He fired me for standing up to him."

Jared chewed on this for a moment. "Maybe it's best," he replied. "That bunch is trouble any way you look at it."

"He still owes me," Mooch said. "I'm not gonna let him get away without paying me."

"Okay. I'll see that it's done," Jared assured him.

"Thanks, Jared. People like him make me want to go back to driving trucks."

"Comes with the territory, Mooch," Jared said with a laugh. "Taking care of any tourists—and especially movie people—is no easy job."

"You got that right," Mooch agreed.

"Anyway, I'll go out to the motel and talk to them," Jared promised. "Try to smooth things over."

There was silence on the other end. Jared sensed that Mooch had something else to say.

"Yeah, Mooch?" he prodded

"Well, you better go out to Standing Rock." Mooch paused. "George is mad as hell. He was calling the Navajo Police."

With a pained look, Jared nodded. For an anglo to go out on the reservation, pick a fight with a young Navajo, and kick him when he was on the floor—hell's bells! Jared had always had good relations with the tribal police, and meant to keep it that way. He decided to head out the next morning and try to smooth things over—at least to let the Navajo Police know that they cared about such things. Right now he better get to the filmmakers' motel and talk to Alex Carlton.

*   *   *

A few minutes later, he was halfway to the Cinnamon Cliffs Inn, which sat two miles out of town on a bench, against massive red cliffs, when frantic honking behind him caused him to glance in his rear-view mirror, slow down, and pull over. With a chuckle he recognized the red Bronco of Katherine Thompson. He had often joked that he would rather tangle with a gunnysack of wildcats than with Cattle Kate.

Slowly, he got out and ambled back toward the Bronco. Kate sat staring straight ahead behind the steering wheel. She was obviously seething from something.

"Howdy, Kate," Jared greeted her. "How're things now?"

She turned to glare at him, anger turning the corners of her mouth white. "Worse, Sheriff. What are you gonna do about it?"

"I don't know what anyone can do." He raised his hands in helplessness.

"You know they're plannin' to sell our cows at auction tomorrow. Well, the Cranstons and Smoots and Lees an' some of us are not gonna let 'em get away with it." She jerked herself out of the Bronco and drew herself up to her full height of just over five feet as she confronted him.

He mulled over what she had said. "Better be careful, Kate," he cautioned.

Her eyes grew wide, and Jared almost took a step backwards when her face turned red and she thrust a finger toward his nose. "It's only September!" she yelled. "We always graze those lands until December. Those cows gotta eat, Jared!"

"Well, the drought, Kate. It seems pretty bad, and you know the range is in bad shape."

She snorted. "What does the BLM know about range? Those college boys don't know sage brush from alfalfa."

Hers was part of a continuing struggle between local ranchers and the Bureau of Land Management officials. For four generations these cattlemen had run their stock on public lands during the summer—some with permits, some without. Inevitably through the decades some of the ranchers had developed a sense of proprietorship over their particular grazing territory. When the Grand Staircase-Escalante National Monument was established, grazing was still allowed, but with stricter controls that rankled the cowmen.

After several ignored warnings to remove the cattle from the federal land because of deteriorating range conditions, two weeks earlier the federal marshals had simply rounded up and impounded all of the cattle that they could catch on monument lands.

"They got 'em in Panguitch, an' they're gonna auction them off tomorrow, Jared," Kate said grimly. "So we're gonna go get 'em—come hell or high water."

Jared blinked. "That's not a very good idea, Kate," he warned. "Those are federal marshals."

"Ever'body's going armed, sheriff," Kate said, looking doleful. "Somebody's going to get hurt."

"When?"

"Tonight."

With a groan, Jared considered this. "Well, Panguitch is out of my jurisdiction, but I'll get in touch with Sheriff Calder. I got to take care of something here, and then I'll drive up. Maybe we can head off trouble."

As he drove away, he watched the angry woman, her jaw set, jam her truck into gear and spin a U-turn. Indeed, Cattle Kate was a formidable voice. When she was young, she had taken a husband from Phoenix to the ranch she had inherited, and then kicked him out after three years—with a tow-headed boy as her only souvenir of the experience. She became local legend during World War II when her son was drafted. She sat down and wrote President Franklin D. Roosevelt a letter explaining how in tarnation did he expect her to run this cattle ranch without her son when she had no electricity to help make things easier. It was seven miles to the nearest power lines.

Neighbors snickered when they learned of her letter. Then,

three weeks later, there came a knock at her door. A Utah Power truck was parked under her willow tree. "President Roosevelt sent us," the leader of the power crew explained. They installed power for her without cost.

*   *   *

At the motel, Jared was stopped by a trilling voice as he got out of his Jeep. "Hey there, aren't you lost?

It was Chandra Maroney, hurrying toward him from the pool. She was wearing a skimpy bikini and a huge smile. Her dark hair flowed down her back. With a start, Jared realized that the cascading hair reminded him of Sunny, even though she had been blonde, with luxurious hair that he loved so much falling over her shoulders. Of course, that was before the chemotherapy. It was a painful memory, and he shook it off.

"Hi," he called. "I see you're still here."

She stood a little too close and turned her eyes up to him. "Sure, still here," she said coyly. "This heat's awful. Why don't you join me in the shade?" She pointed to a table under an umbrella where her drink waited.

He took half a step backward. "Maybe later" he said. "I've got to talk to your boss. Is he around?"

She laughed, and in a scolding tone said, "I'm not sure I have a boss. But Alex and the others are in the dining room. They're just going over plans for scenes to shoot. Pretty boring stuff." Standing in the sun, she lowered her dark glasses, shifted her hips, and watched him stride toward the motel entrance.

When he went inside, Alex Carlton rose to greet him.

"Ahh, our sheriff." Carlton extended a hand in greeting.

Jared wondered why he was so friendly all of a sudden. "Mr. Carlton," he said, "you seem to be in a good mood."

Carlton spread his hands and laughed. "Of course. We just returned from shooting some great film. Found some gorgeous sites that will knock people's eyes out. It's all coming together beautifully, so why wouldn't I be in a good mood?"

Jared frowned and gave a little nod. "Well, I hear there was some trouble over at Standing Rock," he began. "We try to avoid those situations."

"Situation?" Carlton scoffed. "Pshaw, there wasn't any situation." He pursed his lips and gave a little shake of his head. "Just a little misunderstanding," he explained. "A few words spoken too hastily, I'm afraid. Nothing more."

"That so?" Jared asked with narrowed eyes. "I heard you hit the young clerk—and he's just a kid—and then kicked him when he went down."

"Nahh." Carlton denied the accusation with a determined shake of his head. "More like a playful push. No harm done."

"I hope not" Jared replied. The Navajo Police may not look at it that way. You were on their territory, you know."

"Of course. I sent Winslow back in with a few dollars. That should smooth it over."

"Maybe. Maybe not." Jared wondered if Mooch had actually delivered the money. "In any event, I'd like you to be more careful, especially when dealing with the Navajos. We have a good relationship, and we want to keep it that way."

Carlton smiled broadly, ingratiatingly. "Of course, sheriff," he said pleasantly. "Of course. We wouldn't want it any other way."

Murdock rose from across the room and approached with a smile. "Mr. Buck, we had the most wonderful tour," he said, jubilantly. "Sights I didn't know existed. No wonder Everett Ruess was in love with this country. It's going to make a beautiful film." He spread his hands across in front of him as if drawing a panorama. His voice took on the tone of a narrator: "A mysterious young artist," he intoned, "in love with a mysterious, beautiful land. Then the land swallows him up. We'll follow his trail. Interview some who still remember him. Especially one old Indian we heard about. Sundance Film Festival, here we come!"

"That Indian is probably dead by now," Jared observed. He liked Murdock. He wasn't overbearing like Carlton, with that ebullient Hollywood manner that was so superficial.

Murdock chewed on his lip for an instant. "Perhaps. But we can still tell the wonderful story of Ruess, with these marvelous canyons that so obsessed him." He was like a child who had discovered an astonishing new world.

At the same time, Jared wondered if somehow Carlton was looking to milk the banker of his money. The flamboyant Carlton had all the marks of a scam artist. One of Jared's college buddies had gone into the movie-making business, and through the years Jared had marveled at his tales of the various scenarios that existed in that dreamland that separated investors from their money. Murdock was obviously the money man in this deal.

"You think you guys will be around long?" Jared asked.

Murdock shook his head. "This was just a preliminary venture to see if it was feasible. We'll make some final arrangements tomorrow, and then the real work begins. So, probably late tomorrow or the next day we'll be gone. There's some paperwork to be done before I go back to San Francisco and they go to Los Angeles. In two months we'll be back to start shooting for real." The banker rubbed his palms in anticipation.

Outside in the parking lot, Jared took a deep breath as he strode past the Hollywood limousine. He wouldn't be sorry to see them go. He knew that he would have to go out to Standing Rock tomorrow to try to smooth things over with George and the Navajo Police. But right now he had to head to Panguitch to help Sheriff Calder face some angry cattlemen.

CHAPTER 8

The sun was low over the mountains as Jared headed northward. The highway to Panguitch rises high above the red-rock desert to wind through the pines and finally drops into a large valley with the orange spires of Bryce Canyon looming eastward. The hour-long trip always put Jared in a somber mood. Inevitably, he relived the night during his senior year of high school when a jarring tackle by a Panguitch High linebacker had smashed his nose and sent him to the sidelines with his head reeling. When the game ended in a two-point loss, he moped wearily toward the locker room behind his teammates, his head throbbing. As the Panguitch cheerleaders passed him on a celebratory trot around the track, one of them, her blonde pony-tail tossing, stopped and approached.

"Wow," she said gently, her deep-brown eyes intent. "You really got smacked. Does it hurt?"

Gingerly, Jared reached to touch his throbbing face. "Only when I laugh," he joked.

"Good!" she chirped, whirled, and shot back over her shoulder as she ran to catch up with the cheerleaders, "Get better."

* * *

It was the following month when Jared, Craig Yazzi, and two of their teammates traveled back up into the mountains to a church dance in Panguitch. Since pioneer times, dancing had been a mainstay of Mormon recreation. Each church building usually had a recreation hall that featured not only a stage for drama, but a basketball court that doubled as a dance floor.

That night the four friends, high school seniors who were outwardly blustering and cocky, stood on the sidelines watching the crowd as a small band belted out suitable dance tunes. Jared was never totally at ease dancing, but he always tried and nobody seemed to notice that he felt clumsy.

When he and Craig made their way to the refreshment table, he picked up a paper cup and surveyed the girls as he sipped on the pink punch. When someone touched his elbow, he jerked, sending a cascade of liquid sideways. Turning, he grimaced when he saw Sunny McEwen laughing as she held up her arm, dripping now.

"Hey, is that any way to act just because Panguitch beat you in football?" she teased, grabbing several napkins from the table and dabbing her arm.

With his face turning red, Jared reached to grab more napkins. In doing so, his sleeve brushed another cup of punch on the table, toppling it. "Man, I'm sorry," he said, his face contorted in embarrassment. He quickly began to sop up the spilled punch as she nearly doubled over in laughter.

"I'm such a klutz," he apologized. He looked at her closer, and then blinked, and his eyes lit up in recognition. She was the brown-eyed cheerleader. "Hey, I know you!"

"No, not yet," she countered. "But you should. I was just coming over to see if your nose had recovered."

"Ah, the Panguitch game. We was robbed!" he joked.

"Not hardly. But how's the face?"

He shrugged. "Ah, good. I can almost smell again."

She took his face in her hands, and examined him critically. "Well, I think a little bit of a crooked nose adds character to a guy's face, don't you?"

He didn't know whether to be insulted or flattered that she noticed. "Gosh, I hope so," he managed. "Looks like I'm stuck with it. Hey, I'm sorry I splattered you."

She gave a toss of her head and held up her arm. "Look, good as new. Tell me, do you dance as well as you drink punch?"

He laughed. "Worse, I'm afraid. But if you're game, I'll try not to wound you."

They danced, him feeling the stickiness of her hand from the spilled punch, and they talked of football, of mutual friends, and of the comparative merits of their towns. By the end of the evening, his head was spinning from the repartee.

That was the beginning. The road to Panguitch subsequently became a weekly jaunt. And when he traveled north to the university, she was there—living in a dorm and thinking of becoming a veterinarian. He was in wildlife management, hoping to become a game warden and to spend his days in the mountains watching over game animals. They studied together, dated every weekend, and drove back to southern Utah together on holidays, planning their future together.

Never had Jared known anyone who was so vivacious, so inevitably cheerful, so challenging, and yet so informed and caring for others. Sunny was president of the campus chapter of the Food Coalition and of her ward Relief Society.

So, on a bright May morning in Cache Valley, the couple had knelt and joined hands across the altar in the Logan LDS Temple and were married in the Mormon way, "for time and all eternity." It was the great anchor of Jared Buck's life—even now.

*   *   *

From the beginning they had known it was a possibility—had recognized that the beautiful mountain town of Panguitch had served as a sacrificial lamb of sorts for the frantic American efforts to keep up in the Cold War. These were patriots, the ranchers, lumbermen, and townspeople who had gladly marched away to fight in World War II, suffering the highest casualty rates of any Utah community. Patriotism was mandated by their Mormon beliefs, and community celebrations inevitably centered around honoring the flag and the nation.

Never mind that President James Buchanan had sent the largest part of the U.S. Army marching westward in 1857 to put down a supposed rebellion of Brigham Young and his colony of barely-settled Latter-day Saints in Utah. One officer of that army swore to his men that they would not return until they had hanged Brigham Young from the temple wall.

As it was, Brigham Young sent his frontiersmen eastward to meet the army, burned the available forage along the way, captured most of its supplies and livestock, and forced General Albert Sidney Johnston's men to spend the bitter winter at Fort Bridger in what is now Wyoming, suffering from cold and hunger. In the meantime, Brigham simply moved his thousands of followers lock, stock, and barrel southward one hundred fifty miles to Fillmore and abandoned the capital. Then, after efforts in Washington to straighten out the misunderstandings, the Mormon leaders sat down with General Johnston at Fort Bridger. It was agreed that the army would be allowed to enter the territory to keep order, but would pass through the capital city without stopping and would set up a fort forty miles southward.

In one of the eerie scenes of the opening of the West, the beleaguered army forces rode silently through an abandoned Salt Lake City, where sentinels stood with torches where straw had been piled against buildings, ready to set fire to the entire city if even one soldier dismounted or tried to harm the temple, then under construction. All day the parade of soldiers passed in silence through the city toward a barren valley forty miles south. In the end, it was all peaceful, with no casualties.

Yet by the end of World War II, the citizens of Panguitch considered themselves the most patriotic of Americans. So, in January 1951, when an orange, mushroom shaped cloud erupted from the Nevada desert one hundred fifty miles east of the town, folks applauded the testing of atomic weapons to keep ahead of the Russians in the nuclear arms race. They went out and sat on the hillsides to watch history being made. For twelve years the citizens of southern Utah gathered in the early mornings to watch the glow rise from over the mountains in Nevada as test after test of nuclear weapons continued—marveling that they could see an event taking place in another state. For those who worried, the assurances came steadily from government officials that the amount of radiation was harmless.

Sunny's grandparents took their children out in the yard to watch the events. There were no worries, simply trust.

Then, the year following the first test, the cancer deaths began. The McEwen's neighbor, then his son, and eventually five members of his family. People in the area began to develop throat and lung cancer, and a vague uneasiness slowly rose among these patriotic families. When the girls' gym class expressed concerns about going outside for class because of a detonation one morning, the principal assured them there was nothing to worry about. He even went along to show that he had no concerns. By 1955, he was dead from cancer. During the next ten years there was hardly a family that had not been touched. This was among a people that had the healthiest lifestyle and lowest cancer rates in the nation—eating healthy, without smoking or drinking alcohol. Finally it became apparent that Panguitch and other southern Utah communities had been lied to—had become victims of the Cold War hysteria. Lawsuits were brought against the government and dragged through Congress for decades. But the people remained under a threatening cloud.

Worse yet, it persevered through generations. Sunny lost an aunt, and finally her mother to cancer.

That was why, when Sunny finally became pregnant in their eighth year of marriage, Jared felt like he had climbed Mt. Everest—had conquered half the world. But in her fourth month, she was told that she had lung cancer. They consulted ten cancer specialists, traveling to Houston, to the Mayo Clinic, and to specialists in Salt Lake City. Five of the ten doctors told her that she would have to have an abortion to have a chance to live; the others told her it wasn't necessary. She was left with the decision.

"I have to have this baby," she told Jared, "No matter what."

She gave birth to a baby boy, who lived two hours before he

died, and then she died as well. With an aching that had never stopped, Jared named the baby boy Aaron. On a rainy spring afternoon, Jared buried them together—Sunny with the baby in her arms—in the hillside cemetery in Kanab. He declined the suggestion from her brothers and sisters that she be buried in the family plot in Panguitch. There was just too much pain there, he had told them. Yet, in his grief he could find no tears. For two months, numb and unfeeling, he barely functioned—until he gradually almost rejoined the world.

Even after all these years, it still hurt to drop over the pass and into the pretty mountain valley where Panguitch lay so serene and so forboding.

*　*　*

When Jared drove up to the cattle corrals, Sheriff Calder welcomed him and motioned to a group of townspeople, who stood lolling around the corral gates. Inside, the impounded cattle were mooing restlessly.

The town sat in a natural basin surrounded by a line of high peaks, and in the distance, the last remnants of sunlight reflected on the brilliant cinnamon-and-yellow cliffs that led to Bryce Canyon National Park.

Jared leaned on the cedar rail and studied the cattle. Among others, he recognized the T-Bar brand of Kate Thompson on several of the cows. Next to him, Sheriff Calder took a step forward as three trucks pulled off the highway.

"One heck of a mess," Jared opined to Sheriff Calder. Calder was a heavy-set man with a round face and by a bald head, with huge ears that stuck out beneath his hat. He was an easy-going sort and the townspeople liked him.

"You got that right. I'm afraid there ain't no easy way out," Calder said. "No matter what I do, I'm wrong on this one." He watched as the trucks bounced down the lane toward the corrals. Several pickups followed along behind. "Well, here they come. Looks like the fat's in the fire now."

"I'm here, Jake. If you need me," Jared assured him.

Sheriff Calder gave a strong nod, his thumbs tucked in his belt. He was not wearing his pistol. "Main thing is, there's no shooting."

Jared nodded. "You're right. Few cows not worth that."

The trucks pulled to a stop and a dozen men got out, milled together momentarily, and then Cattle Kate led the way toward the two lawmen. Jared knew about half of the men, but he had heard others that were coming from Arizona and Nevada.

"Evening, Kate," Sheriff Calder called as they approached. "You folks out for a stroll?"

Kate drew herself up as the group paused before the lawmen. "You bet your boots we're strolling, Jake Calder. Right out of here with our cows!"

Behind her others muttered their agreement.

"Sheriff, it'll hurt me bad to lose my eleven head," called one of the ranchers. Others chimed in with various complaints.

Jared saw that several of the men carried rifles. But they didn't seem angry enough to use them. *Bluffing,* he decided. Nevertheless, he glanced around to see where he might take cover if shooting started. As usual, he carried no sidearm himself. An incident early in his career had caused him to keep his pistol in his office drawer except in extreme emergencies. He had nearly fired on a fleeing figure who flashed a shiny object in his hand after a break in, only to find out when he cornered the fugitive that it was a teenager carrying a Pepsi can.

Sheriff Calder rubbed his chin in thought. "Well now, I can't say I don't sympathize with you folks," he said. "But you know how the feds are."

"But they're gonna sell 'em, Jake," said a lanky rancher with a leathered face. "You know where that will leave us?"

"Well, I feel for you folks. I truly do. Trouble is," replied Sheriff Calder with a shake of his head, "I told 'em I'd take care of these cows until the auction. Puts me in a hell of a spot."

Cattle Kate drew close and thrust her face close to his. "Jake, they're wrong," she said firmly. "You know that. These Washington cocktail bureaucrats don't know anything about this country—an' even less about cows."

Sheriff Calder shrugged and crossed his arms. He shook his head. "Maybe so, Kate," he replied, "but they got the law on their side. And me and Sheriff Buck here, we gotta stand up for the law."

A long silence ensued, broken by the ominous sound of a shell being levered into the chamber of a rifle. Sheriff Calder glanced at Jared, who gave a little shrug.

From the back of the group, several of the ranchers crowded closer, muttering.

Kate laid her hand on sheriff Calder's arm. "We can't let them ruin us, Jake," she said, her voice uncharacteristically soft. "We have to do this. So please stand back. We're taking our cows. You can't stop us." She turned to the ranchers and waved her arm forward. "Load 'em up, boys!"

Sheriff Calder's eyes narrowed beneath his thick, bushy eyebrows, and his mouth twitched as he surveyed the surly men before him. Obviously they were determined, and two of them were already working the gate. He glanced desperately at Jared Buck for support.

Jared shifted on his feet uneasily. He knew that the ranchers had received ample warning to remove their cattle early to avoid overgrazing the land. But he also realized how desperate these ranchers were. It probably wasn't worth an ugly confrontation now. He shrugged at the other lawman and gave a slight shake of his head.

Sheriff Calder took a step backward. "Well, you're doin' this over my objections, folks," he said. "An' the feds sure ain't gonna like it."

With a gesture of triumph, Cattle Kate waved the trucks closer to the gate.

* * *

It was late when Jared had finished consulting with Sheriff Calder about how to handle the federal marshals, who were sure to be livid when they arrived for the auction the next day. By midnight he was driving through the mountains near Asay Creek, halfway to Kanab, when his cell phone rang and the raspy voice of Angus came on.

"Jared! Jared! Are you there?" Angus was excited, even rattled.

Jared was tired. "Sure thing, old man. You sound flustered. What's up?"

"Something bad! Just got a call—somebody's been shot out at the Cinnamon Cliffs Inn."

Jared exhaled deeply. "Oh, no. Who?"

"I think one of that Hollywood bunch. I'm headed there now. It sounded serious."

Jared could hear the wail of a siren over the phone.

CHAPTER 9

Twenty minutes later, Jared's own siren was screaming as he pulled up to the knot of people in a dark corner of the parking lot at the Cinnamon Cliffs Inn. From the somber crowd, Jared figured half the town had rushed out to the motel to take in the excitement. The onlookers melted away to make way for him as he scrambled from the Jeep and hurried toward a figure on the ground. Angus met him with a shake of his head.

"He's dead," he said, motioning to a shape that was covered by a gray blanket. The three deputies had blocked off the scene with yellow tape. "It's that movie guy, Murdock."

"Murdock?" Jared winced, and felt his brows tighten. Murdock was the last one he would expect to have trouble. "Whew. How'd it happen?"

"Nobody saw, I guess," Angus replied. "Haven't had much chance to interrogate them yet."

"Well, there's too many people too close, Angus," Jared said irritably. "Let's move these tapes back." The deputies had set up the tape only a few feet around the body. With a motion to Ray Ferguson and Porter Cannon, he called, "Let's get these people back and get some pictures."

Angus, looking doleful, waved the people back as the tall, sagging figure of Alex Carlton stepped forward to confront Jared. "What a terrible thing," he blustered, but he looked as if he might cry. "Do you know what this does to our film?"

Jared studied the man before answering. "I guess that's the least of Mr. Murdock's worries now," he replied. "Why don't you go back inside, Mr. Carlton. I'll be wanting to talk to you in a few minutes."

The rotund figure of Maury Peralto stormed toward them, waving his arms. "Sheriff, better get out roadblocks right now!" he demanded, red-faced and wide-eyed, almost shouting. "What kind of place is this?"

Ignoring him, Jared studied the crowd that was pressing against the police tape. About half of them were people he knew from town, and the others were most likely from the motel. "Did anybody see anything or hear anything?" he called out. "Anybody hear any shots?" There were only shrugs and a shaking of heads. He nodded. "All right, folks. Let's move along then," he directed. "Those of you who were here at the motel or anybody who saw anything at all, we'll be wanting to talk to you. There's nothing more to see here." He turned to his deputy. "Angus, let's get these people out of here."

He ducked under the yellow tape, squatted by the covered form, and pulled the blanket back.

*   *   *

After a few brief interviews, Jared was puzzled. No one had seen or heard anything. Of course, most guests were already asleep at that hour. And the occasional automobile backfires on the highway in front of the motel might explain why nobody paid attention to the gunshots.

The most obvious motive was a simple one: robbery. Murdock's wallet and watch were missing. It looked like a trigger-happy thug had been lurking outside when Murdock had the misfortune to leave his room and go out into the parking lot to retrieve something from the limo. The wrong place at the wrong time. *Had someone in the motel seen him flash a wad of money and lain in wait for him—or perhaps lured him outside?* Jared wondered. As one who seldom had more than twenty or thirty dollars in his own wallet, Jared nevertheless knew that some men delighted in carrying large amounts of money. It made them feel important.

If that had happened, the shooter would probably try to leave town as fast as possible. There were only a couple of ways to leave Kanab. To try an intercept the thief, he phoned the highway patrol in Panguitch up Highway 89 and across the Arizona border in Page and Flagstaff to alert them what had happened. About all he could tell those officers was what had happened and to be on the lookout someone acting suspiciously.

* * *

"That's all you got?" Patrolman Hank Sellers in Flagstaff asked on the phone with a wry chuckle as Jared explained the situation. "No vehicle description? Nothing?"

"That's about it, Hank," Jared replied apologetically. "We don't even know if the guy left town. But it looks like a murder-robbery. Murdock's wallet and Rolex are gone. It happened in the parking lot at about midnight, so it looks like maybe a chance encounter."

"How'd he get it?"

"Two shots," Jared answered. "Once in the chest, once in the head. The shooter could even be hitchhiking. Just have your troopers keep an eye open, will you?"

"Will do. We'll set a roadblock at Cameron," Sellers said. "I guess all we can do is check for hitchhikers or somebody who's extra nervous." There was a pause. "Who was it that got it?" he asked. "Anybody we'd know?"

"Nope. A San Francisco banker named Murdock," Jared answered. "Part of a movie-making company here to do a film about Everett Ruess, the kid that disappeared years ago in the canyons."

"That so? I sorta figured maybe one of those red-neck ranchers up there got himself a federal agent. I heard they was taking the ranchers' cattle off the monument."

"Luckily, not that bad yet. Hope it doesn't get there."

The Utah Highway Patrol offices in Panguitch and St. George and the Tribal Police in Window Rock each promised the same cooperation.

*   *   *

By the time Jared got off the phone, Angus had gathered the members of the movie company together in the motel conference room, along with the night manager—a fortyish woman with long, braided hair and turquoise jewelry adorning her wrists, neck, and ears. She looked close to tears when Jared strode in.

The people in the group were in various stages of disarray. Chandra Maroney sat curled in a chair, half asleep, wearing a robe over red silk pajamas.

"I know it's late," Jared said in a soft voice, "but we need to talk to you while this is fresh in your minds."

"What's fresh?" Carlton objected. "None of us heard anything or saw anything. Some vicious thug ruined our project—that's all we know."

Jared nodded. "We're covering that angle. But maybe somebody saw something. Does anybody know why Murdock went outside?" he asked.

There was a shaking of heads around the circle. "No. Last I saw of him was about 11:30," Carlton said. "We were all in the restaurant talking about how to proceed with the film. He was leaving tomorrow, and we were going back to L.A."

"Who was there?"

From her curled-up position, Chandra waved a hand.

"Well, all of us," Carlton said. "Myself, Murdock, Peralto, and Chandra. All of us, that is, except for Silvis, our cameraman. He's not involved in the planning—said he was going to bed."

"Did you all leave at the same time?"

Peralto nodded. "Sure. Like Alex said, it was about 11:30. Except I stopped at the desk—chatted with Velda there," he nodded toward the night manager, "for quite a while. I never saw

Murdock after that. Velda and I were talking when we heard all the commotion."

"That's right," the night manager sobbed, her face wrenched in dismay.

"Well, somebody saw him," Chandra put in sleepily.

"He didn't have his wallet and watch on him, but we haven't had a chance for a thorough search of his room yet," Jared said. "So there's a good chance it was a stick-up. Maybe even a chance encounter. Tell me, did he carry a large amount of cash?"

Alex Carlton thrust up his palms to show that he thought it was a stupid question. "Of course—he wasn't poor, you know."

"So, I hope you've got those road blocks up," Peralto said, his face hardening.

Jared scowled. "The highway patrols in every direction have been alerted, but there are hundreds of dirt roads in this country."

Peralto crossed his arms and looked grim. "Speaking as an officer of the East Bay Bank, I can say we've been hurt badly by this, and we're determined the murderer not get away." He paused a moment, considering. "So I'm sure I'm on solid ground, Sheriff," he continued, "when I say that the bank will put up a reward of five thousand dollars for information leading to an arrest and conviction. You can publicize that."

Jared acknowledged the offer with a nod. He turned to the motel night manager, who held up her hands in dismay. "Sheriff, this is *awful*," she said. "Do you know what this will do to our business? When I took this job, my husband told me we'd get robbed and maybe I'd get shot. But this is just *awful*. My boss is going to be really unhappy."

Momentarily, Jared considered reminding her that it was somewhat worse for Ron Murdock, but he let the opportunity pass. "Tell me, Velda," he said. "Did Mr. Murdock have any calls through your switchboard this evening?"

She stifled a sob, and brushed the back of her hand across her cheek. "N-not that I know of."

He turned to Alex Carlton. "Did Murdock have a cell phone?"

"Of course," Carlton responded curtly. "Why?"

"Just trying to figure out why Murdock was out in the parking lot so late," Jared answered." He let his gaze slip across their faces. "Do any of you have any idea what Ron Murdock was doing out there?"

Peralto rolled his eyes. "The guy probably just forgot something he needed from the limo. He had a key."

"What would that *something* be?"

"Hell, I don't know," Peralto said, annoyed. "Maybe he ran out of cigarettes."

"He didn't smoke," Carlton said glumly.

A frown wrinkled Peralto's broad face. "Could've been anything. A book, a pen he needed, anything."

Jared wondered how long he should keep these people up. Their resentment was already apparent. He gave a deep sigh. "Well, from the looks of it, Murdock probably just ran afoul of somebody out to rob him," he said. "Most likely just by accident. Could be one of the local folks, or just somebody who happened to be passing through. We've got roadblocks set up that could nab somebody like that. But we have to check all the possibilities."

"You're not going to make us hang around this hick town, are you?" Carlton asked.

Jared considered this. "A day or two," he replied. "There are some details. How well did you folks know Murdock? We've got to notify the San Francisco authorities and have his family told. Does he have a wife?"

Peralto shook his head. "He was divorced two years ago. No kids. He's got a mother though."

Jared pursed his lips in thought. "I guess that makes it easier. What about the bank? What was his position there?"

"He's . . . was a senior vice president. Influential. His old man started the bank half a century ago," Peralto replied.

"You'll take care of notifying the bank authorities?" Jared asked.

Peralto nodded and rose, shaking his head. "He was important. He'll be missed."

*   *   *

When he interviewed each person separately, Jared learned very little. Most claimed either to have been asleep or watching television at the time of the shooting. When Angus knocked, the cameraman Silvis came sleepily to the door wearing his perpetual scowl. He waved them inside, yawned, and offered them a drink from a bottle on his table.

When they declined, he poured himself one. Jared noticed the distinctive odor of marijuana in the room.

"So, when did you see Mr. Murdock last?" he asked.

Silvis screwed up his lips, shrugged, and sat on the bed with a sigh. "About ten. The others had business. Me, I just shoot the locations. I watched Leno, then went to bed. I heard nothing until all the shouting started."

"How'd you get along with Murdock?"

The cameraman considered this, and gave a little toss of his head. "Me? Okay, I guess. I do good work. He, uh . . . he didn't like some of my habits."

"What habits?"

"Oh," Silvis gave a nervous little laugh, and raised his glass. "You know. . . . And sometimes I sleep late."

"Okay," Jared said.

When he was through with Silvis, he and Angus went from room to room in the motel, waking those who were not already awake from the commotion, and questioning them regarding what they had seen or heard. Nobody seemed to have had any inkling of anything wrong until one of the motel employees got off duty shortly before midnight and found the body in the parking lot.

After the county medical examiner arrived and made a cursory examination in the parking lot, he sought out Jared. Murdock's death had been instantaneous due to two bullets—one in the chest and the other in the head, he reported. Because the bullets hadn't been recovered yet, they didn't know the caliber of the weapon.

When Jared and his deputy wearily slipped under the tape marking Murdock's room, the bed was still made, but was slightly rumpled from someone sitting on it. A newspaper lay scattered about the bedspread. On the bedside table near the phone sat a half empty plastic cup of water next to a folded handkerchief and the television remote control. Donning latex gloves to protect whatever fingerprints might be there, Jared picked up the cup and smelled it. He shook his head. "Just water." He walked to the bathroom sink, emptied the cup, and placed it in a plastic evidence bag.

"What are we lookin' for?" Angus asked, stifling a yawn as he tucked his thumbs in his belt and surveyed the room.

"Probably nothing special," Jared answered with a shrug. "But I wonder what he was doing in the parking lot." If Murdock had been nailed by an opportunistic hold-up man who chanced to run across him in the parking lot, whatever was in the room would have no bearing on what happened outside. On the other hand, if he was set up . . . if a visitor came to his room and lured him out to the limo, then there might be some tiny clue. Jared was looking for two glasses, or any other sign that two people had been in the room.

On the table near the window were an empty ashtray, a can of unsalted almonds, several neatly stacked travel brochures detailing the grandeur of southern Utah, and the two Everett Ruess books that Murdock had bought at Navajo Bridge two days earlier. The bathroom was equally lacking in anything out of the ordinary. A brush, toothpaste, and electric razor sat next to a travel kit, alongside another plastic cup. Jared carefully picked through the contents of the kit. He wondered if he would find drugs, but the only unusual item was a bottle of prescription medicine. He recognized the name of a popular allergy medicine.

"Not much here," he admitted to Angus, who had stopped to

thumb through the sports section of the paper.

"What did you expect if the guy got whacked by a hitchhiker or somebody working the parking lot?" he asked. "People who travel in limos are usually someone with bucks—easy pickings."

"More than likely that's what happened," Jared said, sliding open the closet door. Inside was a dark suit, a sport coat, and a jacket, along with a half dozen shirts and some gabardine and wool slacks. On the floor were a pair of sneakers and a pair of high-top boots neatly aligned.

Angus ambled over, examined the suit, and let out a low whistle. "Bet that cost a couple weeks of my salary."

"Yeah, well maybe he can be buried in it."

"He's probably got a couple dozen like it back home," Angus mused with a wry grin. The deputy did not own a suit himself. Each of his former wives had complained that getting him into a sport coat and tie was the equivalent of getting a saddle on a skittish horse.

Angus got onto his knees to peer carefully beneath the bed, searching the corners with his flashlight. "Not even dust devils under here," he said.

Jared lifted the suitcase onto the bed and slowly began to take inventory. There were several handkerchiefs, some underwear, a *Forbes* business magazine, and a camera and extra film. Carefully, Jared turned the camera crank to remove the film, then slid the camera and roll of film into an evidence bag. "We'll get this film developed. Never can tell what might show up."

Angus gave a shake of his head. "Like I say, nothing here that points to anything other than Murdock wanted something from the car—maybe a beer out of their cooler—and ran across a mugger with a light trigger finger."

With a last look around the room, Jared stretched and yawned. "That's probably right," he agreed. "But that's why they give me the big bucks, to check things out." Their salaries were a standing joke with Angus and Jared. They often said if they moved only a few miles across the border to Arizona, their pay would go up fifty percent.

It was nearly daylight when they finished interviewing anyone who could possibly add anything to the account of the shooting. With a weary sigh, Jared sat in his Jeep and pondered the situation. So far none of the highway patrols had reported stopping any suspicious vehicles at their roadblocks. That was always a tough situation, he admitted to himself. What does an escaping murderer look like, other than being extremely nervous at being stopped?

He mulled other possibilities. Had Murdock been marked from the beginning, starting with those shots at Mooch Winslow's Land Rover? That could have been a warning, he told himself, and maybe someone had finally caught up with Murdock in a vulnerable spot. Perhaps the assailant had been waiting and watching until the right time and place.

Mooch Winslow was another potential suspect. *Had he come demanding his money for his guide services, maybe drunk and losing control when an argument ensued?* Jared wondered. *Or maybe he saw how much money Murdock was carrying and couldn't resist taking it.*

What about Carlton? He seemed devastated by Murdock's death, probably because of seeing the financing for his movie evaporate. Carlton had definitely lost out financially when Murdock died. But perhaps Murdock had learned something about Carlton, something so drastic that the producer had felt compelled to silence him.

Then there was the other matter of Chandra Maroney, whom Carlton treated as his own property. Jealousy was sometimes an overwhelming emotion for certain people. Jared had seen no sign of Murdock showing interest in the leggy brunette, but that didn't always mean that he wasn't interested. Chandra Maroney could have been carrying on with Murdock behind Carlton's back. The wealth he represented would have been a powerful attraction for her.

She herself was not without suspicion, Jared told himself. Affairs of the heart and the pocketbook were not always what they seemed. He guessed that Chandra Maroney was one of those women who attracted men and trouble with equal felicity.

If it turned out that there was more to this than a simple rob-bery-murder, he bet himself that somehow Miss Maroney had been a factor.

Motive, of course, was always the key. In the back of his mind, he had been considering the possibility of the young Navajo, Sam Begay, from the Standing Rock trading post, who had been attacked by Alex Carlton earlier that day, being involved. Revenge could be a powerful motive. Perhaps young Begay had come to get even, but upon not finding Carlton, had settled for Murdock when he wandered outside where Sam was watching. The Nava-jos were a proud people, and did not take easily to insults. With a sigh Jared admitted that he would have to travel to Standing Rock the next day to explore that possibility.

CHAPTER 10

The next morning the town was in an uproar. Knots of men gathered on street corners to wrangle over the two major events of the previous night—the murder in their town and the local ranchers commandeering their cattle away from the federal marshals in Panguitch.

The prevailing sentiment was that the murder had been committed by a transient passing through on Highway 89, and that the guilty party was probably in Los Angeles or Phoenix by now. Nevertheless, an uneasy feeling lay over the town that a murderer could be among them. In Kanab, nobody locked their doors, and there was tongue clucking and head shaking as neighbors admitted that the world was changing. Not only was the government going to hell, but even in their own town it was now time to keep a sharp lookout and lock doors.

As for the cattle, there was general agreement that this time the Bureau of Land Management had pushed too far and that the ranchers were only taking their own cows back after being harassed unnecessarily. There was talk of gathering a defense fund for the ranchers.

For Jared, he was expecting to hear from some angry federal marshals for his part in allowing the ranchers to take the cattle, but this morning that was the least of his worries. With little sleep, he and Angus had gone over and over the site of the murder, looking for any evidence that might help tell what had happened. There was little there but a matchbook cover from the Luxor casino in Las Vegas and a burnished penny that had obviously been in the asphalt for some time.

*   *   *

After two hours of sleep Jared had returned to the motel to inspect the parking lot in the daylight. A hillside rose from the back of the motel onto a sagebrush flat and then rose again sharply to a cliff. First, he scrutinized the edges of the parking lot, concentrating on the brushy hill that adjoined it. One thing he was looking for was evidence that someone had lain in wait—a spot sometimes marked by several cigarette butts or other signs of someone loitering. In addition, he examined every scrap of paper he found there, but the motel workers had kept the place clean, and he found little that would point to anyone having waited.

Then he returned to the spot where the body had lain, still marked by chalk. The limousine was there also, only a few feet from where Murdock had fallen. Several curious onlookers watched him analyze the scene from behind the yellow crime-scene tape still in place. The body had lain slightly behind the rear passenger's door, which was ajar when Murdock was found. Jared surmised that Murdock had gone to the car, retrieved something from inside, and was just turning from the limo when he was accosted. Any thief would be interested in a man who traveled in a limousine. What had Murdock been after that would take him from his room that late at night? Whatever it was, the thief had apparently taken it, for he had nothing on him other than the things he normally carried.

Another possibility was that Murdock was lured outside to the limo, either by someone he knew or by a stranger. But no phone call had come through the desk.

During the night search, Jared and Angus had found no spent shells in the parking lot, which would have been ejected from a semi-automatic pistol. Of course the shooter might have calmly taken the time to look for the cartridge cases and retrieved them in the dark. But empty shells usually flew several feet and upon hitting the pavement would have rolled a ways away. It was more likely that the murderer had used a revolver, in which case no spent shells are ejected. Just to be sure that they had not missed the cartridges in the dark, Jared spent a half hour combing the parking lot and nearby bushes in case some of the early arriving onlookers had inadvertently kicked them out of the way.

By mid-morning the next day, Jared glumly decided they were making little progress. The various highway patrols had removed their roadblocks without results. After all the interviews and collecting every scrap of possible evidence, he was left with little to go on. When he got back in his office that afternoon, Myra came and stood in his doorway with a worried look.

"Jared, these people are driving me crazy," she said. "You've got to talk to some of them. My heck, we're getting calls from California, Texas, all over."

He gave a tired laugh. "Okay, put the next one through." Already he had fielded calls from several media outlets, but he had managed to be out of the office for most of them. When a television crew from Salt Lake had caught up with him that morning, he had spent a half hour answering questions. A few minutes later, when a competing station had shown up and requested an interview, he had turned them over to Angus. The deputy had a showbiz personality and loved to put on his best Dragnet interview, calmly analyzing the situation in a matter-of-fact voice, all the time implying without saying so that they were making considerable progress in solving the case at hand.

Now, as he glanced out the window, Jared stifled a groan when he saw Alex Carlton and Maury Peralto marching solemnly up the walk. A third person that he did not know was leading the way—a heavy-shouldered, square-faced man in a two-piece charcoal suit. He had a jutting chin that gave him a bulldogish look. Jared stood as they entered, and the square-faced man stepped forward and extended his hand.

"Sheriff, I'm Coy Martin, just got in from San Francisco,"

he said. "Chief investigator for the East Bay Bank. Mr. Peralto called me as soon as it happened. Damn shame about Murdock, eh?"

Jared shook his hand, nodded, and welcomed them. He wondered if Martin had come to take over the investigation from what he considered a hick sheriff.

Peralto nodded a grim greeting, and then spoke in a firm voice. "I hope you've caught the SOB by now," he said.

Unlike earlier, Carlton stood in the background, looking miserable. "What a loss," the producer sighed.

Jared shrugged. "Well, we've had bulletins out all over the West. Nothing yet." He felt quite sure that Carlton was calculating the loss in dollars.

"You think it was really robbery?" Martin asked, his eyebrows raised.

"So far it looks that way," Jared said with a sigh. "But I'm checking out a couple other things. Not much to go on. No weapon. No other motive. And Highway 89 here is a main route for drug runners from Mexico to Chicago."

Carlton's eyes went wide. "You don't think he was mixed up with drugs, do you?"

"No, I didn't mean that," Jared said with a quick shake of his head. "Just that a lot of strange people pass through here. Almost anything could have happened in that parking lot. But we're still questioning people."

He turned to Carlton and Peralto. "In fact, I'm asking you two to stick around a couple of days until we can sort some of this out."

They shot a glance to Martin, and he gave a quick nod.

"That's smart," he said. "I'll be wanting to talk to people too. And I'd like to look at any evidence you've gathered so far, Sheriff."

"That's fine." Jared nodded toward a file on his desk. It contained the preliminary medical report, and photos from the death scene, along with his and Angus's notes of what they had learned so far. "We can make you some copies." Jared hesitated, and then looked Martin in the eye. "May I ask exactly what your role is in this, Mr. Martin?

Martin gave a laugh, and reached to slap Jared's shoulder. "Of course," he replied. "Murdock was an important figure at East Bay Bank. I was asked to come watch out for the bank's interest, that's all."

He reached for the file, but Jared quickly pulled it away. "I'll make copies of these and get them to you this afternoon," he said.

For an instant, a flash of anger crossed Martin's eyes, and then he smiled. "Of course. I'll be around later today. In the meantime, I'll be talking to the people at the motel."

*　*　*

When they had gone, Jared reached for his hat and turned to Angus. "Have Myra make copies of the death reports and the photos, will you? But don't give them our interviews or our own notes—not yet."

"Sure thing," Angus replied. "What are you up to?"

"Looks like I've got to head over to Standing Rock," Jared answered. "That young clerk there may have gotten even with the Hollywood bunch this way. Probably not, But I've got to go check it out before that bank dick makes trouble over there. You handle things here, okay?"

Before he could get out the door, however, his secretary Myra nodded to a young man who stood by her desk. He looked barely out of college, with a large nose, black-frame glasses, and an excitement dancing in his eyes. Before she could introduce him, he strode over to offer his hand to Jared.

"Gary Rydalch, Sheriff, from the Deseret News," he said, identifying a Salt Lake newspaper. "Anything new about the Murdock shooting?"

A wry smile twisted Jared's lip, and he shrugged. "Not much yet. Mr. Murdock was here to make a film. He's from Oakland. Just before midnight, night before last, he was found in the motel parking lot. Two bullets in him. We don't have the full medical examiner's report yet. Most likely it was an opportunistic robbery, but we're not discounting anything."

"No suspects? No fights or disagreements or anything here?" Rydalch was furiously scribbling in a small notebook that he had pulled from his pocket

"Nope. Not that we know of." Jared omitted mentioning the altercation with Sam Begay until he could check it further. "We had roadblocks put up, but so far they've turned up nothing." He turned and motioned to Angus, who was at his desk filling out reports. "Would you mind talking to Deputy Terry here for anything further? I've got to be off to an interview myself. He'll fill you in on everything."

"Oh, who's the interview with?" Rydalch asked with a slightly raised eyebrow.

Shoot, Jared mentally chided himself for making the mistake. He would just hope the press didn't ask too many questions yet. He didn't want to make it sound like the Navajo kid was a suspect.

"Just some preliminary questioning," he dodged. "I'll be around this evening if you want."

"Sure thing," the reporter said, eyeing Angus Terry.

"Oh, one more thing," Jared said, pausing as he opened the door to leave. "You might want to talk to a Mr. Martin. He's an investigator with the bank Murdock worked for. It seems his bank is offering a reward."

Anything to get the reporter off my back, he thought.

But as he strode past Myra's desk, she motioned to him, shrugged, and handed him the phone. "It's the attorney general's office," she said apologetically.

With a tiny groan, he nodded and picked up the phone.

"This is Sheriff Buck."

"Sheriff, this is Kenneth Harman—Utah Attorney General."

Jared felt a little of his breath slip out. "Yes, sir?"

The man's voice was friendly but official. "Well, Sheriff," he said. "We're concerned about the murder that took place down your way. It seems that Mr. Murdock was an important person in California. We're getting heat from all sorts of people out there. What does the situation look like?"

"We're doing everything possible, Mr. Harman," Jared answered. "There's not much to go on. Most likely it was a robbery—probably by someone passing through. All the highway patrols here and in Arizona had roadblocks out, but they came up empty. We're watching to see if any of the credit cards show up. And we're looking at other possibilities."

"Could you use some additional help?" the Attorney General asked. "We can send an investigator or two from here down there for a few days."

Jared bit his lip. He could see them stumbling around, getting in the way and trying to take over. "No sir, I don't think that's necessary," he replied. "My deputies and I are following up the leads we have."

He could hear a grunt on the other end. "It seems that the FBI is also interested in this. The report is that Murdock may have ruffled some feathers out on the Navajo Reservation. And that someone tried to kill him on federal BLM land a few days earlier. So you will probably be hearing from them."

"They're welcome, I guess. But there's not really much to go on right now." Inwardly Jared felt a blow to his stomach. Having the feds come would only roil the waters further.

"I understand," the Attorney General said sympathetically. "If some transient or wetback happened by and blew the banker away for his wallet, he wouldn't leave much trace behind. Could be on the beach at Acapulco by now."

"We're hoping something shows up."

There was a silence, then Harman said in a quiet voice, "It better. It could be bad for all of us—tourism and all. If these things go unsolved, it makes the whole state look bad."

Jared chuckled to himself. There was a veiled threat there from Harman. The next sheriff's election was still two years away, but he didn't feel intimidated even if help from the state officials was a factor in getting votes.

"We'll give it everything we've got," he assured him.

"I'm sure you will. Keep in touch with your progress."

"I'll do that." He made ready to hang up.

"Oh, and one other thing," Harman continued. "This mess about the cows on the Escalante Monument—what the devil's going on with that thing?"

Jared almost laughed to think of the hullabaloo a few cows were causing off in the mountains of southern Utah. "Seems the BLM is particular about having their exact dates followed to get the cattle out. Some of the ranchers are really upset about having them confiscated. For a while it looked really ugly, but it seems to be simmering down."

"I hear one rancher even got a helicopter and shot his own cows. Good hell, that's crazy!"

Jared hunched his shoulders. "I agree. What's even worse is that the feds are talking prison sentences for some of the ranchers—even Cattle Kate, a woman who runs her spread west of town."

"Do you know what kind of national publicity this is getting us?" Harman asked.

"I know."

Jared heard a deep sigh from the attorney general. "It's that damn Clinton," he said. "He started all of this."

Jared smiled. He had voted for the president twice. Even when some of the local citizens had hung Clinton in effigy after he had established the Grand Staircase-Escalante National Monument, he had watched with amusement. Personally, he had thought that the monument would bring tourists, resulting in revenue, in addition to offering protection from huge coal developments that would scar the land. But he was careful not to wear his environmental opinions on his sleeve. Right now, he was not about to offend the Attorney General of the state.

"It's the ranchers I'm concerned about, he said. "But I think we can work things out peacefully."

"We'd better," Harmon said, his voice hardening. "But keep in touch, Sheriff."

When he hung up, Jared stood for a long minute, pondering how many more headaches would result from all of this.

Through the glass, Myra had seen that he was no longer on the phone. She opened his door and made a helpless gesture of apology. "There's something else, Jared," she said. "That was Kate Thompson on the other line. She needs to see you today or tomorrow."

With a grin, Jared leaned back and clasped his hands behind his head. "If it's not one thing it's two, isn't it? I'll get out there in the morning. Right now, I'd better get out to the reservation to check on that Navajo kid. He may be our most likely suspect."

He checked his watch, and then picked up the phone and dialed the offices of the Navajo Tribal Police.

CHAPTER 11

When Jared Buck pulled his Cherokee into the shade of a cottonwood tree at the Standing Rock Trading Post, Craig Yazzi of the Navajo Police was leaning against one of the porch posts, waiting. The store was a squat, rock building with a tin roof. Two old men sat placidly on a log bench in the shade at the end of the porch, their hair tied in traditional buns, watching the sun work its way down a clear-blue sky.

The Navajo officer pulled his broad hat lower and hopped from the porch, moving with that high-shouldered walk that Jared knew so well. With a wide face and coal-black eyes, Yazzi was solidly built and moved with the agility of the rodeo rider he had once been. He wore the green uniform of the Navajo Tribal Police, but carried no badge or gun. As they came together, Yazzi laughed and threw a friendly punch at Jared's shoulder.

"*Ya-teh*," Jared said, dodging. "You're still too slow."

"*Ya-ta he* yourself," Craig Yazzi said, laughing. "You know I can still whip you, Jared."

With a shrug, Jared nodded. "Probably so. I been slowin' down a little lately."

Craig Yazzi had been Jared's roommate at Utah State University after they had played football together at Kanab High School. When he was only twelve, the young Navajo had come to town as part of a Mormon program in place at that time that gave reservation youth a chance for a solid education by living with town families during the school months. Craig Yazzi had arrived as a shy, twig-thin youngster who spent the first months pining for his family a hundred fifty miles eastward at the bottom of Lukachukai Mountain. Then when a high school English teacher took him under her wing, after a few months he had begun to blossom intellectually and physically. By his senior year, he had starred in wrestling and football, and the latter won him a scholarship to the university. After a stint in the U.S. Marines, he had returned, tried law school at Arizona State, and then had gone to work for the legal department of the Tribal Police.

With a gesture of his chin, Yazzi motioned to a pine log bench that sat at the other end of the porch from the old men. "So what's this you been telling me about a shooting?" he asked as they eased onto the bench. The old men had turned to watch them curiously, but were out of hearing distance.

"Like I said, someone killed a banker in the parking lot of the Cinnamon Cliffs Inn last night. He was part of a Hollywood film group up here getting ready to make a movie."

Yazzi nodded. "I heard they came up here and made some trouble. I been talking to George."

They didn't speak for a long moment, and Jared watched a red-tail hawk working above the sagebrush on a distant hillside. "What do you know about Sam, George's clerk?"

"I've been checking. Sam Begay. Seems like a nice kid. No trouble that I know of. But . . ." he shrugged. "You think he did it?"

Jared shook his head. "I've got to check. I realize what a jerk the guy is that hit him. Do you know if he owns a gun?"

Yazzi rose and motioned toward the door of the trading post. "Let's check. He's in there."

The old owner, George, welcomed them, and then stepped back as Yazzi explained that they had to talk to the young clerk.

Sam Begay was in his last year of high school—a tall, gangly youth with a thin face and short cut hair beneath a cap that read "Page Pizza" above the brim. His face bore the scars of acne. He was busily sorting rugs in a pile, but he gave an apprehensive glance at the two men as they approached. He straightened stiffly to greet them.

His eyes went wide when Yazzi explained that one of the Hollywood men who had visited yesterday had been shot and killed the previous night. "Who . . . who did it?" Sam asked, breathing hard.

"We don't know yet," Jared said. "Sam, you were in a fight with one of the men?"

Sam glanced desperately from Yazzi to George, who was watching solemnly from behind his oaken counter. "Well . . . sort of. But he hit me. I didn't hit anybody!"

"We know," Jared assured him. "Sam, where were you last night?"

As the implications of the question hit him, Sam sucked in a deep breath and his mouth came open. "You think I did it?" he asked, wide-eyed and incredulous. Again he shot a desperate look at George, who only shrugged.

"And last night, Sam?" Yazzi prodded.

Flustered, Sam took a moment to collect his thoughts. "I went over to see my girlfriend, over near Kaibito. I borrowed my brother's truck."

"What time?" Yazzi asked.

"Oh, left here about eight." He paused, and then exhaled in dismay. "She wasn't home. Nobody was. Probably gone over to visit her sisters at the Gap."

"Anybody see you there?" Yazzi asked, idly picking up the corner of one of the rugs to study it. "Or coming or going?"

"N-no. I don't think so." The young clerk said miserably.

"So when did you get back, son?" Jared asked in a friendly tone.

"Well," Sam said with a shrug, "I messed around a while up on a mesa there—had a couple beers." He glanced at George to see if he had heard. "Then I had a flat tire comin' back. Took a while to change it. Guess I got back to my brother's about midnight. Ever'body was asleep."

"I see," Jared said. "Do you own a pistol, Sam?"

For the first time, Sam brightened. "Nope. Got a twenty-two rifle, and a single-shot sixteen gauge, but no pistol."

*   *   *

Outside, it was growing dark as Craig Yazzi leaned through the Cherokee window. "What about Sam? Look like you're going to pin this on him?"

Sitting behind the wheel, Jared pursed his lips. "I don't know. What do you think?"

Yazzi gave a little grunt. "Don't think so. Seems harmless. And scared."

"Well, I had to interrogate him. I may be back." He turned the key and the Cherokee purred to life. "Come see us, Craig." Jared caught himself still using the plural. Now there was no "us," unless he counted Sitka.

"Happy to do that," Yazzi said. But he did not step back from the window. "By the way, old George told me what started all this—them wantin' to know about the young anglo that disappeared way back."

"Everett Ruess?"

"Yeah. They thought someone remembered him here."

"That's right," Jared said, turning off the motor. Yazzi seemed ready to tell him something.

"Does that figure in this somewhere?" Yazzi asked.

"It might. Somebody took a couple of shots at that Hollywood crew the first time they went up Cottonwood Canyon. They'd been asking around about Ruess. Do you know something about Ruess?"

Yazzi gave him a wry smile. "Well . . . not for the *belakonas*, no." He used the Navajo word for white man. "But I remember my father telling about a strange white kid coming through here when he was young, drawing pictures."

Jared knew that Yazzi's father was dead. "You think anybody knows what happened to him? It's been a mystery for years."

Yazzi shrugged. "Rumors only. I don't think anybody knows. But." He paused to measure his words carefully. "There is one old man, the one George said they wanted to find, who may know something about that lost kid."

Jared narrowed his eyes and pursed his lips. For some reason, this news excited him. He realized that he had grown more obsessed with the puzzle of Everett Ruess's disappearance than he had realized. "And who's that?" he asked.

With a sigh, Yazzi pulled himself halfway out of the window. "Usually we keep these things to ourselves, among the people," he said, and then added with a broad smile, "but because you and I have become brothers of the Bitter-Water Clan—you may want to talk to Horace Tom over by Navajo Mountain sometime."

Jared reached and gave Yazzi's forearm a squeeze. "Thanks, brother," he said. "Once this murder business settles down I'll do that. Right now, I think a couple of federal marshals may be looking for me in Panguitch."

"I heard."

"News gets around fast, even out here, doesn't it?"

"It's those smoke signals my people use," Yazzi joked. "Of course the radio helps." The whole time he had been at the window, the huge head of Jared's Alaskan malamute kept pushing forward to lick his hand. "I see you still got this big oaf of a dog. Pretty worthless, ain't he?"

Jared reached and rubbed behind the dog's ears. "Heck, gotta have somebody to talk to."

Yazzi looked genuinely concerned. "What about that waitress at Houston's—the skinny one?"

Jared groaned. "Not you too! Hey, my dog and I are doing just fine. At least, we'll be okay if I can get these federal marshals off my back—and find out who shot Murdock."

Satisfied, Yazzi stepped back from the window, a grin on his face. "Well, there's a squaw dance Saturday night out at Oljeto. Some pretty girl might pick you."

Jared returned the grin. "Never can tell. I might do that. If the feds don't toss me in the pokey by then."

CHAPTER 12

On the two-hour drive back from the reservation, Jared fought sleep as he once again considered the facts he knew regarding Murdock's murder. If it was a simple, random robbery, he had to hope that Murdock's expensive watch or his credit cards would turn up somewhere. Jared and Angus had examined trash bins and tromped the sagebrush along the highway for two miles from the motel in case the wallet had been tossed away after being emptied. They found nothing. The reality was, the later it got, the colder the trail became.

On the other hand, there was the possibility that it was done by someone who knew Murdock and had a reason to kill him. It could still be robbery. Mooch Winslow might be the best suspect in that case. Mooch always needed money, and sometimes he wasn't too careful on how he got it. Jared knew of a couple of complaints when Mooch was guiding on the Colorado River from people whose valuables had turned up missing. It was mostly rumors, and there was never any solid evidence, but he had heard that that was one of the factors in Mooch losing his Grand Canyon guide job.

The Indian kid? Jared wondered. *No alibi. But he didn't seem likely.*

The cameraman Silvis, Chandra Maroney, Peralto, Carlton—any of them was a possibility. He'd have to find out more about any undercurrents of conflict, any hidden reasons strong enough to result in a shooting.

Jared had been involved in murder investigations before, but they were usually more clear-cut than this one—a wife who shot her philandering husband; two rival gangs involved in Easter celebrations at the Sand Dunes state park that resulted in the beating to death of one of the motorcycle riders; and a jealous lover in another case. When he had first started his job, there was a rancher who took exception to his neighbor fencing off what he considered his own land who used a crowbar to enforce his opinion, resulting in the death of the fencer.

But this was different. The randomness of it made it difficult to interpret. All he could do was keep looking—keep asking questions.

*　　*　　*

Angus was waiting by the door when Jared got back to the office after dark. The remnants of a burger and fries were on the deputy's desk, and he had his personal coffeepot perking. He waved some papers as Jared hung up his hat.

"Medical examiner's report from Salt Lake," Angus said wearily. "The fax just came in."

Jared took the papers without looking at them, sighed deeply, and hoisted his boots up on the desk.

"Long day," he said.

"You learn anything out on the rez?"

"I dunno," Jared replied. "The Navajo kid could've done it, but he didn't seem like the type. No alibi though. Said he went to see his girlfriend, and she wasn't home. Anything happen here this afternoon?"

Angus rolled his eyes. "You wouldn't believe it! The press is driving me nuts. The feds been calling every hour, half of Hollywood's been in here threatening to sue us, and that private detective from the bank think's he's James Bond or somethin'. If you're smart, you'll go back and hide out on the rez 'til this blows over."

"Any word from the highway patrol?"

"Yeah, but nobody saw any suspicious cars or hitchhikers. That looks like a dead end."

Jared sighed, laid his head back, and massaged his tired eyes. "Bad deal. If it was a transient, he's long gone. We might never know what happened." With a yawn, he sat up and leaned over the medical examiner's report After a moment, he let out a low whistle of dismay. "Uh-oh, those two shots?"

"Yeah?"

"Twenty-two caliber." He raised his eyebrows.

"So what?"

Jared hunched his shoulders. He had hoped it wasn't Sam Begay. "Only that the Indian kid told me he has a twenty-two rifle."

Angus nodded with interest. "Could be. But it may not mean much. I'd guess half the guys on the reservation have a twenty-two for rabbits and prairie dogs."

"That's right. So we'll have to check the ballistics. In the meantime, I guess that makes him a suspect."

Angus yawned again and stretched. Neither man had slept more than a couple of hours since the shooting. "So where are we? What do we know?" Angus asked.

With a pained look, Jared shook his head. "Not much. Let's see. One, most likely some dope-head passing through, looking for a strike to support his habit. Murdock was a likely mark, especially going or coming to a limousine. He usually carried a wad of cash with him. His wallet and watch are gone. Maybe Murdock struggled, so the guy panicked and whacked him, then grabbed the stuff and ran. Maybe he had his car parked nearby. Maybe he hitchhiked."

"Or maybe he simply hiked south, a backpacker," Angus grinned. "Or took his bicycle, maybe an ATV, and is off in the boonies somewhere laughing at us."

It was brainstorming, kicking around all possibilities when they couldn't figure something out. Angus, with his hippie, drug-tainted background, brought a different set of ideas to any problem. Jared felt like they made a good team.

"Could be," he said. "But not likely. Could show up, though. Most likely is if it was a stranger passing through, the wallet or watch might emerge sometime in a bust."

Angus shook his head in disagreement. "Maybe in five years or so, or the guy is in the joint and he brags about a hit he once made in the little town of Kanab, Utah."

Jared exhaled. "Or, if it wasn't a transient, then maybe it was somebody who knew Murdock, or a local who spotted an easy mark."

"There's always our friend Mooch Winslow," Angus said.

"Yep. I'll talk to Mooch—see where he was that night. Any other local characters who might've wandered by?"

Angus named three other men who at various times had been in trouble with the law, but Jared shook his head at each name. None seemed capable of carrying a gun in a crime. "Then we have our Hollywood bunch. What's your reading?"

"We got a couple of faxes in from the California police like you asked." He tapped a manila folder with his thumb. "Not much violence, but a whole can of worms there," Angus said. "Who knows what's going on. Maybe he was diddling somebody's wife. Maybe he left somebody money in a will. Hard to say."

"Of course, we don't know a whole lot about them," Jared said, scanning the two faxes from the folder. "About what I expected."

"Not as much as I wanted to know about that little brunette. Not that I didn't try," Angus said with a chortle. "She seemed to cotton to you, though. By the way, they've all been in here chompin' at the bit. Say they're going home tomorrow, no matter what you say."

Jared nodded. "I expected that. But I want to talk to them again first. And I want to make a few more calls to L.A. and San Francisco."

"What about that Martin guy?"

Jared pursed his lips. He wasn't exactly insulted that Martin had showed up as if he were taking over the investigation, but at the same time, he knew that as an outsider Martin probably didn't have the foggiest notion about how things worked here. For instance, he undoubtedly had no idea that a Navajo kid with a twenty-two rifle may have lain in wait to get even for an insult on his dignity earlier in the day. But if Martin could come up with something, then fine. More power to him. In the short time he had known him, Jared Buck had liked Ron Murdock and his ideas. In fact, he was the only one of the California group that he felt at ease with. So he had some personal involvement in settling this murder.

"Speak of the devil," muttered Angus, swiveling his chair to stare toward the window.

Striding up the walk was the detective, Martin. He swung the door open, nodded to the two officers, and plopped down in an oak chair across the desk from Jared Buck. "Hoo boy, Sheriff," he said in a half groan. "Gets hot down here, don't it?"

"It's September. Next week we may have a blizzard."

Martin looked amused. "That so? In San Francisco it doesn't change much. Cool all the time." He reached in his pocket, pulled out a pack of cigarettes, and saw a slight shake of the head from Angus. A small "No Smoking" sign hung on the wall. "Forgot," he apologized. "Found anything new, Sheriff Buck?"

Jared shook his head. He had no intention of sending this guy off to the rez to interview Sam Begay and screw things up there. "Not much. Highway patrols in Arizona and Utah say nothing out of the ordinary, although Angus tells me they did nab a carload with twenty pounds of pot headed up from Flagstaff. Going the wrong way, though. I'm still looking to talk to some local people. Just got this in though." He slid the medical examiner's report across the table.

Martin took a minute to peruse the report. "Hmm. Twenty-two. One in the back, one in the head. Could be a hit."

"Could be. Or it could be one of the locals," Jared said. "Most homes in this town probably have a twenty-two rifle in them. That's the first gun any kid gets. Kills anything from rabbits to deer. No kick and little noise. Dangerous as heck."

Martin folded his arms and pursed his lips in speculation. "Maybe teenagers after some spending money? And they put the guy away? Who knows these days."

"Tell me, what do you make of this filmmaking bunch?" Jared asked. He wanted to learn how much Martin knew.

"I've been checking. So far they seem okay," Martin said with a shrug. "That Carlton guy has faced a couple of fraud charges. No convictions. Peralto seems to check out. He's been with the bank thirteen years. The woman?" He raised an eyebrow. "Candy for the eyes, but you probably wouldn't want to take her home to mother."

Jared nodded. It fit with what they had received from the California police. "What about the camera guy?"

"He's a moody bastard, but no record. Doesn't talk much. Him, I don't know about."

Jared nodded again. "I still want to interview them again. I hear they're clamoring to head back home. Seems no point keeping them here unless something turns up. Did you learn anything in talking to them?"

"Nope. They seem convinced it was a random robbery gone bad, with the creep who did it heading for Vegas or L.A."

Sucking on his lip, Jared sighed. "Now long gone. It's a good possibility."

Martin rose, put his hands on the desk and leaned forward. "Well, I'll stick around a couple of days. See what else I can turn up. The bank wants this thing solved, if possible. Murdock was a key figure in the company. His father started the thing years ago." He looked grim. "I think the directors feel like if it can happen to Murdock, it could happen to them."

Jared gave a little nod of farewell as Martin headed to the door. When the detective was gone, Angus stood up. "Okay boss, now what? More playing interrogator, or are you gonna let us get some sleep?"

"Ah, we better go see Mooch Winslow. An' then we need to corner the Hollywood gang once more before we send them back to California."

*   *   *

The lights of Mooch Winslow's trailer were on when they drove up. It sat in a vacant lot near the warehouse of a river-running company in Fredonia, just ten minutes south of Kanab across the Arizona border. When Mooch was a boatman for the company, he had set up his trailer nearby; after he lost his job, they had allowed him to remain on the condition that he pay for his electricity.

The twangy sounds of Willie Nelson's music vibrated through the thin walls of the metal trailer as they knocked. There was a shuffling inside.

"Probably hiding his pot," Angus muttered.

The cheerful sound of crickets echoed through the vacant lot. The country song that drifted from the trailer told about Pancho and Lefty in Mexico. Jared liked the song, but had never figured out what had happened to Lefty down in Mexico.

After another minute, the door opened and Mooch stood in his undershirt with a puzzled look on his face. When he recognized them, he stepped outside into the warm night air. "Jared, Angus," he greeted. "You guys are out late, aren't you?"

"Sorry, Mooch," Jared said with a nod. "Just needed to talk to you for a few minutes. You know, about what happened out at the Cinnamon Cliffs."

"I been expecting you," the guide said solemnly. "Hell of a thing, eh? You found who did it yet?"

"We're workin' on it," Jared said. "Probably somebody passing through, but we have to check everybody out."

"Okay," Mooch said nervously. "I got nothin' to hide."

It was obvious that Mooch wasn't going to invite them inside, so Jared leaned against the side of the trailer. "It happened between eleven-thirty and twelve. Where were you then, Mooch?"

Mooch looked startled, then swallowed. "I . . . I guess I was here, watching TV," he answered.

"Anybody with you?"

It took a moment for him to answer. "Well . . . no. I . . . I was kind of celebrating. I went to see Alex Carlton over at the motel yesterday. I was afraid they might cut out without payin' me, so I asked him for the money he owed me for guidin' them. I expected an argument, but he wrote me a check right off. I was kinda surprised, to be honest. So I picked up a bottle in Fredonia, and came right home. I was here all night."

Angus sidled closer and asked with a grin, "You cash that check yet, Mooch?"

Mooch looked puzzled, and then alarmed. "I deposited it in my bank today. Why?"

"No reason, just wondering," Angus replied.

"Then nobody saw you about eleven-thirty. Is that right, Mooch?" Jared asked.

"Well, yeah, but I didn't even know about Murdock until I went to town today. Then I heard."

"I see. But we're checking everything out. Tell me, do you own a twenty-two pistol?" Jared figured that while Sam Begay or a local teenager might use a rifle to pull a stick-up, Mooch Winslow would not be wandering through a motel parking lot with such an obvious gun. It would be a pistol.

Again Mooch looked puzzled and a little frightened. "Sure. I got a sweet little Colt Woodsman. Had it for years. Haven't shot it in months, though."

Jared nodded. "I wouldn't worry then. Mind if we take a look at it?"

Mooch glanced at the interior of the trailer. "Well . . . no. Only take a minute. I keep it under my mattress."

When he emerged, he handed over a leatherette pistol case. Jared carefully slid out the automatic by the scored grip, removed the full clip, pointed the muzzle at the ground, released the safety, and pulled the slide action open. The silver shape of a live bullet flipped to the ground.

Angus clucked his tongue in disapproval. "Mooch, that's dangerous. Keeping one in the chamber."

"When you need it quick, you need it," Mooch said resentfully at Angus's scolding.

Jared moved closer to the light from the door to examine the pistol. It had been one of Colt's finest, one he coveted in his younger days. The model was no longer manufactured, but remained a sought-after classic. With the action open, he smelled the barrel. It had not been recently fired, or else had been cleaned thoroughly.

"Mooch, you mind if we take this for a day or two. We have to check."

"No. That's all right." He chewed on his lip for a moment. "Got him with a twenty-two, huh? I got to admit, that makes me a little nervous, Jared. Somebody could be settin' me up."

"If you're clean, you got nothing to worry about," Jared said, tucking the pistol under his arm. "You sure there's nobody that could verify your whereabouts?"

Mooch looked dismayed. Again he chewed on his lip a long while before answering. He shook his head. "Nobody I'd want known," he said sadly.

The sheriff and his deputy exchanged glances, and then turned and went back to Jared's truck.

*   *   *

When they knocked on room 241 at the motel where Willie Silvis was registered, there was no answer. It was only nine-thirty, so they guessed that he might still be having dinner at the motel restaurant or in town. At Chandra Maroney's room down the hall they had better luck.

"Well, hello there!" she said with a wide smile as she opened her door. She smelled of springtime lilacs, and her hair was loose over her shoulders, once more reminding Jared of how Sunny used to smell after she had showered. Chandra Maroney was wearing tight Levis and a western shirt that clung to her, with a classic Navajo squashblossom and turquoise necklace, along with a turquoise and silver bracelet that gave her a touch of elegance.

She appears fashionably wholesome, Jared decided. "Looks like you've gone native on us."

She spread her arms and stepped back for inspection. "When in Rome—or Kanab," she said. "You like it?"

Angus stifled a low whistle, and then said approvingly, "Maybe not in Rome, but in Kanab, definitely."

She motioned them in, and she sat on the bed. "I guess this is about . . . what happened to Ron?" She looked disconsolate.

"Yeah, we need to see if you've remembered anything else since I talked to you after the shooting," Jared said. "Even any little thing."

She rolled her eyes heavenward. "*Oi,* I laid awake all night trying to put it out of my mind. I tried to think of anything. Like I told you, after dinner we sat out by the lobby talking about the film. About eleven thirty, I came here and went to bed."

"You heard nothing at all?" Jared asked.

"Nothing important." She knitted her brow in concentration, dredging up the memory. "Only some people moving into their room. I think a mother was hollering at her kids. That's all. I had the television on. I was watching the news."

Jared was surprised that she would be watching the news. Many of the Hollywood people he had run across through the years had no notion of anything happening beyond the city limits of Los Angeles. "You talked about this film? About where this left the project?"

"That's right."

"What did Carlton have to say about that? Is the film dead now without Murdock's money?"

She looked puzzled. "Is that important?"

"Probably not, but we're looking at all angles."

"Well . . ." She paused, leaned over the nightstand, and tinkered with a half-full glass of water. "As you might guess, Alex is devastated. Thinks his life is ruined. And the project may be dead, which pretty much puts Alex down the tubes with it. He was banking on this to pull him out of some financial problems."

Angus had begun to scribble in a notebook he carried in his pocket.

"And with Ron's death—" She held up her palms in futility and made a face. "But Alex still has hopes of salvaging it."

"Another backer?"

She nodded. "Maybe the bank directors can still be convinced this is a good project. He's optimistic about it."

"If that doesn't work?"

She flashed a winsome smile. "Alex is a most resourceful person. He's been courting some Arab money for the project also. Seems a young man from Saudi Arabia was in film school at USC, and Alex impressed him. Showed him around Hollywood. Actually introduced him to a couple of budding starlets. The kid has oil money, so who knows?"

"I see." Jared shuffled his feet. "Miss Maroney . . . Chandra, can you think of anything Mr. Carlton would gain with Murdock's death?"

"Gain?" she asked incredulously. "Most likely he lost his ass."

"I see. What about personally? Did he or Peralto or your cameraman have any conflicts with Murdock? Anything at all? Please think carefully."

She knit her brow, and shook her head. "Sure, there were little arguments—what we were going to eat, where to stay—that kind of thing. But they were all excited about this Everett Ruess project. The future of Majestic West looked really good." She threw up her arms in pained exasperation. "Alex even promised me a little part in it."

Angus gave a sympathetic little laugh. "Too bad. I'd have paid to see you."

"Thank you, sir," she said, with a little flip of her wrist.

* * *

When nobody answered at Carlton's or Peralto's doors, Jared and Angus ambled toward the lounge. Sure enough, the two men were seated at a table in the restaurant, which was nearly deserted at this hour, huddled in somber conversation over glasses of beer. With them, leaning back in his chair and looking bored, Willie Silvis studied the deer heads on the wall. Jared guessed that Carlton was making a pitch to Peralto to keep the bank involved in financing the film.

Carlton did not appear pleased when they walked up, but he gave a nod. Peralto took a sip of his beer and glowered at Jared. "We assume you've got the guy by now, Mr. Buck," he said coolly.

"Not exactly," Jared said with a shrug. "But we're workin' on it." He wondered how many beers Peralto had nipped. He was not usually so antagonistic.

"And we're working on getting out of this god-forsaken place and getting back to California," Carlton said, defiance in his voice. "When we come back this time, it will be with a full film crew, ready to shoot."

Jared nodded. "I may have some more questions until this is settled."

"Settled, schmettled," Peralto replied. "You know if you ain't caught him by now, he's long gone down the road."

Angus pulled up a chair and flopped to sit in it backwards.

"Maybe," Jared said. "I'll want phones and addresses where you can be reached. When do you leave?"

"In the morning," Carlton said. "I'm going to Frisco with Maury here for a few days. Willie there is heading straight for Las Vegas and L.A."

"*San Francisco*," Peralto corrected Carlton.

"And Miss Maroney?" Angus put in.

Carlton regarded him coolly. "With us to *San Francisco*." He emphasized the proper name, with a glance at Peralto. "Not that it's any of your business."

A little smile worked across Jared's face, and he pulled up a chair at the table and sat down next to Carlton. "Our business is to find out what happened. Now, just a couple more questions." He turned to Willie Silvis. "I believe you said you left the others and went to your room to watch television about an hour before it happened."

"That's right." Silvis said it cautiously, as if expecting a trick question.

"You hear anything at all in the hallway in that time—a commotion, an argument, even anyone passing by?"

Silvis narrowed his eyes and pondered. "Nothing but Leno, like I said. Quiet as a tomb out there. Course I wasn't listenin' for nothin'."

"Did you hear the others," he motioned with his head to Carlton and Peralto, "pass by on their way to their rooms."

Silvis shrugged and gave Carlton a nervous glance. "Well, yeah, I guess. Seems like I heard Chandra and Alex talkin'. Couldn't tell much. I wasn't really listenin', you know!"

"Okay, how long have you known Murdock, Mr. Silvis?"

The cameraman jerked back and his hands went up defensively. "Hey, I just met the guy on this shoot. I'm just a tagalong here."

"You ever have any disagreements? Words or anything like that?"

Silvis vigorously shook his head.

Jared turned to Carlton. "What about you, Mr. Carlton? How long have you known him?"

With a little sigh, head hanging, the producer said softly, "Nearly a year. I met him at a film festival—up at Sundance, as a matter of fact. We found we had a common interest in this famous, disappeared young adventurer. We've been putting together the project for the last six months." He looked up and thrust out his jaw. "But you better believe this isn't the end of it. We're going to go ahead. It's too good a project to lose."

Jared had to fight back a smile as Carlton struck the pose. It was like a gesture from an old Errol Flynn movie. He turned to the bank official. "And Mr. Peralto, you've been in the bank business with Murdock, I understand?"

"That's right. About ten years now. He was just a young buck when I first met him." Peralto grinned. "There was this meeting, and his old man told us we had a new vice president. Just like that. Fresh out of college with an MBA."

Jared considered this. "I see. Did people resent that?"

"Naw," Peralto said with a shake of his head. "That's business. People understand about family. And when Mr. Murdock senior died three years ago, that left Ron a senior vice president."

"Anybody get their nose out of joint about that?"

Peralto's little laugh showed yellowing teeth. "Like I said, business is business."

Carlton drew himself up, an annoyed look on his face. "Why all the questions? You don't think it was any of us, do you?"

Jared stood up. "Course not. Just have to cover all the bases, that's all. Thanks for your cooperation. Before you leave, stop by the office and leave a note with our secretary, Myra, where you can be reached. I may see you again. Sorry for the intrusion."

As Jared and Angus wound through the empty tables on their way out of the door, Alex Carlton looked at his companions, groaned mournfully, and lamented with a doleful shake of his head, "Murdered out here in the sticks of Utah. What a way to go."

CHAPTER 13

The tables at Houston's Café were nearly filled with the lunch crowd when Jared and Angus plopped down next to the window. Mostly it was tourists, and Jared recognized a few of the motel guests he had interrogated two nights earlier following the murder. When Hannah scurried up, pencil in hand, she took a deep breath before greeting them with a broad smile.

"Busier'n a beehive in June here today," the waitress said, leaning her ample hips against the corner of the booth where they sat. Then she frowned in concern. "I guess you gents been up to your armpits in that murder thing. Wasn't that awful? Who'd a thought it here in Kanab? I tell you, this town is goin' to hell in a handbasket. Ever'body's nervous as a cat on a hot tin roof. I haven't locked my door in ten years, but I do now."

"It happens, Hannah," Jared said with a shrug. "We're just hoping we can catch the guy that did it."

"Not likely, I imagine," she answered with a scowl, "what with all o' these drug runners comin' through here. You think it was somethin' like that?"

"Doesn't look like drugs, Hannah," Jared replied. "Robbery's a good possibility."

She seemed to sag at the thought and gravely shook her head to dismiss the whole thing. "So what do you boys feel like today?"

Jared was halfway through his shepherd's stew when a thirty-something man in a dark suit, white shirt, and red tie came in, briefly surveyed the room, and strode up to their booth. Jared recognized him from a Salt Lake television broadcast dealing with the controversy over the cattle on the monument.

He nodded as he came up. "You're Sheriff Buck, aren't you?"

"I am." He nodded but didn't offer to shake hands. "Can I help you?"

"Cameron Taylor, from the U.S. Attorney's office. We need to talk. Mind if I sit down?"

Jared motioned to an empty chair nearby and Taylor pulled it close.

"We have a problem, Sheriff. And maybe you have a problem also. I'm speaking, of course, of the affair in Panguitch."

Jared gave him a wry smile. "I thought that might be the case."

The federal official cleared his throat. "This is a serious matter, you realize. Some of these people are facing a federal fine of $10,000 and ten years in prison."

Angus's jaw dropped. "For taking their *own* cows?" he asked incredulously.

"These were animals that were impounded by the Bureau of Land Management," Taylor said sternly. "They were to be sold at auction to recover the federal costs of impounding them."

"That's pretty tough on some of these ranchers," Jared said. "They're just scraping by now."

The attorney squared his shoulders. "If they feel somewhere in the federal process they were treated unfairly, then take care of it in the courts." He narrowed his brows. "And you, Sheriff Buck, were an accessory to Sheriff Calder in letting them illegally take that federal property."

"That so?" Jared asked softly, staring straight into the attorney's eyes. "Would you rather have had a shoot-out? Maybe somebody killed?"

Taylor gave a quick shake of his head. "Of course not, but

this is a matter of law. We can't have vigilante actions rising above the law."

"I agree. But you need to realize that there were ranchers there from Arizona and Nevada as well as the local cattlemen to support those whose cattle were taken. There are strong feelings that the BLM is riding rough-shod over these folks. There could be real trouble brewing."

"I hope not." Taylor leaned back and threw out his hands in dismay. "We certainly don't want another Waco shoot-out down here."

"Nope. That's the last thing. But isn't the monument director being a little hard-nosed? After all, that country where Kate Thompson has her cows doesn't have a road for twenty miles. It's tough country to negotiate."

"We're working on a compromise."

Jared considered this, took a long sip of his Coke, and glared with raised eyebrows over his glass at the attorney. "I heard that Mahonri Jones hired a helicopter yesterday and went up on Fifty Mile Mountain and shot twenty-seven of his cows rather than pay the BLM the thousand dollars apiece they're charging the ranchers to get them off the monument."

Taylor looked grim. "I'm afraid so. That's unfortunate."

Jared pushed his plate away. "The whole thing is unfortunate. But right now, Angus and I've got a murder investigation to run." He started to slide out of the booth.

Taylor rose. "One thing. Uh . . . we want to avoid further trouble. You have a good reputation with folks around here; we'd like to ask you to see if you can talk some sense into them. They can't win, you know. I'd hate to see them hurt further, maybe spend years in prison."

"Me too. I'll try. But the whole thing is kind of foolish."

Taylor arched an eyebrow. "And there's the matter of your own involvement."

"I guess I'll chance that." Jared picked up the check and slid three one-dollar bills under the salt shaker for Hannah.

With a shake of his head, the agent stood, watching as the

two officers paid their bill. When they turned to leave, Chandra Maroney burst through the entrance, followed by the other members of the film company. Coy Martin tagged along behind.

Chandra's face lit up when she saw them. "Well, we caught you after all," she said.

Alex Carlton pushed his way by her and shook Jared's hand. He ignored Angus. "Sheriff Buck, your secretary told us you might be here. Just wanted to say goodbye and give you these." With a broad smile and an animated motion, he thrust a list with their addresses into Jared's hand. "And I'm expecting we'll be back in force to begin shooting by the end of October."

Jared took the list and checked to see that phone numbers were included. "I guess that means things are working out financially," he said.

Carlton laid a hand on Peralto's shoulder. "As soon as we get to San Francisco, they will."

Peralto offered a weak smile.

"If you're going to film," Jared offered, "I wouldn't wait too late. The high country here gets locked up with snow, sometimes early. And I'll probably be in touch about the investigation."

As the others turned to meet the hostess, Chandra Maroney took his hand and held on. "So long, Jared," she said coyly.

"It's been nice," he said with a nervous laugh.

She arched an eyebrow at him. "It could've been a lot nicer."

Angus ignored her flirtation with his boss and edged closer to her. "I hope we see you back here."

She released Jared's hand, and as she waltzed to join her friends, shot back over her shoulder, "If Alex can work his Hollywood charm on the bankers, you will."

* * *

Outside in the parking lot, Angus slouched against the Jeep and studied his boss. "Now what?" he asked. "You look like you need some sleep."

"Later." Jared shook his head. "Right now I got to go back to the rez and pick up that kid's twenty-two. Then we can either jail him or eliminate him as a suspect."

As Jared slid into his Cherokee, Angus turned and motioned to two men approaching them. Jared frowned when he saw the dark suits, the official dour looks, and the determined strides. These men didn't bode well, he was sure.

The oldest, whose hair was prematurely gray and had a thin face and a gold tooth that showed when he spoke, nodded as he walked up to the Cherokee. Jared got out to meet them.

"You're Sheriff Buck?" He didn't wait for an answer, but flashed a set of credentials. "I'm Richard Summers from the Federal Bureau of Investigation." He reached to shake hands with Jared and his deputy, and then nodded to his companion. "Harley Stewart." Stewart was a stocky, athletic-looking man who dressed as if he had stepped from a Hathaway shirt ad. "Sheriff," Summers went on, "this murder you've got going here, we want you to know we're available for help."

Jared rested his hands on his hips. The last thing he needed was the FBI getting in his way. "This looks like a local matter. We're on it."

"Yes," Summers admitted, "but we've heard there may be some other factors. A shooting on the monument lands, and perhaps some problems with the Navajos. "

"Oh, we're checking those things. I don't think there's any federal violations—not that we know of, anyway."

The younger agent handed Jared a card. "Maybe not. But if anything turns up, we'd like to know about it. You can reach us at this number."

Summers gave a smile and reached to shake hands again. "We probably don't need to get involved. But we'll be around a couple of days."

The agents turned and walked briskly to a dark Mercury, waved once more, and were gone. Jared stood staring after them and shrugged. "More help. That's all we need."

Angus gave a shake of his head. "You never know," he said.

Jared exhaled deeply and hopped back into his Cherokee to return to his office.

"Now I got to hustle out to the rez before those guys get there. They could foul things up royally."

CHAPTER 14

An hour later as Jared put on his hat to leave for the reservation, he was brought up short by the sight of a familiar figure waiting at Myra's desk. It was VerNell Whiting, the county attorney with whom he worked closely in making cases ready for disposition by the courts. Whiting was a slender, intense, and near-sighted lawyer, a couple of years younger than Jared, with ambitions that seemed to keep him in constant motion. He was efficient, but Jared found him annoying in carrying out his duties—too by the book, too much in love with his record in court. He kept a careful account of all their cases, and periodically sent Jared an accounting of missteps they had made in preparing the failures—just so they wouldn't repeat their mistakes, he said.

It was common knowledge that Whiting had political ambitions far beyond the county lines, reaching not only to the state capital but also to Washington as well. After his graduation from law school, he had served as a congressional assistant, and he made no secret that he had found the atmosphere there so stimulating that he was planning one day to return in a position of influence. He was the kind of man, Jared knew from experience, who wore a white shirt and tie even when working in his garden at the edge of town. Jared felt sorry for him.

Now the attorney walked in and slid onto the chair opposite

Jared's seat. "This Murdock shooting," he said without greeting, fanning himself at the same time, "how close are you to getting a handle on it?"

"Afternoon, VerNell," Jared said with a smile, setting his hat on the desk. "Well, we're doing everything we can. Not much to go on. No witnesses, not even the sound of the shot. Not much evidence to go on, but we're still checking things out."

"I came by the motel," VerNell said. "That's an awful thing, you know." He leaned forward as if to speak in confidence. "The Attorney General called me a while ago. He's very concerned." He sat back with a shake of his head. "This is not good, Jared. We better do something fast."

"What do you suggest?"

Whiting looked flustered. "Well, do you have a list of everyone who was at the motel—names, address, and all?"

Jared nodded. "We've done that."

"Does anybody look promising?"

Jared shook his head. "Not yet." He sat forward. He knew Whiting was only doing his job. "The bad thing is, it was more than likely somebody passing through who saw a chance to make a score, and then lost his head. Maybe Murdock fought back instead of just giving them his wallet."

The county attorney furrowed his brow in thought. "Of course you've alerted all the surrounding states and the credit card companies?"

"Done that."

"No other suspects?"

Jared chewed on his lip as he considered this. "I wouldn't say that. There are a couple of possibilities I'm checking out."

"Oh, and who are they?"

"Well, you probably know that Murdock was with a movie company getting ready to make a movie about Everett Ruess, the kid who—"

"I know who Ruess was!" snapped Whiting.

Jared frowned. "Anyway these guys from Hollywood are not the nicest guys around—although Murdock seemed like the best of the bunch. One of them got into a fight with a young Navajo when they went out to Standing Rock on the reservation. I'm going to check him out."

"That so? Be careful of jurisdiction, you know."

"I'm aware of that," he replied without rancor, although he disliked the ability Whiting seemed to have of making people seem small. "Then there's another thing. These Hollywood characters have been going to some of our local ranchers—Cal Oxborrow and Ira Crahorn. Seems a magazine article says that their grandfathers may have killed Ruess way back when he disappeared. They're not too happy to have the whole thing thrown in their faces now."

Whiting looked troubled. "I've heard. We don't want to get Cal Oxborrow's feathers ruffled if we can help it. He can pack a lot of power."

"There's another thing. Saturday, when Mooch Winslow was hauling the Hollywood gang around, somebody shot their tires out up in Cottonwood Canyon. Kept them pinned down a few minutes. When I got there, he was gone."

"I heard. Probably the same shooter, don't you think?"

"As killed Murdock?" Jared asked. "A good chance, but not necessarily."

Now Whiting looked annoyed. "I suppose you don't have any idea who shot at them there either?"

Jared shrugged. "Not yet. They didn't leave much behind. I walked that mesa top for two hours. Didn't even find the spent cartridges."

Whiting took a deep breath, removed his thick glasses, and looked grim. "Jared," he said, "we've got to make some progress here. It makes us look bad when we can't come up with something. The Attorney General was emphatic."

"I know. He called me too."

Whiting winced. "Then there's the matter of the cattle on the Escalante Monument. I hear *60 Minutes* is even going to do a piece on it. The governor is tearing his hair out over everything that's going on down here." He narrowed his eyes to search Jared's face. "Now Jared," he continued, "you've got an election coming up in two years. If you still want to be sitting in that chair after that maybe you better rachet this thing up a notch or two."

Jared leaned back again and smiled. "Guess I'll just take my chances, VerNell. What more do you suggest this office should be doing?"

Whiting rose, his jaw set. "Get cracking on checking out the leads you have. But just be careful you don't jeopardize the case with sloppy methods. Remember the Salazar case."

Two years earlier one of his deputies had stopped a car with Arizona plates traveling through the town in the dead of night. The car was weaving, and the deputy suspected that the driver was under the influence. The veteran deputy, Ray Shurtleff, asked the occupants to step out, and then to open the car's trunk. He arrested them when he found two bales of marijuana—nearly a hundred pounds of it.

Whiting had prosecuted the case, only to have it thrown out because the deputy had violated Salazar's Fourth Amendment rights against search and seizure. The courts ruled he did not have sufficient grounds for searching the car, and had implied that ethnic profiling was a factor. To keep well-informed on avoiding such debacles, Jared had attended week-long clinics for lawmen, once in Florida and twice in Washington D.C. These seminars dealt with such matters as ensuring rights for suspects. He felt on solid ground in these situations, and he had seen to it that his deputies had also gained the proper sensitivities. But he resented that the county attorney reminded him so often of that particular case.

"I think our deputies learned a good lesson there," he said.

"I hope so. Now I'd like to ask that you put everything you've got on this case to get the governor off our necks." Whiting rose to go, and then turned back. "And what the devil is going to happen with the Escalante Monument cattle? It just keeps going. It's even on the national news."

"Of course that's a federal thing," Jared answered. "All I can do is to try to keep our local people out of jail."

Standing in the doorway, Whiting frowned. "From what I hear, you may be there yourself. Maybe that wasn't smart, helping the ranchers in Panguitch—flouting the federal authorities."

Jared shrugged. "Maybe not. But I'm not sorry."

"Keep me informed," Whiting said. He went out the door without a farewell.

CHAPTER 15

At the Standing Rock Trading Post, Jared found Craig Yazzi waiting on the bench in the shade, his broad black hat pulled low over his eyes and his feet up on the hitching rail. Besides Yazzi's Navajo Tribal Police vehicle, two pickup trucks were parked in front of the store. Jared smiled noting that the same two old men who had been seated on the log bench the day before were still seated there, as if they had never left.

Yazzi rose, stretched, and ambled toward Jared's truck. "Hello again," he said as they shook hands. "You must like George's trading post. You keep coming back."

"It's okay. Come on in and I'll buy you a Coke," Jared said, heading toward the door. "Were you able to pick up the kid's rifle?"

Yazzi held the door open as they entered. There was no air conditioning, and old George was leaning over the wooden counter examining a silver and turquoise bracelet when they entered. He didn't look up at them.

"Not exactly," Yazzi said, massaging his chin where some thin whiskers were attempting to become a goatee.

At the red and white Coca-Cola machine, Jared slid in a dollar bill. After a *thunk*, he handed the drink to Yazzi. When he retrieved his own drink, Jared said, "What does 'not exactly' mean?"

Yazzi pursed his lips and slowly nodded in speculation. "It means he's gone to visit his grandfather. He's scared."

"Does that mean he did it?"

"Nope. It means he's scared. He thinks a poor Indian kid will probably get blamed no matter who did it."

"You know that's not true," Jared said, scowling. "Can we find him? If his rifle checks out okay, he's probably cleared."

Yazzi shrugged his shoulders. "Maybe. And maybe we can find him—if you want to bad enough."

"What do you mean?"

"He's at his grandpa's place. Fifteen miles from any road. Do you want to beat up your truck? Mine's brand new."

"Where is it?" Jared calculated all the things he had waiting to be done back in Kanab.

The tribal officer made a motion northeastward with his chin. "Almost to Navajo Mountain."

After a moment of speculation, Jared nodded. "Let's go. Who's the grandfather?"

Yazzi raised his eyebrows and pushed his hat back. "Old Horace Tom." He paused, and then said softly. "He's the one I told you about."

"Who?" Jared asked, puzzled.

Yazzi scratched his chin as he considered how much he should say. Finally he gave a little nod. "The old Navajo those Hollywood people were trying to find. He remembers the Ruess kid that disappeared."

Jared's eyes widened in surprise and he gave a little whistle. "Mmm," he grunted. "Let's go talk to them both."

* * *

After he filled up at the post's gas pump, Jared and Yazzi headed east on the highway to a dirt road that turned north through sagebrush flats and stark mesas. For another hour they bounced along toward the sacred mountain, leaving a trail of dust behind them, until Yazzi indicated a group of boulders at the side of a mesa covered with cedars. There were the faintest of signs that this was occasionally used as a road.

"Turn here, " Yazzi instructed.

After another mile the faint trail disappeared, and Jared gave his friend a questioning glance. Yazzi just pointed straight ahead. Jared shrugged, and the Jeep careened this way and that as they crawled among the boulders. Occasionally they had to back up and choose another route.

"You sure you know where we're going—and how to get there?" Jared asked after he eased the Cherokee over a rock and heard a grating sound. "If we don't knock a hole in our gas tank, we're liable to get stuck in this sand. Not many tow trucks out here."

Yazzi laughed. "Why do you think I didn't bring my truck? It's not too far now. Only six miles or so."

Jared winced. He hated to beat up the county's truck, but he did have to check out Sam Begay's rifle. The crime lab in Salt Lake City would tell in a few minutes if the fatal bullets matched the rifle.

When they passed the second mesa, the way dropped onto a flat of yellow slickrock that made the going easier. Then after a few miles the bedrock ended and Yazzi motioned to a narrow creek-bed that meandered northward between some rugged cliffs.

"Through *there*?" Jared looked dismayed.

"Sure. It's the only way," Yazzi said. He motioned to some tracks in the sand that showed that another vehicle had come this way recently.

"Okay." Jared exhaled. "We'll try." After a few minutes of grinding, climbing, and bouncing over large rocks, they emerged. He glanced at Yazzi. "Tell me, brother," Jared asked, "how do you know the way to Horace Tom's hogan, anyway?"

A wide grin creased Yazzi's face. "Oh, it's my business to know where everybody on the rez lives," he said in mock serious-ness.

Jared shot him a withering glance and cleared his throat.

After giggling, Yazzi shrugged. "Okay. I been here with my

father. He and old Horace were friends. They were in World War Two together. Both Navajo Code talkers for the army in Guadalcanal. My dad was a kid, and Horace was older, but he took him under his wing."

Jared knew that his friend's father had been dead several years. He marveled that Yazzi could still find his way over mostly unmarked country that looked essentially the same in any direction. "Oh," he said. "I guess that explains it."

It was late afternoon when Yazzi pointed to a plume of blue smoke that rose above a six-sided log-and-mud hogan that sat against a bluff where a few cedar trees struggled to survive. Jared breathed a sigh of relief.

As they pulled up to the hogan, they saw a battered, turquoise Ford pickup parked nearby. Two figures seated near a fire in the shade of a cedar tree rose to greet them. The tallest tucked his thumbs into his belt and watched them without moving. He stood straight, his face brown and crevassed like old oak bark. His thick, silver-white hair, bound behind his head in the traditional bun, was pulled back beneath a straight-brimmed black hat with a silver conch band. A luxurious white mustache turned down around the corners of his mouth. In the afternoon light, the old Navajo made a picturesque figure.

"Wow, how old is he anyway?" Jared whispered as they rolled to a stop.

Yazzi laughed. "I think he's a hundred and two. Could be older, for all I know."

At the side of the old man, Sam Begay glanced warily around as Jared and Yazzi approached. Jared wondered if the boy was going to run. He knew that fugitives could hide for months in this wild land. He hoped it wouldn't come to that.

"*Ya-ta-heh*," Yazzie greeted the old man.

He shook hands and sized up Jared. Young Begay looked as though he would sink into the ground, staring at his feet.

Craig Yazzi explained in Navajo that the sheriff had come to get evidence of the rifle to clear Begay's name. Solemnly, the old man nodded and reached to shake Jared's hand. "Okay," he said simply.

Then the old man moved stiffly to the door of the hogan, said something in a quiet voice, and a middle-aged woman appeared, avoiding the eyes of the newcomers. She wore a heavy print skirt and a velvet blouse, and carried a pot and a covered pan, moving with a solemn grace. With a nod the old man motioned them into the hogan.

With a slight motion of his chin, Craig Yazzi indicated the woman. "Daisy Begay, the kid's mother," he whispered. Jared nodded that he understood.

It was stifling inside. Old Horace eased himself onto a sheep-skin and gestured for the others to sit on blankets. For Jared, it was nothing new, for he had been with Craig to sings and squaw dances. He glanced at his watch. First, he reminded himself, he had to get the rifle—then he was bursting with anticipation to learn what the old man knew about Everett Ruess. But he had learned not to be too direct out on the reservation. He knew that the older Navajos liked to take their time about things. He sat back against a rolled-up sheepskin and listened as Craig Yazzie and the old man conversed in the throaty, quiet tones of Navajo. He could catch an occasional word he knew of the language, but could not follow the meaning of the conversation. In the mean-time, young Begay sat listening intently, rocking on his heels, occasionally nodding in agreement.

Finally Yazzi turned to Jared. "He says it looks like it will be a good crop of pinion nuts this fall."

Jared agreed with a deep nod. "Yes, I've seen lots of cones."

They sat silently for a time, and then the old man laid his hand on Yazzi's arm and spoke intently. After a time Yazzi turned to Jared. "But the drought is not good for sheep feed. Very dif-ficult without grass."

Again Jared nodded his assent. "Tell him the cattle are having a hard time on the Escalante range too."

The old man raised his eyebrows at him. "I heard that too," he said in a quiet voice in English.

Jared was not surprised. It would be hard to go to war with the United States Army without speaking English. He guessed that Horace simply preferred his native language.

Again there was a long silence, then the woman appeared in the doorway bearing food and plates. She was shy and avoided their eyes as she proffered fry bread, and then a plate of beans. She served Craig Yazzie first, then the old man, followed by Jared, and then the youth. The meal was, in fact, one of Jared's favorites. He had eaten it often with his friend. After serving, the woman left the hogan without ever looking at Jared.

"Daisy's a good cook," Yazzi said. Sitting quietly, young Sam Begay nodded his agreement.

When they finished, Horace Tom turned to his grandson and spoke in Navajo. Yazzi gave Jared an approving glance, rose, and went out with the youth.

In the silence that ensued, Jared felt guilty for having come to disturb this old warrior. He felt the man's eyes on him.

"He didn't do anything bad," Horace Tom said.

"I think you're right," he agreed. "This way the police will know for sure. I apologize for the man who hit Sam. He caused the trouble."

The old man gave a deep nod, and then sat staring into the cedar logs on the side of the hogan.

In another minute Yazzi stepped in holding a small rifle. Jared took the gun and examined it. It was an old, bolt-action Winchester model 69, one that had been around for half a century. "I'm sure it'll check out okay," he said, laying the gun aside. Craig Yazzi sat down and another long silence ensued.

Finally, Jared cleared his throat and looked at the old man. "Uh, Mr. Tom, I have another question," he ventured. "Something that happened a long time ago. It is said that you may have seen something—way back when you were young." Jared glanced at Craig Yazzi to see if he was on firm ground. His friend gave a tiny nod. Jared took a deep breath. "Many years ago, a young man came through this country, walking. He was an artist. He drew pictures of the land—of the rocks and the desert. He went through the towns, and he went to some of the hogans of your people. He went to Escalante and talked to the people there, and then he came south toward the river. He disappeared then. Nobody saw him again."

The old man showed no sign of having heard.

"We don't know what happened to him," Jared continued. "Many people would like to find his bones." He paused. "It is said that you may have seen him at some time when he wandered through here. He was in this country for nearly two years."

Another long silence ensued, broken only by the buzzing of a fly.

Old Horace Tom sighed deeply, shifted position, and continued staring into the charred remnants of the previous night's fire.

Finally Jared cleared his throat again. "His name was Everett Ruess," he continued. "He was about nineteen or twenty, with brown hair. He had a burro that he used to get around."

The old man turned to look long at Jared, and finally nodded. "Two burros," he corrected.

Jared felt his breath stop. Could this old man know something nobody else had discovered all these years? *It's entirely possible,* he reasoned, *given the Indian proclivity for silence.* He reminded himself that he was hip-deep in a pressing murder investigation. Nevertheless, he felt caught up in this decades-old disappearance. He knew that he shouldn't be messing around with this now, but the temptation was great, since he was already here. He leaned forward, anticipating what the old man would say.

But Horace Tom turned instead to Yazzi, and began a long explanation. When he was finished, he sat back and gave a grunt.

Jared reached to tug at Yazzi's sleeve. "What'd he say?"

His friend worked his lips into a shrug. "Well . . . he says he seems to remember something about a boy with two burros." Then Yazzi grinned. "And he says he might be able to remember if you can put on a sing to help him remember. He says a few years ago he dreamed about a bear up on Navajo Mountain. In his dream he laughed at the bear, and that made the bear mad. So he got the bear sickness, and it made him forget things. He says the medicine man at a sing is very good for helping people remember things."

Jared was flustered. "What? I can't get involved in a sing. I got that murder to work on."

"Okay," Yazzi hunched his shoulders. "When you bringing that rifle back?"

With knitted brow, Jared figured the time it would take to get the rifle back from the Salt Lake lab. "Probably about a week." The thought came that he might be back sooner to arrest Sam Begay if the match with the bullets was positive.

"That'll work," Yazzi said. "You want me to line it up?"

Jared looked nonplussed, and then shrugged. He had plans to follow up on the Everett Ruess disappearance after the Murdock murder settled down. "How much will it cost me?"

"Oh, it'll probably be only a two- or three-day sing. There's lots involved. Gotta have lots of mutton. Medicine men aren't cheap. Maybe about fifteen hundred bucks."

Making a wry face, Jared let out a whistle. "Holy cow, Craig, I don't have it."

In earlier years, Yazzi had taken Jared to two healing sings to view the sacred ceremony. In it, the medicine man used ancient chants and invoked special blessings with spirit-laden objects while dribbling different-colored sand between his fingers onto the cleared floor of the hogan to create a beautiful sand painting. In order to avoid offense to the deities watching, the sand painting had to be erased by sundown.

Yazzi turned to the old man, who sat staring off to the west where the dying sun was singeing the line of cumulous clouds into purples and reds that filled the horizon. After a few moments of earnest conversation, Yazzi gave a grunt of satisfaction.

"He says it's too bad. He would like to have a sing for him to get rid of the bear sickness. Then he could remember everything."

"Heck, I have the same problem sometimes," Jared said with a laugh. "Will he settle for something less?"

Again Yazzi engaged Horace Tom in a quiet debate, and then

he faced Jared. "He says that some people say strawberry soda pop is very good to help somebody remember," Yazzi said without laughing. "He says maybe two cases of strawberry soda pop would bring back the memory of that kid. And four cases would make sure."

Jared stifled a laugh. "That I can probably do."

The old man said something in Navajo, so quietly that Jared could not hear the words.

Yazzi nodded, and then addressed Jared again. "And no cans. He wants bottles. Cans take the spirit from the pop, he says."

"Bottles. Okay, bottles."

Horace Tom's hat bobbed as he nodded his assent. But once more, he added something aside to Yazzi.

"Nehi. He wants Nehi strawberry pop."

Jared blinked in surprise, than gave a nod. "Nehi," he said, frowning. "I haven't seen it in years. I hope they still make the stuff."

At a sign from Yazzi, Jared put on his hat, rose, and took the old man's bony hand in his. It felt frail and he was careful not to squeeze too hard. Still seated, the old man gazed up into the anglo's eyes and would not release his hand. For a long moment he stared as if he were searching for something hidden there; then, still grasping the hand in a grip that was surprisingly strong, he began to speak in Navajo without looking at Craig Yazzie. He spoke intensely, his voice not wavering, in a low sing-song that sent chills down Jared's back, as if it were from some primordial recounting that had been chanted for millennia among these barren mesas. As the old man spoke, his free left hand made a slow, broad sweeping gesture across the horizons beyond the hogan where they sat. A gentle glow appeared in his eyes, deep with intensity, as he searched Jared's face. His voiced cracked with the urgency of what he was explaining. Awed, Jared held the hand, listened, and did not try to pull away or avert his gaze from those charcoal eyes buried deep in a face that had weathered so much.

After what seemed like minutes, Horace Tom squinted,

raised his arm toward the tribal officer, gave a deep nod, and dropped Jared's hand. Craig Yazzie slowly lowered his chin in understanding.

Jared glanced at his friend, puzzled. "What did he say?"

With a wry smile, Yazzie hunched his shoulders. "He says you are okay. But there is something he wants you to know—to understand." He paused for a moment, and made a gesture toward the north. "Here . . . in this land . . . is the place that is sacred ground. He says that here where the three sacred rivers come together—the Colorado, the Green, and the San Juan—this is a spiritual place. A place where the spirits of the Old Ones still live. A place where the ancient people left their drawings on the rocks to remind us they are still here." Yazzie paused to trace a figure on the rug on which he sat, as if gathering courage to go on.

"And he says this place is sacred because it is the center of the universe. In the beginning the creator had the first humans in a bag to place them on earth, but the Trickster Coyote tipped over the bag that held the world's first humans. This trick scared some of the humans, so they scattered to live in other places around the world. But the wise ones, the Dineh, remained and waited for instruction and light from the Creator. And this is where they are today, in this special place, where the spirit people still walk to show us the way." He paused and studied his boots. "He says there are powerful forces here in this land."

Jared did not know if his friend was embarrassed or solemn. After a long silence, Yazzie looked up, pursed his lips, cocked his head, and in a slow, soft voice said, "He says this is why the young boy artist was drawn to this place. Here, where the four sacred mountains point to the sky, the boy witch came to find his soul." Yazzi glanced at the old man to check his reaction. The grandfather lowered his chin in solemn affirmation.

Yazzie stopped, took a deep breath, his eyes narrowed, and he stared intently at the rug between his knees as he said in a near whisper, "Horace Tom believes the spirit people took him with them."

*   *   *

When they stepped outside, the sun was nearly down, and Sam Begay was loitering near the turquoise pickup. Looking hangdog, he ambled over as they got into the Jeep. "You gonna take me to jail?" he asked morosely.

Jared reached to shake his hand. "I hope not, Sam. If your gun checks out, you'll be okay. But stay close, all right?"

Jared had never seen anyone look sorrier or guiltier as the youth shook his head.

"Okay," Sam Begay said without looking up.

As they bounced away through the sagebrush, Jared looked back in his rear-view mirror. The two stood together by the hogan watching, the tall dignified grandfather and the grandson who feared he was going away to prison.

CHAPTER 16

Angus was already in the office when Jared arrived at eight-thirty. It had been early morning when Jared had finally gotten back from the marathon trip to Horace Tom's hogan. Now, after three hours of sleep, Jared ached all over. As he moved stiffly toward his desk, his secretary, Myra, cocked her head and gave him a look of disapproval.

"My heck, you look awful," she said.

"Thanks. I feel like I been rode hard and put away wet," he admitted. "Remind me to get some sleep one of these days." He didn't mind Myra's mothering, but at times it was embarrassing.

"I'll sure enough do that," she said, frowning.

Angus looked up from the morning newspaper with a grin. "Did you have a good time out on the rez?"

"Well, I got what I went after—this." He held out the large, plastic garbage bag that held Sam Begay's rifle. "But it was one crazy road getting there."

"So now we've got two possible murder weapons," Angus said grimly, "but maybe no real suspects."

Jared lowered himself into his chair and stretched out his legs. In addition to lack of sleep, the hours of bouncing over rocks and sandhills had left him sore and weary. "That's about the size of it."

Angus scratched his balding head. "So what do we do now?"

"I guess we step back and take a look at what we got," Jared said. He reached down, pulled open the bottom drawer of his desk, and set the plastic evidence envelopes they had gathered onto his desk. Briefly, he examined their contents. He held up the one that contained the matchbook cover he had picked up near the body.

Angus put down the newspaper and ambled over to lean on the desk.

"The Las Vegas Luxor," Jared mused. "Pretty fancy place. Think it means anything?"

"Nope," Angus said with a shake of his head. "Half the tourists at the Cinnamon Cliffs probably came here through Vegas. Possible, but not likely, that it was the guy who shot Murdock."

"Granted. So it's probably meaningless. The lab said the prints were too smudged to be any help." He examined the matchbook again. "But it *could* have been the shooter who stopped in Vegas."

Without answering, Angus went to his desk and returned with a colorful envelope that he dropped on Jared's desk. "Got the pictures back from Murdock's camera."

"Anything interesting?"

"Don't know. I waited for you. Didn't want to spoil the surprise."

Jared slid the prints out and spread them across the desk. Only about half the roll had been shot. One by one, Jared ran his finger over the figures. Four of the prints were from their first day in town, standing in front of the motel or seated in the restaurant. Three were from their stop at the visitors' center at Navajo Bridge over the Colorado River. One shot was of Murdock standing next to the solemn-faced park ranger, Al Coots. The other pictures were of various members of the film group climbing pastel-colored rock or making their way through the narrow passages of one of the slot canyons. These were darker than ideal, obviously a result of the high canyon walls that cut out the sunlight. Jared paused on two pictures—one of Mooch Winslow with his arm around Chandra Maroney, pulling her close, and the other with

Murdock leaning against Mooch's shoulder. In his short-sleeve safari shirt, his Aussie hat at a cocky angle, and with the sun playing on the blonde ends of his handlebar mustache, the guide appeared to be doing his very best to come across as the great adventurer.

"No surprises," he said, sliding them back into the envelope.

"Just your average cast of beautiful people," Angus observed with irony.

Jared began to chew on his lip in speculation. He leaned back with his hands behind his head and stared out the window at the red cliffs beyond town, just visible through the trees of the parking lot. "Let's analyze it. First, we got a movie group that comes to town to make a movie that some of the local folks may not want made."

"Yeah, but you don't—"

"Wait," Jared raised a forefinger to stop the objection. "So somebody takes a couple of shots at Mooch Winslow and the filmmakers. Maybe they're after Mooch, and maybe Murdock. Or maybe they just want to scare the whole bunch away from something. May or may not be connected. Then these film people go talking to half the people in southern Utah about the Ruess kid. That Carlton guy picks a fight with young Sam Begay out at Standing Rock."

Angus folded his arms in resignation. He was used to Jared ruminating about any puzzling situation to try to come up with answers. Sometimes it helped to talk it out.

"And then there's Mooch Winslow, who might have even more financial problems than we know about," Jared went on. "Could he be desperate enough? No real alibi, you know."

"You think Mooch could really be that wacko?"

"Maybe. Not likely, but a possibility. The ballistics might show us something. But let's ask some more questions. More than likely it's a random robbery that turned bad. But the final bullet to the head bothers me." Jared gave his head a shake as if to clear cobwebs. "Wouldn't a hitchhiker or opportunistic thief settle for grabbing the wallet and leaving him wounded?"

"Sometimes. Not always," Angus said.

Jared began to stare at the ceiling, his fingers meshed behind his head. "Let's assume just for the heck of it that it wasn't a chance encounter. That Murdock was in someone's way. So who gains with Murdock's death? Maybe somebody we don't know about. By the way, I'm phoning a friend in San Francisco to have him check on Murdock's family and friends. There could be heirs. Could mean something."

Angus' face lit up. "Follow the money. That's what Deep Throat said. Turned out he was right."

"Yep. Never underestimate the power of an inheritance, I hear. Murdock was undoubtedly worth *mucho dinero*. I'm checking on it."

"Send me out there, Jared," Angus said with a grin. "San Francisco's wonderful this time of year."

Jared ignored him. "And then there's Carlton . . . and Peralto . . . Chandra . . . and the cameraman—who knows what kind of intrigue might be there under the surface. I'm still waiting to hear more from L.A." He paused, sat up, and pushed the rifle in the garbage bag, butt first, across his desk toward Angus, taking care to keep the muzzle pointed to the wall. "Get this and Mooch's pistol off to Salt Lake this morning, will you please?"

Angus rose and picked up the rifle and sat it in the corner. "Wouldn't it be easy if one of these matches the bullets in Murdock?"

"I really don't expect that to happen. But we have to check." He held up the evidence envelopes one by one to inspect them one more time. "What we don't have," he said with a glum shake of his head, "is Murdock's wallet and watch—and maybe the murder weapon."

*   *   *

An hour later Jared looked up to see Coy Martin coming up the walk. He sat back from the report he was filling out. When

Myra ushered Martin in to his office, he saw that the private detective was sunburned.

"Looks like you've had a little sun, Mr. Martin."

"You could say that," he answered, reaching to tenderly stroke his cheek. "I've tromped over half of Utah and Arizona."

Jared swivelled in his chair to face him. "What'd you find?" he asked, curious. He wondered if the detective had turned up something that he hadn't.

"Not much. Yesterday I traveled clear out to the Standing Rock trading post looking for that kid that Carlton had the fight with. Couldn't find him. Folks are pretty close-mouthed out there."

Jared gestured to Sam Begay's rifle standing in the corner. "I talked to him. There's his twenty-two rifle. We're sending it to Salt Lake for ballistics tests."

Martin glanced at the rifle, and then glared accusingly at Jared. "You could have saved me a lot of time, you know."

"Never thought of it. What else have you found?

Martin hunched his shoulders. "Not much. There's not much to go on. May have to go back and report 'Death by person or persons unknown.'"

"Almost looks that way," Jared agreed with a sigh. "But it's not over yet. We're still checking on some things. I'm sort of starting over. Tell me, who do you think would profit from Murdock's death? What about his family?"

Martin cast a glance to the table where Angus kept a coffee pot on a hot plate. "Anything in that?"

Jared rose, poured a cup, and delivered it to the detective. "Cream and sugar there." He pointed. But the detective shook his head, and took a sip of the coffee.

Balancing the cup, Martin eased himself into Angus's chair and sat back. "Not much there that I can find. As I told you, Murdock's divorced. The bank's got a half million insurance on him. I don't know what else."

"No kids?"

Martin took another sip of his coffee and studied Jared over the rim of his cup. "Good chance that Murdock was gay—which might explain the divorce and why there were no kids."

A pained expression grew on Jared's face, and he let out a low whistle. "Whew. I didn't think that." He paused, considering. "I wonder if that changes anything. Any jealous boyfriend?"

Martin shrugged. "Not likely in this case, way out here."

"Hmmm," Jared began to rub his chin in speculation. Carlton, Peralta, or Silvis? Maybe Carlton was too casual about Chandra. He didn't seem very concerned when she carried on her flirtations. But he appeared to have too much to lose in Murdock's death. After a moment of pondering, he shook his head. "Doesn't seem much to go on there. It looks like robbery is still the most obvious bet. Too bad something didn't turn up in the roadblocks."

Martin set down his cup and rose. "That's what I'm going to report back to the bank—person or persons unknown in what was probably a random robbery." He reached over to shake hands. "I'm leaving this afternoon. If anything turns up on the ballistics evidence from the guns you've got, I'll be grateful if you'll let me know." He handed Jared a card. When the detective left, Jared glanced at the clock, and then placed a call to San Francisco.

"*San Francisco Examiner*," a pleasant voice said.

"Umm, yes, this is Sheriff Jared Buck, calling for Paul Crichlow. I think he's in the business section."

"Mr. Crichlow? I'll connect you to city desk."

There was a click and soft music came on. After Jared had ruined his knee playing football at Utah State, Sunny had convinced him to keep his hand in sports by writing for the student newspaper, the *Statesman*. Reluctantly, he had wandered in and offered his services. To his surprise, he learned that he enjoyed the interviewing and the bylines. After a few months he had his own weekly sports column, where he had the chance to vent his opinions. At the same time, he had become friends with a skinny, mop-haired Californian with wild ideas who became editor during Jared's final year. He knew that since then Paul Crichlow had started reporting for a small-town daily newspaper in Texas and then had jumped to a big-city daily, the *Examiner.* The guy had always had a flair for investigative reporting that sometimes ruffled feathers. But some editors loved his inquisitive nature and dogged determination in ferreting out hidden facts. For several years after graduating, Jared and Sunny had exchanged Christmas cards with Crichlow and his wife. The reporter had called with condolences when he heard about Sunny's death.

"City desk—Crichlow," said a crisp voice.

In the background, Jared could hear the muffled sounds of people talking. "Hey, you old Aggie son-of-a-gun, I thought you'd be editor by now."

There was a moment of silence, and then an exhaled breath when Crichlow recognized the voice. "Jared Buck, that you?"

"You betcha. Long time, eh? How're things going, Crichlow?"

"Good. But how about you? I was going to call you. Here in the Bay Area, there's been big news out of your little podunk town. Somebody out there murdered one of our bankers. Your name was mentioned."

"Yeah, well, that's why I'm calling. Mr. Ronald Murdock got himself shot twice in a motel parking lot about midnight Wednesday night. So far, we've got nothing."

"That's what I hear. Some people are muttering," he paused to chuckle, "about hick-town police. Of course I know better."

Jared drew a breath. "Well, most likely it was some hood passing through who saw an easy mark as the guy went to his limousine—late at night, nobody around. Used a twenty-two, so there was no noise to speak of. Nobody heard anything."

"That's a tough one, " Crichlow said. "So what do you do?"

"That's why I'm calling you, old buddy. There's a small chance this wasn't just a robbery gone bad."

"A hit?"

"We don't know. But the second shot to the head—the *coup de grace*—makes me wonder. Can you do some checking for me?

"Sure. What do you want to know. Could be a story in it."

Jared had been making notes as he made the call. "Well, first, who stands to gain by Murdock's death? The bank had him insured for half a million, but what else did he have? Any impatient heirs? Did he have enemies? Was there any personal intrigue going on with him? I hear he may have been gay."

"I heard that too. Not unusual in this town."

"He was going to put up money for a film set here in Utah where a young guy disappeared years ago down in the canyons. Not everybody wanted that film made, so I'm still checking out some local people."

He could hear Crichlow let out a little laugh. "Hey, this sounds fun. Sure, I'll do some checking over in Oakland at the bank. I'll get back to you."

Jared thanked him, asked him to pass along regards to his wife, and then hung up. He felt empty when Crichlow told him they were expecting another child. For a long moment he sat staring at the wood grain on his desk.

CHAPTER 17

Ira Crahorn had not mellowed. As Jared turned off the dusty Johnson Canyon Road toward Skitarumpah Creek where Mose Crahorn had homesteaded a century ago, he watched the pink cliffs that towered northward where the Paunsugunt plateau became Bryce Canyon National Park slide by. Here below, it was scrubby country with cedars, sagebrush, and deer brush, only good for running cattle. Jared didn't look forward to interviewing Ira Crahorn again, but the old curmudgeon was someone who might be bitter enough to be a possible suspect.

Pulling up to the Crahorn gate, Jared studied the run-down house for a minute before he got out of his Jeep. At the side of the porch, several deep-orange chrysanthemums were blooming—the only sign of color around the place. He decided that the woman must not have entirely given up hope. No one was in sight, but Crahorn's pickup sat at the side of the barn. When Jared knocked on the door, he heard a shuffling noise inside. After a minute, the door opened a crack and the drawn face of Velda Crahorn peeped out. With a suspicious glare, she nodded her recognition without speaking.

"Afternoon, Mrs. Crahorn," Jared said, removing his hat. "I was wondering if I might speak to Mr. Crahorn."

She opened the door another foot, studied him silently for a moment, and then said, "Ain't here." Her voice was a husky whisper, with a slight crack, as if she didn't use it often.

Jared shifted his feet. "Well, when do you expect him? I need to talk to him." The woman would not meet his eyes. Through the door he could see that the furnishings were bare and worn, but they appeared to be spotlessly clean. He wondered what her life had been like, to leave her so timid and beaten down.

She considered his question, working her jaw as a deep cough gripped her, and she fought to gain control of her breathing. "Might find him out back inside the barn," she finally offered, and gestured with a bony finger.

"Thanks, Mrs. Crahorn, I'll look." He started to leave, but then turned to face her. "How are you feeling these days?"

She seemed startled by the question, as if it had never been asked before. She looked down and clasped her hands, and then seemed to study the veins there before answering. "Tolerable, I guess. I expect I'll live."

"Good luck," he said with a smile.

She nodded gratefully, and then said with what was almost a twinkle in her eye, "You gonna put him away again?"

"No—I don't think so," Jared replied with a wide grin. "Just need to ask him a couple of questions."

"Hmmph," she muttered with a shake of her head. "Too bad. Might improve his disposition some."

Beyond the corral, Jared could see the stooped figure of Ira Crahorn leaning over a small all-terrain vehicle. He had pieces of the engine spread out on the ground around him.

"Halloo," Jared called as he approached. He had no intention of startling the man.

Without answering, Crahorn turned slowly and appraised the sheriff. Straightening, he wiped his hands on his pants, and then planted them on his hips as a challenge without speaking.

Jared nodded as he approached, but didn't offer to shake hands. "Ira," he said. "How're things?"

Crahorn cast a glance around at his place. Behind the barn, the bodies of two old cars sat rusting in the afternoon sunlight.

"Not a helluva lot better than the last time you came," he said with a grunt.

Jared cleared his throat. "I uh . . . I guess you heard what happened in town Tuesday night—to one of those Hollywood people."

"I heard," Ira said with a deep nod, his jaw taut. "Now I suppose you're lookin' at me for that too?"

"Not really. But I got to ask you where you were Wednesday night."

Crahorn's brow furrowed as he considered this. "Hellfire, where would I be? In bed that time o' night." He made a gesture toward the house. "My wife can tell you."

"I see," Jared said, rubbing his chin. It was what he expected Crahorn to say, no matter where he had been. And he knew Ira's wife would back him up—out of fear, if nothing else. "Tell me, Ira, you have a twenty-two pistol or rifle?"

"Course. Who doesn't?"

Jared chuckled at this. The man was right. He couldn't go around gathering up rifles without any evidence on the off chance one of them might match the markings on the bullets from Murdoch's body. Jared shrugged. "Just looking for anything that might help us find out who killed Ron Murdock."

"Well, you sure came to the wrong place," Crahorn said, glaring. "I mind my own business out here—and I wish you'd do the same."

"Problem is, this *is* my business," Jared said with a shrug.

Picking up a wrench, Crahorn turned back to the machine, picked up a part, and began to attach it back onto the ATV. "Then I'll be obliged if you'd take it someplace else."

*   *   *

Because it was a Friday afternoon, Jared knew that the Oxborrow family would be at the football game in town. With two of their boys on the team, and with Pine Valley High School in town for the game, he knew that the whole family would be there to root for them. High school sports rivalries in the small Utah towns were a binding force for the communities—a source of pride and fervent competition. Jared calculated how long it would take him to reach their place. If he dawdled, they should be home from the game and have supper over by the time he got there.

It was nearly seven when he pulled up to the cement driveway and got out. The Oxbow Ranch sat on a bench at the mouth of a canyon some dozen miles from town, where a creek during the spring watered the flats below to allow two hundred acres of alfalfa to thrive. Using modern methods, with deep wells and a sprinkling system, Cal Oxborrow had built the family ranch into a model for others in the area.

The large home itself was proof that he didn't mind showing his prosperity. The ranch house had been built twenty years earlier with a Taos Pueblo motif—a flat roof with pine logs protruding from thick plastered walls. It looked like it belonged in northern New Mexico rather than in southern Utah. Inside, a great stone fireplace with a carved cedar mantle was flanked by a picture window that overlooked the cinnamon cliffs north. It was a house that Jared envied, but he knew that on a sheriff's salary, such a home was only a dream.

The door was opened by a husky youth when Jared rang. "Hi, Sheriff, come on in," Kelly Oxborrow said with a smile. "You want to talk to my dad?"

Jared landed a mock punch on the youth's muscular shoulder. "Sure. But first tell me—did we beat Pine Valley?"

The boy smiled broadly and spread his hands. "Heck yes! Twenty to seven. What'd you expect?"

"Great! Go Kanab!" Jared laughed, then cocked his head. "Did you score?"

The boy blushed and touched his chin on his shoulder. "Well, yeah—twice." He looked pleased that Jared had asked.

Jared put on a mock scowl. "Hey, careful there. We don't want you setting any records." In his senior season, Jared had run for thirteen touchdowns. That had won him the football scholarship at Utah State.

From the doorway behind them came the deep voice of Cal Oxborrow. "Evenin', Sheriff Buck. Come on in. We'll grab you a plate."

Jared followed him into the kitchen, where the family had just begun to eat. "No thanks, I've eaten," Jared fibbed. He was embarrassed that he had intruded at supper time. After seeing Ira Crahorn earlier in the afternoon, he had hoped to catch the Oxborrows after their dinner.

"Missed a great game, Jared," Mrs. Oxborrow said. "Sure you won't eat a bite with us?"

"I'm fine, Amy." Jared stood holding his hat in his hand. He nodded to the other Oxborrow boy. "Did you get in, Curtis?" He shared a bond with the boys because he had played on the same team two decades earlier.

"Sure. Nearly two quarters." Curtis was taller and more slender than his older brother.

"But he dropped a pass," Kelly chortled.

Curtis stared at him, furious. "It was over my head," he shot back.

"It was," Cal Oxborrow put in to end the discussion. Then he turned to Jared. "What's up, Sheriff Buck?"

Jared shifted nervously. He needed to talk to Cal alone. "Oh, we're just trying to piece things together. You know what happened Wednesday night . . ."

Oxborrow made a wry face. "Awful. Right in Kanab. Are you making any progress?"

"We think it was a crime of opportunity," Jared replied with a shrug. "Just somebody traveling through who saw a well-heeled man in the parking lot. Mr. Murdock carried quite a bit of cash with him. Maybe somebody saw him with it. We're looking at all our leads."

Mrs. Oxborrow gave a mournful shake of her head. "Used to be we didn't lock our doors. Guess we'll have to change our ways."

Cal Oxborrow rubbed his chin in speculation. "So, what can we help you with, Sheriff?"

Jared tried to think of a way to avoid asking what he needed to in front of the family. "I'm just checking out a few things—if you've seen anything suspicious, like when you were in town that day or anything."

After a moment's thought, Oxborrow shook his head. "I was in Panguitch that day, trying to work things out with the feds about the cattle on the monument."

"That's where I was too," Jared sighed.

Amy turned from where she was gathering up dishes. "I didn't even go to town that day, so I can't help you."

Both the boys shook their heads and said that they had seen nothing unusual after school.

Jared fingered his hat. "Well, thanks anyway. Guess I'll go along then."

Amy came and gave a firm handshake. "Come have dinner with us next time, Jared."

"Thanks. I'll try, Amy," he said.

Oxborrow came and led the way outside. At the sheriff's car, Jared turned and faced him. "Cal, I have to ask you—where were you Wednesday night about eleven thirty?"

The rancher laughed. "So I'm a suspect am I? Why's that?"

"It's just that I've got to check, that's all. One possible motive, if it wasn't robbery, is that some people don't want this movie made. I told you about the shooting of Mooch Winslow's tires last week."

Oxborrow's face clouded, and through a clinched jaw he said, "Oh, I see. And because of something my grandfather may or may not have done, that puts me in the category of those not wanting the movie. Pretty slim, Jared."

"I know. But I've got to check everything. It's my job."

"Well, that day after I came from Panguitch, Amy and I had a late supper, watched television, and then went to bed about eleven. You can check with her."

Jared nodded. "All right. Uh, one thing more, I guess you own a twenty-two rifle or pistol?"

Oxborrow's eyes narrowed. "Sure. A couple of twenty-two

rifles. No pistols. Don't want them around, what with the boys."

"I see." Jared rubbed his temples. "Speaking of the boys, do you know where they were that night?"

Oxborrow caught his breath and even in the fading light Jared could see his face turn red in anger. "Now wait a minute!"

Jared held up his hand, palm first. "Sorry. Again, I have to ask."

"Hey, they're kids. I'm pretty certain they were in bed. That was a school night and they're in training."

"I thought so," Jared responded with a sigh of relief.

The sun was going down behind the cliffs as he drove through the gate of the Oxbow Ranch, the light playing on the sandstone bluffs behind him. A sense of discouragement settled over him, for he seemed to be making no progress, and somewhere in Phoenix or Los Angeles or maybe Mexico, the shooter was probably wondering how long the money that he had taken from Murdock's wallet after he had popped him would last. In the meantime, Jared reminded himself, he wasn't making any friends among the locals he had to question.

CHAPTER 18

By mid-morning on Saturday, Jared was knocking on the door of Kate Thompson's ranch house. In the back of the Cherokee, Sitka sat with pricked ears watching. The massive, two-story frame home had been built early in the 1900s, with a dormer and balcony on the upper story that opened to the south, similar to the widow's walk of sea-facing homes in the East. Jared knew that Kate's grandfather, Jedediah Thompson, had joined the LDS Church when he was young, had migrated westward to this settlement of the Saints, and had brought his ideas of architecture with him. From the upper walkway, the owner could gaze over the lands where he had built a small cattle empire.

The place had been kept in good repair, its window boxes brimming with red and blue petunias. Jared wondered how she managed alone, but he knew that back in the cottonwoods from the main home, there sat a two-bedroom house painted a pastel blue where Epifanio Ortiz and his family lived. They had worked on the ranch for two generations, doing most of the ranch work and seeing that a garden produced much of what both families ate.

When the door opened, Kate greeted him with a large smile. "Come on in, Jared," she said warmly. "About time you're getting out to see me." She was wearing a faded pair of Levis and a leather vest over a denim shirt. He smiled to himself when he saw that her boots were flecked with mud and barnyard manure.

He followed her into a roomy kitchen, where he was surprised to see the lanky figure of Mahonri Jones slumped over a cup of coffee. Jared had called ahead and Kate was expecting him, but he didn't know that the other rancher would be there. Jones was a solemn man, with prominent cheek bones that seemed to jut nearly to his bushy grey eyebrows beneath the broad hat that he hadn't bothered to remove. Naturally of a melancholy disposition, he appeared even more depressed now.

"Mahonri," Jared acknowledged, "good to see you."

"Sheriff," Jones said with a nod.

Kate motioned to a chair, and then pointed to her stove. "Cup of coffee, Jared?"

He shook his head. "I've eaten, thanks."

She lifted the coffee pot and glanced at it. "You know, Jared, you can still get a temple recommend if you drink Sanka. Bishop Heaton told me that."

Jared grinned. He wondered if the coffee pot held the decaffeinated or regular coffee. "Sure, Kate."

"Now Mahonri here," she gestured at her guest, "he won't drink anything unless it's black and strong enough to float a horseshoe. Ain't that right, Mahonri?" She gestured at him for confirmation.

He pushed his hat back and a grin crossed his face, showing a missing tooth in front. "More or less. Gotta get my heart started in the mornin' with it, or I'm no damn good at all."

Jared sat down, fingering his hat. "I heard you had some problems up on Fifty Mile Mountain," he said to Jones.

"Trouble? Guess you could say that," he mused with a shake of his head. "Just cost me eight thousand dollars to hire a chopper to go up and slaughter twenty-seven of my own head, that's all."

Jared drew a deep breath. "That's a heck of a note. This whole thing about the cattle on the monument is a big mess."

Kate slammed her fist against the table with a resounding thump. "The dang government is being totally unreasonable,

Jared. They got no business runnin' us off like that and givin' us no chance to get our cows out."

Jared looked glum. "It's the drought, I guess. But I agree; they are being unreasonable." He wondered if Kate just wanted to complain in person to him or if she had some specific request.

"So what are we going to do about it?" she demanded, staring him in the eye.

He pursed his lips and blew in frustration. "I wish I knew, Kate. Don't know there's much that we can do."

Mahonri Jones looked up with a furrowed brow. "We can go bankrupt, I sure as hell know that!"

Kate slumped in her seat. "Oh, I guess we'll survive. But it sure makes it hard." She turned with pleading eyes to the sheriff. "Jared, can't you talk to them again? Make them let up a little."

"I'll try, Kate," he said. "But they're bureaucrats. Makes it hard to communicate." He sighed again. "Then I got this murder investigation. That's eating us up down at the office. It's been a real hullabaloo."

"I know," Kate said, staring into her cup. "Seems the whole world's changin'. Things used to be a lot simpler."

Jones grunted assent. "Back when I was young, no television, no computers, no cell phones, no airliners leavin' a trail o' smoke up in the sky. Seems like ever'thing was easier. We worked, went to dances, courted, had kids, ran the ranch without ever'body tellin' us what we could and couldn't do. Sometimes I wish we could go back."

"I guess it's too late for that," Kate said mournfully.

Jared looked at them. The two seated before him were about the same age, both from families that had been in the area for at least three generations. He sympathized with their longing for the world they had lost, but he appreciated the progress that had enriched lives around the world, so he said nothing.

"Well, Kate, Mahonri, what can I do for you now?"

She gave a shake of her head. "Just that—see if you can't reason with them, will you? They're even talkin' about us goin' to jail."

He could see that she was fighting back her emotions.

"I'll do that. A Mr. Taylor from the U.S. Attorney's office came to see me. Told me that I might get charged with obstructing justice for what happened in Panguitch. But I'll call him, try to get him to use some sense in all of this."

"Sure appreciate it," Jones said.

Jared rose. "I have to get back. I'm expecting a call."

The old woman rose, shook off her melancholy, and with a smile, put her arm around him. "When you getting' married again, Jared?" she asked. "Good man like you shouldn't go to waste."

"Why, Kate," he said, giving her a sly wink, "I'm gonna come courting you—just as soon as this murder investigation is over."

She was still laughing as she followed him out onto the porch and waved goodbye.

*　　*　　*

Back in the office, Jared found a fax from Paul Crichlow in San Francisco. With a nod of appreciation, he read:

Hey, this is fun. Seems that W. Ronald Murdock was a reluctant banker. Didn't like the business. Instead gave his time to causes like Save the Whales and the Redwoods. Wasn't cutthroat like his old man, J. Murray Murdock, who started the bank. Was kind of a playboy, yacht races, etc. But when Murray was killed in a car wreck four years ago, W. Ronald became one of the principals through inheritance. Took a hand in the bank business. Probably worth about eight million bucks—maybe more. Married and divorced, no children. Far as I can see, had insurance of about a million, most goes to his mother. She's in her sixties and lives in the Bay Area. One policy, about a hundred thousand, goes to a sister who lives in L.A. His will—and this took some doing—leaves most to his mother and sister. But the rest of it goes to charitable organizations, including a hundred grand for AIDS research.

As far as I can tell, he wasn't infected. Like you guessed, he was probably gay. So there, old buddy, if you're looking for a motive, I don't see one there—yet. But I'll keep looking. Anything developing on your end? Keep me informed. Talked the editor into putting me on the story. Didn't make the guy happy who was covering it. He wanted to come out there. If anything develops, maybe I can talk them into sending me back to Zion. —Paul

Jared studied the message, reading it again to see if there was anything that might offer some insight into what had happened to Murdock. In this town that was in an uproar over the case, a town that hadn't had a murder in a half century, he wasn't making much progress. He knew that there was a sense of unease, and of wariness in a community when a murder went unsolved. It was natural for people to wonder if a killer still lurked in their community. A pervading sense of distrust could tear a quiet town like this apart.

He looked up in surprise to see Cal Oxborrow with his two sons coming through the door. Cal nodded as he strode into Jared's office, pausing at the door and removing his hat. Both his sons, following his lead, doffed their hats and stood, looking abashed.

Jared was puzzled, but rose from his desk to greet them. "Cal, Kelly, Curtis. You boys look like you've been on a bear hunt and the bear won."

Cal had a grim look on his face. "Too bad it isn't something like that, Jared."

A chill went through Jared, and he wondered if the Oxborrow family's world was about to fall apart. "What's up?" he asked, catching his breath in dread.

Cal gestured toward the boys, who hunkered against the wall as if they'd like to sink into the floor. "The boys here have something to say."

Kelly stood fingering his hat as he glanced at his brother. But Curtis elbowed his older brother in supplication, not looking up from the floor.

Kelly cleared his throat, glanced away, but finally looked directly into the sheriff's eyes. "I'm afraid we . . . we did something bad, Sheriff."

Jared leaned forward, both hands on the desk. "What happened, Kelly?"

The boy took two deep breaths, glanced at his father, then his brother, and then said, "Curtis an' me . . . last week we were out shooting, getting our rifles sighted in for the deer hunt." He glanced at his father for encouragement. Cal Oxborrow gave a grim nod. "We were on our bullet bikes—you know, shooting some, chasing some rabbits up on a mesa down in Cottonwood Canyon." He paused. "That's when we seen Mooch Winslow down below on the road. He . . . he'd brought the Hollywood people to the ranch the day before." He looked at Jared again, a pleading for understanding in his eyes. "They were real jerks, acting obnoxious and saying they were going to make this movie that would call Grandad Oxborrow a murderer."

Jared slowly exhaled. He was relieved for them because he had been afraid that they were going to admit to Murdock's slaying. "And . . . ?"

Kelly Oxborrow shrugged. "So we stayed up on top on our bikes, cut across some gullies, and came out where they had stopped to have a picnic or somethin'. Then . . ." He turned to his brother, who shook his head vigorously. "Come on, Curtis, you tell the rest."

Curtis swallowed and stared hard at a picture on the wall of an arch silhouetted against the snow-capped Las Sal Mountains. Finally he gulped and began, "We uh, we . . . we figured maybe if they got scared they'd go away. Forget about making a movie."

Jared made a face. "So you got your deer rifles . . . gave them a scare. Shot the devil out of Mooch's truck. Smart, boys," he said, shaking his head.

Both boys nodded in assent. Their father stood in grim resignation.

"Yes, sir," Kelly finally said.

Jared gave a low whistle and ran his hand through his hair. "Well, at least that clears that up." He then looked straight into Kelly's eyes and asked, deadly serious, "But what about Murdock? Did you carry it on that far?"

Kelly gasped in denial, and his father stepped forward, his hands raised in protest. "No, Jared, they wouldn't do that."

Both boys had stepped back, as if in defense. "No, sir! We wouldn't do anything like that! Sheriff, I'm getting ready for my mission next year. I wouldn't kill anybody."

"Me neither," Curtis quickly put in.

A thought had struck Kelly, and his hand came to his mouth. "At least, I'm going on a mission unless . . . unless . . ." He searched Jared's face. "Am I going to jail?" Like most young Mormon men, he would have to have his life in order to be able to serve two years for his church, often in a foreign land, teaching, performing service, and paying his own expenses.

Cal worked his mouth as he considered this. "Could be you've thrown your chances away—both of you." He studied them accusingly.

Jared hunched his shoulders and leaned back. "Well, shooting up Mooch Wilson's truck certainly wasn't the brightest thing you've ever done. We figured maybe it was the same person who came back to finish the job and murder Murdock."

Both boys once again raised their hands in denial.

"However, this really helps us to know that the two things aren't connected," Jared said, leaning back and beginning to relax. "We couldn't figure out the relation if it was somebody passing through. We've been looking for the connection. It really helps us out if we can eliminate the truck shooting from the equation. Makes it more likely it was a simple chance robbery." He paused a moment to consider the ramifications this had on the case.

"And the boys?" Cal asked through tight lips.

With narrowed eyes, Jared sternly examined the two youths before him. "You've certainly committed a crime. It's pretty serious, fellas."

"Are we gonna go to jail?" Kelly asked once more, breathing rapidly.

Jared looked down at his desk, studied a moment, and then shrugged. "I guess we could charge you with 'reckless endangerment,' 'discharging a firearm carelessly'—maybe even attempted murder. Let me think about it. And you've got to make good with Mooch Winslow for getting his truck fixed."

After a moment of silence, Cal asked, "What about jail? Are you going to arrest them?"

Jared pursed his lips. "Like I say, let me think on that a while, Cal." He rose from his desk. "In the meantime, you better see Mooch Winslow and make it right with him."

Oxborrow looked at each of his sons. "You'll have to earn the money yourselves to pay it."

"I know, " Kelly said. "We'll pay it. I'm going to sell my motorcycle for my mission anyway." A worried look crossed his face again, and he turned to the sheriff. "That is, you think they'll let me go . . . with this?"

Jared shrugged. When he was young, he hadn't gone on a mission, choosing instead to stay in college and marry Sunny—a decision he had regretted at times. He knew that she would have waited the two years for him. "I think you can probably work it out with Bishop Heaton."

"So now what?" Cal asked, stepping forward.

"Now, see Mooch Winslow and make arrangements with him. I'll get in touch about any charges." Jared turned to the boys. "And I know it took courage to come in and volunteer this. I appreciate that, especially how it helps us in finding out what happened to Murdock. Your dad taught you well."

"Apparently not well enough to keep them from going around shooting at people's trucks," Oxborrow said with a dismal shake of his head.

Jared came out from behind the desk. The boys, looking tremendously relieved, even happy, shook his hand enthusiastically.

When they had gone, Jared leaned back in his chair and

stared at the ceiling. This changed things considerably, lending even further weight to the "random robbery" theory. But there was that second bullet to the head. He wondered if there were other rocks that he had yet to look under in this messy affair.

CHAPTER 19

Heavy clouds were gathering in the west as Jared pulled into the parking lot of the red-brick church. He paused to consider the sky, calculating how soon the storm and cold weather would arrive. Then he hurried inside, carrying scriptures and a lesson manual. When he was available, he team-taught the twelve-year-old boys, sharing the duties with a young building contractor who had moved to town from California three years earlier.

Today, the seven boys in the class were more rambunctious than usual, all on fire with wide-eyed excitement at the murder that had shaken their town—and bubbling with rumors and speculation. They were sure that Jared would soon be involved in a shootout, and each one had tales of how his own family was locking doors and had firearms ready to repel any home invader. Jared used the occasion to focus them on the day's lesson regarding the courage necessary to keep the commandments when under duress, using the example of the persecution of the early Church members when the Governor of Missouri had issued an official order to the state militia to exterminate all Mormons within the state after a certain date. Eventually, saner heads rescinded the order, but in any event, the Saints were forced out of the state to a bend of the Mississippi River, where they built Nauvoo, the largest city in Illinois, before once more being forced to move—this time to the refuge of the Rocky Mountains.

After the class, Bishop Morgan Heaton caught Jared's arm in the hallway. "Jared, you got a minute?" he asked, motioning to his office. Heaton was two years younger than Jared—a friend who worked as a game warden for the Division of Wildlife Resources. It was the job that Jared had cherished when he graduated from college, but he had ended up in law enforcement instead after becoming disillusioned with the political entanglements endured by officers at the wildlife division. Nevertheless, there were times when Jared envied his friend.

"Jared, this is quite a mess, isn't it? I mean that murder." Bishop Heaton said as he waved him to a chair. He was a stocky, brown-haired man with intent dark eyes. "You've got a tough job sometimes."

During the sacrament meeting, he had cautioned the members about picking up hitchhikers, but at the same time had reminded them of their long custom of friendliness and had encouraged them not to lose their trust in their fellow human beings.

"Comes with the job, I suppose," Jared replied.

"I'm sure," the bishop said, leaning back. "How's everything else going?"

A grin crossed Jared's face. He thought of all the other enforcement problems right then that seemed a long way from being solved. "Well, if I can keep myself out of jail over this Panguitch cattle affair, and keep Kate Thompson out too," he took a deep breath, "and help Cal Oxborrow get his boy on his mission—but I guess that's your responsibility too."

The bishop looked glum. "I heard. They came in and talked to me this morning."

"Oh, I suppose we can work something out that won't be too devastating on them. They didn't really mean anything by it. But it could have been very serious."

"Sure," the bishop agreed, looking down at his hands, but then straightening to gaze into Jared's eyes. "But that's not why I asked you to come in."

"What else?

"Well. . . ." the bishop paused, reluctant to go on, "It's your father," he continued, raising his hands in apology. "Now I know Levi's a good man; I like him—he's got a good spirit about him. But—and I should put on my other hat for this—there's a rumor from another officer that he may still be poaching elk and deer."

Jared screwed his face in pain as he sucked in his breath. "I know," he admitted. "He thinks if he just shoots enough for his winter meat, it's his right."

Conservation Officer Morgan Heaton rubbed his hand across his chin, pursing his lips. "Lots of old-timers feel that way. Fact is, I don't worry about that as much as the professional poacher or the wanton waste of wildlife. But still . . . it's the law."

Jared gave a mournful shake of his head. "Yeah, I'm well aware of that. So," he said, searching the game warden's face, "how does it stand now?"

The bishop rose, extended his hand, and smiled. "Heck, Brother Buck, go talk to him, will you? He's a friend, he's pretty careful, and he hasn't done that much damage. But in the future . . . ? Well, just tell him to pick up a few steaks at the market, okay?"

*   *   *

After he picked up Sitka, Jared headed for his father's place. When he got out of his truck, he carried a bag that was warm against his hands to the door. When the old man saw him, he stepped out onto the porch and his face lit up. "Well, hell, look who's here!" he said aloud to nobody. "I thought you'd be out catchin' that murderer."

"I'm working on it, Pop," Jared replied. In one corner of the porch an unpainted table, warped with weathering, sat against the railing. He set the sack down on it, and eased himself onto a bench. "I brought some chicken from town. Have you eaten?"

"Not so I couldn't eat again," his father answered. "Here, I'll get a couple glasses."

The old man brought two glasses and Jared filled them from a carton of milk he had brought.

The clouds had drifted over now, cooling the day, and a breeze had sprung up so that it was pleasant to sit on the porch looking out over the hillside.

When they had eaten, Levi Buck leaned back and studied his son. "You gonna get him?"

With raised eyebrows, Jared shrugged. "The guy who murdered Murdock? Don't know. Not much to go on. He hasn't used any of the credit cards in Murdock's wallet."

"Have to be pretty stupid to do that anyways, wouldn't he?"

"You'd be surprised how often it happens. It leaves an immediate trail, but some guys can't resist." Jared finished the last piece of chicken, wiped his fingers on a napkin, and then turned to his father. "Pop, you still got that elk hide around?"

A wry grin creased the old man's face. "Hauled that off to the dump. Told you it was roadkill."

Jared shook his head. "Well, I saw Morgan Heaton in church this morning. He asked me to pass along that they're watching you. Said you need to start buying your steaks at the market."

"Hmmph!" Levi buck snorted. "Seems like they'd have other things to worry about."

"It's his job, Pop. You're lucky he's a friend."

He scratched his ear and sat pondering a long moment. "Guess it beats getting' nailed for a big fine."

"Sure does. I can drop by some meat from time to time. Or come on the elk hunt with me—we'll get meat."

"Maybe."

After a moment's silence, Jared cleared his throat. "There's somethin' else I need your help on."

"What's that?"

"Well, I was over at Ira Crahorn's place the other day. He hinted that old John Lilly the lion hunter had something to do with that Ruess kid that disappeared."

The old man considered this, rubbing his stubble. "Could be."

"I remember years ago you talked about Lilly. I've run across him a few times myself. What do you know about him?"

His father looked away, pausing to rub his hands briefly as if conjuring up past scenes. "Tougher'n whang leather," he said, cocking an eye at his son, "an' twice as mean. Lives with his pack of hounds. Guides lions, of course. Nobody ever kilt more lions than John, 'ceptin' maybe his father, Old Ben. John lives in the canyons most of the time. That is, if he's still alive. I been to his place maybe ten years ago, the last time."

Jared nodded.

"He made a living huntin' lions back when there was a bounty," the father went on. "And he guided dudes who wanted to brag about baggin' a dangerous beast." He made a snorting noise. "Course that was back before the damn Fish and Game decided mountain lions needed to be protected—now we hardly got any deer left on account o' that. Can't hardly find a deer or elk track 'thout findin' a paw print trackin' 'em."

"You said he was ornery?"

"Meanest son-of-a-gun you ever seen when he was drinkin'. That's why he stays away from town."

From his vest pocket, Jared drew a folded map. He spread it out on the table. "Where do you think I could find him now?"

After a questioning glance, Levi turned the map toward himself. "Probably dead. Last time I saw him was near the North Rim."

"I think I better have a try at looking him up. Where do you think the best chance of finding Lilly is?"

His father squinted at the clouds, considering. "Well, his favorite place was the Paria Canyon. South. Hell of a country. Can't hardly get there. No roads, deep canyons all over. Has a little rock house down there, can't hardly see it. Blends in."

"Can you show me about where it would be?" Jared pushed the map closer to his father and handed him a pen.

Levi Buck retrieved his glasses, adjusted them, narrowed his eyes to study the map, and ran his finger over the Paria Canyon area. After a minute's study, Levi traced the riverbed with the pen, identified some landmarks, and explained how two chimney-like buttes lined up at the mouth of a side creek. He noted a group of tamarisk and mesquite that set an almost-hidden canyon mouth apart from numerous others. "Three miles up that dry creek bed on a flat bench," he said.

He looked up and cocked his head. "Take plenty of water, hear? People die down in that country."

Jared looked up at the scurrying clouds. Cooler weather would be ideal to explore the area. "I know. I'll be careful."

He rose, called his dog, who had been frolicking in the bushes, and reached to shake his father's hand. Instead, Levi Buck pulled him close and squeezed his shoulders in a hug. Jared blinked in surprise.

"Thanks, Jared. Thanks for the chicken. That's what your ma and me used to celebrate Sundays with."

"I know, Pop. I remember."

As Jared walked to his truck, his father called out to him from the porch. "You gonna go try to find John Lilly?"

Jared paused and then nodded. "Yeah, soon as I get a couple of days. Got to return a rifle out to the reservation tomorrow. And it depends on if anything breaks on this murder investigation. Right now we're kind of stalled."

"Well, be careful. Old Lilly is a little crazy. No tellin' what he might do."

Jared waved. "I will be."

CHAPTER 20

When Jared came into the office to retrieve Sam Begay's rifle, Angus was wearing a broad grin.

"What's with you this morning?" Jared asked. "You look like you swallowed a canary. A successful weekend, was it?"

"I don't kiss and tell," Angus said with a smile. The deputy rose, poured himself a cup of coffee, and went to the window to gaze out toward the cliffs beyond town. "But Jared, I was just thinking. This Murdock case seems to be getting us nowhere. And nothing we can do about it, unless something happens like the perp using one of Murdock's credit cards. And you're all caught up in this Everett Ruess disappearance." He turned from the window and held the cup aloft. "Now it looks like they're both going to end the same way, not with a bang but a whimper."

Jared smiled grimly. "We're not done yet."

"Maybe. But it looks like the fat lady is about to sing unless something happens."

"You're in a cheerful mood this morning." Jared sat at his desk and shrugged. "Besides, we got one problem solved—the Oxborrow boys are going to pay Mooch for his tires they shot up."

Angus acknowledged this with a shake of his head. "Yeah, but I was just thinking, we're now going to have *two* great mysteries of southern Utah—whatever happened to the Ruess kid, and who killed the banker in the parking lot in Kanab? Just think, Jared, we get to be part of it."

Jared gave him a sour look. "Any more word—from anywhere?" His voice showed the discouragement he felt. More than a week had passed since a national alert had gone out about the credit cards, watch, and ID in the wallet. So far, they had little to go on. And Angus was right. With every passing day, the likelihood of catching the murderer was getting slimmer. Eventually, life would resume its normal pace, and this would go on the books as an unsolved footnote. And it would remain a burr in his saddle that would keep Jared Buck awake nights trying to figure what he might have done differently.

"Not a thing. Looks bad," Angus said. "So, you're going to take the kid's gun back to him today?" He pointed to a long cardboard box sitting on the sheriff's desk. It was the two guns they had sent to Salt Lake for ballistics checks.

Jared answered with a nod.

"Too bad Mooch Wilson's didn't match," Angus said.

"Mooch has got enough problems as it is, I guess. What else is going on?"

Angus shrugged. "The usual. A rollover yesterday up by Gobbler's knob. Nobody hurt bad. There was a break-in at some Salt Laker's cabin up by Afton. But nothing much going on today."

Jared went and hefted the box from UPS. "You want to take Mooch his pistol? I'll get this back to Sam Begay. He'll be relieved. When I took it, he looked like he was sure he was going to be wearing leg irons."

"Want me to come along out on the rez?"

"You better stick around here." He picked up the phone and dialed. "I told Kate Thompson I'd make a pitch to Cameron Taylor to lay off a little. And also maybe keep me out of jail at the same time."

Angus edged closer, cup in hand. He wanted to hear how the sheriff would handle this.

When the phone rang, a recording led Jared through a series

of frustrating options until finally a live feminine voice came on the line. "U.S. Attorney's office," a woman said.

"Morning, ma'am, this is Sheriff Buck from Kane County," he said. "I need to talk to Cameron Taylor, please."

"I'm sorry, but Mr. Taylor's out of the office. Can someone else help you?"

Frustrated, Jared growled, "No, but tell him I called."

With a shrug at Angus, Jared hung up and dialed Attorney General Ken Harman. There was a moment of silence as the secretary considered the sheriff's place in the pecking order.

"He told me to call him," snapped Jared, his exasperation showing.

"Oh. Just a moment, please."

After a long delay with elevator music, a gruff voice said, "Sheriff Buck? I hope you've got good news for me."

Jared swallowed. He wished he'd reached Taylor. "I'm afraid not, sir. The Murdock murder is a tough one. We're hoping the killer uses one of the credit cards that will put us on his trail."

This time the voice was irritated. "What the devil are you calling me for then?"

Jared took a deep breath. "It's the cattleman. Cameron Taylor from the U.S. Attorney's office was down here threatening everybody. If he gets nasty, he could send them to the Point of the Mountain for just taking their own cows."

He could hear Harman ponder for a moment. "Considering this murder, that seems a minor problem right now."

"Not to those facing jail."

Harman made a gutteral noise. "Look, Sheriff, I want you to get your tail busy on the murder of Ronald Murdock. We're taking heat on this."

"We're covering all the bases, sir. Some things take time."

There was a sigh. "Okay. But renew your efforts, will you?" It was a command, not a request.

"Sure thing. But what about the cattlemen?"

"Hells bells, the governor tells me we're getting bad publicity on that one too—nationwide." He paused, weighing his words.

"I'll ask Taylor to ease off a bit. But we can't have people defying authority like that!"

"I understand. Thanks."

When he hung up, Jared examined the box that held the rifle, slid out the plastic bag containing Mooch Winslow's pistol, and laid it on his deputy's desk. "Okay, take this to Mooch, please, and I'll get this back to Sam Begay." At the thought he grimaced. "Dang, I forgot about the soda pop." He told Angus about old Horace Tom's request for Nehi strawberry.

When he phoned the local market, the manager only laughed. "Somebody probably handles Nehi drinks, but we don't. Try St. George or Flagstaff."

It took another half hour before he found a small store in Flagstaff that had some Nehi drinks, but they were able to promise only two full cases of strawberry and two of orange soda. This would add three hours to his trip out to Horace Tom's, but he decided he had better make the effort if he was going to learn anything further from the old man.

* * *

By late afternoon his mud-splattered Cherokee emerged from the canyon near Horace Tom's hogan. It had rained the previous afternoon and in spite of using four-wheel drive, Jared had nearly gotten stuck in several places. At his side, Vince Yazzi leaned back in the seat, enjoying watching his friend struggle with the trace of a road.

"Sure glad I didn't have to bring my truck out here," he said for the tenth time.

Jared grunted. When he had phoned Vince, he had suggested that they deliver the rifle to Sam Begay where he worked at the Standing Rock Trading Post.

"Are you kidding?" Vince had said. "That kid is so afraid of going to jail George hasn't seen him for days. He wants to be with his grandpa, close to the jumping off place so he can disappear into the San Juan country if things look bad."

It was true. North of Navajo Mountain the land was rough and untamed enough that a person could disappear for months there without being seen. Only four years earlier, three survivalists had shot and killed a police officer at a road check just across the border in Colorado. They had sped southward into Utah with a host of police in pursuit. On the edge of the Navajo reservation they disappeared into the canyons. A massive manhunt ensued— FBI, police units from Utah, Colorado, and the Navajo Tribe, and special trackers from around the nation. One of the fugitives took his own life when cornered. As the search dragged on week after week and became the nation's largest ever, speculation was that the remaining two had escaped to Brazil or some other international haven. Two years later, the desiccated body of the second fugitive was discovered in one of the lonely canyons. The search for the third still continued.

When they pulled up in front of Horace Tom's hogan, he was sitting on a weathered wooden chair in the sun, watching them come. He nodded as they got out and greeted him.

"*Yah-tah-hey, ya-sho,*" he said, eyeing the case of soda pop that Jared was carrying.

They chatted for a time in their own language, and then nodded to the anglo. Jared looked around for the youth whose rifle he was returning. There was no sign of him. He set down the box of sodas and reached to shake the old man's hand. "I . . . I brought back Sam's rifle. It's okay. It isn't the gun that killed Mr. Murdock."

"I knew," Horace said with a deep nod of his hat.

"Is Sam around? I'd like to apologize."

With his lips, the old man motioned to the hillside beyond the Hogan. But his eyes remained on the drinks that Jared had brought. Winking at Vince, Jared brought the other cases, set them by the door of the hogan, and then retrieved the rifle. He leaned it against the Hogan.

"Tell Sam he can go hunt rabbits again," he said.

The old man had risen and was inspecting the cases of drinks. He was frowning. "Two strawberry?"

"I could only get two strawberry and two orange," Jared apologized. "Finding Nehi strawberry wasn't easy. I had to get it in Flagstaff."

Horace Tom grunted acceptance, took his seat again, lifted a bottle of strawberry soda, and pried off the cap with a knife he fished from his pocket. After he took a huge swig, he sighed with satisfaction.

Jared wondered how he could enjoy the soda warm like that. But Vince had told him that in the early years the trading posts had no refrigeration and many Indians had become accustomed to drinking it that way.

Vince squatted alongside the old man's chair and began to chew on a piece of dead grass. There was silence as Horace Tom took deep swigs. Jared glanced at Vince, wondering if this was the time to ask about Everett Ruess. But his friend had warned him not to rush the old man. After a time the venerable Navajo squinted at the remaining two fingers of soda remaining, drained it, and sat examining the bottle. Still squatting, Vince Yazzi took a pinyon twig and began to doodle in the dirt at his feet.

Following Vince's lead, Jared squatted. He swallowed and licked his lips, wondering if the old man had changed his mind or had forgotten about Ruess. After another long silence, Jared could wait no longer, and blurted, "Mr. Tom, do you remember the boy we talked about last time? The one from a long time ago, when you were young. He had his burros."

Old Horace Tom turned and studied Jared's face, searching his eyes, and then gave a curt nod.

A raven flew by, its croaking voice gurgling in the afternoon sun. Jared was beginning to sweat, and he tipped his hat to wipe his forehead. Vince did not look up, but chewed his grass and contemplated an ant that was passing near his foot. After another minute dragged by, Horace Tom finally cleared his throat and motioned with his chin. "They say . . ." he paused to stare after the raven that had alighted in the top of a pinyon, "They say that one day over at the Dinnehotso trading post some old Dineh men were standing around, talking. There was Hosteen Chee from

Two Gray Hills, and a Bitterwater man from Lukachukai, and an old man from Marble Canyon," he said in a quiet, confidential tone, his voice scratchy with age.

The Navajo sheriff nodded, listening with great interest.

"They say Hosteen Chee said one of Joe Blackhorse's boys showed up two . . . three weeks ago. They say he brought back from California, he brought a white man, a big fat white man with white hair that stood up all over his head. They say he came to watch the Dineh." A wry smile almost crossed his lips. "Joe's boy took him to a sing over by Dinnehotso."

Still squatting, Jared gave a nod to show his attention, but wondering if the old man was avoiding his question.

Horace Tom paused to squint into the sky. "They say Joe's boy took him into the shade house, and he ate fry bread and stew. Some say he was all the time writing in a little book. They say the big man went into the cedars to the outhouse then. Well, there was a goat that lived by that house, a billy goat with big horns. That goat had never seen a big white man with standing-up hair before. They say that man was gone a long time, mebbe three or four songs, mebbe an hour. So Joe's boy went to find him. See if he was sick or something."

The old man paused to pry open another bottle of strawberry soda, drank, and then resumed in his soft voice. "So Joe Blackhorse's boy saw that goat by the door of the outhouse. They say every time the man tried to open the door, the goat butted it, and he was afraid. So Joe's boy chased away the goat."

Horace Tom turned and gazed at Jared Buck to see if he was listening. Jared met his gaze and gave a slight smile, still puzzled where all this was leading.

"That was near the Dinnehotso trading post," he squinted into the fading sun as he continued. "The old men stood there listening to Hosteen Chee tell of the man. The Bitterwater man said, 'what happened to the white man?' Joe's boy laughed and said the man was afraid of the goat and he ran to hide in the car and wouldn't get out. So Joe's boy took him to Gallup." He paused and nodded somberly. "That was over by the Dinnehotso trading post. They say that when that white man came out to watch the Dineh again, he was called the Goat Man."

With a knowing sigh, Horace Tom sat back in his chair, and Vince Yazzi looked up and grinned at him. Jared didn't know whether to laugh or not, wondering if there was more to come. He shifted position to ease his cramped legs.

Vince Yazzi reached to pluck another piece of dry grass. "Yesterday it rained. We were nearly stuck in the sand coming out here," he said.

Horace Tom nodded in agreement. "It will bring the frost soon. Then we can gather pinyon nuts." In spite of himself, Jared glanced at his watch. It was nearly five o' clock, and a three or four hour drive back to Kanab—that is, if they didn't get stuck in the creek bed. With a deep breath, he began, "Mr. Tom, I hope you like the soda pop. I'm sorry I couldn't afford a sing to help you remember about the boy who made pictures and walked with his burros."

"Okay," Tom said simply. He began to rise with some effort and Vince sprang to assist him to get up from the chair. Then without a word he shuffled toward his hogan and disappeared inside. Jared glanced inquisitively at Vince, but his friend only shrugged and said, "Wait."

They could hear the old man puttering around inside. After another minute he emerged into the afternoon sun, carrying a book. He came and stiffly sat down again, motioning to Jared to come closer. The book was a history of World War II, and Jared wondered if he was in for another long tale. However, the old man reverently reached between some pages and brought out a piece of stiff artist's paper. The drawing on it was pen and ink, of a young Navajo man sitting with his dog.

Rising, Jared studied the drawing over the old man's shoulder. Then he caught his breath as he saw the signature at the bottom: "E. Ruess, 1933."

In awe, Jared Buck knelt by the old man's side. "You knew him, then."

Horace Tom nodded, his finger tracing over the part of the

drawing where the dog sat next to its master, his head on the owner's lap.

"Is that a picture of you, Mr. Tom?" Jared was overwhelmed that here was solid evidence of the mysterious Ruess legend.

"And my dog," he said ruefully. "Buster—my best dog ever."

Jared studied the drawing again. It was very good, stylized but with a realism that caught the spirit of the place and of a young man facing the world. "How did you meet him? How did you get him to draw a picture of you?"

Horace Tom leaned forward. "My wife was cooking supper when he walked into the hogan. Not a word at first, just came in and sat down like we had invited him. We thought mebbe he was a witch, but mebbe okay. My dog didn't bark, not even at the burros. So my wife gave him fry bread and beans. He slept under our cedar tree by the hogan. Next morning he ate coffee and fry bread. He saw me sitting with Buster, my dog. So he drew us. I was afraid mebbe he was going to steal my spirit, but he was drawing the dog good."

Jared looked at Vince Yazzi. "This could be worth a lot of money, you know. A lot of people think this kid was a hero. It would end up in a gallery."

A grin spread on Vince's face. "You want to sell this drawing, Hosteen?"

The old man blinked in surprise, and his face clouded. "*Do-tah! No!*"

"It could be worth quite a bit," Jared said.

A grim smile came over the weathered face. "If I sell this picture of my dog, pretty soon I have no money and no picture of my dog." His eyes grew glassy. "Sometimes I get this picture and sleep by it, and mebbe dream of my dog. I remember how that dog used to chase coyotes. How he slept against me every night. And I remember when I was not old—like this." His skinny finger traced the figure of the young man in the picture.

For a long time there was silence and no one moved.

"When did you see him last?" Jared asked, abashed that

he was intruding into pungent memories.

Still the old man remained staring down into the recollections brought by the picture, and Jared thought he wasn't going to answer. Finally, though, he made a noise in his throat and looked at Jared. "Next day he left with his burros. I don't know what happened then." He paused to once more run his finger around the edges of the drawing. "But some say . . . they say that the lion man may have killed the boy white man who walked with burros."

Jared caught his breath. After all these years. Could it be? And there is no statute of limitations on murder. He knew now that he had to search out John Lilly—if he was still alive—and find out what his dealings were with Everett Ruess.

"But I think," the old man added with a resolute nod, "that the spirit people took him."

CHAPTER 21

A fly buzzed against the window in the sheriff's office, causing the new deputy to reach for the morning paper to take a swat at the insect. He was unsuccessful, and moved to intercept the darting path of the fly. Angus leaned back and watched the pursuit with a grin.

"It's no use, Porter," Angus said dryly. "I think he's smarter than you are—or at least quicker."

With an annoyed glance, the deputy returned to his chair and spread the newspaper out once more. "It's the weather turning cooler. It senses fall is coming."

Angus glanced out the window. "I sure hope it's cooler. Jared told me we're gonna be traipsin' some low country today." He turned back to the deputy. "You sure you and Shurtleff can handle things here for a couple of days?"

Deputy Porter Cannon seemed to swell inside his sharply pressed shirt. "Oh, I think Ray and I can handle anything that might come up."

Ray Shurtleff was a fifty-year-old, overweight deputy who was quietly efficient, but so docile that he had been passed over for promotion. Yet Jared trusted his judgment enough that he often left him in charge when he and Angus were both away.

Just then the door opened and Jared hurried through and motioned to his chief deputy. "You about ready to hit the trail?"

he called. "Long way to go today."

"Just about," Angus replied. He picked up a backpack, hefted it, and then as an afterthought, began to add a few things from a pile in the corner. "So how'd things go out on the rez?"

"Good. I got the rifle back to the kid. He was the happiest guy north of Window Rock. How was Mooch?"

"Plenty tickled to get his pistol back. You know," Angus screwed up his lips, "he's a no-good cuss. I think he's still one of our suspects. Maybe he has two pistols."

Jared considered this and shrugged. "Could be." He sat down as Angus fiddled with his pack. "You know, I've been thinking." Jared said. "The gun that killed Murdock must be somewhere. If it was someone just passing through here, that's one thing. But if it was someone at the motel, or someone waiting to kill Murdock, then where did that gun go?"

Angus eased himself onto his desk. "I guess we could have searched everyone's luggage." He raised his hands at the futility of the thought.

"Not practical," Jared said with a shake of his head, and sat pondering. "Maybe they simply walked up on the hill behind the motel and buried it. Wouldn't be hard, at night, and nobody alarmed yet."

Angus considered this, paused for a final tug at one of the pack's straps, and frowned. "I dunno. If I whacked somebody in a public place like that, I'd think somebody was going to walk out any second to see what happened. I wouldn't want to be seen going up the hill."

"So he'd want to get out of sight right away. Where would he ditch it quickly? The trashcans? We checked those. Laundry? Toss it out along the highway? We checked for five miles."

In fact, they had examined nearly every possible hiding place in the motel. Jared had even sent Angus up on the roof in case the killer had simply tossed the gun there after the murder. "You know," Jared mused, "it might pay to get a metal detector and go up that hillside behind the motel. If the perp was a guest, he could have slipped there after everything quieted down here and in two minutes buried the thing without being seen."

"Why do I feel like that's my assignment when we get back?" Angus asked with a grin.

Jared rose and turned to Cannon. "Not much happening right now. If anything drastic comes up, you might be able to reach us on my cell phone—but down in the canyons, probably not."

Cannon gave a confident nod. "Don't worry, Sheriff. We can handle whatever happens."

Outside, Angus gave a doubtful shake of his head. "You sure you want to do this—headin' off to hell's half acre or somewhere on the off chance you can find an old lion hunter who's probably dead by now."

"If he's dead, it's our job to report it."

Angus sighed as he heaved his water bags and a backpack into the Cherokee. "It's the Everett Ruess thing again, isn't it? Looks to me like one murder investigation at a time would be enough for you."

"That's right," Jared agreed grimly. "But it looks like nothing is going to happen with the Murdock case for a few days anyway. I told you about old Horace Tom and what he said. We have to at least look into John Lilly."

Angus made a face and let out a little groan. "Yeah, but . . . oh, I hate hiking cliffs and slot canyons."

Jared jerked a thumb at the sky, which was graying with clouds. "Be grateful it isn't a couple weeks ago. We'd be half roasted. Got plenty of water?"

"Course. I know what happens to people who go into the canyons without it." He turned to fend off the licking of an enthusiastic Sitka, who was leaning over the back seat. "Do we have to take this beast?"

"Hey, Sitka loves you. Besides, he may have to lead us out if we get lost."

Angus eyed the dog critically. "I guess if it came to that, we could always eat him. At least we wouldn't starve to death."

Jared laughed as they pulled out of town and headed east

toward the primitive area of the Paria River that ran southward into the Grand Canyon.

*   *   *

Two hours later they had come to the end of any passable trace of a road. They had passed through gray sand hills, past Bucksksin Mountain, up onto cedar-covered bluffs where the rock had turned a cinnamon color streaked with striations of blue and yellow. Perched on the edge of a mesa, they could see far below a maze of canyons, upthrust mesas, and rock formations, all in muted reds, oranges, blues, and grays where little vegetation grew, and further to the south, the dim outline of the San Francisco Peaks.

In recent years the trend toward outdoor activities had brought hordes of hikers into the area searching for solitude, scenery, and adventure. They had left boot-worn trails through the popular canyons, and often into inhospitable places where a mistake could mean disaster. Every summer Jared and the sheriff's department had to undertake rescue expeditions to pluck stranded climbers from cliffs, or to carry out hikers who had not realized that a forty minute walk down into a canyon could mean an eight-hour struggle to get back up. With temperatures nearing one hundred twenty degrees at times, dehydration was sometimes a fatal problem.

But there were other nearly impassable areas that were still so cut by slot canyons and vertical walls that they were seldom penetrated. Now, with packs on their backs, Jared and Angus stood on the edge of the Paria Canyon-Vermillion Cliffs Wilderness area and studied what lay ahead. The malamute forayed ahead of them, pausing at the precipice. Angus surveyed the steep, red-rock canyon into which they were descending and shrugged. "You sure this is worth it? We probably can't even find the guy."

"We have to try. And just think," he said, needling Angus, "we might even find that missing guy who shot the cops up in Colorado."

"Fat chance."

"Anyway, we might as well get started."

* * *

Six hours later they had left behind the trails made by legions of hikers. Jared had followed his father's instructions that led them far up one of the side canyons of the Paria. Somewhat nervously, they had traversed a slot canyon for a mile that grew so narrow that their shoulders at times touched on both sides, with the smooth rock reaching skyward high overhead to block out the sky. The colors were undulating bands of reds, yellows, browns, and grays, much like taffy that had been twisted by some giant hand.

On this afternoon Jared was in no mood to appreciate the aesthetics, though, and he breathed a sigh of relief when the canyon widened. On a little rise they paused to drink from their water bags. Jared started to call Sitka to provide him a drink, when he saw that the dog was licking from a trickle that made its way down a tucked-away declivity in the shade of a cliff. It formed a tiny pool at the base, and Jared made a mental note that here was water if they became desperate.

Angus plopped himself down on a rock to rest and shook his head in mock dismay. "Some country you drag me to."

Jared laughed. He was winded himself. "You just don't appreciate it." He eased his pack down and sat alongside Angus, pausing to fish out a small paperback book, the letters of Everett Ruess. He held it up. "Now, here, Angus was somebody who appreciated this land. Listen. Here's what the Ruess kid found out here." He began to read aloud:

I have been fighting my way up tall hills, between canyons of skyscrapers, hurling myself against the battling night winds, the raw, swooping gusts that are like cold steel on my cheeks. I am drunk with a searing intoxication that liquor could never bring—drunk with the fiery elixir of beauty, the destroying draught of power, and the soul-piercing inevitability of music.

*Often I am tortured to think that what I so deeply feel must
always remain, for the most, unshared, uncommunicated. Yet,
at least I have felt, have heard and seen and known, beauty that
is inconceivable, that no words and no creative medium are able
to convey.*

Jared paused, then went on:

*Alone I shoulder the sky and hurl my defiance and shout the
song of the conqueror to the four winds, earth, sea, sun, moon,
and stars. I live!*

Angus let out a little moan. "No wonder the kid got done in
out here. He was a little crazy."

With a smile, Jared rose, replaced the book in his pack, and
studied the trail ahead. "Maybe," he said, leading out again with
long strides.

The way had turned more difficult, with a maze of dead-
end box canyons and precipices slowing their progress. Among
the sagebrush and clumps of grass, occasional colonies of prickly
pear perched alongside the rocks, bringing a wide berth from
Sitka, who had long ago learned that the poisonous spines were
not to be smelled.

The sun was reaching the canyon walls when Jared spotted
the twin spires that his father's map indicated, bringing a heaved
sigh of relief from each of the men. It was easy to find oneself lost
in such a tangle of rock.

Far up the little hidden canyon, the dog scented it before
the two law officers knew that they had found John Lilly's place.
Ranging ahead, Sitka stiffened, barked twice, and trotted forward, sniffing the air.

Jared stopped to catch his breath. "Sitka, what?" Then he saw
the barely discernible outline of a rock house, tucked away at the
base of a cliff. It was small, made of pieces of the same cinnamon
sandstone as the cliff around it. A roof of cedar logs overlaid with
sod blended into the surroundings. Sitka barked twice more, and
this time was answered from the cabin. Jared could see a brown,

long-eared dog peer over the edge of the rise and begin to bark furiously.

"Think this is it?" Angus asked, looking relieved.

Jared nodded. It was as his father had described it. "Yep. I think we've found our lion hunter."

Sitka streaked ahead as the men made their way up a little trail to the house. The two dogs met, briefly circled and smelled each other, and then Sitka came bounding back to the men. The hound stood bristling, head lowered, watching the men and the dog approach.

A few yards from the doorway, they stopped and waited while the hound eyed them suspiciously and gave a few half-hearted barks. "Halloo the house!" Jared called.

There was no answer and he called once more. Finally, a movement showed in the doorway, and a graying, stooped man peered at them beneath a hand held to shield his eyes from the evening sun. His hair was a startling white, tied in a pony-tail, while his beard was gray mixed with streaks of black. The part of his face that showed was gaunt, with splotches of pink against burnt-brown skin. He carried a short lever-action rifle in the crook of his arm.

"Who's there?" he called. His eyes swept the canyon around them, and Jared knew that he must have lost much of his eyesight.

"We're friends, Mister Lilly," Jared called.

John Lilly shifted the rifle he held, and Jared could see that his thumb was on the hammer, prepared to cock and fire. He squinted at them. "I got no friends," he growled.

Jared tucked his thumbs in his belt and smiled. "Well, let's say we're friendly then."

"Who the hell are you?" Lilly demanded, still glaring.

"Jared Buck, Mr. Lilly. County sheriff. And this is Angus Terry, my deputy." He saw the old man loose his grip on the hammer and shift the rifle to a more comfortable position in the crook of his arm.

"What do you want?" He coughed into the back of his hand.

Jared took a dozen steps closer that put them face to face. The dogs were still examining each other. "Just came out to check on you, John. I think you know my father, Levi Buck."

The old man arched an eyebrow at him. "Old Levi? Yeah. Still alive, is he?" Beginning to relax, he looked around behind him and sidled to a log, where he eased himself to a sitting position. He leaned the rifle against the log. "Years ago got drunk a couple of times with Levi. Couldn't hold his liquor."

"I know," Jared said. "He quit drinkin' a few years ago."

Lilly looked amused. "That so? Pity."

Angus leaned back against the rock wall of the house in the shade. Jared examined the rock home and the little bench on which it sat. A cottonwood tree grew from a declivity at the side of the house, apparently where a spring provided enough water to provide a precarious existence in a patch of green. It shaded part of the house. On the tree trunk hung a string of rusting traps and some harness. Clumps of sagebrush grew along the bench.

"You moved since I saw you last," Jared said. "Maybe you don't remember, but I ran across you a few years ago down in the Vermillion Cliffs.'

The old man pulled at his ear, striving for recollection. "Seems like I do recall."

Jared wondered if he really did remember. "There were a couple of others with me. We were looking for a downed plane."

The old man nodded. "So what'n hell you doin' here now?" He said it in a friendly way.

Jared laughed. "Just looking you up to see how you're doing."

A deep scowl crossed his face. "Don't need nobody checkin' up on me. Still kicking . . ." He paused, licked his lips, and his expression softened. "But jest barely sometimes."

Angus was studying the little canyon. Farther ahead several cottonwoods and mesquite grew along the canyon bottom, and patches of green grass stood in contrast against the red earth. "Kind of tough living out here, isn't it, John?"

The old man eyed him critically. "Lonesome, you might say,

and that's the way I like it. Ain't tough at all."

The dogs had made a truce after the customary inspections of each other's backsides, and Sitka was exploring the strange smells emanating from the house and the cottonwood tree nearby. The hound had been hanging back, eyeing the newcomers suspiciously, with an occasional, unenthusiastic "woof" to remind them that they were on his turf. He was black and tan, with a touch of red along his shoulders.

Jared snapped his fingers toward the dog, beckoning it. "You used to have more dogs, didn't you?"

Lilly shrugged. "That's Hambone. Used to have eight, sometimes ten. But they got used up, died—all of 'em but Hambone there. And he's gettin' on—like me. And," he gave a futile shrug, "No use for 'em now, anyways. Lion business is shot all to hell."

"That's what I understand." Jared said sympathetically.

But John Lilly turned and stared at him. "Still plenty of lions, you know. Maybe more'n ever. But the gov'ment protects 'em now. Throw your ass in jail they catch you killin' one."

Jared nodded in agreement. "That's what my pop says."

They sat in silence. After a minute Lilly slowly and stiffly eased himself to his feet. He motioned to his doorway. "If'n you gents don't mind pork an' beans, come in an' sit. Don't get much company out here." Then he added, "Don't want much."

The sun was still an hour high, and Jared calculated where they might sleep. He nodded assent.

Inside, through the gloom, Jared saw that the walls had been lined with clapboard, giving the place a rustic but cozy feel. Two tanned lion skins hung on one wall. A bed was at one end of the room, with a stove and small table at the other. A series of wood shelves lined the end of the building behind the stove. It was stocked with canned goods, flour, and other odds and ends. There were two bare wooden chairs, and Angus sat on one and began to examine an old *Reader's Digest* that was lying there.

While Lilly busied himself gathering dishes, Jared leaned over the bed to examine a photo that was propped in the windowsill in a wooden frame. It showed a middle-aged man on one side and a youth on the other, both holding rifles, with two large tom mountain lions hanging on a pole between them.

"This you?"

Lilly paused and glanced at the photo. "My old man and me. He was the real lion hunter. Nobody better ever lived," he said, holding a spatula. "Famous. Teddy Roosevelt came and hunted with him once."

"That so?" Angus put in, rising and coming to look at the picture. "What happened to him?"

Lilly frowned at him. "Died of TB. In a Phoenix hospital. Then they planted him in a cemetery there—green grass all over. Stacked shoulder to shoulder with ever'body else." He gave a vigorous shake of his head. "Not me. Don't want no cemetery. Don't want nobody crowdin' me." He turned on them. "Why, do you know they're stackin' 'em two and three deep in those cemeteries these days?"

Both men nodded in understanding, and Lilly returned to his shelves.

"Where do you get your supplies, John?" Jared asked.

He was rummaging among the shelves, pulling out various cans. "Mostly the tradin' post. Sometimes get into Page. Navajo friend brings some stuff out to me." A new thought came to him and he stopped and turned to search the men's faces. He gazed out the small window. "Used to have a mule," he reminisced. "Name was Sweetheart. Got that name from the old mining song. You know it?" Without looking at them, he began the simple tune in a scratchy voice:

> My Sweetheart's a mule in the mines
> With her I don't use any lines,
> On the bumper I sit
> While tobacco I spit
> All over my sweetheart's behind.

He turned with a shy grin to see if he had made a fool of himself. Both the officers were laughing. "I liked that song, John," Jared said.

Lilly's eyes were glazed as he slipped back into the past. "Best mule I ever had." He turned to eye them. "Don't ever use a horse to chase cougars. Mules are the thing. Smarter'n most people. Don't get scatterbrained like a horse. Horse's liable to dump you off a cliff as not. Get wild-eyed and turn idiots. Mule knows better," he said with an emphatic nod, and then turned and cocked his head. "But chasin' big cats, lots of places even a mule can't go—or even dogs sometimes."

"I've heard, " Jared said.

"Now Sweetheart," he almost choked, and began coughing again, before he caught his breath. "She was goin' on thirty when she gave out. Took me a full day to bury her." He looked sheepish, and then shrugged an apology. "Didn't want the coyotes or the buzzards to get to her, you know."

He finished with the can and dumped the contents into a frying pan.

From a woodbox at the side of the stove, he picked three pieces of cedar and carefully laid them inside. He inserted some kindling around the larger pieces, and blue smoke curled up when he applied a match.

Lilly stirred the beans with a large spoon, spilled a bit on his finger, and paused to lick it.

They ate on the bare wood table from enameled tin plates. It was pork and beans, with canned peaches for dessert. The old man and Angus drank coffee from the same enameled cups, while Jared settled for water that tasted amazingly cool and refreshing. He guessed that it had come from the spring at the base of the cliff.

After they had eaten, mostly in silence, Jared rose and went to the window.

"John," he said, "there's a movie company been down in this country looking around. They want to make a movie about the young guy who disappeared down here years ago—Everett Ruess." He turned to gauge the old man's reaction to the name. Lilly was busy opening a can, and he paused briefly, and then replied, "That so?"

"You've heard of him?" Jared asked.

"I've heard."

"Did you know him?" Jared asked.

The old man sighed and looked sad. He eased himself back into his chair, and sat staring at the back of his hands. "Ran across him one time," he said. "One fall night he showed up, come along singing, towing two burros, walked up like he was home. Came right in," he reminisced in a soft, lilting voice. "The dogs went crazy about them burros. I had a mule then, sounded like a circus with the dogs barking and the burros and the mule braying like long-lost brothers. Didn't bother him none, though. A likeable kid. He had a spirit about him that, well, we kinda got along. I fed him, stayed up half the night, tellin' lies. He liked bein' alone out here. Clean-cut kid. Didn't even smoke." He looked up at them to see if they understood. "I was young myself then, only a few years older." He smiled at the memory. "Huntin' lions, making a living, heading for Flagstaff or Phoenix for a fling with the ladies when not huntin'. It was before the war."

He fell silent, lost in the memory.

"What happened then?" Jared asked quietly.

John Lilly looked up, smiled, and again studied the back of his hands. "Well, he stayed two nights. Had bacon and beans and flapjacks. Then he packed up and headed up the trail following his burros." He pointed out the window southward along the canyon wall. "Few months later I heard he's disappeared. Course he prob'ly fell. One of these slot canyons, no country for somebody who's careless." He drew a deep breath and turned to Jared. "I guess you know that. How many people you lose here a year?"

Jared swallowed, touched by the old man's memories of a person with whom he had come to identify. "Sometimes too many," he said with a sigh. "Mostly falls or dehydration in summer."

"Damn fools," Lilly said with a snort. He raised his head to eye them shrewdly. "Or flash floods. Sometimes drown a man, and then bury him under fifty feet of sand. Ever'body wonders then what happened to 'poor ol' Harry.'" His voice lapsed into a sing-song as he mocked. "Poor Harry. We seen him yesterday. Hiking off to the wonderful Grand Canyon north rim. Somebody musta done him in.'" He shook his head in dismay. "This is no country for fools." He paused, and then shook his head. "Course, the Ruess kid wasn't no fool. Probably just fell someplace." He looked up. "They found his burros over in Davis Gulch—a ways from here."

"Yes, I know," Jared said. "You never saw him again?"

"That's what I said, wasn't it?" he answered testily.

Jared pursed his lips. "I guess so." He shrugged. "Well, it's been so long now, I guess it's no use worrying about it now."

*   *   *

An hour later it was dark. A kerosene lamp burned on the table, casting a soft glow around the cabin. Angus had settled in at the table close to the lamp where he thumbed through an old magazine he had found. The old man sat in his doorway with the dog at his feet, staring out over the canyon below them. He had grown less talkative, and Jared figured it was time to let him go to bed. He rose, and then stopped when he noticed another photograph behind the larger one of Lilly with his father. It was of a young Lilly in uniform, his arm around a brunette girl who was staring up at him.

"You were in the army?" Jared asked.

In the doorway John Lilly turned, looked at him a long moment, and then nodded. "Drafted in 1942." He rose and came to the bedside, reached and took the picture, looked at it a long moment, and then slid it out of sight behind the large photo.

"She didn't wait," he explained quietly. Then, as if in apology, he added, "It was a long war."

As he moved his hand away, a third picture, brushed by his faltering hand, fluttered onto the blanket of his bed. In spite of himself, Jared stared at the aging black and white photo, creased and torn around the corners. It was of a young man, seated with his arm around a pretty woman and two children around his knees. They were Japanese.

Slowly John Lilly sank down onto the bed, held the picture a moment, turned it face down on the covers, and heaved a deep sigh. He looked up at them. "Shoulda thrown this away years ago," he said in a weak voice. He turned to the wall and sat staring at the boards.

"Someone you knew?" Jared asked, feeling as if he was intruding into a private place, but curious, nevertheless.

A slow shake of the head, and his eyes squeezed shut. He turned toward the wall, and in a hoarse, halting voice said, "My unit got cut off—left behind when the Japs closed in on us in New Guinea in 1943. About three hundred of us in the outfit—trapped there. No way out, except crossin' the Owens Stanley range through thick jungle."

Jared felt his breath slow, and Angus laid down his magazine and turned to listen. A softness filled the air, as if the moment had captured another time, another place.

"Seemed impossible," John Lilly almost whispered, caught away in his recollection. "No way out. Didn't want to surrender. We knew what the Japs did to prisoners. So we set out to walk two hunnert miles over the mountains—all jungle. Impossible, all of us knew it. But it was our only chance. They dropped a skinny little Kiwi soldier to lead us. We started out, him in the lead, little chicken legs on him. And my friend Whitey leaned over and said, 'That little bastard won't get us far. Looks weak as my grandma.'" A grin crossed his face, and he sought their eyes.

"You know who that was?" he continued. "Years later I saw his face on the cover of Life Magazine, and I recognized him. Same little guy. From New Zealand, I guess it was. It was Edmund Hillary. He was the first man up Mount Everest." He laughed at the irony of it, and the two lawmen nodded in agreement.

"That was something," Jared agreed.

But the old man's face clouded. "But Whitey never got to find that out. All those years we were together—basic, Guadalcanal, then New Guinea. He always said he'd never make it back, and we always told him he was wrong. But," he gave a broad shrug, "turned out he was right. A sniper got him while we were lookin' fer something to eat one night. Had to fight almost the whole way. Lots of 'em just gave out. Couldn't get up, and just lay there and died. No water, bugs eatin' us alive, cuttin' our way almost ever step."

He looked as if he would cry, his head slowly moving back and forth. "Only about a fourth of us made it over the mountains to Port Moresby." He paused to turn over the picture that lay on his blanket. Slowly his finger traced around the little family. "One day, Johnson and I were scouting ahead, came on this young Jap soldier, so hot it made your eyebrows crawl. He had on only a cloth wrapped around his middle. He had a rifle, but he threw it down when we surprised him. Had his hands up. When we came close he reached down into his crotch to get somethin'.'"

He stared into Jared's face, as if pleading for understanding. "He coulda pulled out a grenade, anything. So I . . . I shot him. He fell down, didn't make a sound. I walked up and saw it was a picture he was tryin' to pull out. This picture here." No one spoke, and he looked hard at the picture.

"Don't know why I kept it all these years. To remind me, I guess." He turned, gave a wan smile, and shrugged. "Hell of a life sometimes, ain't it?"

No one moved or spoke, and the silence lay over the room like a heavy fog.

A few minutes later the old man finally yawned, fed his dog, and told them to throw their beds wherever they wanted. Jared spread his sleeping bag outside under the cottonwood tree, where Angus joined him after a few minutes. A cool breeze sifted up through the canyon. The long hike there had left them both sore and stiff.

"He's somethin' else, isn't he?" Angus said.

"One of a kind these days, I expect," Jared answered.

They lay there with the wind rustling the yellow leaves of the cottonwood above them.

Angus stirred and leaned up on his elbow. "Well, did you

learn anything important enough to get us down here halfway to hell and gone?"

Jared smiled, but did not move. "Not much. Guess we'll never know what really happened."

"I coulda told you that before," Angus said, resignation in his voice.

They could hear the old lion hunter coughing spasmodically. Jared wondered how much longer old John Lilly could last. He had to be ancient. With a start he realized it would be his job to bring the body out when the old man finally gave out. It was a task he didn't relish. The long walk back out, mostly going up steep, barren hillsides was going to be tough enough as it was.

When they woke just after sunup, the old man and his dog were gone.

CHAPTER 22

Myra was waiting impatiently when they trudged wearily back into the office late that afternoon. At the doorway, Jared paused to brush some of the dust from his boots and clothes before entering, but he could see that his secretary was impatient. She shook her head at the disheveled appearance of the two men after their long hike back from John Lilly's place.

"You two look awful beat up," she said.

"You might say that," Jared said with a sigh, easing himself into his chair.

With a clucking sound, she slid a piece of paper across his desk. "Before you get settled, you better call your friend from San Francisco. He said it was important."

"Paul Crichlow?" He glanced at the note.

"Yes. He says you're old buddies."

"Yeah, at Utah State." Jared felt his pulse quicken. Maybe Crichlow had come up with something. "When did he call?"

"This afternoon. I stayed around so you'd be sure to get the message." She glanced at the clock. It was nearly six. "And that federal attorney—Taylor—he called too. Said he'd get back to you."

Jared nodded, studying the name and number. "Anything else go on while we were gone?"

"Just Cattle Kate tried to get hold of you. And Sheriff Calder.

Then one of those environmentalists that you jailed after the monument demonstration last week called to complain. I put him off."

Jared reached for the phone.

"He gonna be there this time of night?" Angus asked.

"It's a morning paper. This is the middle of the day for them." He dialed the string of numbers, got the receptionist, and was connected.

"Crichlow."

"Paul, Jared Buck. My secretary said you called. Anything new turn up?"

"Of course. I've been digging for you while you're out gallivanting around the mountains. Your secretary said you were off on a wild goose chase. Did you have fun?"

"Just checking something out. I already returned a rifle to a kid out on the reservation a couple days ago. Turned out it didn't match the murder bullet, so he was very relieved. What did you turn up?"

There was a sigh at the other end. "Man, you're lucky I worked for a while on the business desk. Made some contacts there. They're a quiet little fraternity in the banking business."

"And . . . ?" Jared couldn't hide the eagerness in his voice.

"Well, nobody likes to talk bad about any other banks. Makes them all look bad, they say, and they depend on public confidence or people will stop trusting them with their money. So it took some doing to even get some hints."

"What kind of hints?" He tried to keep his annoyance from showing.

"Not sure exactly," Crichlow said, pausing. "But in this business you get instincts. It's like the hair on the back of your neck goes up when you know people are bullshitting you to avoid the real issues. You get the runaround, but you know something's there."

"And what was there, Paul?"

"I can't say for sure, but something is cheesy in Denmark with East Bay Bank. It turns out that it has gone through some interesting changes in the last four years or so. It started when old man Murdock was killed in a car wreck. There were some new partners came in from the East. Some of the local people dropped hints that they didn't really fit in with the scene here."

"What does that mean?" He was puzzled at what Crichlow was getting around to.

"Not sure. There were implications that the new management wasn't particularly happy with the young Murdock and some of his wild ideas about what made for good investments. But nobody would say anything definite."

"I see." Jared chewed on this a moment. "How—" he searched for the word, "unhappy were they?"

"I couldn't say. But a woman at Bank of America—an old friend—says she's heard rumors about bank investigators being interested in what's been going on at East Bay."

"Hmm, that's interesting. You think it's worth checking up on?

"Like I say, we get instincts."

Jared laughed. "And what do your reporter's instincts tell you this time?"

"That you better get your tail on the next plane to the Bay Area and see for yourself."

* * *

As the plane banked over the Oakland airport, Jared watched the bay slide by below, the reeds and the saltgrass fading away from the water to the freeway and homes beyond. He looked eastward and saw the white spires of the Oakland temple looming out of the mists on the mountainside, a beacon to ships at sea, he had been told. Sunny had always wanted to attend that temple, but they had never gotten around to making the trip, and now he regretted their procrastination

A grinning Paul Crichlow stood by his wife's side as Jared emerged from the runway carrying his bag. The reporter had lost some hair since Jared had last seen him, but his wife Susan was as he remembered her—had gained a little weight, but was still the same vivacious redhead who was a favorite friend of Sunny's. That had made his association with Paul the more enjoyable, as they had occasionally double-dated.

"Wow, Jared, you look great," Susan said, giving him a hug. "But I thought you'd be in a uniform, with a big sheriff's badge."

He reached to shake Paul's hand. "I'm traveling incognito," he joked. He reached to touch Paul's receding hairline. "Paul, we're both getting older," he said, reaching down to pat his own stomach, which was starting to show signs of gaining a paunch.

"Heck, man, we're just kids yet. This San Francisco air keeps you young."

As they headed through the terminal, Jared shifted his bag.

Susan gave him a nudge in the ribs. "You're staying with us, you know."

He had expected this. "Hey, I appreciate that, but I've already got a room reserved at the Durant in Berkeley. I'm going to be coming and going at all hours. It's best."

"Oh." She made a face. "The kids will be disappointed."

"Besides, Paul is going to be introducing me to some unsavory types that you wouldn't want hanging around."

Paul glanced at his watch. "I've got a couple of extra hours before I check in. You want to get started right away?"

Jared nodded. "The sooner the better."

After they rented Jared a Ford Thunderbird, Paul made several phone calls and they drove to a bar that sat at the edge of Jack London Square. They took a booth where they could see the boats tied up to the wharf and the pelicans soaring out over the bay. The tourist season was still in full swing and the place was nearly full. The buzz of conversation filled the air around them.

Jared was not sure what he was looking for, or what he hoped to learn, but the intriguing fact was that Murdock's apparently-strained relation with the bank offered possibilities that demanded some exploration. He suspected that some of the townspeople in Kanab would wonder if he had cadged a vacation to the Bay Area at their expense, but there was so little else to go on in this case that he felt impelled to investigate.

For an hour the two friends sat eating pastrami sandwiches and nursing their drinks; Paul sipped beer while Jared downed two large Cokes. Jared had been hungry, and he was considering ordering another sandwich when a hefty woman with a freckled face and thick glasses came in, saw Paul, and strode toward them. She was dressed in a tailored blue-wool suit, and Jared guessed that she was one of Paul's bank contacts. She wended her way through the other customers with the confidence a woman who is used to being in charge.

"Sorry, Paul, I was held up in traffic," she said, sliding into the booth as he made room for her. She extended a hand to Jared. "Jocelyn," she offered. "Jocelyn Jacobs."

"Jared Buck."

Paul Crichlow smiled broadly. "Jocelyn here is one of the toasts of the banking business in the Bay Area. Over at Bank of America, she keeps them on their toes. Not much goes on in this town that she doesn't keep her finger on."

She aimed a mock scowl at him. "Flattery will get you . . . almost anything, Paul." Then her expression changed. "Welcome to San Francisco, Mr. Buck. But one thing, Paul—this is strictly off the record."

He laughed. "I was afraid you were going to say that. Okay, if them's the rules you want."

A waitress approached, but the banker waved her off.

She turned to Jared. "Paul tells me you're investigating the murder of Ron Murdock."

"That's right."

She considered this for a minute, chewing on her inside lip and staring at the table. Finally she sighed, reaching for one of Paul's French fries. "As Paul knows," she began, "the Bay Area is changing. Used to be it was a friendly business place. Families owned most of the businesses, along with the major corporations of course, but most everyone knew everyone in the financial community and we pretty much got along. Then," she shrugged, "we entered the global economy. Asian interests bought up half the businesses. And there were others—" Here she made a face.

Jared leaned forward. "What kind of others?"

She looked up and frowned. "Like all big cities, there is organized crime."

"The Mafia?" He looked at Paul, who shrugged.

She sighed in resignation. "Every city has it. Don't let anybody tell you different."

Paul Crichlow sat listening, playing with two French fries that he balanced on the ash tray in front of them. "Do you remember reading that J. Edgar Hoover insisted there was no Mafia back in the investigations thirty years ago?" he chipped in.

"I heard that," Jocelyn Jacobs said. "Wrong, wasn't he?"

Jared sat speculating, his lips pursed. "And how does this fit in with Ron Murdock?"

She regarded him with narrowed eyes. "Nothing for sure." She paused, and then continued, "I only hear rumors. A tidbit here, a word dropped there. It's like a jigsaw puzzle, but some suspicions get aroused."

Jared nodded. "That's my job—trying to fit the pieces together." He sighed, thinking of this investigation. "Sometimes they never quite make it together. Never get the picture complete and clear."

She studied their faces for a time, and then said, "There was even a hint a time or two—and you never reveal where you heard this, because it's only a rumor—that old Murray Murdock was in the way of people who wanted to take over his bank. That he wouldn't give in to pressure." She paused to watch their reaction to see if they fully understood.

Jared blinked in surprise, but Paul gave a slow nod. "I've heard rumblings about that. Tried to talk my editor into letting me spend time on it, but he said there was no evidence of any wrongdoing." He sat back and ran his tongue around his cheek in speculation.

"But I thought it was a car accident," Jared said. Then he

realized the banker's implication. He let out a low whistle. "Wasn't there an investigation?"

"Sure," said Paul. "His car went off an overpass on the Nimitz freeway, catapulted down and he was dead on impact. Not much to investigate. It was late on a rainy night, not much traffic. No witnesses."

With a deep sigh, Jared mulled what he was hearing. "How did that affect the bank?"

The banker smiled gimly. "That's when certain people from Florida were able to complete their purchase of a controlling interest in East Bay Bank. Since then. . . . Well, the word is that some strange things have gone on. There's a rumor that bank examiners are taking an interest."

CHAPTER 23

That night Jared Buck left the small hotel across from the university in Berkeley and ate at a food court where he remembered the wonton soup and shrimp curry was excellent. Fifteen years earlier he had accompanied the Utah State basketball team as a sports writer covering a game against the University of California at Berkeley. For a small-town sophomore from Kanab, wandering the campus and the adjoining streets was an eye-opening experience. He had been in awe of the vitality of the place—the free-speech demonstrations, the liberal causes espoused on nearly every campus bulletin board, and the excitement of Telegraph Street, with its strolling musicians and meandering, unfettered youth with flowing hair. He had gawked at the garish clothing and homemade jewelry hawked by sidewalk vendors, and then gazed in awe at the hand-lettered signs calling for various rebellions.

When he had described the place to Sunny on his return, she had loved it immediately. That was a few months before they were married, and after her death he regretted deeply that he had never brought her to experience San Francisco for herself.

Now on this warm September evening, as he strolled after dark, listening to the Telegraph Street sounds, he saw changes. There were still nearly as many dogs as people, and Blondie's still had customers lined up for the sliced pizza, but an air of seediness had replaced the vitality of a decade and a half earlier. In some places, bearded, aging hippies burned out on drugs sat on the sidewalk in front of boarded up storefronts, strumming out-of-tune guitars in a fruitless attempt to relive better days. The era of protest had withered, with only remnants marked by an occasional poster advocating some social cause.

America's youth had changed, Jared mused. They had turned away from soul-expanding pilgrimages dedicated to social justice, and instead now aimed for a secure future in the corporate world with an MBA in hand. It was a poor trade, he muttered dourly as he turned back toward his hotel. On Bancroft Street on the southern edge of the university, he stopped at a wooden phone pole to study a poster that said in broad red letters, "OFF A PIG TODAY!" *Not total change,* he admitted. It made him sad rather than angry. Such hostility vented at a system could well become an obsession, with the potential of ending in something as stupid as a terrorist bombing.

He took a deep breath, turned, and scrutinized the stores he was passing. Two doors down was a coffeehouse. He studied the customers inside, and then entered. Almost all of the patrons were students, some with long hair, but mostly not much different than those at Utah State—jeans, sweatshirts, T-shirts with messages. A few were engrossed in reading books at their tables, but most were simply chatting.

A waitress ambled over, wearing a purple apron with yellow sunflowers.

She was slender, with her dark hair pulled back. Her face was thin and intense, as if she worried too much. She wore a nametag that read, "Alyce."

"Hi," she said.

"Hi. I need a Coke without ice, a dark marker, a sheet of paper—any color—and a piece of scotch tape," Jared said.

She blinked. "What?"

He smiled. "A Coke without ice, a sheet of paper, a marking pen, and a piece of scotch tape."

She cocked her head. "The Coke we got. You'll have to go somewhere else for the other stuff."

He lifted an eyebrow and gave a kind smile. "Now Alice, or is it Alees?"

"Alyce." She pronounced it with the long "e". She was beginning to look annoyed.

"Well, Alyce, I know this is a restaurant, or at least a coffeehouse. But I'm buying the Coke, and if you'll check the office back there, I'd also like to buy a marker, a sheet of paper, and a small strip of scotch tape."

Alyce squeezed her lips tight. "I told you, this isn't a bookstore."

He kept his tone amiable. "I know that, Alyce. But I bet if you tried, you might humor a hick cop from Utah."

She licked her lips nervously, eyeing him up and down. "I'll see," she said finally.

In less than a minute, a tall young man with mutton-chop sideburns and a spindly goatee strode from the kitchen. He looked puzzled. "What is it you want?"

Jared was beginning to enjoy this. "I just said I want a Coke without ice. Then, if you'll be so kind as to find me a sheet of paper, a marker, and a small piece of tape, I'd like to buy those too."

The tall man gave an amused laugh as he gestured at the customers. "This isn't an office supply, you know. There's one around the corner, and they open tomorrow morning."

Jared saw that he wasn't making progress. He leaned forward across the table and motioned with his finger for the manager to lean close. "I know that," he said in a whisper that caused the man to draw nearer. He reached for his wallet and flipped it open to show his sheriff's badge.

Frowning, the tall man put his nose close and studied the metal insignia, and then drew back. "Hey, get real. I can buy those anyplace."

With a grim shake of head, Jared said, "Not this real, you can't. This is official business. I'm on a murder case from Utah."

He showed his Utah Lawman's credentials opposite the badge. "Now, I need those items—a sheet of paper, preferably colored, a heavy marker, and some scotch tape. I'll pay." By uplifting his palms, he lent an urgency to his request.

The tall man glanced at the open wallet, swallowed, gave a curt nod, and disappeared into a back room. In another minute he was back, and he plopped the requested items on the table before Jared Buck and walked a half dozen steps away before turning to watch.

To begin, Jared drew a wavy border around the purple sheet of paper he had been given. Then he carefully began to print.

Five minutes later, he stepped to the post and above the sign that read, "OFF A PIG TODAY!" He carefully used the tape to fasten the sign he had just made. With a grunt of satisfaction, he stepped back to survey what he had accomplished. His sign read:

FIND EVERETT RUESS!

THIS YOUNG POET DISAPPEARED

IN THE WILDS OF SOUTHERN UTAH IN 1934.

WHAT HAPPENED TO HIM?

SOLVE THE MYSTERY!

As he walked away, Jared chuckled to himself. At least it will give the little nerds something to think about.

Walking on to his hotel, he took deep breaths of the cool sea air with its refreshingly salty tang. Back home, the evening breezes that crept off the high cliffs with the scent of sage and piñon always made him feel good. But tonight in his hotel room he lay awake, at first plotting what he would do the next day to perhaps bring some resolution to the Murdock affair, and then, half asleep, imagining Sunny and what she would do walking along Telegraph Street with him. As likely as not, he decided, she would organize a rally to attempt to bring justice to some African dictatorship.

Then his imagination slipped into a dream where Sunny walked with him down Berkeley's University Avenue to Spenger's, a nineteenth century fishing warehouse that offered the best seafood that Jared had ever tasted, all in a rustic, seafaring environment. For some reason she seemed drawn to the huge iron anchor there that was taller than Jared, and she kept hugging it while Jared urged her to come inside to eat. Next thing he knew, he was following her inside one of the huge rooms where patrons were busy eating, and she leaped onto one of the tables to demand attention to a sign that she held up. "Ban abortion!" it read. While those around them turned to stare and heckle her loudly, Jared tried to whisper to her that they were in Berkeley, where that sentiment was sure to be unpopular. A swift jump in the dream had them fleeing across the green hills above the university, darting through shadowy trees and clinging shrubs as angry students and townspeople pursued them. The forest was dark and forbidding, but Sunny wore a bright yellow dress that seemed to light up everything around it as she ran. Just when the mob was closing in on them, he woke up sweating, missing Sunny. In an effort to have her show up once more, he closed his eyes and tried to imagine her again, but this time he slept soundly without dreaming.

CHAPTER 24

Fighting the traffic on the freeway toward Oakland the next morning made Jared appreciate the uncrowded highways around Kanab. He was ten minutes late to meeting Paul Crichlow, and his friend was waiting in the parking lot of a bank when Jared drove up.

The bank was of red brick, with a colonial look, which, Paul explained, was probably due to the fact that J. Murray Murdock had come from Boston, bringing enough of the family fortune with him to establish himself in the financial community of the Bay Area. In talks with Jocelyn Jacobs and others, Jared had also learned that the elder Murdock seemed above reproach in his business dealings, and the bank had never had even the whisper of any irregularities. In the newspaper accounts of the man's death that Paul had provided Jared, he had learned that J. Murray Murdock was the subject of accolades from numerous business and political leaders of the area. The stories lamented the road conditions the night of his death, but there was also the slightest intimation that alcohol might have been involved in the accident. Even more important was the mention of the discovery of a smudge of gray paint on the left front fender of the car Murdock was driving. It was not known, the newspaper accounts said, if this had occurred earlier or if Murdock had been involved in an accident with a hit-and-run driver that had been a factor in his car going over the railing.

"So what's the plan?" Paul asked after teasing Jared about being late.

"One of the bank officers is expecting us. I just told him we need more information to be able to carry out this investigation in an orderly fashion."

The bank lobby was a combination of marble floors and dark walnut walls, obviously to give the place a sense of stability. When they approached a receptionist seated at a long, glass-topped desk, she quickly dialed a number and motioned toward the second door.

"Go right in," she said. "Mr. Tregaskis is expecting you."

They were greeted by a younger man with dark hair worn down to his collar—very Ivy Leagueish.

"So you're investigating the murder of Ron Murdock?" he said as they introduced themselves and shook hands. He gave a doleful shake of his head. "Terrible thing. These days. . . ." He spread his hands in a helpless gesture. "What can I help you with?"

Jared took a chair and leaned forward. "I'm not sure. We're just trying to find out as much as we can about Mr. Murdock's situation—anything that might help shed some light on what happened."

Michael Tregaskis frowned. "I don't know what I can tell you." He searched Jared's eyes. "We've understood it was a robbery, maybe by a transient."

"That's entirely possible," Jared said with a nod. "We're following that up, but we also have to look at other possibilities. Tell me," he paused, trying to phrase the question correctly, "do you know of any enemies that he may have had? Or anyone who might have reason to want the man dead?"

A look of shock flashed over Tregaskis' face. "Why, no—at least none that I can think of. He was well-liked here at the bank." A slight twitch made him blink. "Now, his personal life—that's something I wouldn't be of much help about."

Jared considered this. "Any rumors of a jealous *boyfriend*?"

he asked. "I understand Ron Murdock may have been gay."

Tregaskis shifted uncomfortably in his chair. "That I couldn't say."

"Did you hear anything?"

The banker shrugged, and glanced around, as if afraid that someone might hear his answer. "Well—some hints, I guess. But I always ignored it." Then his face took on an official look and he scowled. "The bank has a non-discriminatory policy, you know."

"I guessed that," Jared said with a wry grin. "Do you know of any other problems that might have existed?"

Tregaskis gave a curt shake of his head. "Nothing I know of," he said grimly.

Paul leaned forward. "What about the insurance? Who would benefit? We heard there was about half a million."

"Who told you that?" He seemed troubled that they knew.

Paul shrugged. "It's not a secret."

"No. No, I guess not. But nobody benefits personally. It was in the corporation's name. Standard policy for businesses, you know."

Jared pondered this. "So nobody personally got the money?"

"Of course not," he shot back with a frown." Surely you don't think somebody here—"

"We're just checking every possible lead," Jared explained. "Up 'til now we haven't had much to go on."

The banker rose to signal that the interview was over. "Well, if I hear of anything I'll be sure to let you know," he said blandly.

But Jared didn't move. Instead, he leaned back in his chair and drummed on the banker's desk with the fingers of his right hand. "Oh, there's one more thing." He said. "How did people here at the bank feel about Mr. Murdock's involvement in financing the movie about the Everett Ruess kid?"

Tregaskis quickly looked away, and Jared thought he saw a slight flush of his cheeks. "I couldn't tell you that. You might speak to our president, Abraham Schuh. But he's in Washington this week."

"Oh," Paul spoke up. "What's he in Washington for?" For a second he made a move to pull out the slender notebook he carried from his inside coat pocket, but then thought better of it.

"Nothing that concerns the bank or this case," Tregaskis snapped, his unease apparent. Just then his phone rang.

After a moment of listening to the receiver, he hung up. "That will have to be all, gentlemen. An important meeting is waiting."

Outside, Paul leaned against Jared's rented Thunderbird and grinned. "Ah, the things you don't learn from bankers," he said.

"Not much help, was he?" Jared said, slouching alongside his friend. "Except that he reacted to our question about the film."

"You noticed, eh?" Paul said with a laugh. "Looked like you hit a tender spot."

"Maybe so," Jared replied. "But investing ten million or so in a movie shouldn't break a bank like this, would it? Even if the movie went bust." He looked inquisitively at Paul.

The reporter shrugged. "One thing I've learned in this town—especially on the business beat—is that things are seldom what they seem."

"How does that apply to this situation?" He watched as Paul carefully considered his words. At that instant, he heard his name called by a warm, feminine voice.

"Jared! Jared! Sheriff Jared!"

Shocked, he turned to see Chandra Maroney waving frantically from the bank entrance. She was trailing Alex Carlton, who was engrossed in scanning some papers as he left the doorway of the bank. The woman began to pull Carlton toward them.

"I'll be darned," Jared sighed.

"You been busy since you been here," Paul kidded with a nudge to Jared's side.

"No. They were in Kanab. They're with the movie company."

She was beaming as she approached, leading Carlton by the hand. "I swear, Jared, I didn't think they let you out of little Kanab," she teased. "What a pleasant surprise!"

When Jared introduced Paul Crichlow, Carlton perked up at the mention that he was from the *San Francisco Examiner.* "We're doing a blockbuster movie, you know," the producer said, sidling close to the reporter.

"Jared told me."

By this time, Chandra had Jared's arm firmly in her grasp. "I can't believe this good luck. I didn't know if I'd ever see you again."

"I guess I should have known you'd be around the bank. How's it going, Mr. Carlton? Is your financing going to work out for the movie?"

With a deep breath, Carlton drew himself up to his full height, and addressed Crichlow rather than the sheriff. He waved the sheaf of papers he held. "Without doubt," he said. "There's just some routine hoops we've got to jump through. And I kid you not that we're not only going to make a movie—but a movie that will knock their socks off at the Sundance Festival." He looked directly into Paul Crichlow's eyes. "This is going to be big. Really big."

Chandra beamed. "Alex has promised me a part—if we get the bankers to sign."

He shot her a withering glance. "Oh, they'll sign. No worry there." He turned to Jared. "And that means, Sheriff Buck, that you'll be seeing us in a few weeks—months at most, with a full crew, ready to shoot."

"I'm sure the mayor will be happy," Jared replied.

Carlton eased over to the reporter and began to regale him with details of the stars they expected to sign for the Everett Ruess film. From time to time he let his arm sweep high in a gesture to emphasize the magnitude of what they were planning.

As they talked, Jared felt Chandra give a firm squeeze to his forearm. "And I'll be happy too," she said softly. "We'll be there several weeks. You owe me a sightseeing trip."

He laughed nervously. "I'll see if we can't work something out." He could always send Angus to go tripping with her over the red rock country.

"We're at the Fairmont in San Francisco. Where are you staying?" she asked him, her eyes scanning his face.

"Just a little hotel in Berkeley," he replied vaguely. "I stayed there once years ago and I liked the place."

Carlton motioned with a nod that it was time to go, started to pull her away, and then as an afterthought turned back to Jared. "By the way," he said, "I assume you're here about Ron Murdock. Have you made an arrest yet?"

"Not yet," he answered with a shake of his head. "But we're working on it."

When they had gone, Paul Crichlow stepped back and appraised his friend. "So you're wowing the Hollywood crowd now, eh?"

"Nah, that's just movie-people come on. Doesn't mean anything."

"Okay, but that woman obviously likes you. That producer isn't the jealous type, is he?"

Jared considered this, chewing his lip. "Nope. I wondered about that too."

As he turned to go, Paul caught his arm. "Jared, Susan wanted me to find out if you're seeing anyone." He shrugged in apology. "You know, women."

"Nobody special. Tell Susan my dog and my job keep me busy."

Paul slapped his shoulder. "Well, we worry about you, pal."

"Right now, I'm worried about this Murdock murder." Jared thanked his friend, got in the Thunderbird, and extended his hand for a farewell shake. "So what do you think? Anything in the East Bay Bank muddle that might include murder?"

Paul took a deep breath and slowly exhaled. "Not on the surface. Could be more to it, though. I'll keep checking."

"Anything else I can learn here?"

"Maybe talk to a bank examiner."

* * *

By late afternoon, Jared sat across from Stanley Morton in the Federal Building, where the bank examiner glowered at him over horn-rim glasses. He was nearing sixty, paunchy, with striking gray hair that was cut evenly across the back of neck. A long, thin nose gave him a perpetual look of ill humor.

"You understand, don't you, Mr. Buck, that in no way can we divulge sensitive information about any bank?"

"I understand that, yes." Jared had identified himself as a lawman working on a case, but had not said which bank he was concerned about.

Morton leaned back and regarded Jared with a patronizing look. "Of course I sympathize with your curiosity about any of our banks, but—"

"It isn't curiosity," Jared quickly corrected. "It's a murder investigation."

"Yes, yes, of course. But still . . ." He held up his palms in helplessness.

Jared put both hands on the desk and leaned forward. "Let's just say, for instance, hypothetically, that a bank might be having money problems. Would your office know about it?"

Morton quickly sat straight. "Of course. That's what we do, protect the public's money."

"But there are ways of hiding it?"

Morton shifted uneasily. "Well . . . sometimes. Sometimes it slips by for a while. But it always catches up to them."

"Okay. Then what?"

"Then, of course, we take proper steps to make things right—to straighten up the ship, you might say, in order to protect the public's interest." Morton was on more familiar ground now, and he launched into an enthusiastic explanation of how, step-by-step, a bank in financial trouble could be guided back to solvency. Or, in extreme cases, shut down by the federal government.

Jared pondered this for a moment. "And are any banks in this area in that condition?" he asked, searching Morton's face for any signals of alarm.

"Here? Of course not," he answered quickly, not wincing or blinking.

Ignoring Morton's obvious glances at his watch to signal that his time was up, Jared leaned forward. "What about the East Bay Bank in Oakland?"

At that, the examiner looked shocked, sat back, and then stood up. "As I said, we can't discuss specific cases. I hope you enjoy your stay in Oakland." Morton turned his back and began to examine something on his file cabinet.

When Jared went out into the cool afternoon air, he stood for a while, watching the seagulls wheeling overhead on the rising breeze.

CHAPTER 25

It was three that afternoon when Jared Buck stepped into the main reception room of the Oakland Police Station. He felt frustrated by the dead ends he kept running into in this Bay Area expedition, and he was beginning to grow weary of the bustling sounds and shouts around him in the city. He watched as a young black man with dreadlocks wearing handcuffs was loudly protesting to the sergeant at the desk that he was just strolling by when a purse was snatched from a tourist in Oakland's Chinatown.

After they led the young man away, Jared sidled up to the desk, showed his credentials, and said, "Jared Buck from the Kane County Sheriff's Office in Utah. I believe Lieutenant Bascom is expecting me."

With a weary sigh, the sergeant sat back and inspected the newcomer. A heavy-set man with flushed cheeks that shone beneath a balding head, he was evidently annoyed that nothing was going right today.

"Oh yeah, the Utah Matt Dillon, right?" he said sourly. Then, before Jared could respond, he jerked a thumb at a corridor. "Second door on the right."

"Thanks," Jared said with a chagrined smile.

The door was slightly ajar, and on the first tap a gruff voice shouted, "Come on in!"

Lieutenant Gene Bascom leaned back in his chair and

arranged his hands behind his head to study the new arrival. He was only slightly older than Jared Buck, a slender, dark man with bushy eyebrows and sunken cheeks that gave him worried look.

Jared slid into the proffered chair, introduced himself, and explained that he was simply in town checking into some possible loose ends in the Murdock case.

When Jared had finished, Bascom swiveled in his chair to stare out of his window that looked over the parking lot. "Well," he said finally, "we'll help in any way we can. A lot of people here are disturbed by what happened to Murdock out your way. Didn't know the guy myself, but he carried a lot of weight in the community."

"Yes, I've heard."

Bascom turned back to search Jared's face. "Anything solid yet?" he asked. "Sounds to me like it was probably a robbery gone bad."

"Most likely," Jared agreed with a shrug. "But a couple of questions have come up that I want to check out."

"Questions?" A new interest flicked across Bascom's face.

"Yeah. Like why the second bullet to the head? Not like someone who panicked during a robbery."

Bascom nodded. "Makes sense."

"Then there's the matter of Murdock pushing for spending ten million of the bank's money to finance a motion picture. They were in Utah checking it out. Now it sounds like not everyone was enthusiastic about spending the bank's money that way."

Bascom sat up, stroked his chin in thought, and said, "I see. Anything else?"

"Just rumors that maybe everything's not right at the bank."

The lieutenant raised his eyebrows. "Maybe not. I've heard whispers too, but nothing solid to go on. So what can I do for you now?"

Jared considered a few moments and then asked, "Do you know of anybody who'd want Ron Murdock dead?"

"Nope. Course we haven't opened an investigation. Heaven

knows we got plenty of murders here in this town to keep us busy." Bascom leaned back in his chair and again entwined his fingers behind his head. "We had some calls from people wanting us to get involved, but they've pretty much died down now. But we figured it was most likely a transient—a crime of opportunity that got out of hand."

Jared nodded. "Most likely that's the case." He paused for a moment and added, "By the way, was there anything strange about how the senior Murdock got killed a few years ago?"

Bascom blinked in surprise. "Funny you should mention that," he said. "I looked into it a little myself. Something didn't seem quite right, but there was nothing I could pinpoint. These freeways take a lot of lives. People drive too fast, especially in the rain. Easy to lose control like that."

Jared leaned forward. "Do you know a guy named Maury Peralto, who works for the bank?"

Bascom shook his head. "Don't think so."

"Doesn't seem to have a record. He was there with Murdock—in Kanab when he was shot. But . . . ," he shrugged helplessly, "not much to go on in any direction."

Bascom rose. "Is there anything I can check on for you?"

Jared laughed. "Yeah, you can see what your police have on these names—if anything." He slid him a paper with the names of those who had arrived to make the film.

The lieutenant studied the names a moment, laid the paper on his desk, and cocked his head. "By the way, you're from Utah," Bascom said. "You LDS?" He used the common initials for the Church of Jesus Christ of Latter-day Saints.

"Sure thing, card carrying."

A wide grin spread across Bascom's face. "Me too. My wife's folks are from Richfield." He stood up and they shook hands. "We'll give you all the help we can in this."

Jared felt himself relax. It would be good to have a bond with the Oakland police. He might need help as this part of his investigation progressed.

It was raining when Jared left the police station. When he

pulled into the line of cars creeping on the freeway, he wondered if this whole trip had been a waste of time.

* * *

As he unlocked his hotel room, the phone was ringing. It was Paul Crichlow.

"Hey, Sherlock, I may have turned up something," the reporter's voice said with the sounds of the newsroom in the background.

"Good, Paul. What's up?"

"Well, Jocelyn called me back. Off the record, she told me she had checked and it seems a couple of years ago there was a move to get an intensive audit going on the East Bay Bank, but somehow it got sidetracked. Seems that somebody pulled some strings. She didn't know or wouldn't say who was behind it, but it seemed interesting, and she seemed pretty pissed off about the whole thing."

"Hmm. Make you wonder, doesn't it?"

"Yep. My editor wants me to follow up on it. I'll keep you posted."

"Paul," Jared said with a chuckle, "if you have any money in the East Bay Bank, I'd think about changing banks."

"Heck, on a reporter's salary, it wouldn't be enough to worry about."

When Paul Crichlow hung up, Jared sat on the bed for a long while, considering the unfolding possibilities. He had just decided to hop in the shower when the phone rang again.

This time it was Angus. "Hey, Jared," he said. "I've been calling you. You been out on the town?"

"Just business. What's happening?"

He could hear Angus take a deep breath. "Well, first, Cattle Kate is bringing a lawsuit against the federal marshals that took her cattle. That only made them mad, so that federal guy has a subpoena for you."

Jared sighed. "I half expected that. I'm just glad it isn't a warrant for my arrest."

"Oh, he'll get around to that. Just give him time. How's San Francisco?"

"The seafood's great, the weather's cold and nasty."

"Naturally."

"What else is going on?"

"The usual. Had to arrest two more protestors at the monument headquarters. Obstructing the tourists again. They like the publicity. And there was a big fight caused by some bikers out at Coral Dunes. Arrested three drunks. Oh, the other thing is that one of the Navajos brought a message for you. Seems that old John Lilly wants to see you."

Jared frowned. He wondered what old John could be up to. Maybe he needed a doctor or some medicine. He determined he'd get there as soon as he could—when all of this settled down. Right now he had a few more people to see.

CHAPTER 26

The locked gate at the community where Madeleine Murdock lived baffled Jared. He got out of his rental car and stood staring down at it. As he pondered the situation, a cold wind whipped at his coat and gray clouds scudded overhead.

He greatly disliked the idea of class differences in a supposedly classless society, and this practical reminder of such elitism galled him. It seemed downright un-American. He had developed strong egalitarian ideas in college, and found in his religion what he considered a firm basis for the idea that people were meant to live more or less equally and not try to set themselves above one another.

Indeed, just twenty miles above Kanab on Highway 89, the little town of Orderville that Brigham Young had established under a system of shared prospects, which he called The United Order, still stood. In the Order, everyone was to share equally. However, human nature being what it is, The United Order did not succeed, and the Mormon prophet determined that the Saints were not yet ready to live this higher law.

Whenever Jared drove through the little town, set amid farms and orchards in the narrow canyon, he always recalled the pants story. When the town was in full operation of The United Order in the 1870s, a mining boom was going on in the area, and those from other towns who worked in the mines sported store-bought clothes and made fun of the homespun duds worn by the people from Orderville. One romantically inclined young man in the settlement petitioned the town board for a new pair of pants, even though those he wore had no holes nor patches. His petition was declined. So, when the lambs were docked that spring, he gathered up the amputated tails, sheared them, and traded the wool for a new pair of pants at a store in Nephi, several days ride to the north. When he showed up at the town dance in his new, store-bought pants, one young lady ran up, embraced him, and gave him a kiss. The president of the Orderville council demanded to know where the lad had gotten the pants and was told the truth. At a hearing the next day, the young man was commended for his ingenuity, but was told that the pants belonged to the community. The pants were then unseamed, and became the pattern for all pants produced by the community. The young man received the first pair.

So it always amused Jared Buck that some of his right-wing, Mormon friends enshrined unbridled capitalism and railed against any form of division of wealth, when their own prophets had preached that to live in this way was the ultimate goal of the Saints. He liked to explain to them how one of his professors, a Democrat, had defined unfettered capitalism: "'It's every man for himself,' said the elephant as he danced among the chickens!"

Behind the gate lay huge homes with manicured lawns, gardens, and stone statues. He could imagine what kinds of people lived in them, hiring armies of gardeners and servants to take care of them. He thought of his own little place where he struggled to keep a few fruit trees and a tiny patch of grass growing in the red earth, and of the Navajos he knew who had to haul water several miles in barrels just to be able to drink and cook. Standing there in the wind, he studied the gate, not with envy, but with a sense of repulsion at the waste when so many people had so little.

With a sigh he pulled the paper from his pocket on which he had scribbled down the phone number and address of Ronald Murdock's mother. He dialed her number on his cell phone. He was prepared not to like this society matron, and he grudgingly approached the task of interviewing her.

A pleasant voice answered.

"Hello, Mrs. Murdock?" Jared asked.

"Yes?"

"Ma'am, I'm Sheriff Jared Buck from Kanab, Utah, where I knew your son."

"Oh," came the subdued reply.

"Sorry to bother you like this. But I'm in town investigating his death. I know this is a hard time for you, but—"

"You're investigating?" she said quickly. "I'd like to talk to you."

"I'm at your gate, Mrs. Murdock."

"Oh? That's fine. Come right on in." She gave him the code for the gate. "Second house on the left—the one with the big trees."

There was no mistaking the house. It was a three-story brick home with several chimneys and an expansive yard with stone benches and two large fountains. A curved walk led to a carved-walnut door.

When she answered his knock, he was surprised. She stood before him in a blue, two-piece wool suit, a comely, slender woman who in no way resembled the dour matron he had expected. Her hair was auburn, and he wondered if it was dyed. Sunny would have been able to tell at a glance, but he was not good at such things. She looked young enough that he guessed she must have had plastic surgery. She smiled and her gray eyes sparkled. He had expected her to be red-eyed and weepy.

"Come on in, sheriff," she said, stepping back. "I'm glad you came. Maybe you can help us make some sense out of this thing."

She directed him through a hallway into what he would have called the "sitting room" in Kanab. A glowing fireplace at one end was flanked by shelves of leather-bound books. She directed him to a soft chair where he was touched by its warmth, while she sat across a small table from him.

"So you're looking into my son's murder?" she asked.

He nodded. "That's right. And I certainly extend my condolences. I met him a couple of times, and I liked him. He came with a group that was going to make a movie there."

"I know. He talked incessantly about the intriguing young man—" she paused to give a little shake of her head, "over that young man who got lost in the desert down there. For several months he was obsessed with it. He wanted to make a film that would be a work of art on the subject."

"Yes. Everett Ruess. I saw how excited he was about the project."

She stared into the fire, lost in a reverie. "It was nice. Ron didn't get excited about a lot of things. I suppose we spoiled him." She paused and sought Jared's eyes, as if in apology.

"He seemed very nice. And the Ruess disappearance has a mystery about it that intrigues a lot of people."

She nodded, and pushed a plate of shortbread cookies across the little table toward him, but he waved them off. She sat up straight then.

"So tell me, Mr. Buck, how can I help you?"

"I'm not sure," he answered in frustration. "Maybe you can't. There's a good chance that your son was killed by someone just passing through who saw a chance to take his money. But his credit cards haven't been used. So, I'm just checking to see if anything on this end had anything to do with his murder."

She cocked her head. "Like what?"

He shrugged. "That's what I don't know. Tell me, can you think of any reason why someone might want your son out of the way?"

She furrowed her brow in thought, and then raised her hands helplessly. "He's made a few enemies along the way, but no more than most people. His lifestyle . . ." she paused and stared down, and for the first time showed a hint of misery, "was not, what you might say, pleasing to some people." She looked up as if searching for support. "But no more than many men. I can't think of anybody who hated him. He became obsessed about the environment too. He wanted to save the world."

"I see." He pondered a moment. "This film, it's too bad he won't be here to see it made. I ran across Alex Carlton at the bank yesterday. He's the producer."

She looked startled. "Oh no. The film won't be made. Charlotte Stohl told me that a few days ago. Her husband is on the board of directors. She said it was definitely dead now."

Jared pursed his lips in speculation. "That's interesting. I wonder if Carlton knows that."

She shrugged, and again Jared noted a lingering look of sadness fall over her. "I suppose it doesn't matter."

"What would it have done to the bank if the film had failed and all the money was lost?"

She gave a little laugh. "Some people said that's what would happen. Oh, it wouldn't have greatly hurt the bank—they have major reserves. I've heard they've had a few problems, but the bank was solid. My husband saw to that."

He digested this, pausing to entwine his fingers. "Speaking of your husband, you've had some bad breaks, losing him also like that."

Her face clouded, and he saw that she fought to maintain control. "Oh yes, that too." For a long moment there was silence before she continued. "I suppose you know of his *accident*."

"Yes," he said. "Seems there might be a few questions about that." He watched her intently.

She met his eyes. "I've had some."

"Anybody you can think of that might have . . . ?"

Her jaw was set. "Nobody in particular. But some strange things happened before—"

"What kind of things?"

"Well," she gave a slight shrug, "phone calls in the night. Nothing definite. And Murray never told me much about business matters. But I could see he was upset."

"Can you think of anything definite that was said?" Jared leaned forward in interest.

She thought a moment. "One night about eleven—just a few days before the accident—Murray was in the hall when the phone rang. He was angry and I heard him say something like, 'I built it'," He swore at whoever it was, and then said, 'and I'm going to keep it. Now leave us alone.'"

Jared gave a low whistle. "What do you think he was talking about?"

"I don't know. Maybe the bank?"

"Did you tell the police this?"

"They didn't seem interested. But I mentioned it. It was the highway patrol who came to inform me, and I met with others in a few days. But they seemed like they wanted to move on. Said it was a tragic result of the rain on the freeway."

"I see. Tell me, who owns the bank now?"

She frowned as the thought came to her. "Murray always held a controlling interest, and the business has prospered. Afterwards, he left a big lot of shares to Ron and his sister, but the controlling interest was bought by a Florida concern. I believe they have other banks in the South."

"Hmm. You know any names?"

She appeared excited. "I could find out." She searched his face. "Do you think somebody may have engineered his death to take over the bank?"

Jared quickly held up his hands in protest. "I wouldn't jump to any conclusions," he said. "It's just interesting, that's all. But I'll look a little further into it."

She breathed a huge sigh, and he wondered if she was going to break down, but instead she gave him a sad smile as he rose to go. She paused by the door before she opened it for him. "Tell me, what's it like to be a sheriff in a small town?" she inquired. "Are you Mormon?"

"Yes, Ma'am," he said with a smile.

"I suppose you have only one wife?"

He laughed aloud. "Not even one, Mrs. Murdock. I'm a widower. You see, polygamists are lawbreakers. They're not Mormons—can't be. Not for more than a hundred years. There are a few nut cases in our neck of the woods I have to deal with at times—incest, welfare fraud, that kind of thing. They have their own little religion—but they're not LDS. Mostly I think it's a . . ." he searched for the right word, "lustful thing."

"Yes, I suppose it is, you men being what you are," she answered with a twinkle in her eye.

She opened the door and he was halfway through when he turned to face her. In spite of his previous notions, he liked the woman. "Ma'am, if you ever get a yearning to tour the national parks, Bryce or Zion, they're in our backyard. Be happy to show you around. It's a beautiful place."

She gave a wan smile. "I'm sure they are. But I don't travel much."

As he walked down her driveway, she stood watching him until he was out of sight.

*　　*　　*

Paul Crichlow was at his desk pounding furiously on his computer when Jared strode into the office of the *San Francisco Examiner*. His friend looked up, pencil between his teeth, and with a nod waved the sheriff to a chair across from him. After half a minute in which Jared watched the activity in the newsroom, Crichlow, with a flourish, hit the key that sent the story to the copy desk and then sat back with a sigh.

"Just think," he said, "if you'd followed your journalistic bent, you could be sitting behind a computer somewhere in a newsroom like this—pounding your brains out on the stupid thing."

Jared looked around him and grinned. At times he in fact did envy Paul Crichlow his work on a major daily, but overall he loved the fact that in southern Utah he was responsible for keeping the law in hundreds of square miles of challenging landscape.

"I was never a good typist," he replied.

"You heading home soon?"

Jared nodded. "On my way now. Paul, I've just been to talk to Madeleine Murdock. You know, the banker Murray Murdock's wife."

Paul leaned back to study him. "So?"

"She says her husband received death threats before his accident." Crichlow considered this as he put his hands behind his head and stared at the ceiling. "I didn't know that. I didn't do the story, but that fact didn't show up."

"She said the highway patrol investigated the accident, but they didn't seem very interested in what she said. She's not sure. She just caught bits of conversation. Her husband wouldn't tell her anything about it, but it sounded to her like whoever it was wanted control of the bank."

"The old squeeze play, eh?" He sat forward and began to scribble on a yellow pad. "That's interesting." He sat back and cocked an eyebrow at his friend. "Could be big news."

Jared nodded. "Or it could provide a motive for two deaths. The senior Murdock and the junior. Maybe junior was rocking the boat."

Crichlow pondered this with pursed lips. "Have you talked to the cops about it?"

He shook his head. "I met with a Lieutenant Gene Bascom from the Oakland police. Seemed okay. But I didn't know then about Mrs. Murdock's suspicions when I talked with him."

"Could be a good story. Let's follow this up."

"I have to go back tonight," Jared said. He rose and put a hand on Crichlow's shoulder. "But keep me in touch with what's happening, will you?"

*   *   *

At the airport, Jared placed a call to the Oakland police. When he was informed that Lieutenant Bascom was not available, he pleaded for five minutes to the dispatcher before finally convincing her that he should have the lieutenant's home phone number as part of an ongoing investigation.

"Lieutenant," Jared said when the officer finally came on the line. "sorry to bother you at home. This is Jared Buck, from the Kane County sheriff's office."

"Sure. I remember." The voice sounded sleepy, but perked up when Jared mentioned his name.

"Listen, I appreciate your help here. I was just out to Mrs. Murdock's place in Berkeley. You know, she's the wife—er, widow—of Murray Murdock, the guy who owned the East Bay Bank, who got killed in what may or may not have been an accident three years ago."

"Yeah? Anything definite?"

"She says her husband received some vague threats a week before it happened. Someone wanted to buy the bank, and he didn't want to sell."

There was silence on the other end, and then he heard Bascom cough. "Interesting. But with the rain we get, these freeways are deadly. There were no signs this could have been intentional."

"But there's plenty of motive there."

"Right." Again there was a long silence, and then he heard Bascom sigh. "Okay, I'll look into it. It could be interesting—somebody knocking off one of the Bay Area's most prestigious citizens."

Jared gave an emphatic nod. "Okay. Please let me know if anything develops. Oh, by the way, could you fax me anything you can find out about a couple of the bank employees—Maury Peralto and Coy Martin? Martin is kind of a bank detective who was sent to make sure I found the killer. Peralto is one of the bank officers of some kind."

"Yeah, I think I saw your request earlier on Peralto. We sent you what we got."

"It showed no record. Would you mind checking a little further? Maybe making a couple of phone calls?"

"You got it. I'll be in touch." The voice was more animated now. Jared wondered if he had awakened him from a nap.

CHAPTER 27

On the short flight from Oakland to Las Vegas, Jared took his window seat and propped a magazine on the tray in front of him so that he would appear occupied. Alongside him, a woman complained about her former husband until he settled back against his headrest and pretended to sleep. Instead, his mind raced over the possibilities of what he had learned in San Francisco. More and more, his gut was telling him that the phantom random killer who had stumbled across an easy robbery mark in the motel parking lot simply did not exist.

Maybe, he told himself, they were thinking wrong about the movie or the bank even being connected with this sordid matter. What if a jealous boyfriend or some other enemy simply followed Murdock, looking for an opportune place and time to do away with him? The fact that the young banker was gay added an intriguing element to that possibility. The motives seemed endless in that direction. Maybe even revenge for someone who felt cheated in a business deal.

Yet, something about the East Bay Bank smelled bad—possibly its involvement in the Everett Ruess movie or some fiscal shenanigans that Murdock was involved in. In his years as a law officer, Jared had developed a sense of when something didn't feel right. During his time in San Francisco he had felt his neck hairs rise a couple of times—when Jocelyn Jacobs revealed that the bank was suspected of having some financial problems and again when Madeleine Murdock told him of overhearing someone putting pressure on her husband before his accident. *Could be coincidence, of course,* he thought, *but what would anyone gain by killing Ron Murdock? And even if someone connected with the bank wanted to knock off Murdock, how would they do it?* Carlton, Peralto, and Chandra Maroney had flown in from San Francisco with the banker, he had learned. Not taking any chances, he supposed, on the banker changing his mind and not showing up. They had landed in Las Vegas, where they had hired a limousine. If it were one of them, how would he get a pistol through the airport checkpoints? Then there was Silvis, who had driven in from Los Angeles—about an eight-hour trip. No problem there of simply packing along a gun, and then hiding it in his car and going back to L.A. with it. Or he might have dumped it anywhere in the desert.

While the woman next to him rambled on about her ex to an older woman seated by her in the aisle seat, Jared let his mind consider other possibilities. Suppose he himself wanted to murder someone who was visiting a town like Kanab. How would he handle getting the pistol there, given the airlines' wariness these days? Yet, he assumed it could be done, perhaps in one's luggage. Or, he might ship it to general delivery and pick it up at the post office. Or mail it to a friend there or nearby. Not likely. He wouldn't want to involve another person, a potential witness. He might simply drive there, as Silvis had done.

He furrowed his brow in frustration as he considered all of the possibilities. The gun—where was the gun? The police always looked for the three ingredients in cases like this—the motive, the opportunity, and the weapon. Finding it would answer many questions. He decided that he would follow up on the metal detector idea when he had time and search the hillside behind the motel.

It was nearly eleven that night when the plane landed. He had planned to make the three-hour drive back to Kanab immediately, but as he walked through the terminal he decided that he needed to talk to the airlines in the morning.

* * *

By eight o' clock the next morning, he was out of the Stardust and striding through the airport doors at the McCarren International Airport east of the city. Twenty years earlier, the airport had sat out in the desert from Las Vegas, but now the famous Strip had sprawled steadily along the interstate until the airport was now almost part of the billion-dollar casino scene.

At the America West desk, a harried attendant looked questioningly at his badge as he explained his mission, and then finally made a phone call and led him back to an office away from the counter activity. Inside, a clerk with a blue blazer bearing the airline insignia looked up at him over a cluttered desk. He was a middle-aged, slender man with thick glasses who nodded knowingly when Jared showed his badge and explained his problem.

"Just a minute," he said, and turned to his computer, checking it against the names Jared had handed him. After a two-minute search, he shrugged. "Nobody by any of these names on those dates," he said. "You can check with American and United. They've got a couple of flights a day to Oakland. And San Francisco."

At American Airlines the answer was the same. At United, however, an attractive honey-blonde about Jared's age regarded him with bright-blue eyes and smiled. "Glad to help, Mr., Uh . . . Buck," she said in a sprightly voice. After a computer search, she turned triumphantly. "Aha! Here they are. Your party of four on September seventh—Mr. Carlton, Mr. Murdock, Mr. Peralto, and a Miss Maroney. They arrived on flight 613, at 11 A.M."

"I see," Jared said. He drummed his fingers for an instant on her desk, reading her name tag. "Uh, Miss Durstan, I'm checking into a murder that happened earlier this month. Suppose I was going to try to smuggle a gun aboard one of your planes. Could it be done?"

She blinked and her eyes went wide. "Heaven forbid!" Then

she shrugged. "As you know, we take every precaution, but you know, there is an occasional slip-up here and there. But our monitors at the entry point are very thorough."

He laughed. "I know. Last night I had to take my badge out of my pocket. But what about in somebody's luggage?"

She was a pleasant and attractive woman, and Jared noticed how trim she looked in her uniform. She reminded him of Sunny.

"Ahh, that's under federal regulation too. Anyone carrying a firearm aboard must declare it, even in their luggage."

"And on this flight?"

Again she turned to her computer. "Nope. Nothing declared on these dates."

He leaned over and put a check by a name below the others he had given her. "How about this man?"

She searched once more and finally pointed to the screen. "Yes, here he is. He arrived on September fourteenth, on our 12:35 P.M. flight." Her face then lit up. "Yes, look! He did declare a firearm. Deposited a pistol with the crew when he got on. Was he a policeman or . . . ?" Her eyes narrowed and her lips pursed in thought. "Wow. Just think!"

Jared shook his head. Coy Martin had arrived long after the murder. "No, he's a private investigator. He's licensed to carry a gun."

"I see," she said. "I thought maybe . . ."

He could think of nothing else to ask, so he thanked her and left.

* * *

Driving into the desert as he left Las Vegas, he welcomed the blast of wind that came in through the open windows of his Cherokee. The storm that had blown over San Francisco a day earlier had made its way into Nevada and Utah, bringing with it cool air and nimbus clouds.

In St. George, he stopped at an outdoor supply store and wrote a check for three hundred dollars for the best metal detector he could find. In the back of his mind, the thought kept recurring that the gun was really the key to finding who killed Murdock. He was determined to search the area around the motel on the off chance that the killer might have quickly buried the pistol in the sand, hoping it would never be found.

For a moment he considered charging the detector to the county, but then decided he could use it himself. He might take up prospecting in the local mountains for who-knew-what.

When he arrived at his place, he half expected Angus to be sitting on his doorstep waiting for him with news that he was being arrested for his part in the Escalante Monument cattle affair. There was no Angus, but an ecstatic Sitka went into a paroxysm of leaps and barks to welcome him. Jared noted with satisfaction that the dog's water dish was half full, thanks to a teenage neighbor boy who fed and romped with the dog when he was away. He was glad the next day was Saturday so he would not have to be up early.

* * *

Shortly before noon, he was puttering with the metal detector when Angus came pounding on his door.

"Holy cow, you sound anxious," Jared said with a grin as he let his friend in.

Angus flopped onto a chair at the kitchen table. "Well, it's about time you got back. What'd you find out in Frisco?"

Jared raised his eyebrows and nodded. "Some interesting things. What's happening here?" He went to the fridge and set two cans of Coca-Cola on the table.

"Nothing much," Angus said with a sour look as he began to drink. "Couple of highway accidents. Some thievery out at the Dunes Park, and VerNell Whiting's been blustering around about getting the Murdock case wrapped up. Anything new?"

Jared considered before answering. "It's starting to look like it wasn't a hitchhiker or a random robbery. There is something rotten going on with Murdock's bank, and it could have been a factor in his death."

"You mean maybe one of our Hollywood friends wasn't so friendly?"

"A good possibility. Murdock may have been set up, maybe lured out into that parking lot at midnight by someone who knew him. I'm not sure why yet."

Angus made a face. "I hope it wasn't that Chandra—she's too pretty for something like that."

"You never know," Jared said with a laugh as his phone rang.

It was VerNell Whiting. His voice was business-like, definitely not friendly.

"Glad I caught you," Whiting said. He took a deep breath. "What on earth is going on with this investigation? We're taking heat like you can't believe."

Jared gave Angus a long-suffering look. "Well, VerNell, I just got back from San Francisco and—"

"I know that! But are you making any progress? We got to do something to show some progress here."

Jared felt his anger rise, but he restrained himself. "There are some leads developing, yes."

"Leads? Well, you told me there was this young Navajo had a fight with Murdock. And you say he has no alibi?"

"That's right. But I don't think he—"

"Well, there's motive and probably opportunity. You better bring him in and grill him a little."

"His gun didn't fire the shot that killed Murdock," Jared said evenly. "We know that much."

"Maybe he had another gun," Whiting said sarcastically. "Did you ever think of that?"

"A possibility, but not likely. And this San Francisco bank thing may lead somewhere." Briefly, he explained the situation with the East Bay Bank. That seemed to quiet the county attorney briefly, but he insisted that Jared take another look at Sam Begay.

* * *

That afternoon Jared and Angus drove to the Cinnamon Cliffs parking lot and got out the metal detector. Angus hefted the mechanism. "I knew a guy once in Santa Monica who spent every weekend on the beach with one of these things," he said. "Found a diamond ring once, but mostly coins and pop can tabs."

Jared studied the hillside adjoining the parking lot. It was red sand with sagebrush, cheatgrass and an occasional mesquite.

"Oh, I guess we won't find any diamond rings," Jared said. "But I'd sure like to find a little twenty-two pistol that got Murdock."

Sitka worked ahead of them through the brush, finally busying himself digging furiously at the hole of a ground squirrel. Five minutes later, a pinging sound stopped Jared as they swept back and forth in the dirt around the perimeter of the parking lot. The sheriff gestured at the deputy, and Angus probed the sand with a short shovel they had brought along. The deputy bent over to examine what he had excavated, then with a wide grin he held up a rusting tuna can.

Slowly they worked their way away from the motel through the brush up the hillside. At ping after ping they unearthed more tin cans, pieces of rusty wire, nails, and an assortment of metal objects of unknown origin. After two hours, when they had worked their way a quarter mile up the hillside, Jared wiped his brow and shook his head.

"Looks like we don't hit pay dirt," he said.

Angus straightened, stretched his back, and said, "At least we can eliminate the idea the guy may have jumped out the back door and quickly buried the gun."

Jared eyed the detector critically. "I spent three hundred bucks for this thing."

"Look at it this way," Angus said with a grin. "You know now it even finds little things like nails. Maybe you'll strike gold one of these days."

"Fat chance."

"Now what?" Angus asked as they made their way down the hill toward the Cherokee.

"Back to the drawing board," Jared answered, discouraged.

*   *   *

That night Jared spread out his notes on his kitchen table to review everything he had learned so far. Perhaps he was missing something, was assuming something that wasn't true. *If the bank issue was a factor in the murder, how would it have been carried out,* he asked himself. Carlton could have done it, but he apparently suffered a huge economic loss with Murdock's death. More likely was Silvis. He had a somber, ugly way about him—but there seemed to be no reason why he would want Murdock dead. Peralto also seemed to have a sinister way lurking beneath his bank connection, but he had been chatting with the desk clerk when it happened. Chandra was only a slim possibility, but on the other hand a twenty-two was a woman's weapon.

Who else? There was Martin, but he flew in after the shooting. And Mooch Wilson was probably someone who could have got desperate enough to attempt a robbery, and just because his pistol didn't match the fatal bullets didn't eliminate him. As Whiting had pointed out, any of them may have had a second weapon.

He sat alone in his kitchen, Sitka at his feet, poring over the notes and pondering until midnight. Then, putting his notes into an orderly pile, he pulled out the book of Everett Ruess's letters and began to read for relaxation.

As he turned the pages, familiar now through dozens of readings, he stopped at two of his favorite passages:

I have loved the red rocks, the twisted trees, the red sand blowing in the wind, the slow sunny clouds crossing the sky, the shafts of moonlight on my bed at night. I have seemed to be one with the world. I have rejoiced to set out, to be going somewhere and have a still sublimity, looking deep into the

coals of my campfire, and seeing far beyond them.
Adventure is for the adventurous. My face is set. I go to make
my destiny. May many another youth be by me inspired to
leave the snug safety of his rut, and follow fortune to other
lands.

With a smile Jared lay the books down. He would have liked to know the young man—so idealistic, and so afire with passion for the same wilderness that Jared loved.

CHAPTER 28

On Monday morning Jared waited until the airline offices would be open in Las Vegas before dialing United. Amid the usual bustle in his office on Mondays, Myra had made him a cup of Postum, and now while he waited, he put his feet up on the desk and leaned back to enjoy it as he waited during the usual recorded messages. When he finally got a live voice, there was a long pause after he asked for Miss Durstan. He considered for a moment that perhaps she hadn't got into the office yet, but then she came on, business-like.

"Miss Durstan. Can I help you?"

"I hope so, Miss Durstan. This is Sheriff Jared Buck from Kanab, Utah. I spoke to you for a few minutes Friday night."

Her voice changed to a lilt. "Of course I remember you, Mr. Buck—the tall, good-looking lawman from Utah."

He laughed, embarrassed. "Well, anyhow—I appreciated your help the other night. I got to thinking, if someone was bent on murder, they might have used a fake ID to get on the plane."

"We check pretty close, Mr. Buck."

"Well, what would they need to get past the desk?"

"Photo ID. We don't allow any exceptions. It's federal law."

He already knew that. He wondered what he had expected to learn by calling her. He was silent for a short time. "For a professional, I guess that wouldn't be much of a problem. I guess it's pretty easy to get fake ID."

He could hear her thinking. "I guess it might be. But we train our agents to watch for forgeries."

They chatted for another minute before hanging up. He sat feeling foolish. Was he just eager to get in touch with her once more? He didn't know.

When he called Oakland to reach his new friend, Lieutenant Gene Bascom, he had no better luck. Bascom was not in the office, but was expected in the afternoon. He left his number.

His call to Los Angeles Police went reasonably well. He was put through to Detective Sergeant Matt Davis, who had cooperated earlier in checking the backgrounds of the three Hollywood figures in Kanab.

"Hi, I know you helped us earlier in investigating the murder up here in Utah of an Oakland banker, Ronald W. Murdock."

"Yeah, I remember. So what's happening with the case."

Jared sighed. "We've got a long way to go, I guess. But there's progress."

"So what can I do you for?"

"You've already checked on some people for us, Hollywood people who could be possibly suspects. Would you go back and see if Alex Carlton, Willie Silvis, or Chandra Maroney have used another name? It would help us, and we would appreciate it."

He heard the detective laugh. "You know, don't you, that half the people in Hollywood have taken another name," came the slow answer. Jared could almost hear him calculating the extra hours it would take him.

"Yeah, I suppose so. And they may have tried to hide the other ID," Jared reminded.

"I had already assumed that," the officer said dryly, "but I'll see what I can find out."

Jared said goodbye, feeling foolish once again, and hung up.

* * *

That afternoon Jared had better luck with his next call to Oakland. Bascom was in the office, and he was in a good mood.

"Good trip back?" he asked.

"Sure, but this thing is eating at me."

"I know how that feels," Bascom commiserated with him, and then changed the subject. "Hey, do you fish Lake Powell?"

Jared could hear the excitement in the officer's voice. "Of course. It's only an hour to Wahweap Bay."

"Fishing's good?"

Jared allowed himself to grin. "You bet. Fantastic in the spring and fall. Stripers that herd the shad into the little bays. You watch the birds, and then drop a shad imitation near the boils and—you're on!"

"Sounds great. So now what's happening with you?"

Jared sighed. "I need another favor. You still have the names I gave you to check for records up your way?"

He heard some shuffling, then Bascom came back on. "Sure, Alex Carlton, Maury Peralto, Willie Silvis, Chandra Maroney."

Jared nodded. "That's them—especially Peralto. He uh . . . he gives me a funny feeling. But one other—Coy Martin? I don't think he was here, but it doesn't hurt to check."

"Oh yeah, the private eye. What's he got to with this?"

"Probably nothing. The bank sent him here after Murdock was killed. I don't think he found out anything I didn't already know."

"Okay, but what do I check on these guys? I've already checked for rap sheets."

"Oh, go beyond the computer search, will you? Sometimes there's some extra stuff that doesn't get on the computer—maybe some details on the arrest sheet—if they have any." Jared fidgeted in his chair, wondering if he was making too much of a vague hunch.

Bascom gave a little grunt. "Makes sense. I'll check—something might not show up on the computer."

"I'll appreciate it, brother."

He heard Bascom laugh. "On one condition: next time we're

in Utah, you have to take me fishing down at Powell."

"Hey, you're on!" Jared hung up, breathed a deep sigh, and settled back. He might be barking up the wrong tree, maybe even in the wrong forest, but he didn't have anything else to go on.

His reverie was interrupted by Myra, who stepped into his office holding a sheaf of papers. "It's the Mark Herrington arrest again. I think that young man likes going to jail."

Jared shook his head. "He likes the publicity it gets his causes."

"He's due in court this morning. You're supposed to appear to testify."

He leaned back again and grinned. "He's already got what he wanted—newspaper coverage. A couple of days in the pokey hasn't hurt him."

Myra raised her eyes skyward.

* * *

By late afternoon Jared was back in his office. Herrington had been chastised by the judge for ignoring the court order to keep his anti-grazing efforts away from the Escalante Monument headquarters, sentenced to time already served, and released with a stern warning.

Myra was on her way out, lunch pail in hand, when she picked up the ringing phone. She motioned to Jared. "It's that Los Angeles policeman."

"Sheriff Buck here," Jared said into the phone.

"Yeah, uh, Sheriff, Lieutenant Davis here, LAPD. Say, I checked further on that guy Silvis like you wanted. He's had some troubles with the law, all right."

Jared sat up straight. "What kind?"

"Oh, mostly spousal abuse. One charge of theft of electronic equipment about ten years ago."

"How much violence?"

"Well, only the spouse abuse. But there was a broken arm. His wife brought charges but dropped them."

Jared sighed. "I wonder why women do that."

"Security, I suppose," Davis said slowly. "Does that help any?"

"I don't know," Jared answered. "It's not like he's been up on attempted murder or anything."

"Okay. But you never know. Did this guy have an alibi?"

"About like everybody else at the motel that night—in his room alone, watching TV or asleep."

"Well, let me know if I can check anything else."

Jared thanked him for his cooperation, and then sat thinking. Silvis drove to Kanab from Los Angeles; therefore he wouldn't have had to worry about getting a weapon through airline checks. Perhaps he should go there—or send Angus—to check him out further.

CHAPTER 29

It was Bascom on the phone from California. Jared motioned to Angus to shut their office door so he could hear better. Bascom sounded out of breath.

"Hey, Buck," the Oakland lieutenant said. "I've been checking for you. Just got back from across the bay. San Francisco, Sacramento, here in Oakland—looking for stuff that's not on the wire. I may have something."

"What'd you find?" Jared felt his own breath coming a little faster in anticipation.

"Not much there, but this guy Peralto just joined the bank four years ago when the bank changed hands. We've been a little suspicious of that whole deal anyway. Anyway, I talked to a detective in Miami who knows him. Peralto's been the subject of a couple of investigations—fraud and an assault case, but he got off clean. So, no, he isn't your typical banker type."

Jared chewed on a pencil as he mulled this over. "You think he's maybe got connections?"

"Could be."

Jared took a deep breath. "But what the heck motive could he have for knocking off Murdock?"

"Good question. We'll have to dig a little deeper."

"Okay," Jared grunted. He pondered this a moment before asking, "What about Martin? Anything on him?"

"Not much either. He does have a couple of assault charges. But these private eye types get a lot of those by the nature of their work. Guys see they're being followed, so they get tough. They defend themselves, and *voila*, somebody brings a charge against them. He has a permit for a Walther PKK .380, kind of standard for those guys. Small, easy to conceal, but packs a punch."

"Yeah," Jared sighed, "and Murdock got it with a twenty-two. Of course, I wouldn't expect the guy that did it to go carrying it around."

"Never turned up at all, eh?"

"Nope. Course it's not hard to ditch a gun, I guess."

"Well, anyway, next spring I hope to get out your way fishing."

"Sounds good to me. By that time we better have this thing wrapped up."

The detective sighed. "Me too. You're not the only one taking heat on this.

"Talk to you later."

"Oh, almost forgot," Bascom said. "One other thing, probably means nothing. But on one of those assault sheets that Martin got, it mentions he had some ID in his pocket for a George Grant. No picture, just ID. He said it was a client he was helping."

Jared knitted his brow. He wrote the name in his little notebook he carried in his shirt pocket. "Probably nothing," he agreed.

* * *

Later that day when he called United again, she was in the office. "Miss Durstan," she announced when he finally got through.

"You won't believe this," he laughed, "but this is that pesky Utah sheriff again, bothering you."

She laughed with him. "Always happy to help out the law. What can I do for you?" She did not sound irritated.

He cleared his throat. "You've already helped lots. But can I ask one more thing?"

"Sure."

"Would you check your computer again and see if a George Grant caught a plane into Vegas about September 10 from Oakland or San Francisco?'

He could hear the working of her computer and her typing. After two minutes, she said, "No, nothing I can see for the week before or after September 10."

He was not surprised. He thanked her again and hung up. For the briefest moment, he wondered if he wouldn't look her up sometime, but he knew that he wouldn't.

Next he dialed the Las Vegas offices of American Airlines. After a ten-minute wait a gruff voice came on that made him picture a burly woman with short hair and a dour look on her face. He wasn't sure if it was a man or a woman, so he carefully avoided the issue. Reluctantly the voice on the other end said that he or she would check the airline's records. Finally, the gruff voice came back on the line and said, "Nobody by that name on these dates." Before he could explain further or thank the person, there was a click on the line and he or she was gone.

"Thanks anyway," he said into the dead phone.

On his next call to America West, he got a better reception. A friendly male voice answered, listened carefully to his request, and said, "Just a minute—I'll check."

Jared could hear the sounds in the background of customers complaining, and he wondered if the man had been side-tracked by one of them. But shortly the voice came on, "Yes, here it is. A Mr. George Grant on September tenth. He arrived on the 3:30 P.M. flight, and returned on—let's see—the next morning at 11:10." The voice was cheerful. "Both flights on time, I might add."

Jared felt his pulse quicken. For a moment his breath came in little gasps as he considered what this might mean. "Thank you, thank you *very* much!" He sat back and blew a deep breath before turning to Angus and giving him a thumbs-up.

*   *   *

All the way across the mountains to St. George Jared was lost in thought; if he intended to murder someone, how he would carry out a killing like this? If it was Martin—and that was starting to look likely—he would have flown in to Las Vegas the day before the murder, probably rented a car, driven the three hours to Kanab and simply hung around, taking pains not to be noticed, waited for an opportunity at the motel, and whacked the banker when he went out to the limo. He could get through airport security by packing his pistol in his luggage, or perhaps having false ID as private investigator George Grant.

But after the job was done, then what? The murder was at midnight. He had to be in Vegas by ten in the morning. He had to sleep somewhere—likely at a motel. Maybe, considering the hour, one of those in St. George or across the Nevada line at the booming little town of Mesquite in Nevada. Or, he may have driven back to Las Vegas to meld into the mass of tourists there. But there was a chance that at two or three in the morning he may have felt confident enough to have taken a room for a few hours of sleep before catching the plane for his return trip. Then, back in Oakland, he would be available when the bank called to ask him to fly to Utah to go help find the killer of a key officer. A solid alibi, Jared admitted, because for all anyone knew, Martin wasn't even in the state when the murder was committed. But now Jared's job was to gather proof.

It was supper time when he pulled up in front of the Hilton in St. George. He was always amazed when he passed through this town that twenty years earlier had been a relatively sleepy hamlet on Interstate 15, a natural stopover between Salt Lake and Los Angeles. Now subdivisions seemed to have sprung up on top of every red rock outcropping. Winters were mild, which is why Brigham Young had his winter home here. But summers, Jared knew, were atrocious. A century earlier one of the Mormon high officials—noted for his humor—had said when called to speak at a conference there, "If I owned St. George and Hell, I would rent out St. George and live in Hell."

At the registration desk, the clerk, a young man with thinning hair and thick glasses, studied the pictures that Jared laid out on the counter. "No. No, I can't say any of these look familiar," he apologized. "I was working that night, but it's been more than a week. We get lots of customers."

Jared had placed the pictures he had received by fax from Bascom and Lieutenant Davis of Los Angeles, taken from the driver's licenses or other applications in a plastic folder. There were pictures of Silvis, Martin, Carlton, Peralto, and Chandra Maroney. He thanked the young man and slid the plastic folder back into his briefcase.

Bluff Street in St. George boasted several hotels—a testimony to the popularity of the route to summer travelers and the scarcity of other towns across the desert. As usual in September, the afternoon was uncomfortably warm despite the winds of an approaching storm. Jared sighed as he contemplated how many more desk clerks he had to interview.

He checked the Hilton off his list and traipsed to the nearby Holiday Inn—with the same results. Three hours later, he was discouraged. With the exception of an older woman with badly dyed platinum hair, none of the clerks could place any of the faces. The platinum clerk squinted at the pictures, pursed her lips, and nodded emphatically. "This one here." She held up the picture to catch a better light. "Why, I'm almost sure she came through here about a week ago." She laughed, seeming delighted that she had made a hit. "Brassy woman, talkin' all the time. Bossin' around the little guy she was with."

"What did the guy look like," Jared had asked.

She had furrowed her brow in concentration, melding it with the other wrinkles. "Oh, little feller—about your age. But bald as anything."

When she had shown him the motel registration, it was a couple from Illinois. Jared nodded and thanked her. He doubted that she had the right woman. Besides, by now he had essentially written off Chandra Maroney as having any involvement in this matter.

It was dark when he made the half-hour drive through the dramatic Virgin River Gorge that had been hacked through solid stone to shorten the route south to the Nevada line. In the night, garish neon lights advertising the casinos in Mesquite lit up the sky for miles before he reached the town.

At each of them, however, he received the same negative response when he showed the pictures. He had decided to bunk down himself in the Casablanca, when he recalled that there were a couple of other small, rundown motels on the outskirts of town. At the first, a floozy woman eyed him critically when he showed her his badge. She gave a furtive glance to the back room where a television was blaring and a baby was crying. Then she explained that the clerk who had been on duty that night had quit and moved to Seattle. When he checked her register, none of the names matched.

At the Sundown Motel, a cinderblock, one-story building of questionable age and reputation, a wizened little man with rheumy eyes and a chronic cough reluctantly studied the pictures. He kept running his hand through what was left of his hair. He stroked his chin, and studied the sheriff. "We don't have much truck with the law here," he said in a gravelly voice. "What've they done?"

"It's a murder investigation," Jared said.

The man continued stroking his chin as he studied the pictures. "I was here all night, all right. Don't remember too well though." He shifted the pictures around at an angle to study them.

"Mighta been this one. He looks kinda familiar." His finger was on the picture of Coy Martin. He squinted. "Seems like I noticed that ugly chin."

"Can I see your register?"

With a grunt the man shoved the register across the counter. Several coffee stains marked some of the pages. Jared thumbed through to find the page for September 11. There were only five names before a pencil line marked the change to the next day.

Sheriff Jared Buck froze and held his breath. There it was: "Grant Smith, Sacramento, Calif." It wasn't the same name, of course, but close enough that it held promise.

The motel clerk peered over Jared's shoulder. "Yeah, that's him," he said, letting his own finger rest on the picture of Coy Martin. "I recall him now. Said his name was Smith. We get lots of those here," he added with a grin.

CHAPTER 30

The sun was breaking over the craggy hills to the east of Mesquite when Jared pulled to a stop two miles from the Interstate on the Beaver Dam road. Alongside him sat the rheumy-eyed little motel clerk, whose name was Chauncey Burns.

It had not been easy to convince Burns to come. He appeared to be wary of recriminations. First Jared had to pressure him into letting him search the vacant room where "Grant Smith" had stayed that early morning two weeks earlier. They found nothing.

"Any place else around here a guy who was in a hurry might hide something like a gun?" Jared had asked when they had finished searching the room.

Burns had scratched at a scab on his balding head as he pondered. "Hell, might be a thousand places. The desert, up in the hills, one of the casino dumpsters—" Then his face had brightened. He pulled at his chin. "But sometimes I see things. I allas keep an open eye," he had said shrewdly.

"And that morning a week ago Wednesday? Did you see something?"

The clerk had raised his eyes and considered. "I might have. Not certain."

"Like what," Jared had asked, trying to keep the edge from

his voice. He was getting frustrated with the man, who as likely as not was jerking him around.

"I might have seen some guy putterin' around over on the Beaver Dam road that mornin'. I was goin' home to Beaver Dam about six thirty, just got off work. I passed the guy's car, a gray Chevy, looked near new. It was pulled off the edge of the road, and I wondered what it was doin' out there that time of mornin'. I noticed it cause it's like my wife's sister's car, and at first I thought maybe it was her. She's a waitress at the Virgin River— makes good money."

Jared had perked up, but he wondered if the little man was pulling his leg, trying to get paid for information that may or may not be worth two green chili peppers. Or maybe he was simply after some attention. Jared was familiar with the type. "Did you see anybody?"

Burns had narrowed his eyes as he remembered. Then he had taken on a shrewd look. "Seems like I did see somebody, looked like it coulda been him," he motioned to the picture of Coy Martin, "comin' down the hill out over there. It mighta been him."

Jared had caught his breath. "Can you take me there?"

Burns had screwed up his mouth and had given a slow shake of his head. "I don't know. Awful lot of snakes out there. I hate snakes."

"I'll take care of the snakes. You just show me where it was."

The man had shifted his feet, thrust his hands in his pockets, and looked away. "I dunno. What's in this for me?"

In the end they had settled on two twenty-dollar bills, and at first light they were on the hillside where a little pullout led off the main road. Jared gathered his metal detector from the back of the truck and looked to Burns for directions. He was not sure that Burns had seen anything—other than a chance to make a few bucks with little effort.

"Where to?"

"The car was parked about there," Burns said. "The guy I

saw was coming back down that hill." He shaded his eyes with his hand and pointed up a sloping hillside. It was a barren, sandy slope with only scattered sagebrush and a few strands of grass here and there. An occasional dark-brown outcropping of rock showed against the gray sand.

Jared studied the hillside and nodded. It was a long shot, but he had to look. There was a good chance, he knew, that Burns was making it all up. As he strode toward the hillside, he turned on the metal detector and began to arc it back and forth

"Them things really work?" Burns asked, trailing along.

"They seem to. I've only used it once."

Burns pointed farther ahead and together they trudged along upwards on the hill, sweeping in little zig-zags to cover the ground as they went.

"Chauncey, where you from?" Jared asked after twenty minutes of fruitless search.

"Lodi, out in California," he answered with a shrug, wiping his brow with the exertion of the climb.

"What the heck brought you out here to Nevada?"

"Too hot out there in that Central Valley," he joked with a feeble laugh. Then he said, "My wife. She's got family here."

Jared laughed along with him. He knew that most summer days in Mesquite ranged above a hundred degrees. Then his detector buzzed, and he stooped to dig with a little trowel he had brought along for the purpose. With a grin he held up a foot-long piece of pipe. "See, it sort of works."

A half hour later they had worked their way to the top of the hill. They had unearthed two scraps of metal, three tin cans, and the remnants of a rusted spur some cowboy had lost decades ago. Atop the rise, Jared studied the rolling desert that stretched away to distant rocky hills and realized with dismay that burying something here was like tossing it overboard in the ocean. He wondered how far a man trying to get rid of a gun would walk from his car before he buried it.

An hour later, the sun had grown hot and they were both sweating. "I thought you said you were afraid of snakes," Jared said as Burns ranged ahead of him.

Chauncey grinned. "Oh, I am. But that was mostly to raise the price a little." He brightened. "Say, did you know there're turtles here in the desert?"

"Yeah, I knew that. Learned it in college."

"Desert tortoises, they call 'em. Used to be thick. They tell me gas stations would give you one with a fill-up. Now they call 'em an endangered species." He grinned widely. "Ain't that somethin'?"

By ten that morning, Chauncey Burns begged to be taken home so he could go to bed, loudly complaining that his asthma would probably kill him after being on the hillside so long with little sleep. Advising him that they might need his testimony, Jared drove him the five miles to a little bungalow in the desert settlement of Beaver Dam. Then he returned to the hill.

Jared chewed his lip as he surveyed the landscape. It was growing hotter, and he had other things to do. But he decided that he'd better continue searching a while longer on the chance that it was Coy Martin who had stayed briefly at the Sundown Motel, and that Chauncey Burns was right about whom he had seen on that hillside two weeks earlier.

After another half hour, on the far side of the hill from where they had been searching, down on the edge of a steep gully where erosion from flash floods had cut deep channels into the earth, he stopped and let out a little groan. His khaki shirt was wet with sweat, and the canteen he always carried was nearly empty. He pushed back the wide-brimmed Western hat he wore and sighed. He determined to work to the bottom of the gully before admitting defeat.

When he started again, his detector beeped near a large sagebrush. He could see signs the earth had been disturbed recently. Of course, it could have been old. In the desert, scars on the land last for years because there is little rain to change them.

On his knees he began to pull the sand away, and then heard a clang when his trowel hit a piece of metal. He sucked in a breath as a flash of blued steel shone through the sand. With a feeling of thrilled awe, he slowly brushed the dirt away little by little to expose the outline of an automatic pistol. A shout of triumph erupted from him, echoing along the hillside. He pulled a pen from his shirt pocket, inserted it through the trigger guard, and as sand dribbled from the barrel as he held aloft the pistol. "Look at that, would you!" he shouted.

On the frame were stamped the words: "Ruger Mark II .22 Caliber." The pistol was like new. Jared held it up into the sun to examine the weapon without touching it. He recalled that in one of the Florida law-enforcement seminars they had mentioned that that model of Ruger was the hit-man's favorite because it was relatively quiet and thoroughly deadly. Kneeling there in the sand, he considered his find. Obviously whoever had buried the gun was in a rush, because it was no more than four inches deep in the sand.

At least now he felt an assurance that it was Coy Martin, the private detective who worked for the East Bay Bank, who had shot Murdock. Things were falling into place at last. Martin had apparently used the name of George Grant to book himself a flight to Vegas, rented a car, shown up in Kanab somewhere, waited in the parking lot, and did away with Murdock when he went to the limo. Then he must have driven as far as Mesquite, got so tired that he got a room at that flea-bag motel as "Grant Smith," and drove on to Las Vegas where he caught a plane back to San Francisco. That way he was available when bank officials asked him to go investigate Murdock's murder. Or, Jared wondered, was it a bank official or officials who sent him on the grim errand?

Proving all this was another matter, of course. The testimony of Chauncy Burns would be critical to put him in the area at the right time. And they could probably find the car rental agency, where they had a good chance of getting further identification. But questions remained. How was Murdock lured into the parking lot? What was Martin's motive?

One thing bothered Jared slightly: why would Martin wait until morning to bury the gun, instead of dumping it that night?

Nevertheless, he stood with a sigh of satisfaction and grinned. "Aha—got you, you son-of-a-gun!" he said in a hoarse whisper. Carefully he slid the pistol into a plastic bag he had brought for that purpose.

CHAPTER 31

The state crime lab in Salt Lake City was located in a low brick building on Capitol Hill behind the other state buildings. In a small, dimly lit room Jared stood looking over the shoulder of pudgy, balding Jerry Sorenson as the technician prepared to fire the twenty-two pistol into the water of the firing tank. After phoning the lab to inform them that he was coming and would arrive after closing hours, he had driven all afternoon to pull into Salt Lake a few minutes after seven.

A few minutes earlier he had presented the Ruger in the plastic envelope to Sorenson. Jared had watched with interest as the technician dusted the pistol barrel and frame for fingerprints. "Clean as a baby's behind," Sorenson pronounced as he set the gun parts on a table. "Not a smidgeon of a print."

"I didn't expect any," Jared said. "This guy's a pro."

As they prepared to fire, both wore ear protectors, for even the small caliber weapon made an explosion that echoed in the enclosed room. Jared watched intently as Sorenson, donning protective goggles, inserted a fresh cartridge into the chamber, looked away, and pulled the trigger. With rubber gloves Sorenson fished out the spent bullet, cradled it in cotton, and walked across the room to slide it under a microscope.

"Uh-huh, uh-huh," he kept repeating as he studied the lead projectile. On a plate at his side, he had the spectroscope printout of the bullet that had killed Ronald Murdock. His gaze swept back and forth from his microscope to his computer screen. Finally he punched a key and waited for the latest printout to emerge.

Jared fidgeted nervously. "Uh-huh what?"

The technician didn't answer, but his eyes squinted intensely as he studied the computer printout of the Murdock murder bullet, and then that from the bullet brought in by the sheriff of Kane County. Finally, Sorenson heaved a huge sigh, sat back in his chair, and held up the bullet he had just tested.

"Well?" Jared demanded impatiently.

Sorenson gave a big nod. "There you are, sir. This fine fire-arm you retrieved out of a sandy grave produced a bullet with exactly the same markings as the one that killed Mr. Murdock." He examined the bullet with a satisfied smile. "In short, you have a match—one that will hold up in court."

"Great!" Jared brought his hands together in a giant clap.

"It's as good as a fingerprint—at least to establish that this weapon did the killing." The technician then arched an eyebrow. "And you have an owner of said firearm in custody, do you?"

Jared shook his head. "Not yet. But we will. Right now my deputy is in Las Vegas gathering evidence that should snap the cuffs on the guy." At noon after finding the Ruger, Jared had phoned Angus. He had explained the situation, and sent him hurrying to Vegas to tour the car rental companies with Coy Martin's picture. It was probably not essential in building a case, but he wanted all the evidence possible to make a sure case, establishing that Martin, traveling as George Grant, had come to Las Vegas, rented a car, traveled toward Utah and several hours after the murder had slept at a motel in Mesquite. Plus, he was seen where the pistol was buried—it was close to irrefutable evidence.

In his elation, Jared felt like giving the technician a grateful hug. Instead, he pumped the man's hand. "Sorenson, you're a good man," he said enthusiastically. "Now all we got to do is go get this guy and bring him back so he can take up residence at the

Point of the Mountain. Thanks again for waiting for me."

Sorenson leaned back against a file cabinet, a smug look on his face. "Glad to do it. Now you get to do *your* job. Good luck."

CHAPTER 32

When the plane touched down, Jared roused himself. As a law officer, he had checked his pistol in with the crew during the flight, and would retrieve it when he got off the plane. The bulk of the holster on his shoulder was a reminder of the seriousness of his mission. With that reminder came the haunting memory of the face of the young Rasmussen kid that he had almost shot that night ten years earlier in Kanab.

He had been driving through town late one summer night after checking out a cattle theft. When he glimpsed a shadow by an opening behind the hardware store, he had stopped, got out, and silently approached the back of the store. The sound of breaking glass brought him around the corner of the building and he shouted, "Hold it right there!" A dark figure broke from the side of the store fifty yards away, barely visible in the moonless night. Jared drew his gun when he saw the man turn. Something flashed in his hand, and then he turned and ran off with the sheriff in hot pursuit. "Stop or I'll shoot," Jared shouted in full sprint.

The man slowed, turned, and again Jared saw the glint of a faint light on steel. He brought up his own pistol, aimed, and hesitated. At the last second he decided not to fire and slowed to a walk. Before he got close, however, the figure wheeled and fled again. Once more Jared pursued the man, gaining ground quickly, his gun held ready. He sprinted near enough to bring the man to the ground with a flying tackle, pinning his arms as the two men fell. Breathing hard, Jared slowly rose, covering the man with his gun, and shined his flashlight into the man's face.

It was sixteen-year-old Dane Rasmussen, a youth he knew from the new subdivision on the edge of town. Jared caught his breath, almost unable to speak because of the irreparable error he had almost made. A few feet away lay a silver Pepsi can the kid had been carrying. Since that night, Jared had rarely carried a pistol. Soon the community learned the reason and they were supportive.

But now having a gun with him felt natural and reassuring as he prepared to arrest a killer. Even though he preferred not to, he knew he could use the gun if necessary. During the flight, he had dozed while pondering what steps he might have forgotten to make this all legal. On returning to Kanab from Mesquite and the Salt Lake crime lab, he had immediately notified VerNell Whiting in the County Attorney's office. He could almost hear Whiting rub his hands together in glee as he gave him the news that it looked positive they had found the murderer of Ronald Murdock. Jared was quite sure the main reason Whiting was so happy was that this would provide a big boost for his political ambitions. Whiting had prepared the proper arrest papers and the affidavits needed to extradite Martin from California.

"What a piece of luck!" Whiting had exclaimed when Jared told him of Martin being sighted near where the gun was hidden. For an instant Jared was tempted to remind Whiting that it wasn't luck that had turned up the pistol after they had established the general area. He was still sunburned from the hours of searching with the metal detector in the Nevada sun.

But he stifled the urge, and simply said, "Yes sir. A piece of luck." In fact, Jared himself had wondered what had kept Martin from ditching the gun that night instead of waiting for daylight. He decided he would ask him once the arrest had been made.

Now as he left the gateway in Oakland, he saw the smiling

face of Gene Bascom waiting for him. Bascom shook Jared's hand. "By golly, that's the best news I've had in months," he said. Jared had phoned him from Kanab and explained that he was coming to make the arrest, with extradition papers in hand.

"The only thing is, you've got the guy who put away one of our prominent citizens of Oakland. I don't know if they'll let you take him out of the state or not," he joked.

"Well, I gotta tell you," Jared answered, "he insulted the fair people of Kanab when he shot Murdock. They're not used to things like that. We're a quiet, civilized society out there."

The lieutenant shook his head. "No society is quiet and civilized anymore. I can testify to that."

"Okay," Jared laughed. "What's our plan for arresting this guy?"

"Bad news," Bascom said, looking glum. "Seems he's disappeared."

"Got wind, did he?"

"I don't know. At the bank they said he had accumulated vacation time. Supposed to be in Mexico."

Through Jared's mind there flitted a momentary vision of himself wandering the beaches of Mexico with Martin's picture in hand, trying out his limited Spanish to locate the fugitive. "That's a bummer," he said.

"He probably just got worried and decided to cut out. He might even come back if we don't make waves."

"Don't think so," Jared said. "He's too smart for that. Let's talk to some people."

*   *   *

When they marched into the East Bay Bank, Bascom flashed his badge and they were shown immediately into the president's office, where Michael Tregaskis regarded them with a puzzled brow. "Why are you looking for Martin? He's our investigator. He's not a suspect in this matter, is he?"

Jared offered a noncommittal smile. "We're just exploring all the avenues, trying to answer some questions he might help us with."

Tregaskis cocked his head and took on a condescending expression. "It seems to me you might better spend your time out where the murder took place. We didn't even send Mr. Martin out to your state until the day following the . . . the event."

"That's so," Jared agreed. He glanced around him at Tregaskis' door. "You don't suppose Mr. Peralto is anywhere near do you? We'd like to check a couple of things with him also."

With a frown, Tregaskis picked up the phone and in a low voice asked his secretary to find Peralto. He then turned to them. "He'll meet you in the lobby," Tregaskis said stiffly.

"Nice guy," Jared said when they left the office and stood watching the activity in the bank. It was mid-afternoon and several people were lined up at the teller windows. In another minute the portly figure of Maury Peralto came smiling toward them.

"Well, the gendarmes are back in action, I see," he said to Jared, extending his hand. "What brings you back to our fair bank by the bay?"

"Just trying to wrap some things up," Jared responded. He introduced Bascom, then said, "I don't suppose you know where Martin might have got to? I just had a couple of questions to ask him."

Peralto shrugged. "Said he was going to Mexico with his girlfriend. I don't know where. Say," he looked puzzled, "haven't you got the guy yet who shot Murdock?"

"Still looking. But we've got some clues. I just wanted to say hello while I was passing through."

Peralto looked concerned. "You don't think Martin . . . ?" He let the sentence hang.

"Well, he didn't even get out to Utah until two days after the murder," Jared said as if that fact eliminated Martin. No sense sending out any other signals.

*   *   *

A palpable gloom settled in the car as the two officers drove toward the address the bank had given them for Martin.

"Mexico," Bascom sighed. "Big place."

"And my Spanish is not that good," Jared said. "His next stop is probably Brazil." They both knew that Brazil does not have an extradition treaty with the United States.

"Not so sure," Bascom said. "My experience with these guys, even the serious criminals, is they hate to leave home too far. They don't like the foreign food, the customs, what have you. Even if they leave, they usually sneak back."

They pulled to a stop before a large stucco apartment complex that featured a row of smooth-barked eucalyptus trees and blazing flower beds. For a long moment they sat staring at the building.

"What do we expect to find here?" Jared asked. The floral landscaping made him think once more of his own part of the country where the color was mostly in the sand and rock.

"You never know," Bascom said as he got out.

After five minutes of searching, they found the apartment number, went up the stairs to the second floor, and rang the bell. As expected, no one answered. They rang again and waited.

"We could get a warrant," Jared suggested.

"Better do it," Bascom agreed. "But let's talk to the neighbors first."

At the door to the left of Martin's apartment, a Hispanic man in an undershirt and sporting a beer belly regarded them sourly. He had obviously just awakened. "I never see them, I work shifts, so we don't talk." He shut the door without further ado.

Jared regarded the closed door and chuckled. "Guess I'd be grouchy too if I got woke up like this."

At the door on the other side, a young blonde wearing shorts answered and stood blinking in the afternoon sun. Jared guessed she was about twenty-eight. She had a pert nose and small hazel eyes that seemed to blink perpetually. She eyed Jared appreciatively. "Yes?"

Lieutenant Bascom flashed his badge. "Gene Bascom from

the Oakland police. This is Sheriff Buck from Utah. Could we ask you a couple of questions about your neighbors—the Martins?" He gestured toward the Martin apartment.

"The Martins?" she blinked in surprise. "They're not home. Went to Mexico, I think. What about them? Are they in trouble?"

"We just have a couple of questions," Jared said. "Could we come in a minute?"

She glanced once more at the badge that Bascom still held in his hand. "I guess it would be okay." She stepped back and they entered a room filled with the sound of a daytime soap opera. With an annoyed glance she turned the sound down but not off. Then she turned to face them and motioned to the sofa. "I'm Rosalie Proust. Sit down, why don't you? Can I get you a cup of coffee or anything?" She nervously wiped her hands on a tissue she had pulled from the pocket of her shorts.

"We're fine," Bascom said as they sat down. "You said you thought they were in Mexico. Are you good friends with them?"

She blinked and slowly gave a little nod. "Just with Jeannie. In the few months they've lived here we . . . we've gotten to know each other quite well. Go to the movies, things like that. Mr. Martin's gone lots. Oh." She looked embarrassed. "They're not really married, you know. And I'm divorced." She said it with a pained expression.

"I see," Jared said. "Did they give you any idea where in Mexico they might have gone?"

"Oh, Acapulco," she said with a smile, as if envious. "Talked about it lots. Jeannie had never been there—me neither."

"Did they give you any idea where they might be staying—mention any hotel?" Bascom said, leaning forward in anticipation.

She shook her head, obviously concerned. "No, just Acapulco. Is it important?"

"It could be," Bascom said. "Mostly we just wanted to ask them a few questions to help solve a case."

"I see," she said, pursing her lips. "They seem like nice

people. Jeannie, especially." She looked up, brightening. "Funny thing though—a few days ago I overheard them talking. They mentioned Trinidad. I thought maybe after Acapulco they were taking a cruise, but I didn't ask. I don't think I was supposed to hear that."

The two officers exchanged glances. Trinidad. Add that to Mexico and the task got daunting.

"Trinidad?" Jared said. "You're sure she said Trinidad?"

Rosalie's face clouded for an instant, and then she nodded. "I think so. They were talking low in another room, but it sounded like Trinidad. I decided they wanted a quiet getaway there so I didn't mention it."

"Anything else you can think of?" Bascom asked.

She pursed her lips and thought. "I don't think so. Jeannie's just been a good friend. I hope they're not in any real trouble." She ran her hands down her hips to dry them.

The two officers rose. Bascom handed her his card. "If you can think of anything else, Mrs. Proust, please call me at this number."

She showed them to the door, and stood leaning against the knob as they went toward the stairwell. "Oh," she called after them. They turned to hear. "Is Acapulco cold this time of year?"

"Cold?" Jared called. "I don't think so. Why?"

"Then it must be Trinidad that's cold. I saw Jeannie pack two sweaters. I thought it was strange for Acapulco, but I didn't say anything."

Puzzled, the officers exchanged glances. "That could be helpful, Mrs. Proust," Bascom said. "Thank you very much."

"No problem," she said, her glance lingering on Jared as she began to close the door. "No problem at all. If you have more questions, I'm here."

They went down the stairs silently, chewing on what she had said. In Bascom's car, Jared leaned back and sighed. "First Mexico, and then Trinidad. Where to next?" Something was prodding from the back of his mind and he couldn't identify it.

Bascom leaned over the wheel of his car, tapping his fingers.

TO DIE IN KANAB

"Acapulco's probably a smokescreen. They seemed to have talked to everybody about it. Too obvious if they're trying to hide."

"And Trinidad? It sounds like the lady here was not supposed to hear that. Why Trinidad—maybe get lost in some Caribbean paradise?'

"A fair bet," Bascom agreed. "I'll get in touch with the Trinidad police." He reached to start the car. "One of us might get to the Caribbean. I've never got that far from home."

"Me neither," Jared said, settling back in the seat and studying a eucalyptus leaf that had settled on the windshield. His mind was whirling with all the developments in the case. He was desperately trying to snag the thought that kept flitting around his mind, something forgotten, maybe important.

Suddenly he sat up, catching his breath in a gasp. From the dim memories of his past, something had flashed to the top of the pile. "Wait a minute, Bascom," he said in almost a shout, "This might make sense. You know, when I was at Utah State, I wrote on the paper. I'd blown my knee out in football, so they sent me traveling to cover the basketball team. One time we played Humboldt State, up the coast by Eureka. In the redwoods almost to the Oregon border. Well, we had an afternoon free and they took us on a tour. A state park out on a point, and then to a little town on a bluff with a lighthouse that looked out over the ocean. Beautiful little town. But the wind off the sea is colder than blue blazes. That town, I'm almost positive, is named Trinidad! The sweaters—it might make sense."

CHAPTER 33

As they drove northward from San Francisco through the rolling grape country, a somber mood fell over the two officers. Jared was well aware that this was a long shot. Yet, if they lost Martin in Mexico or someplace else in Latin America he might never be brought to justice. It would leave everybody feeling unfulfilled. For Jared, it would be the bitterest of pills to swallow.

Obviously this five-hour drive northward could well be a fool's errand, a hunch brought about by a chance remark. But much of his success on the job, Jared had learned, often leaned heavily on hunches and instincts developed through the years.

When they entered the redwoods, Jared felt better. He was attuned to wild things, and the soaring, majestic conifers that had been growing for a thousand years lifted his spirits. The Trinidad hunch was not just a wild hair, he had decided, but was based on enough information to make the trip worthwhile. But if it failed? Well, maybe a trip to Mexico or the Caribbean in search of Martin might not be all that bad.

An hour south of the Oregon border, the little town of Trinidad sat in the redwoods on a bluff overlooking the sea, with a lighthouse that warned of treacherous cliffs and rocks. It looked pretty much as Jared remembered it from those momentous college days when he had visited the area. Small homes lined the narrow streets, and there were sea-craft shops in the tiny business section. Seagulls were wheeling on the wind overhead against a gloomy sky as the two officers eased to a stop before the one market.

Jared got out of the car and watched the gulls playing. They seemed not to have a care in the world. "We should have it so good," he commented with a gesture at the birds.

Bascom glanced up and shook his head. "They don't have to carry a badge."

Inside the market, they were pointed to the manager, who sat in his office doing paperwork. He was a mountain of a man, whose belly overlapped his belt. He looked up and frowned as Bascom identified their mission and handed the grocer a picture of Martin. Squinting, the man held the picture at arm's length and scowled.

"Don't think I've seen him in here," he said. His jowls jiggled when he shook his head.

"This looks like a nice town you got here," Jared said, motioning to the window that looked out over the street. "Anyplace else around here where someone might have seen this guy?"

The grocer worked his jaw, still eyeing the picture. "What'd he do?"

"We're not sure. Just want to locate him."

The grocer rubbed his chin in thought. "There's some little shops, sell seashells—stuff like that. Couple of cafes. Oh, and there's a pizza place back near the main highway."

Outside, Jared studied the few shops that lined the street. "If you were on the lam, what would you do in a place like this?" he asked Buscom.

Bascom hunched his shoulders. "If I was wanted on a capital charge, I'd lay low. I wouldn't go gallivanting around like a tourist."

Jared pursed his lips in agreement. "Too bad we don't have a picture of the woman. He'd likely send her to do the shopping."

"If this *is* the Trinidad the woman mentioned," he said, arching an eyebrow. Bascom had never been thoroughly convinced this was a good idea. Jared had to spend several minutes convincing him it might be worthwhile. The lieutenant had wanted to concentrate the search for Martin in the Caribbean.

Jared shrugged. "Well, we're here. Might as well check these places."

No one in the shops and cafes in the little town recognized the mug shot they showed of Coy Martin. When the officers finished asking at the shops, they stopped at the lighthouse to gaze out at two ships passing on the sea beyond the whitecaps. A line of darker clouds loomed westward above the horizon, promising foul weather shortly.

It was growing late in the afternoon, bringing a refreshing ocean wind, when they returned to their car and drove back toward the highway.

Bascom turned in and parked near a large sign that read "Pete's Pizza Parlor." Their feet made crunching sounds as they made their way through the gravel parking lot toward the entrance. It was a near-new wooden building, neatly trimmed in white and blue with two window boxes filled with blooming flowers.

Inside, they sat in a booth near two other couples as a teenage girl in a checked apron and pigtails sidled toward them. She grinned, showing braces, as she greeted them. "What would you guys like?"

Bascom pushed aside the menu she put before them. "How about a medium pizza—and a root beer for me. How about everything on it?" He looked at Jared, and then turned back toward the girl. "You got anchovies?"

She nodded.

Jared scowled. "Sure, let's split a medium. But no anchovies."

Bascom chuckled. "You a coward or something?"

"In fact, make half that medium just mushroom and sausage, okay? And I'll have a Coke, no ice."

"You don't want ice?" She seemed incredulous.

"No ice," he repeated.

She scribbled the order and scurried away.

"You don't like ice?" Bascom asked with a chuckle.

"Ice is a gimmick to water down the drink. It's cheaper for the owner." Jared nodded toward a couple sitting across the aisle from them. There were two tall glasses of beer sitting before them as they ate their pizza. "See that? You ever wonder why nobody ever puts ice in their beer? Nobody raises an eyebrow, either. It's because beer drinkers wouldn't put up with it. We softdrink people have let them put one over on us."

Bascom broke into a laugh. "I'll have to remember that."

Jared turned and motioned the girl with the braces toward them. She looked startled when Bascom showed his badge, and then nodded and carefully studied the picture that he held out. After a minute she shook her head. "I don't recognize him. And I usually remember people."

Jared had a thought. "Do you deliver?"

"Sure." She gestured back behind the partition where the pizza was prepared. "Eddie handles most of those. You want to talk to him?"

Eddie was a tall, slender college student with an ongoing attempt at a goatee and sideburns. He wiped his hands on his apron as he came out from the kitchen and approached them. "Sarah says you want to see me. You're cops?"

"Yep," Bascom said. "Just tryin' to find a guy. You ever see him." He held out the picture.

Wiping his hands again, Eddie took the picture, pursed his lips in thought as he held it at an angle to the light, and gave a quick nod. "Yeah, I think so. That's Mr. Martinez. Moved into one of the Seacliff Cottages by Trinidad last week."

Jared caught his breath. "You sure?"

Eddie cocked his head, eyeing the picture from a different angle. "Pretty sure."

"Anybody else with him?" Jared asked. He licked his lips. Maybe this thing would end here, in a little town smaller than Kanab up in the redwoods.

Eddie shrugged. "Just his wife. Anyway, I guess she's his wife."

262

"A blonde?" Bascom asked, his eyes narrowing.

Eddie brightened. "Yeah, not bad looking." A sober look came over his face. "What's this guy done?"

"We're not sure. Just want to talk to him."

"Can you show us where he's staying?" Bascom said, looking grim.

"Sure—just let me tell the boss." He rose and disappeared into the back.

The girl was approaching with their drinks as they rose.

Jared licked his lips. He could feel his pulse racing, but he told himself he had to remain calm to handle this right. "So much for pizza," he said with a grin. He laid a twenty-dollar bill on the table, thanked her, and opened the door for Eddie as he emerged pulling on a coat.

*　*　*

On the far edge of the seacoast town, sitting back in the trees, a row of small bungalows sat back from the sign that declared in wooden letters "Seacliff Cottages." Smaller letters proclaimed that rental was available by week or day. All the rentals bore the names of seabirds.

"Back there," Eddie pointed, seated in front by Bascom. He indicated the farthest of the six cottages, the one that bore the name "Osprey." The cottages were separated and each had a parking space in front. Two small redwoods grew along the south side of the cabin. A dark blue Lincoln was parked in front.

For a long minute they sat in Bascom's car, sizing up the situation. "You sure that's it?" Bascom asked.

"Sure I'm sure," Eddie beamed. "I delivered there twice. A five-buck tip both times, so I remembered it. Wow, this is exciting."

Bascom cast him a sour glance. "Kid, don't you move your ass from right where you're sitting now—or I'll break your neck." He nodded to Jared, and began to back up until he pulled to a stop behind a tree just out of sight of the Osprey. In front of the third cabin a slender gray-haired man was puttering with an outboard motor on a wooden bench.

Jared got out of the car and stood surveying the scene as Bascom came around.

"Let's take this nice and easy," Bascom said, "And not alarm these folks. Keep your piece out of sight until we're there."

Jared nodded. "You know, I think I know something that'll work." He explained what he had in mind, and they disappeared behind the first cottage and began to work through the trees. In Bascom's car, Eddie was leaning out the window, the wind whipping at his hair as he strained to see what was happening.

Jared felt his blood pounding in his ears as they sneaked along. He had pulled his Browning from its shoulder holster. The wooden grip felt good in his hand, and he was glad for the security it offered, although he hoped he wouldn't have to use it. He hadn't shot anybody yet in this job, and he didn't want to start now.

He felt the sting of a branch that whipped across his cheek as Bascom let it go. Jared felt a slight shiver, and he didn't know if it was from the tension or from the rising wind that had taken an edge to it. Now he knew why the blonde had wanted to bring a sweater.

At the side of the Osprey, they paused. Jared felt his breath come faster, and he inhaled deeply twice to calm himself. His hope was that Martin was not watching out the window. With a nod, Bascom slipped around behind the cabin toward the other side. Jared tucked the Browning into his belt, turned, went back toward the next cabin, and then strolled out as if he were emerging from that cottage toward the street. Once there, he ambled along at a leisurely pace, hands swinging at his side.

When he reached the Lincoln, he glanced around. No one was in the window of the Osprey, and the old man at number three was engrossed in the outboard's problems. Quickly he leaned against the car, gave a shove, and an ear-splitting whine of the car alarm erupted in the evening stillness. At the sound, Jared sprinted for the side of the Osprey, opposite where Bascom stood waiting, gun in hand. He barely reached the side of the cottage when the door burst open and an angry man stepped out onto the porch. He stood there, hands on his hips, looking for an intruder.

"Don't move, Martin!" Bascom called out from the far side of the cottage.

At the same time, Jared stepped forward in the grass from his side, his Browning leveled. "Don't even think of it!" he called.

In a reflex motion, Martin's hand had jerked toward his jacket, but now his head whipped back and forth as he evaluated the situation. After a tense moment, he shrugged and raised his hands. "What the hell you guys want? I'm on vacation," he called loudly.

Jared stepped around to confront him, his gun still leveled at Martin's belly. "Just some questions, Martin."

Martin grinned as he recognized Jared. "Well, what have we here? Small town sheriff comes to big California. Why aren't you back in Hicksville chasing down that guy that got Murdock? You run out of things to do, Buck?"

From behind Martin, a blonde head appeared. "What is it, Coy? What's going on?"

"Nothing, Babe," he assured her. "Just some friends from the police. Go on back inside." Frowning, she slowly pulled the door almost closed.

Jared smiled. "We've made considerable progress in that case, Martin. It turns out it wasn't a random robbery by somebody traveling through Kanab, after all. Now, turn around. Hands on the wall."

He stepped back and covered Martin as Bascom hurried up, holstered his own firearm, and frisked the man. With a grunt of satisfaction, the detective snatched a semi-automatic pistol from Martin's jacket holster. He produced cuffs and snapped them onto Martin's wrists behind his back.

Jared pulled out his Miranda card and faced the man. "Coy Martin, we're placing you under arrest for the murder of Ronald Murdock." From the card he finished reading him his rights guaranteed by the Constitution.

The lieutenant glowered at the prisoner. "Folks in Oakland will be happy to know, Martin, that nobody gets away with knocking off one of our prominent citizens."

But Martin was undaunted, almost jovial. "Hey, you got the wrong guy," he protested. "I didn't even get out to Utah until two days after Murdock was shot."

Jared pulled him close, face to face. "No? What about George Grant? The guy who flew to Las Vegas, rented a car, drove to Kanab, shot Murdock, slept in the Sundown Motel, buried the pistol, and then got back on the plane to be ready when the bank wanted you to come out and investigate. They wanted you to investigate the murder *you* committed!"

Martin's eyes narrowed, and his face grew ashen. He was clearly shaken. "Hey, you don't even have any jurisdiction here. Get these things off me," he demanded.

"Afraid not," Jared said. He patted his breast pocket of his sport coat. "These papers say you're coming to Utah. We can go through a long court process, or you can waive extradition proceedings and come back with me immediately."

He gave Bascom a pleading look. "You guys can't prove a thing. You're just guessing."

"Not now," Jared said. "We've got witnesses that put you on the airline as George Grant, and the motel manager identified your picture as the guy he saw burying the gun. You've had it, Martin."

For a moment Martin stood taking deep breaths, working his tongue around his lips. "That bad, eh? I guess I wasn't too smart."

"I'm afraid they get first crack at you," Bascom said with a shrug. "But we can scrape up some charges here too."

The air seemed to have gone out of Martin. He licked his lips and faced Jared. "How'n hell you ever find that gun? I figured it would be a hundred years before it surfaced."

"Pure luck," Jared said. "The guy from the motel saw you and wondered what anybody was doing there on that hill in the morning." He thought a moment, and then added, "And I've got a question. How come you didn't bury that pistol that night on your way?"

Martin made a sour face and groaned. "Pure stupidity. That's what I was going to do. But there was no moon at all. I got out to bury it in the desert, and about broke my leg trippin' over a rock. Couldn't see my hand in front of my face. So I decided to wait until morning when I could see where I was going." He aimed a kick at the porch post in frustration. "Stupid damn mistake." Then his face clouded as he considered his situation.

"It happens," Bascom said in mock commiseration.

Martin drew himself up. "I want to talk to my lawyer."

Bascom glanced at Jared, and then nodded. "Back in Oakland, you can."

CHAPTER 34

The Oakland police conference room was stifling hot the next afternoon as Jared Buck sat waiting for a decision. Next to Jared, Lieutenant Eugene Bascom was whispering to the district attorney. Across the long table, Coy Martin sat looking bored. At his side, his attorney, Joseph Waldrop, distinguished-looking with a shock of graying hair that kept falling down over one eye, pursed his lips and gave a little shake of his head as he contemplated the papers before him.

"I don't see any reason why my client should sign these," Waldrop said with just a touch of a curled lip toward Jared. "He's fine here in California until—and unless—your people can show that he belongs on trial in Utah."

Jared scowled. He didn't like the condescending way that Waldrop seemed to regard everyone in the room. "There's plenty of evidence," he said, "and we're eager to get him on trial."

Again the attorney shook his head with a benign smile. "That's your opinion. A California judge may differ."

Jared leaned back and nodded. "Well, if we have to, we can wait for the court process to get Mr. Martin."

"Or you may want to think about dropping—or pleading— the charges," Waldrop said, oozing confidence.

With a shake of his head, Jared looked at Martin. "That's not for me to decide. My job is just to get the prisoner back to Utah.

It's quicker and easier if he waives extradition."

"Well, I certainly wouldn't advise that. In fact, I think it would . . ."

Suddenly Martin made a loud groaning noise, leaned forward, and motioned to the extradition papers that Jared had given to the lawyer. "Let's cut the crap," he said curtly. "I want to sign those and get the hell out of this state."

Shocked, Waldrop pulled the papers away. "That would be a major error, Coy!" he blurted.

Martin stared defiantly at his lawyer. "I know what I'm doing," he said gruffly. "Give me those papers."

Reluctantly the lawyer slid the papers toward Coy Martin. " Well, I certainly think you better analyze this carefully, Coy. They use a firing squad out in Utah, you know."

Jared sat forward and slid a pen to Martin. "Not necessarily. There's injections also."

Martin looked back and forth between the two. He made another grunting noise, and, with a few quick strokes, signed the papers that would allow the Utah sheriff to take him from California to face legal action in Utah. He stared Jared in the eye for a long moment. "Just so you know," he said, "I ain't planning on using either of those options."

His lawyer sat back and raised his hands in disgust. "You just threw away your best chance," he almost spat the words as he rose, his long hair flying.

Martin rose. "We'll see," he said. He extended his wrists for the handcuffs Jared had ready. "When can we leave?"

*   *   *

On the plane, Martin seemed to relax. As the lights of Salt Lake City came into view, he pressed against the window to watch. "Never been to this city," he said.

"You'll probably be seeing quite a bit of it in the next few years—from a window at the Point of the Mountain," Jared said.

Martin shot him a shrewd glance. "Don't bet on it."

"How's that?"

Martin leaned back and folded his arms, looking self-satisfied. "You can forget those options you talked about."

Puzzled, Jared licked his lips. "Why would that be? You admitted killing Murdock."

"Sure, but I got somethin' to trade. That somethin's going to spring me."

"What do you mean?"

Martin sat back with a smug smile. "You'll find out. But you don't think I whacked Murdock for the fun of it, do you?"

Jared considered this, chewing his lip in thought. Martin was probably just blowing smoke like a lot of prisoners do. But when the rumbling of the engines changed as they prepared to land, what Martin had said sent an unsettling feeling through him. He leaned forward to study Martin's face.

"I'm curious, Martin," he said. "Do you mind telling me how come you came to Utah so easy. Waldrop thinks you made a stupid mistake in waiving extradition. Frankly, I was a little surprised."

Martin smiled with a tip of his head. "That's cause you don't know how things work. Too many people don't want me talking. I wouldn't have lasted a week in some California jail."

"And here in Utah?"

"A better chance, friend," he said, settling back to once more stare out of the window at the approaching lights.

* * *

As the plane pulled up to the gate at the Salt Lake International Airport, Jared waited alongside Martin as the rest of the coach passengers filed out. Then he followed as Martin, whose coat covered his shackled wrists, bid the crew goodbye with a smile, and went up the jetway into the terminal.

As they emerged into the waiting area, Jared blinked in surprise. Lights flashed, and a half dozen reporters crowded close around four television cameramen who battled to get a close shot. He should have known, Jared told himself. In front, smiling, VerNell Whiting elbowed forward to shake Jared's hand so that they both faced the cameras. Jared inwardly groaned. The Kane County attorney had made this a media event to launch his own political career.

Martin raised his arms to cover his face with the coat.

"No comment at this time," Jared repeated in reply to the bombardment of questions from the reporters. He pushed on through the crowd, in spite of a tug at his arm by the county attorney.

With a disapproving glance at Jared, Whiting stepped before the cameras. "As officials of Kane County, we're pleased to see justice being done by an efficient legal system. We'll have more for you tomorrow," he said. He trotted to keep up with Jared, his face angry at the public relations opportunity that the sheriff had caused them to miss.

*   *   *

Shortly after eight the next morning, Jared Buck sat in the conference room at the Hall of Justice in Salt Lake City. At his side was Angus, who had arrived at midnight, eager to help escort the prisoner back to the Kane County jail. Now he yawned as they sat there waiting for the prisoner to appear.

"It's about time you got back to work," Angus joked. "Folks in Kanab thought you'd maybe given up and moved to California."

Jared gave a shrug and smiled. "I'm ready to get back home. And maybe now people back in town can relax without worrying about a murderer being loose."

They turned as the door opened and a slick-bald, portly man entered, followed by a smiling Coy Martin, dressed in street clothes and wearing handcuffs, and a jailer. Two men in dark suits came trailing along behind. Jared was startled as he recognized Richard Summers and Harley Stewart, the two

FBI officers he had met in Kanab the previous week. Kenneth Harman, the Attorney General of Utah, filed in at the end of the group. Jared knit his brow in consternation, trying to decide what was happening here. The Attorney General nodded to Jared and Angus, and then motioned for them all to sit around the table.

Jared let his glance sweep over the group. He was puzzled by what was happening. He had expected to come pick up the prisoner and leave with him in handcuffs for the trip back to Kane County to await trial. Martin caught his eye and gave a little wink.

Harman stood at the head of the table, looked around the group, and cleared his throat. "Gentlemen, these proceedings won't take long. Jared, Deputy Terry." He motioned to the two officers from Kanab, "You know Mr. Martin. His attorney here is Mr. David Reid, of Los Angeles. These gentlemen here," he nodded toward the two federal agents, "are representatives of the federal government."

Curt nods acknowledged the introductions.

Harman looked weary as he turned toward Jared. "These gentlemen will be taking custody of Mr. Martin."

Jared came halfway out of his seat in surprise. "What? Martin is our prisoner. No way are we going to let these guys . . ."

Harman stopped him with an upraised hand. "No. Unfortunately," he paused, "in spite of the gravity of the crime committed, it's out of our hands."

Feeling the breath go out of him, Jared slowly settled back and let his gaze wander back and forth. The two federal agents looked uneasy. Finally the older one, Richard Summers, nodded. "I'm afraid that's how it is, Mr. Buck. At times the interest of the federal government and the citizenry of the United States outweighs that of a local entity."

Angus had sat with his hand to his mouth in shock. "Hey, this bozo killed a guy, right in our town. What are you goin' to do with him? He belongs in prison—or worse."

The agent gave a slight nod. "I can sympathize with your

feelings in this matter, deputy. But Mr. Martin has critical information that will help us gain convictions in numerous important cases. I'm afraid we need him more than you do."

"We get him back then, right?" Angus blurted.

Jared shot a glance intended to shut Angus up, and then he turned to the agent. "Well, will we get him back for trial?"

The agent glanced at his companion. Both shook their heads. "No. Mr. Martin won't be anywhere after he testifies."

Martin's attorney smiled broadly. "No sense fighting it, gentlemen. It's all been worked out."

Slowly the truth dawned on Jared. He blew a deep breath and looked helplessly at the attorney general. "Mr. Harman?"

Harman seemed to sag. "I know. We've already spent several hours trying to head this off. I personally feel the people of Utah deserve to see justice done here." He raised his hands helplessly. "Our office has done everything we can. But . . . but they hold the trump cards."

The two federal agents rose and faced the attorney general. "If that's all, we'll take Mr. Martin to the airport now. Our plane leaves for Washington in an hour."

Jared sat stunned as the men gathered themselves up. Before they went through the door, Martin turned, strode back, faced Jared, and extended his hand. "I told you I wouldn't be here, didn't I?" Jared took his hand

"But you did okay, nailing me like that," Martin said. "Pure luck, I call it."

Jared allowed himself a little laugh. "Part of it, yes. But you made some mistakes."

"Yeah, but witness protection ain't all that bad, Sheriff. Better than sittin' in the stinkin' joint."

Martin gave way as the younger agent took his arm. He looked back over his shoulder as he went out the door, and once more shot a wink at Jared.

Outside in the morning chill, Jared leaned against a sycamore tree in front of the Hall of Justice and stood breathing hard.

He felt like kicking the tree to relieve the emptiness that flooded over him. Such a gross crime, such a violation of a human being, and of a town. And the killer wouldn't have to pay.

Angus stood on the grass, bent over with his hands on his knees, swearing.

CHAPTER 35

Back in Kanab, two days later, Jared plopped himself down at his desk and heaved a heartfelt sigh. He was tired and a little discouraged. In the outer office Myra was bustling around, helping a deputy who had arrested another environmentalist at the Escalante Staircase Monument that morning. Angus was across the room staring through the window at a wind that was whipping the trees out past the parking lot.

"Looks like a storm coming," Angus said as he turned to Jared. "So, where do you think Martin is now? Aren't we ever goin' to get a crack at that guy?"

Jared let out a long breath of frustration. "Right now he's probably in some air-conditioned office in Washington." Jared had just taken a phone call from the Attorney General and his stomach was still churning. "That was Ken Harman on the phone. The FBI just informed him that the Murdock case is to be considered closed. Martin has gone into the federal witness protection program."

"That really frosts me!" Angus was incredulous.

Myra had wandered in and stood with a puzzled look on her face. "So, what was all this about anyway?"

Jared gave a somber shake of his head. "Our friend Martin had a long history with a Florida mob, I guess. They took over the Oakland bank a few years ago—faked a freeway accident to kill the bank president because he wouldn't sell to them. They've been using the bank to launder money from drug operations in Colombia and Panama."

"Whew," Angus whistled. "Big doings. And Murdock—what was his part?"

Jared shrugged. "Sort of an innocent bystander. Apparently he didn't know about the money laundering, but he was pushing to invest ten million of the bank's money in this movie, which is a sure failure. The bank examiners were already curious about some of the goings-on, and this would have brought an audit—something they couldn't have happen."

Angus made a face. "So our friend Martin was a hit-man then?"

"I guess so." He gave a resigned smile. "Now the feds want his testimony against the cartel. So he'll end up living as a protected witness somewhere with a new identity—and being paid by our taxes." Jared gave a grim smile at the irony of it.

Angus's mouth dropped, and he said in a doleful tone, "That means the bastard's going to get totally away with it—and get paid to boot?"

Jared drew a deep breath, sighed, and nodded. "Looks like it. Sort of sits in your craw, doesn't it? But—" he paused, and then smiled, "I guess witness protection is no picnic—always looking over your shoulder."

The young deputy Porter Cannon had been sitting at another desk, pretending to fill out papers but he was really listening. "Wow," he called over. "That's awful."

Myra agreed with a solemn nod. "It sure is. And to happen in our own little town."

"What about the other people at the bank?" Angus asked.

"My friend Bascom from the Oakland police tells me they arrested Tregaskis, the bank president, but Peralto, the little fat guy with the Hollywood bunch—he's disappeared."

"Holy cow," Angus said. "So he was in on it?"

"Looks like." Jared reached to the stack of unopened mail that had awaited him and retrieved his letter opener from the desk. "It was probably him that made the phone call that got Murdock out into the parking lot. Then he hung around the night clerk during the shooting so he wouldn't be a suspect."

Angus gave an amused chuckle. "Well, what do you know? I never did like that guy. What about our friend, Chandra Maroney—and that jerk, Alex?"

"All clean, apparently. They just lost their movie, that's all."

Angus made his way to his desk, still shaking his head. "What a way to end—but the most excitement to hit Kanab since Frank Sinatra built this town a swimming pool."

Jared leaned back in his chair, his hands behind his head, and studied the mountain scenes on the wall. It felt good to be back and settle into his routine.

Myra started away, and then turned back. "I forgot to tell you," she said to Jared. "That old Navajo man came by again late yesterday. He said that you need to go see that lion man, what's his name?"

"Oh? You mean John Lilly?"

"That's it. He came by about a week ago. Said the same thing—Lilly sent word he wants to see you as soon as possible."

Jared glanced down at his calendar. There was nothing Angus couldn't handle for another couple of days. It would be good to get away, maybe clear his mind from the tension of the last few weeks. If nothing else, Sitka deserved an outing.

He turned and listened to the wind splattering leaves against the window. Storm clouds had moved over the Paunsagunt, and he wondered if the roads would be impassably muddy for the elk hunt.

CHAPTER 36

The throaty croak of a pair of ravens brought Sitka's ears up as Jared, pack on his back, strode down the dry creek toward the rock house of John Lilly. A hundred yards below Lilly's place, as Jared approached several crows took flight from the tamarisk where they had been working on something. Scolding as they went, they rose over the bluff beyond.

No smoke came from the cabin, and Jared halted momentarily. A sense of foreboding flitted over him, and from fifty yards away he called out, "John! John Lilly!"

Immediately he was answered by a flurry of deep-throated barking as Lilly's hound emerged through the open doorway to stand glaring from the porch. Sitka bounded ahead, his tail wagging. The two dogs touched noses and smelled each other's backsides.

Still apprehensive, Jared hurried to the open door and peered through the gloom. "John? John, you there?"

He was answered by a cough and a wheezing voice. "Hell, yes! Who'd you think'd be in here?" A coughing spasm followed the question.

Through the murky light, Jared could make out the figure of John Lilly huddled beneath a pile of blankets. Jared shut the door behind him as he went in. Inside, the room smelled of a mixture of linament, salves, and sour food. The scents brought boyhood images of how his grandmother had smelled in the months before she died. The only light came from the open door and the one small window. Still sweating from the climb, Jared swallowed and stood by the side of John Lilly's bed. The old man was gaunt and gray, with red-rimmed eyes that were half shut. Veins showed through his nearly transparent cheeks.

Jared reached to lay a hand on Lilly's forehead. It felt as warm as a rock in the afternoon sun. "You're pretty sick, John," he said, frowning. "You need a doctor bad."

The old man strained to face him. "No—don't need no doctor." He breathed a deep sigh, and stifled a cough on the back of his hand. "Knew you'd come. You almost didn't make it."

Jared pulled a chair over and sat alongside him. He gave a light squeeze to the man's bare arm that was above the covers. "Sorry. I came as fast as I could. I had some police business out in San Francisco. Now we've got to get you out of here."

John Lilly struggled to reach a half-sitting position. "Nope," his voice was a rasping whisper. "But I need to . . . to ask you a favor."

"John, the biggest favor is to get you some medical help."

The old man gave a vigorous shake of his head that flung his matted hair. "I said no, damnit!" He lay back and stared at the ceiling. "What I want . . . what I need you to do is two things."

"What things? I will if I can."

Without looking at him, the old man gestured with his finger to an ancient dresser that sat against the wall at the side of the bed. "Top drawer. Under some things. There's some govmint mail. Get it."

After a minute's search, Jared spotted a stack of brown envelopes bound by two rubber bands. "These?" He held them up and received a cursory nod in response. Lilly motioned with a bony finger for Jared to take his seat again.

"Open it."

With a glance at the man, Jared pulled back the rubber bands. It was a stack more than an inch high of government checks. Jared frowned. "John—all these, and you never cashed them?"

"Some. There's a note."

Beneath the second envelope was a white paper. Jared opened it and read:

I John Lilly, do hear by leave all my possessions—which ain't a hell of a lot—to Sheriff Jared Buck to be passed out as I explain to him. These checks are signed by me. He's to give them to somebody who needs them. And he's to take care of my dog, Hambone, kind of worthless but friendly.

It was dated and signed: *"John J. Lilly."*

Jared sighed and sat back in his chair. He glanced out the door. The afternoon was nearly gone. "John, we can probably get a helicopter out here to get you to a hospital." He said it with some apprehension, because he knew that in most of the canyons a cell phone was useless.

A stifled chuckle made the old man cough once more. "Not me. Not ever," he said emphatically. He waved a thumb toward the stove where a bucket sat. "I could use some water though."

Jared almost leaped to the bucket, where he filled a glass and returned and watched the old man drink it. Lilly then wiped his mouth and turned to Jared. "Don't have any whiskey, do you?"

"Afraid not."

"Shame. Just when you need it. I'm fresh out—fer the last month." His breath was coming fast.

Jared glanced around the room. "John, don't you have some medicine? Something I can get for you?"

He gave a little shake of his head. "Just water. Had some aspirin, but I outlasted them."

"Well, we've got to get you some help."

The old man turned and stared at him with murky gray eyes. "You're the help I need."

"What do you mean?"

Lilly motioned out the side window. "Thet cottonwood yonder. Where you slept once?"

"Sure, I remember."

"Bury me there."

Jared made a face. "John, we can get . . ."

"No—do it," he said firmly. "I've seen what those cemeteries are like, people layin' cheek to jowl. This is my canyon. I don't want to be taken from here."

"Aw, John, you're going to be around a while." Even as he said it, he knew the old man was probably right.

Lilly ignored him and lay back to stare up at the log ceiling overhead. "Just don't let the coyotes get to me. Use rocks on top."

Jared shrugged. "I don't even know what the laws are about burial on BLM land."

This brought a snort from the old man. "Hell fire, it don't matter out here." He breathed a deep sigh and was still. For a moment Jared thought he might have passed out, but then Lilly continued in a wheezing whisper, "This is my place in the world. My place to *be*—just like him."

For an instant Jared frowned in puzzlement. "Who, John?"

John Lilly raised himself on one elbow and gazed intently into Jared's face. "The Ruess kid. It's what he wanted."

Jared blinked. He recalled the passage in Ruess's letters about wanting to be buried in a lonely place, and he wondered if Lilly had read those books. "Ruess?" he asked hesitantly. "John, do you know what happened to Everett Ruess?" He held his breath as a flicker of remembrance crossed the old man's face.

"Never told nobody, but now—" he said slowly, and then settled back onto the bed, as if gathering strength. "He came that September. I was trackin' a cat near Davis Gulch when I found him campin' there. We ate and talked. Pretty little place, a stream with willows and grass. Showed me some of his pictures." His voice trailed off as he gathered the memories. "I wasn't much older than him. We hit it off. He wanted to go huntin' lions with me," He allowed himself a smile across his quivering lips. "Wanted to take his burros. I told him there's so many jump-ups we'd have to haul 'em up by rope. So we left them burros in the canyon behind a brush fence. Plenty water and grass."

He was silent, and his eyes nearly closed. "Worked our way

around Forty Mile Ridge back this way. Then—" He raised himself up and pointed out the window, "then we jumped a big tom just down the canyon there in Scorpion Gulch. Up a box canyon there." He motioned feebly with his thumb to show the direction. "Not far from here. My dogs run him up a cliff. Thet ol' tom stood looking down from a ledge where a cedar grew. Ruess got excited when the cat went on over the top . . . started climbin' up after him. Reckless as hell, told him I wouldn't go. Got to the ledge, and then found a crack to climb higher up toward the top."

Jared listened breathlessly, not moving, not wanting to break the spell. John Lilly was reliving a moment in time, his eyes closed, his voice barely audible. "He got nearly to the top. It was pink sandstone, and just before he topped out, he turned and yelled that he was going on, and wanted me to come. Then, the rock where his foot was standin' broke loose. For an instant he hung there . . . kind of a puzzled look on his face . . . and he came crashing down along with the rock. Fell maybe forty feet onto that ledge where the cat had stopped."

A cough racked him, and he stopped, caught his breath, and continued. "Course I climbed up then to help him, nearly broke my own neck goin' up. He was in bad shape, blood comin' out of his mouth, and I knew he was a goner. He looked up and said, 'Don't move me. Don't let them take me. Here's where I want to be.'"

Once more Lilly raised himself up to stare into Jared's face. "That's what he said. Made me promise to bury him there—and not tell. So I did." He lay back.

There was silence. Jared sat stunned, hardly daring to breathe. A fly buzzed against the window. He sat back in his chair and sighed. "That's been a long time, John. You kept his secret well."

John shook his head. "You too. Don't let 'em come and take him."

Jared considered this. He wondered if he was legally bound to inform Ruess's next of kin. "I don't know, John. His family . . ."

Lilly half rose and his face took on a fierce expression. "They'd come take him away. He wanted to be left alone. He wanted to stay here." With a deep groan he lay back down. "And so do I."

Jared swallowed as he considered John's request. Finally, biting his lip, he nodded. "All right, John."

"If you don't believe me, I left a sign. You can go check it. The kid wore a blue bandana. I tied it to the cedar to mark it. Course it's long gone now, but I left his Navajo bracelet there. It has three turquoise stones in it. I buried it at the base of the tree by the grave. You check that."

"How will I . . ."

With painstaking effort, John Lilly reached under his pillow and handed Jared a piece of paper. "It's a little box canyon—not far. Here's the way. I been waitin' for you."

*   *   *

The sun was nearly down when Jared found the spot. A large outcropping, nearly purple against the red and yellow sandstone, helped him locate the cliff. Several giant slabs of salmon-colored rock that had tumbled from the cliff provided the landmark he sought. He studied the vertical rock face with awe. From the description on Lilly's note, this must be it. He let out a low whistle. No wonder Lilly had declined to attempt the climb those many years before. He calculated his own risk in attempting the vertical face, but decided he must make a try.

His dog paced below, whining and attempting an occasional jump as Jared worked upward on the rock. For the first few feet, several knobby toeholds offered purchase to allow him to skim upwards. At twenty feet up, he found two slender cracks leading upward, probably the same ones that Ruess had used to ascend in pursuit of the lion. Clutching with fingernails into the cracks, he carefully felt into the declivity with the toes of his boots. He plastered himself against the rock face and wondered if he was tempting the same fate that had felled Ruess.

Halfway to the ledge, he felt his left foothold give way. With a grunt he caught himself by his fingertips, flattening against the face and holding his breath until his right foot found new purchase in a tiny projection of weathered rock. For a time he did not move, catching his breath and reviewing what he had noted when he had studied the rock from below. Finally, he began to inch upward once more. At last he breathed a sigh of relief as he pulled himself up onto the ledge. He half lay against the sandstone, breathing hard and feeling the welcome pain of the hard rock against his cheek. Then he sat up.

The skeleton of a cedar tree remained on the ledge, which was no more than a dozen feet wide and twice that long. A few spindly sagebrush grew in the sand, and the bones of the juniper cedar stood stark against the cliffside.

He rose and studied the ledge where he stood. Over the centuries a declevity in the ledge had filled with sand. He decided that it would have been a shallow grave if Ruess were really here. There was no sunken mark of a burial, but alongside the tree trunk, several slabs of rock were gathered in a casual grouping as if they had fallen that way.

For a long while Jared stood staring down at the spot. So much mystery, so much emotion spent, so much irony in the youth ending up here after such an intense love affair with this lonely land. A chill wind had sprung up from the canyon below, and it rustled the sagebrush near the cedar. He wondered if he should disturb the grave, but he had to know if Everett Ruess were really buried here.

With a little shake of his head, Jared squatted on his heels and probed the sand around the base of the dead tree with his pocket knife. On one side he found nothing. Then, on the side nearest the cliff, he felt a metallic click as he probed. Digging as carefully as an archeologist, he slowly whisked away the yellow sand to reveal a blue shard of turquoise. Tugging gently at it, he pulled out a tarnished silver bracelet, set with three turquoise stones. He brushed away the sand and sat staring at the relic.

He blew a long breath. It was enough. He remembered that in one of his journal entries, Ruess had mentioned how pleased he was to own the bracelet with three turquoise stones that he had bought in his desert wanderings. The bracelet alone would be proof enough that he had been found.

Hardly believing this could be happening, Jared rose and studied the gravesite of the articulate, talented and likable young wanderer who had caused the West and much of the nation to ponder his mysterious disappearance for decades. Now what? Jared leaned back against the cliff and considered his options. Below, his dog was whining and barking up at him and the wind was growing.

He slouched with his hands on his hips, looking out over the little canyon that lay below, where a few sagebrush and tamarisk struggled in the sparse soil. The canyon walls were a mixture of cinnamon and yellow, with streaks of red and gray. To the east he could make out the hump of Navajo Mountain south of Lake Powell. Here there were no boot-worn trails. This was far from the popular hiking areas and about as inaccessible a spot as he knew, with jump-ups and box canyons pretty much blocking the way in almost any direction.

With a deep sigh, he turned and squatted once more by the grave. In his hand he held proof of the fate of Everett Ruess, the young poet, artist, and adventurer who still captivated those who were caught up in his words and his description of the lure of this wild land that was so unforgiving. He fingered the silver bracelet, rubbing it with his thumb until the tarnish began to wear away and the silver began to shine bright. With a handkerchief, he cleaned the decades-old dirt away from the turquoise. It shone blue as the summer sky, with spiderweb veins that accented the color.

Jared knelt and, from his jacket pocket, fished out the paperback copy of the book he carried which contained the letters of Everett Ruess. After a minute search, he found the passage he remembered. It was in a letter to the adventurer's brother in 1932:

I shall always be a lone wanderer of the wilderness. God, how the trail lures me. You cannot comprehend its resistless fascination for me. After all, the lone trail is best. . . . I'll never stop wandering. And when the time comes to die, I'll find the wildest, loneliest, most desolate spot there is.

Jared set the book down and looked around him. The maze of canyons and colorful buttes sparkled in the evening sun, which shone through the gathering clouds. The young wanderer had found his place.

Ignoring the whines of his dog below, Jared sat studying the bracelet for several minutes. He knew family members were still alive who would cherish it, along with proof of the young man's fate. His duty, he knew, was to report the find and bring to a close the puzzle of the disappearance of one who had caught the nation's imagination.

What then? He chewed on his lip as he considered the possibilities. Probably a reburial somewhere in California. Maybe a news frenzy converging on this peaceful spot in southern Utah. Perhaps renewed interest enough to make a feature movie, after all.

The evening shadows had deepened over the canyon by the time he rose. He pulled out his pocket knife again, and began to dig a deeper hole at the base of the cedar. Into the hole he gently placed the bracelet, covered it carefully, and erased all sign of his having been there.

CHAPTER 37

Shortly after sunrise, Jared Buck stood under the cottonwood near the rock house where he had buried old Lilly. He had carried a slab of vermilion-colored sandstone and placed it erect for a marker. Into the sandstone he had scratched the words: "John Lilly—Lion Hunter," followed by the date.

The old man had breathed his last a few minutes after Jared returned from finding the resting place of Everett Ruess. With his last efforts, Lilly had motioned to his stack of government checks that sat on his bedside table.

With a grim sigh, Jared had nodded. "I'll get these to some-body who needs them," he assured. "There's a Navajo woman—Sam Begay's mother over by Navajo Mountain. . . ." He had let it hang there, as John Lilly lay with his eyes closed.

As he stood contemplating the grave, two magpies were squabbling in the trees down along the streambed. Clouds were gathering to the northwest and with a glance, Jared guessed he would be wet before he completed his all-day trek back to his Jeep. Sitka and Hambone lay watching.

He wasn't sure what he should do now. Finally, he removed his broad hat and offered a dedicatory prayer on the grave in the Mormon way, blessing the grave to be safe from animals, asking the Lord to accept the man's spirit until the judgment and resurrection, and to reunite him with his loved ones, even though his life had not been exemplary.

When he finished, he replaced his hat and turned to the dogs. The hound lay with his nose between his paws at the side of the grave, looking mournful. "Hambone, I guess you're family now," Jared said to the dog. "If Sitka can stand you, I guess I can." He hefted his pack onto his shoulders. For a time the brown dog lay resolutely by the grave, looking confused. But as Jared walked away, Hambone finally rose, his tail low, and followed along.

When he reached the rock house, Jared stopped and studied the place. After a moment's hesitation, he stepped through the doorway, ordering the dogs to stay outside.

When he finished, the man and the dogs hiked down the canyon in the breeze of the coming storm. At the turn in the canyon, Jared stopped to look back. The smoke from the burning logs of the rock house swirled upward, and then was lost on the rising wind. It might cost him his job, he knew, but he couldn't tolerate the thought of casual hikers using John Lilly's house as a stopover. It was what Lilly had asked him to do. He would stand by it.

Drained of emotion, he finally sat on a rock and watched the smoke furl upward until it was swallowed by air currents. From his shirt pocket, he pulled out the picture of Lilly and his father that he had rescued from the shelf where it sat. After a long moment of contemplation, he slid out the other photo he had taken from the house. With a painfully slow motion, he ran his fingers over the photo that Lilly had kept of the Japanese soldier who had died in New Guinea. His gaze lingered on the man's children, a boy and a girl, both toddlers. He wondered what they were doing now.

Finally, he removed his wallet and took out the picture of his Sunny, his eternal companion. The sparkle of her presence still burned from the photo, and a dull ache rose in him—as it did almost every day. She had loved such country as this, and had fought at every turn to keep it the way it had always been. He looked around him and could almost feel the whisperings of the rock and the land. She would have been at home here. The bitter wind began to whip at his shirt as he sat there, bringing with it a wave of loneliness—of desolation—that swept over him, and he suddenly felt more empty than he had in years. For a long moment he held it back, and then he let go and sobbed into his arms. Feelings repressed for so long tumbled from him in a torrent, constricting his throat so that he nearly choked. Finally, as the wind grew colder, he felt his dog nudge at him in compassion.

Swallowing hard, he looked guiltily around him, patted the dog's head, and wiped his eyes on his sleeve. For a time he sat studying the sand at his feet, breathing heavily and regaining control. He reminded himself that ultimately Sunny was waiting for him. It was the great stabilizing philosophy of his life. With a deep breath he rose, smiled, shouldered the pack, and with the two dogs at his heels, began to trudge across a bare patch of slick rock on the long trek back toward his truck—and Kanab.

ABOUT THE AUTHOR

The son of a Norwegian immigrant, Jack Nelson grew up in Bellflower, California. However, during college he became a heartfelt Utahn after discovering the wild places of that lonely land. As a youth, he danced the Squaw Dance with Navajos on the Reservation at the prodding of his cousins who ran the Dennehotso Trading Post.

A former reporter, Nelson taught journalism at California State/Humbold, the University of Utah, and then settled in to teach writing for twenty-five years at Brigham Young University. With a master's degree in creative writing from the University of Utah, he has published four other novels with New York publishers.

As an outdoor writer, Nelson served for thirteen years as Utah editor of Western Outdoors Magazine while teaching, along with writing an outdoor column for a local newspaper. He lives with his wife, Patrice, in Provo, Utah.